You Are Cordially Invited...

*to enter one woman's
exclusive world of rare privilege,
extraordinary beauty...
and shocking deception.*

THE
BILLIONAIRE

He had heaped the House of Uni's "show table" with gold and sapphires, emeralds and pearls—earrings, necklaces, jewel-encrusted combs and belts. The table was laden with the loot of ancient civilizations, so many pieces that Cella could hardly see the black silk.

It gave her a bad taste.

"You've passed the seven-million-dollar mark, Mr. Petty," she pointed out.

"I know," Peter Petty answered brightly. "And this is only the beginning. I haven't seen anything yet that I didn't like." He pointed to a glass case in which a gold-and-silver diadem was displayed on white silk. "How old is that? And how much is it?"

"About 4,500 years. And it's not for sale."

"Cella!" her father sputtered with astonishment.

"Nor is anything else in the shop," Cella said with a cool smile. "Listen to me carefully, Mr. Peter Petty. You are not Sears and Roebuck. This is not costume jewelry. We can't call the factory in Hoboken and order two dozen more—"

Other Avon Books by
Davidyne Saxon Mayleas

THE WOMAN WHO HAD EVERYTHING

BY APPOINTMENT ONLY

DAVIDYNE SAXON MAYLEAS

AVON BOOKS · NEW YORK

AVON BOOKS
A division of
The Hearst Corporation
105 Madison Avenue
New York, New York 10016

Copyright © 1989 by Davidyne Saxon Mayleas
Front cover and inside cover photographs by Walter Wick
Published by arrangement with the author
Library of Congress Catalog Card Number: 88-92119
ISBN: 0-380-75362-6

First Avon Books Printing: March 1989

AVON TRADEMARK REG. U.S. PAT. OFF. AND IN OTHER COUNTRIES, MARCA REGISTRADA, HECHO EN U.S.A.

Printed in the U.S.A.

K-R 10 9 8 7 6 5 4 3 2 1

BY APPOINTMENT ONLY

PRELUDE

1989

Gaia Caecilla's bare feet treaded the pathway, noiseless as the moon above. Little golden snakes coiled around her upper arms, licking her, tickling her. In her dark hair, hanging loosely down her naked back, was a diadem of golden flowers and leaves; around her neck chains of gold links intertwined with strands of emeralds and amethysts that reached down over her bare breasts to her waist. The sacred Jewels of the Rites. She breathed in the strong, sweet ritual scent of bodies. The scent of the festival.

At last she stood in a clearing beside the great hollowed stone that was the sacrificial altar. The glade was surrounded by trees and their branches bent down, caressing her with their leaves. Above in the night sky, the great stars wheeled and swung. She saw a star falling and, in a great burst of light, beheld hundreds of her people carrying torches in the sacred grove; many were whirling and dancing in a frenzy of abandonment. She heard their chanting and felt the power of joy and life in them. And urging them on was the sensuous, beckoning music of the double flutes.

The young virgin turned and looked across the altar. Before her stood a huge figure whose body, like her own, glowed in the moonlight, alive with the springtime tide. He moved to her side, his phallus erect, demanding fulfillment. He was the groom, the great stag with seven golden horns radiating from his head, and she felt the surge of life in him calling to her.

Quickly the chanting and dancing ended. A solemn, waiting hush fell over the glade as she stretched out her arms to him. He gathered her to him, and they locked together, sinking onto the stone altar in hallowed surrender to the Rite.

Gaia Caecilla's eyes were dazed with moonlight as she felt his hands caressing her luminous nakedness, inviting her to joy. He had many hands, all touching her everywhere. And many mouths, all greedily drinking from her. Her blood became lines of fire coursing through her body. He mounted her, with his open mouth on hers, drinking in her soul, and their bodies undulated together in an ever-increasing rhythm. The climax between them grew until she cried out from the ecstasy running through her.

So Gaia Caecilla gave up her virginity, and in her exaltation, the signal went forth. Throughout the sacred grove, beneath the fertility torches, the coupling began. Men and women were drawn together by the same throbbing call of their blood. Many children would be sired, and no one would know or care to whom they belonged. All would be precious, all would be cared for. Husbands would exchange wives, brothers and sisters would know each other, strangers would mingle, becoming lovers. . . .

The scene began to break up and ripple as if it were underwater. The sound of the flutes grew softer and was gone. Cella Taggard fought to keep her dream, to hold it tight, but the dream slipped away, back into the past of more than two thousand years ago. Reluctantly, she opened her eyes to her ringing telephone. By the time she answered it, whoever was calling had hung up. She blinked away the sleep and glanced around the room. Everything was as she remembered it. She was not lying on the dried weeds, grass, blossoms and leaves covering the altar, but instead in her splendid four-poster bed, which she'd cherished from childhood and inherited from her mother. And the thick, overhanging branches of trees encircling her in her dream had vanished; instead, sixteenth-century tapestries covered the walls, and hanging nearest the bed was a favorite piece, an ancient Chinese fan inlaid with precious stones that had once belonged to the Empress Lu, mother of the Han dynasty.

No, nothing in the room had changed. Why should it? She had not gone far. Or been gone for long. Only twenty-five hundred years. She'd fallen asleep over the book and dreamed her dream again. Her eyes filled with tears. Once more she felt a strange, mourning cry for all that had been lost with that vanished world of thousands of years ago, and the sorrow of that loss followed her even to the here and now.

Cella glanced at the well-thumbed book in her lap, *The Enigmatic Etruscans*. It was still open to the page that had started her dreaming. She read again the paragraph at the top of the page.

"The world of Etruria is in some ways more mysterious and inaccessible than that of Egypt, Crete or Mycenae, despite the fact that it is closer to us in time than any of those others. For there exists no Rosetta Stone to assist scholars in understanding the Etruscan language. Comparatively little is known of this high civilization that reached its peak about 500 B.C.; it seemed to spring out of nowhere and dominated

Italy when Rome was a collection of mud huts and the Greek Classic period was only dawning.

"What we do know we learn from the writings of Etruscan contemporaries. We know from the Greek writers, who stressed the Etruscan fondness for uninhibited pleasure, that the Etruscans often confused and shocked them. The overall picture we have of the Etruscans is that of a nation of exuberant, life-loving people. The Etruscans loved music. They danced. They made love constantly. . . .

"So it is hardly surprising that they evoked the envy of their contemporaries and the admiration of we who live today; who stand in awe of the vital art we find in their tombs; who honor the craftsmanship of their sculptures, their painters and especially their jewelry makers. . . . Across twenty-five centuries their sensitive, worldly faces regard us with ironic amusement, half smiling, as if they hold some secret. They remain one of the great enigmas of history. Salve.''

It was gone. Forever. The life of joy and beauty. She ought to keep away from books like this. They worked on her like a dangerous drug to which she was addicted. The Etruscan world was for scholars, for archaeologists, for historians. For them, it had the fascination of an ancient mystery. But not to her. To her, when she dreamed it, Etruria was a vividly alive world; more vivid than today's world.

Cella fingered the jeweled-and-gold-chased necklace, the same one she had worn in the dream. Her mother, Spina, had given it to her on their last Christmas together, almost fourteen years ago, when Cella had been not quite fifteen. Her mother had understood so much. There were secrets that Spina had only hinted at. Although she had raised her daughter as a woman of today, Spina knew, as did Cella, that she was once Gaia Caecilla. She was born to the ancient ways. Given time, Spina would have properly trained her daughter to deal with her heritage. But the old gods had willed there would be no time.

The telephone started to ring. Cella glanced at the blond-haired man sleeping beside her. She picked up the phone quickly so as not to waken tonight's lover. "Hello?"

"You were dreaming your dream again."

It was a voice she knew and adored. Anton's. Her unmanageable lover. Her Etruscan mate. A flare of desire rose in her. How she missed his caresses, his strong body. "I was dreaming my dream again."

"What are you wearing?"

"You mean besides my skin?"

"I mean what jewelry?"

"How do you know I'm wearing jewelry?"

"You always wear jewelry when you play games in bed with a friend."

"Who says I have a friend here?"

"I have the ears of a dog. I can hear a high, wheezing snore."

"I cannot tell a lie." Cella gave a teasing laugh. "Actually, I would adore to tell a whopper now and then. But I have this embarrassing handicap. I can never remember my lies. So, yes, I am wearing jewelry. And yes, I have a . . . 'friend' will suffice."

"What's his name?"

"Gorgeous."

"You call them all Gorgeous."

"I have to. I can't remember their names. And besides, they love it."

"I wish you'd be more imaginative." He sounded like a professor dismayed with a favorite student.

"But I haven't forgotten your name, my thrice-gorgeous man," she murmured. "It's . . . don't tell me . . . it's on the tip of my tongue. Mmm, feel my tongue playing with your tongue. I'd know that tongue anywhere. Your name is . . . is . . . is Anton."

"Anton what?"

"Anton, the ass grabber."

"You pass, my bare-assed Cella. And the jewelry you're wearing is the gold chased necklace Spina gave you."

"Who told you? You Peeping Tom. It's voyeurism. Clairvoyant voyeurism. You've been enjoying my every orgasmic twitch."

"I wish I had. We Etruscans have always practiced voyeurism. Watching people make love is highly erotic. But no such luck, my dearest. I know because you told me. Whenever you wear the necklace, you have dreams. Glorious and unsettling dreams." There was a note in his voice that made Cella wonder if Anton wished he could also dream. "When I called a few minutes ago, I let the phone ring ten times and you dreamed on."

"It's not the necklace. I was reading a book. The book put me to sleep."

"I know. Whoever tonight's Gorgeous is, he's also a gorgeous bore, or you would have been doing something more interesting than reading a book."

"Forget Gorgeous. I'll toss him out. Leave your bags in

baggage claim and we'll pick them up tomorrow." Cella's voice was seductive. "How long will it take you to get here?"

"Poor Gorgeous. I feel for him." Anton laughed. "But not too much. Still, I think a little waiting will add to desire. I'm going to give you time to change the sheets to black silk. I'm at Heathrow Airport on my way to Paris. Be back in a week."

"London! I thought you were at Kennedy. Now what does the Villanova Trust own in Paris that you absolutely must look into? Besides the ground on which the Eiffel Tower stands?"

"Paris is a stop-off. I'm driving to the Loire. Then on to Périgord. There are two châteaus with leaky roofs and poor plumbing . . ."

"Châteaus are exceptionally fragile. The old families want to sell?"

"We have been approached."

"And after the Trust makes the appropriate restoration?"

"There are many Americans longing for ancestral homes."

"Darling, are you sure you're Etruscan? Your instinctive American business sense awes me," Cella said thoughtfully.

"So does your father with The House of Uni," Anton half teased. Then his tone changed. "Have you missed me?"

"Don't I always miss you?" A mischievous look flashed through her sparkling eyes. "I've been saving myself for you."

"Saving, maybe. Hoarding, no. Certainly not enough to spend your nights as a nun."

Cella started to laugh. "You're jealous. I'm just keeping in practice for you."

"I am not jealous. Etruscan men are never jealous. Merely taking a head count. After all, we are mated."

"A head count? Ha! Anyway, ours is an Etruscan mating. An engagement, so to speak. Not a marriage. And definitely not an American-type marriage—with all that piety about love, honor and be faithful 'til death do us part. You do know what our ancestors thought about fidelity? Even after marriage. Sexual jealousy was low caste. Fidelity was only used as a punishment for lazy slaves." She ran her long, elegant fingers through her gleaming black hair, pushing it back from her forehead. "And by the way, my sweet, since you bring up the tiresome American obsession with fidelity, how many nights have you tossed and turned alone in bed?"

"Not very many."

Cella smiled. "Enough. Let's stop counting lovers. It's tedious. But I am sorry you won't be here for the Northbie's auction."

"So am I. It should be a three-ring circus." He savored the idea. "Are you bidding on the Aphrodite necklace?"

"How did you know it's being offered?"

"I received a silk moire catalog explaining—with regret, you understand—that they were sorry not to invite me to the auction. But they did not believe any of the items were of interest to me."

"It figures. The best publicity for a private showing is to not invite enough people. With abject apologies, of course."

"Do you want the silver fertility girdle too?" Anton asked.

"It depends on how high we'll have to go on the necklace. Darling, fiancé of sorts, as you well know, we are not buyers for Bloomie's. Or Kenneth Lane. We buy for our own highly exclusive, highly expensive, highly insured House of Uni. The necklace could easily go for seven figures."

Anton chortled. "Are you telling me The House of Uni is tightening its Etruscan belt? Your father is the world's leading dealer in ancient jewelry. How can he—you—let the girdle slip away?" He lowered his voice, becoming conspiratorial. "Unless you have your own ideas for designing silver girdles."

"Shut up, Anton! The Russians are listening."

"Or Maurice Wheelock. Wouldn't he have a hemorrhage if he suspected the truth? Wouldn't the world . . . ?"

"Shut up!" Cella cried out in exasperation.

Anton's bubbling laughter was as clear as if he were in the same room with her. "I'm shut," he said, half choking. "Damn! They're calling my flight. Throw Gorgeous out before I get back. Ciao, my love."

Cella hung up the phone. Anton would be back soon. She breathed a deep sigh of anticipation and glanced at the exhausted man beside her, still sound asleep, softly snoring. He'd been a bore. Most men became tiresome after the first few nights. And although she was always polite when dismissing them, they kept hanging around.

That men spoiled her was inevitable, for nothing about her was ordinary, and everything was seductive. Her shoulder-length hair, silken and straight, was swept back from a high forehead and could be called black until, catching the light, it shot off navy blue sparks. Her eyes were an unusually deep violet. Her face was sensuously high-boned and strong, flaunting a passionate acceptance of her untamed nature. It bore a striking resemblance to the faces of young women seen in wall paintings that decorated Etruscan tombs. Like her ancient sisters, she had firm, high breasts, rounded hips and thighs and well-developed legs that were not oppressively muscular but gracefully long and strong. Her entire body conveyed the languorous seductivity of a woman who enjoyed men. But no man took her against her will. Those few who tried discovered the strength of the muscles beneath her smooth skin. Cella was like steel covered with satin.

She took no credit for her beauty, her vitality, accepting everything as a gift from the gods. Still, she took full advantage of the gift. She wasn't flirtatious or even romantic. Her attitude was simple. She had a permanent inclination toward sex in its endless varieties and used men as a natural resource. She was also irreverent, disrespectful and unwilling to accept any authority but her own. Except, of course, for Spina. Her eyes were drawn to the book on her lap, and she thought again of her dream. What Anton had said was true. She dreamed because she chose to dream. Of Etruria and the ancient ways.

Cella slowly shook her head and exhaled deeply. On the other hand, Northbie's auction was today's business. And indeed it would be a three-ring circus. Dedicated to money and power. Again she glanced at the book. Sometimes it was hard for her to keep her perspective with every daylight hour devoted to the money-power game, while her nighttime heart longed for the joyous life of twenty-five hundred years ago.

PART ONE

TWENTIETH-CENTURY GODS

Chapter One

Sebastian and Marcus Taggard sat in the library of the Taggard gray stone town house, brooding. While waiting for Cella, they made conversation about this and that—the new customers of The House of Uni, the new clients Marcus was getting as a broker for a large Wall Street firm. No hint of the latent bitterness between them was evident, since good manners were as much a part of them as their male good looks and the air of knowing they were welcome anywhere that marks the born aristocrat.

"Tell me again, Father. Exactly what is my lawbreaking sister pulling this time?" Marcus asked, glancing at the six blank CRTs resting side by side on a parsons table. The CRTs were all wired to an IBM AT computer.

"It's not a bad stunt." Sebastian chuckled. "If she can pull it off. She's going to try to break the Northbie code so we'll be able to see the same six faces on those screens"—he gestured toward the CRTs—"as our old friend Maurice Wheelock, the auctioneer, will see. It helps to watch the face of the person you're bidding against."

"Like getting inside information on a stock." Marcus rubbed his chin thoughtfully. "Good for Cella. She promised me a show. I hope she delivers."

"I'll deliver," Cella called out as she entered the room, gliding toward her father and brother. She was wearing a sari of shimmering green brocade embroidered with gold sequins and gold thread. Tightly wrapped around her hips and thighs, it followed the flow of her body as she moved across the floor more elegantly than any model in a fashion show. A triple strand of Burmese pearls swayed with her every step.

Marcus applauded. "You get this year's award for the best-dressed computer hacker."

"Thank you. All compliments are gratefully accepted. Since we're bidding on the Aphrodite—and maybe the silver

13

fertility girdle—I wanted to wear something in keeping with the time and mood. For luck. So I chose a sari—royal and divine and as ancient as the Ajanta caves.''

Cella settled herself on the chair in front of the computer. Her jeweled fingers ran lightly over the keys without depressing them. The triple strand of pearls swung forward, getting in her way. She took them off and flipped the necklace to Marcus. ''Hang on to that for a second.''

''You trust me. How naive.''

''I don't have to trust you. This room has an alarm system tied to the Sixty-sixth Street police station. Captain Conners and I have worked out a barter system. He takes good care of The House of Uni, and when I'm in the mood, I call him Gorgeous. That bauble cost three hundred thousand dollars, so watch your sticky fingers.''

''A mere pittance to The House of Uni.''

''Compared with what the Aphrodite will cost, you're right,'' Sebastian said. Cella glanced over her shoulder at her father, who was peering down at the computer, his eyes round with curiosity. ''Is this really going to work?'' he asked, a mixture of puzzlement and awe in his voice.

Cella grinned. ''I think I have it. I just had to psyche out Maurice.'' She typed in the words MODEM AUCTION? and pressed the return key. Then, NORTHBIE's? And the date, 4/1/89. She pressed the return key again. The screen in front of her asked a question. IDENTIFICATION NUMBER? Cella's fingers flew over the keyboard: 13-1-21-18-9-3-5.

''What are you doing?'' Sebastian stared at the screen.

''The numbers stand for the letters in Maurice's name. Thirteen for M. One for A. And so forth,'' she said. When she pressed the return key, her screen blanked for a few seconds. Then seven different faces appeared on all seven monitors.

''You did it!'' Sebastian exulted.

''Give the little lady a big hand!'' Marcus said.

Cella blew on her fingers, imitating the cliché act of movie safecrackers. ''And now, Marcus, my pearls, if you please.'' Casually, she snared the necklace in midair and draped it around her neck.

''You've earned them, Mata Hari.''

''Yeah.'' Cella grinned at her brother. ''I'm pretty damn good.'' She made no attempt to disguise how pleased she was with herself. She had cracked the ultrasecret Northbie's modem auction code.

* * *

Maurice—he insisted his name be pronounced "Mor-ris," as the English did—Wheelock fingered his Vandyke beard lightly, being careful not to disturb a hair. He straightened his dark-green-and-brown-striped bow tie and checked the brass buttons on his beige cavalry twill jacket as he readied himself for the pitch. His hands were firm, warm and dry; he felt the cold chill of anticipation that only came when the game was for millions. Any minute the cameras would click on and he would be standing alone, facing six bloodthirsty sharks with their shrewd, glittering, acquisitive eyes. The twelve greediest eyes in the world. Among the richest. Hand-picked for their insatiable craving. As the offerings were handpicked for their beauty, provenance, rarity and, naturally, their costliness.

It would be up to him to rack those six with the pangs of starvation, to make their mouths water and their need grow painful. They must itch with desire as he teased and tantalized. They must strain every fiber of their demanding, lustful spirits to get what they couldn't live without. He would tempt and taunt them into a frenzy of bidding, and finally he would discreetly insult their judgment, sneer at their intelligence, at their sacred net worth. It was his style, and only his style. No other pitch man—how his snobbish colleagues resented that crude term—dared to use it.

Maurice now, but once Mannie, the kid from the East Bronx via London; only he could push record-breaking floor prices to record-breaking sales. That was why dear old Northbie's paid him so handsomely. That was why he was known to them as "The Great Persuader." And, in the accounting room of the auction house, as "Money Maurice." He heard the cameras click on, saw six screens light up; and there were his clients, primed and waiting. Maurice smiled at all the screens, at his dearly beloved suckers.

Around the world six computer screens at six different sites, each tied to an AT&T modem, came to life. The auction was under way.

In Georgetown, Washington, D.C., Darlene Moore Schiller, her lustrous blond hair wrapped in a towel, lay naked on her massage table. Roberto, his hands slippery with Darlene's personal rose-scented rubbing oil, kneaded, groped, gouged, punched, pressed, knuckled, rubbed, wrenched, rotated, slapped, squeezed, and even sucked her entire body from her shoulders to the tips of her toes. The Mozart Quintet in C Major, Kochel 515, was playing in the background. Darlene felt she'd entered paradise as Roberto extended his fingers to encompass as much as possible of her lumbar region, pressing inward with moderate force, easing the pressure slightly, then intensifying it. Darlene grew more and more relaxed; she was ready for anything. She was Darlene Moore Schiller, unquestionably the most sensual woman in Washington. She glanced without interest at a newly discovered "find" that appeared on her forty-six-inch-diagonal computer screen. A tiresome Federalist mahogany, Sheraton-style sofa, vintage 1800, was the first course in today's orgy. Maurice was babbling with soft soap.

". . . it was a truly fantastic piece of luck to find this marvelous piece. And your luck too, dear friends, to be able to see it first." Maurice's accent was very British, superior, smug, as befitted his official biography. "This simply marvelous piece turned up during a probate valuation of the Heep family property in Worcester, Massachusetts. Granny Heep was tight-fisted and closemouthed. She lived comfortably on Social Security checks for fifteen years. Hers and her sister's, Abby. Dear Abby had been dead for twelve years, but Granny Heep ignored the fact. Since her ancestors had regularly thrown up on the *Mayflower* crossing, Granny felt Abby's checks were the least the country owed her." Having struck a properly larcenous note, especially appealing to his viewers, Maurice came to the point. "The piece is in mint condition. There are only seven other such pieces in the world. All in museum collections. The floor price for this miracle of perfection that the Heep family must have actually sat on is one half million dollars. A true bargain."

Darlene glanced at the sofa and made a face. Herman would love the sofa. Herman had no taste. But he would particularly love it now that they lived in Washington and he was the White House Chief of Staff. The President was a fool for Americana. So Herman had become a fool for Americana. Darlene sighed, and raised one finger.

"Thank you," Maurice said. "I have five hundred thousand dollars from Washington." To use Darlene's name would violate the unwritten code of this auction. But it served Maurice's purpose to keep all bidders informed as to who the competition was. It raised their hackles. And the prices. So cities did nicely, for those who knew. And these people had reduced knowing to an art form. They knew his "Washington" was Mrs. Herman Schiller III.

The camera cut to a tight head shot of Darlene. Anyone but Maurice, seeing her rapturous expression, might have supposed it was caused by the perfection of the sofa. Maurice knew it wasn't. Having made it his business to know the business of every important bidder, Maurice guessed that something was happening to Mrs. Herman Schiller III off-screen that had nothing to do with the sofa. Bitch! he said to himself with some relish. Served her husband right. He didn't like pompous asses anyway.

In Amsterdam, the "Flying Dutchman" went to six. His name was Hendrick Van Der Velder, but he spent so much time on his three private jets, policing his worldwide holdings, that it was estimated he lived about a total of one year out of seven in Amsterdam. They called him the Flying Dutchman, and the name had stuck. Somehow the Dutchman never missed an important Northbie's auction.

"Thank you, Amsterdam. I have six hundred thousand from my friend in Amsterdam. It's back to you, Washington."

Out of sheer irritation, Darlene raised her bid to seven. Patiently, the Dutchman bid a million. Fat, as round as he was tall, hard of hearing and nearsighted, the Dutchman could be counted on for action, even at age eighty-eight. Maurice beamed, and then Josie raised all ten fingers, closed her hand and pointed toward the camera with the forefinger of her right hand. Maurice nodded. Josie was the prodigal daughter of Moe Frankenberg, the former ambassador to France. She was the Beverly Hills hostess who gave the most "fun parties." It was she who made it "smart" to seat husbands and wives at separate tables. Imagine! Separate tables! Josie, dear child, had topped the Dutchman.

"I have one million one hundred thousand dollars from Beverly Hills," Maurice stated serenely. Nothing chintzy about Josie.

Under her breath, Darlene said, "Shit!" She didn't want the fucking sofa anyhow. She'd wait for the Louis XVI commode. And the jewelry.

Maurice glared and continued. "Going for one million—No! I must protest. One million one for a Sheraton sofa in mint condition? Surely you realize that we are witnessing the greatest steal since the tragedy of the Mexico City museum. Dear friends, I am sorely tempted to remove the sofa from the auction." Crap! If those clowns think I'm letting them off for one million one . . . Dammit! It's a real antique. A genuine piece of junk. Anyone who sits on it is going to have a very sore ass. "Now let us show a sense of proportion, dear friends . . ."

After returning from a baseball game at Candlestick Park

in San Francisco, Toshida Takahashi had slipped out of his Brooks Brothers slacks, sports jacket and shirt and changed into a comfortable silken kimono. Now, sipping tea in the computer room of his penthouse in the chic Pacific Heights district of the city and staring at his one-of-a-kind, liquid crystal, flat screen display, Mr. Takahashi decided it was time to teach the Americans a lesson. He raised the fingers of his right hand three times and added a single finger.

"One million six," Maurice said soberly. "I have one million six from Tokyo. I beg your pardon. From San Francisco." That should make clear even to Josie whom she was bidding against. "It's back to you, Beverly Hills."

Josie Frankenberg scowled. It wasn't for nothing that, besides all that diplomatic garbage, her father was the man who had founded the *Frankenberg Racing Form* and, in his old age, the magazine *Videotape Guide,* which sold over forty million copies every month. Josie sat in her Charity Room, as she described it to herself, and considered the sofa. And the one million six. She would place the sofa in the living room, rope it off, of course, and throw a big party to celebrate the acquisition. A party for charity. Not a blue-chip charity to support the music or medical centers of Los Angeles, which everyone supported anyway. But perhaps a charity party for bag ladies. Or one for the victims of incest. No. She meant abused children; that was the common euphemism. Charities were the way. Then she would donate the sofa to one of her favorite museums and get a tax write-off. The party would be a tax write-off too, and with the money she siphoned off the top for giving the party, she would buy something else. And do it all again. Josie showed her family mettle by using nine of her fingers.

"One million nine from Beverly Hills," Maurice remarked offhandedly. "Do I hear more?"

Mr. Takahashi was chairman of what had been described in business magazines as the General Electric of Japan. He was acknowledged to be one of his nation's most important business leaders. A trendsetter. And these days he had a liking for Early American. Also middle American. In fact, anything American. He wouldn't mind owning America. Someday he might. The inscrutable Mr. Takahashi raised his bid.

Maurice closed the bidding at two million eight with, "Going, going . . . One last chance, Beverly Hills. No? Very well. Gone! This magnificent piece of Americana is yours, San Francisco."

Josie decided the United States had made a mistake dropping only two atomic bombs on Japan. They should have dropped ten.

Money Maurice was starting to hit his stride.

The Flying Dutchman relaxed. While watching the back-and-forth on the sofa, in which he'd lost interest, he had managed to consume twenty-three hundred dollars' worth of Beluga caviar that filled a Meissen porcelain bowl. The bowl rested on a Chippendale mahogany marble-top server. He washed the caviar down with a glass of Moskovskaya vodka as he observed that Darlene Schiller finally got herself the ostentatiously ornate cabinet made in 1788 for Louis XVI. For a mere one and a half million. The woman had no taste. Now that her husband was the White House Chief of Staff, he wondered how Herman would feel about one and a half million dollars for a French king's conspicuous consumption. He was glad he'd never married.

"The old joke goes," Maurice was saying, "that Jean Baptiste Camille Corot painted three thousand canvases in his life. Of that number, five thousand are in the United States. . . ." Maurice studied his audience on the six television screens. Josie Frankenberg could hardly contain her eagerness. The Flying Dutchman seemed more alert. Sebastian Taggard, Mr. Takahashi and Darlene Moore Schiller looked bored. But no matter about them. At long last, thank God, Peter Regis Petty had come alive. The Petty Museum wanted the painting. Peter Petty had been sitting like a broomstick until now. Afflicted with tunnel vision, he cared nothing about furniture. Terra cotta sculpture. Vases. Jewelry. Nothing but paintings. He was fixated on paintings. With his custom-made buttoned-down suit, his long-strand Egyptian cotton shirt and his maroon patent leather Gucci loafers, the man remained something of an innocent. Who happened to have at his fingertips almost fifteen million dollars a month to spend. Courtesy of Rex Regis Petty, his deceased grandfather, seeking immortality. The Petty Museum—an architectural disaster in Maurice's opinion—had the largest collection of the very worst paintings done by the greatest painters who ever lived. The "upset price" for this figure painting by Corot was seven hundred and fifteen thousand dollars.

The bidding began. It became incendiary. Up. Up. Up. Josie dropped out at two million three. The Flying Dutchman bid three million five. He already had two Corots including "La Chanteuse."

Maurice's practiced British public-school accent was perfect as he said, "I have three million five hundred thousand from Amsterdam. It's back to you, Dallas."

Peter Petty crinkled his nose and raised eight fingers.

"Thank you, Dallas," Maurice said. "The bid is now three million eight. Amsterdam? Three million eight? Going . . . going . . .''

The Dutchman raised his finger again. Four million wasn't that much money.

Maurice acknowledged the bid. "I have four million from Amsterdam." He glanced at the Corot. Actually not the master's best work. But respectable. He wondered if Petty had any idea what would happen if he ever bought a truly great painting of a truly great painter. One masterpiece could shatter the perfect harmony of Petty's entire collection. Even this mezza-mezza painting could be a fatal mistake.

Oblivious of the danger, Peter Petty raised ten fingers. With the result that Maurice said, "I have five million from Dallas. Amsterdam, what do you say?"

The Dutchman shook his head.

Maurice pushed a button that shifted the shot of the painting to a close-up. "Look at the freshness of those colors, the natural beauty of the face. It's worth every penny, Amsterdam," Money Maurice pleaded.

The Dutchman stared at his monitor. He hated color television. The reds were always orange and the blues purple. He shook his head again. He had enough Corots. And the best.

"Five million from Dallas," Maurice said sadly. Pity. This had started to be good, clean fun.

Sebastian Taggard was seated in the library of his town house in the East Sixties in Manhattan. In his early fifties, of average height, he was a handsome man with thick black hair, graying at the temples, strong features and a carefully trimmed iron-gray beard. He had not been heard from before. Now he raised two fingers. Maurice raised an eyebrow. Taggard never bid on paintings. Or on furniture. Or on terra cotta.

"Five million two?" said a somewhat baffled Money Maurice. What was Taggard doing? The man was the only professional in the crew. Maurice respected that. The Taggards—Sebastian and his beautiful daughter, Cella—were true art collectors and art dealers. The House of Uni, their shop, was the toniest place in the world to buy antique and ancient jewelry. The pieces were glorious. Necklaces, headdresses, earrings, chokers, bangles. He would give almost anything to be able to auction off a piece of ancient jewelry from The House of Uni, any piece. Classy people, those Taggards. But why the hell was Sebastian Taggard bidding on the Corot? Maurice didn't think the man even liked French painters. Still, a bid was a bid. "I have five million two hundred thousand dollars from New York. Thank you, New York," he said, his voice reflecting only a small part of his confusion.

Cella had the same question. "Father," she said, leaning toward Sebastian, "what do we want with a Corot?"

"We won't get it, dearest. Peter Petty won't let it go."

He didn't. At that moment Maurice announced that he had six million from Dallas.

"See," said Sebastian. "I'm just playing." He raised the bid and Maurice felt his head spin. This was going to be a record sale. "I have seven million from New York," he said. Maurice was awed, but his face showed only good cheer.

Cella waited. Sebastian waited. Everyone waited. Even for these people, seven million dollars for a painting was approaching real money. But Sebastian was confident.

Peter Petty was irritated. He all but poked himself in the eye making his next bid.

"Eight million," said Maurice. He was living up to his name with a vengeance. Money Maurice! "I have eight million from Dallas for this beautiful Corot. New York? It's against you."

Sebastian did not move.

Maurice said, "Going . . . going . . . gone!" He paused to give emphasis to his words. "A new and historic price has been set for a painting by Jean Baptiste Camille Corot. Eight million dollars. For 'La Femme au Petit Chapeau.' You will never regret it, Dallas."

Everyone took a deep breath.

Darlene Moore Schiller felt wonderfully relaxed and only vaguely concerned as to what she would tell Herman. It was hard to concentrate on Herman when Roberto's fingers had moved upward to her gluteus maximus, the main swell of her rump. But she must think of Herman. The commode wasn't his taste. She would say she'd been carried away. It was all a mistake. She'd tell him about the commode over drinks tonight. She wished Maurice would skip all the rest and get to the gold Aphrodite necklace. And the silver girdle! Thank heaven she had Roberto to keep her occupied. She hoped he had a sense of timing. She mustn't have an orgasm on camera.

In the course of time Mr. Takahashi picked up the blue-

and-white Ming bowl and the T'ang horse for two million and three million, respectively. Maurice was glad to have him aboard.

As for Mr. Takahashi, with the purchase of the Ming bowl and the T'ang horse, in his own mind he had conquered China. Something even the emperor had failed to do. What with China and America in his possession, it was truly a splendid day.

With the Dutchman having a malaise, and with Josie having stretched her allowance on a terra cotta piece, Peter Petty acquired a Turner for beans. Ten million three.

This time Sebastian Taggard didn't interfere. He didn't want to call Peter's quixotic attention to the Aphrodite necklace and the silver girdle. Though the Petty Museum did not collect jewelry, in a fit of pique Peter might bid for anything. And only the Flying Dutchman could compete with Peter Regis Petty.

As it turned out, things went to Sebastian's liking. When the Aphrodite necklace—gold links interspersed with pearls and golden pomegranates—came up for sale, Josie dropped out early. It wasn't quite right for a charity party. And she didn't feel justified in buying the necklace simply because she desperately wanted to wear it. Darlene longed deeply for the exquisite piece, but what with the commode, she didn't dare push Herman too far. She stopped at one million. After all, there was still the silver girdle to look forward to. Three of the men had turned off their computers. The Dutchman had given up women years ago. Peter Petty knew that jewelry was not a painting. And the Japanese had no feeling for Aphrodite—a Greek goddess, wasn't she? The Japanese had their own goddesses. So Sebastian Taggard picked up the Aphrodite necklace for only one million three hundred thousand dollars.

Cella Taggard snapped off the computer. "Even if we lost out on the girdle, we have the necklace. It's exquisite." She smiled with satisfaction.

"It's aged well," Marcus said. "Quite a looker for a piece almost three thousand years old."

"A little less flippancy, Marcus. A necklace that cost us as much as the Aphrodite deserves your respect," Sebastian said with mild indignation.

"I'm lousy with respect. That necklace is authentic."

"Exactly. Remember, brother, a diamond is not the only thing that's forever. In fact, the Aphrodite necklace gives new meaning to 'forever.' '' Cella went to the liquor cabinet and opened a bottle of Dom Perignon she'd chilled for the occasion. "Let's hear it for Aphrodite."

They toasted the necklace. The auction. The clients of The House of Uni. Money Maurice. Northbie's. They toasted computer hacking. After they'd finished the bottle of champagne, Sebastian suggested a snifter of brandy.

"Your one-hundred-and-fifty-year-old V.S.O.P. Napoleon brandy, perhaps?"

"Now that you mention it, Marcus, why not?" Usually Sebastian reserved his special brandy for himself, but the children were his own flesh and blood. He poured each of them a generous dollop, and they seated themselves in their favorite spots—Sebastian in his leather armchair, Cella cross-legged on a hassock, Marcus on another hassock.

"I can think of nine women who will bleed for it," Cella said.

"You're not thinking very hard. I can think of twelve." Sebastian smiled. "I've got my work cut out for me."

"Even you can't re-create twelve necklaces." Cella laughed. "It would cause talk."

"Some clod might suggest that they were mass-produced. Not to worry," Marcus said cheerfully. "You'll charge enough for the one to make up for the other eleven."

"Why not?" Sebastian settled himself more comfortably in the chair. "I've already selected the name for our interpretation. We'll call it the Astarte necklace."

"Aphrodite? Astarte? It's all the same," Marcus said. "Both love goddesses. All artists should have your business sense. They'd never need foundation grants."

Sebastian glowed. "The spring season will be very busy. Our customers wear more jewelry than clothes in the summer."

"But we won't have the Astarte ready in time for the spring," Cella said.

"Damn! You're right. We'll show it in the fall. The Astarte!" Sebastian pronounced the name with an exaggerated "Ah" and a long, rolled "r." "The Phoenician goddess of love. Yes. I like the name. I really do. Now let's see. Hmm. I know. It was found beneath the rubble of a bombed-out village in northern Lebanon."

"Great story. Proving that something of beauty can turn up anywhere. Even in the senseless destruction of an entire country. Here's to Astarte!" Marcus said dryly, staring at his shoes.

"Father is a born salesman," Cella murmured, sipping her brandy and looking around the room with pleasure. The room had the elegance only the very wealthy cultivate. And the disorder. A Renaissance painting, unlit, needing a little cleaning, amidst a collection of Victorian watercolors. Equally in need of cleaning. One wall of bookshelves held rows of books with old, gold-tooled, leather bindings, set every which way. Other books lay in random piles, equally disorganized. Faded fabrics, a slightly worn look to the leather chairs, cracked vellum lampshades, a fine Persian carpet frayed at the edges and art objects scattered randomly about—a Chinese vase here, a French commode there, a Greek statue against the wall—all helped set the tone. It was a room full of beauty, casually accepted, deeply loved. Yet it had none of the standard pretensions associated with wealth, or with celebrated art collectors.

Marcus interrupted Cella's reverie. "Father, was the Corot a genuine Jean Baptiste Camille Corot? Or was it our old family friend—Jean Phillipe André Beaumont?"

"I think it was a genuine Jean Baptiste et cetera. The painting was listed in Alfred Robaut's catalog. Published in 1905. But it could be a Jean Phillipe or one of that clan." Sebastian pursed his lips. "That family has some very talented painters."

"It's quite lovely, no matter who did it," Cella said with the merest hint of defiance. "The Beaumonts are remarkable. But I'm glad they don't tackle Vermeer."

"Come on, Cella. They're brilliant forgers—not fools."

"By the way, was the terra cotta *Madonna and Child* that Josie Frankenberg bought done at Uncle Victor's studio?" Cella asked Sebastian.

"You have a good eye. How did you know?"

"It was just a touch too perfect. It's actually more beautiful than many originals I've seen. You know, people have the damnedest fixations. If an artist was born in the fifteenth century and had tooth decay, diarrhea, consumption, syphilis or, even more inspiring, died of the Black Death, they automatically gasp at his genius. Because they soak in Jacuzzis and don't worry about dentistry, or syphilis, but are scared out of their minds about AIDS, they think any misery they don't have is inspirational. It's not. It's just misery. Incidentally, remember the lovely Cycladic maidens they did when Mother was still alive? Those idols have been bought and sold by museums and collectors for over twenty years. I've seen some marvelous work in Uncle Victor's studio."

"We all have," Sebastian said. "And Victor has equally high praise for our work."

"He should. We send him enough clients." Cella smiled.

"As he does us. It's a reciprocal arrangement that works to both our advantage."

"By the way, Father, how do you plan to re-create the Aphrodite?" Cella asked.

"I have a few ideas. Do you have any?" There was an undercurrent of appeal in his voice. "You've not been a very enthusiastic coworker recently."

"Sorry, my mind has been full of straw. But I have thought about the Aphrodite. Or, as you named it, the Astarte. A loop-in-loop gold chain with a large pearl. No, not pearls. Perhaps amber or garnets?" In her mind's eye, Cella could see the necklace forming, circling the throat of a maiden at the altar of the goddess.

"It's a pity diamonds aren't possible," Sebastian said, frowning. "I do like diamonds."

"Diamonds! Father, you know as well I do that the Astarte would never have diamonds. De Beers wasn't even a gleam in a Dutchman's eye for another three thousand years."

"Historical accuracy can be a nuisance. Diamonds are so . . . well, rich in feeling."

"Especially when they're flawless, ten carats and associated with Elizabeth Taylor. Or the Florence Gould collection. Otherwise they're so common they're almost tacky. I gather you think amber and garnets are too ordinary?" Cella asked with a shade too much innocence.

"Too ordinary for our clients."

"They're true to the period."

"Truth is not something we could sell to, say, a sweet young thing like Mari Schlieffen."

"Who, if you'll excuse my saying so, Father, has her taste in her behind."

"But rich," Marcus insisted. "And not chintzy."

"Merely vulgar and totally uneducated," Cella snapped. "She counts on her fingers and toes."

"But she does know how to count. And well beyond ten. The way I heard it is that she was an unemployed starlet who took up mud wrestling to pick up a quick buck and landed— stark naked except for the mud—in the lap of Felix Schlieffen, the hotel king." Marcus looked pleased. "She gave the old bugger his first erection in a year."

Cella made a face. "She makes erection sound like a dirty word."

"Don't be catty. Anyway, you'd better think of ways to appeal to her delicious vulgarity. Not too vulgar or she'll get the hint. Just trendy vulgar—you know the old pizzazz," Marcus said.

"I suppose I do," Cella admitted. "All right, we can do without diamonds. Pure gold pomegranates and pearls and maybe—why not emeralds? Consider emeralds, Father. Those divine chunks of ginger ale bottles quarried from the bug-infested jungles of Colombia. Can't you see those sacks of muddy green rocks on the backs of eight muddy burros being led by eight muddy peasants? Muddy, sweating burros," Cella murmured mischievously.

"I suppose we could use emeralds. Or perhaps sapphires. And gold." Sebastian nodded his head. "I lean toward sapphires."

"No. The Astarte deserves emeralds. Emeralds are heroic. Astarte was heroic. Think of those eight muddy burros picking their way, step by step, through the steaming jungle. Dodging snakes, the jaws of alligators, tarantulas. They plod endless miles to reach the first link with civilization. The Walkashore Natural Bridge. A wonder of nature swaying a mere thousand feet above the raging Walkashore River."

"I can see you have your heart set on emeralds," Sebastian said peevishly. "Personally I prefer sapphire blue to emerald green."

"Not if you appreciate the kinship among Astarte, the emeralds, the burros and the peasants. Bravely, the eight sure-footed, muddy burros and heroic, muddy peasants step across the Walkashore Natural Bridge. Step, step, step. Eight muddy burros . . . oops, there goes a muddy burro." Cella paused and gave her father a dazzling smile. "Reduced but undaunted, our seven muddy burros, seven sacks of muddy emeralds and seven muddy peasants push onward."

"I give up," Sebastian said through his laughter. "Emeralds and gold it will be. Attractive and, as you say, in keeping with the goddess. And maybe small, perfect pearls? Or we could begin with a large emerald in the center."

"That's the old snake oil, Father. Big is beautiful. Big jewels. Perfect pearls. Pure gold. Nothing cheap. No bargain hunters allowed." A grinning Marcus turned to Cella. "You convinced the old medicine man. He's just developed a fondness for muddy burros."

"I'm not unreasonable. Emeralds will bring a good price. Eventually, we'll also make a profit on the resale of the Aphrodite.'' Thinking of the huge sums the two necklaces would sell for pleased Sebastian.

Unlike her father, Cella had been drawn to the Aphrodite necklace by its beauty, not by its resale value. Even if it had not been found on the site of the famous Kenan Erim archaeological dig at Aphrodisias, she would have known it was authentic. It gleamed in a way that kindled pictures in her mind; ancient scenes and voices came to life that were strangely familiar. With Sebastian, nothing happened. He heard nothing, saw nothing. She often thought her father was deaf, dumb and blind; imprisoned, even more than she, in the here and now.

''More important than the resale,'' Marcus said earnestly, ''think how owning it rubs off on every forgery in the shop. Every Minoan toe ring, or Etruscan pin . . .''

Sebastian's smile faded. ''I don't know where you pick up such language. Forgery? Gutter talk. Please don't use that word in my presence. You make us sound like common charlatans. Is this what comes of your working on Wall Street?''

''My mistake.'' Marcus threw up his hands in mock surrender. ''I meant every piece of jewelry you re-create.''

''I would hope so. Our work is often superior to the original.''

As usual, Cella acted as peacemaker. ''You put on a marvelous performance at the auction, Father. That was very clever, letting Darlene get her kicks outbidding Josie. Maurice was ready to close for Darlene at nine hundred twenty thousand dollars. Going . . . going . . . It was all over but the invoicing. Until you stepped in. Maurice almost fainted with pleasure. You outfoxed Darlene. She didn't dare go higher or Herman would spank. A splendid show!'' Cella hoped she sounded sufficiently admiring.

''I did handle it rather well.'' Next to money, there was nothing Sebastian liked better than flattery. ''I suppose people will talk.''

''Thanks to Maurice, everyone in that auction knows who was bidding. You'll be the talk of the art world,'' Cella said.

Sebastian sighed contentedly. ''The Aphrodite is a fine investment in our future.''

''Investment?'' Cella wrinkled her nose as though sniffing an unpleasant odor. ''That must be why the faces on the screen depressed me.''

''Depressed you? That auction included some of the wealthiest collectors in the world. You've known most of them for years." Sebastian was genuinely astonished. "What's depressing about them?"

"Their attitude—pure greed. They have no interest in the beauty of a work of art. Social climbing is passé, there's no longer any society to climb to. So when all they have isn't enough, they become Patrons of the Arts. It's the new status symbol."

"If you were anything but Etruscan, I'd advise you to say five Hail Marys and give thanks," Marcus said. "After all, status is what you sell."

"But I am Etruscan, and I don't understand these people anymore."

"What's there to understand? They have to do *something* with their money," Sebastian observed.

"And all they can think of doing is making more money. So they buy a piece of ancient jewelry for a million or two. Or an ancient Bugatti automobile for six and a half million. They'd buy a fly swatter if it belonged to the Emperor Claudius. Then it becomes great art, and great art is a great investment."

"I find Darlene Schiller's greed inspiring," Marcus said dreamily.

"Sex is Darlene's sublimation for money. And the way Maurice plays on it is a form of bondage and discipline." Cella sounded as disgusted as she felt.

"The trouble with you, my dear sister, is that you are not naturally greedy. It's a flaw in your character. Someday I'll have the money to send Maurice into spasms," Marcus sighed. "He can play on my avarice, and I'll purr as prettily as Darlene."

"I think you both underestimate Darlene. She does love beautiful things," Sebastian said.

"Probably. But it's a secondary consideration to her. Mostly, as Cella said, she wanted the Aphrodite because it's like buying IBM in the early sixties. A great investment." Marcus gave his sister a hard look. "Why do you suddenly care?"

"I don't know. I never cared before. But today something happened. There was an odor of dead fish. Or maybe decaying ideals. I saw too clearly."

"My poor sister. I've often wondered what would happen if you ever saw the Gorgon's head. It doesn't make you blind. It does worse. It curses you with clarity. And now that you see the truth, are you going to spend your life repenting your sins? Or can you learn to live with a bad conscience and make money from your pretty doodads?''

As usual, Sebastian found his son's attitude exasperating. "Our creations are not 'doodads,' '' he insisted. "Our jewelry is exquisite. Each piece sells for hundreds of thousands of dollars. If they're good investments, I'm glad."

"Good show, Father," Marcus said. "I admire your honesty. And what a great joke on a world full of Darlene Schillers. Your Astarte forgery will cost more than the original. And, comparatively speaking, will cost peanuts to make."

"You're becoming tiresome, Marcus. The word *forgery* does not exist in Etruscan language. And at that, your Wall Street world has enough fraud. And fakery. And scams. In fact, if you insist on thinking of us as forgers, think of your work on the Street as preparing you to work with us in the shop. A sort of apprenticeship."

"Sorry, Father. The Street's not a training school for a shopkeeper. The amount of money that you flimflam from customers over an entire year is petty change compared with the shell game that goes on down on the Street each and every day. Remember the crash in '87?" He gave his father a look of smug superiority. "Since I'm doing my damnedest to join the world of big money, Wall Street is a lot better launching pad than The House of Uni. I plan to be a customer of The House of Uni. Like the Herman Schillers, the Frankenbergs, the Schieffens. A buyer, not a seller."

"You think being a shopkeeper is beneath you?" Cella snorted.

"Not beneath me. Just not up to me. I admit that The House of Uni is a pretty tony shop, but it's still a shop. Even if Father wears custom-made suits and you wear designer clothes, you're both glorified shopkeepers." He grinned at his father. "And I want to be a patron of the arts, not a clerk. I look forward to the day when I can stop in and pick up a few trinkets—even if here and there one is a forgery. Or . . .''

"I've had all I can take for tonight, Marcus. I told you I dislike that word." For all his conceit, Sebastian was a courtly man who was very fond of his children. His face had grown pale from the strain of controlling his irritation with his son. "I think you ought to go home."

"If I've raised your blood pressure, Father, I apologize."

"Apology accepted," Sebastian said as calmly as he was able. "I'm going to bed, Cella, and you should too. We have busy days ahead." He rose and leaned over, kissing his daughter on the cheek. "Sleep well. And don't dream. You need to sleep off a good deal of nonsense. Including your brother." Sebastian left the room without saying good night to his son.

"Marcus, don't you have any feeling for our heritage?" Cella asked. "We're Etruscans. Our ancestors were the goldsmiths of the goddess Uni. Father and I re-create the beauty of the past as our way of paying homage to the old gods. How can you compare what we do with forgeries?"

"It's different since Mother's death," Marcus said gravely. "Father's busy enlarging the client list and maximizing profit. Making sound business decisions. He wouldn't allow a non-salable item like our heritage to fuck up the bottom line."

Cella was silent for a moment. Then she said, thoughtfully, "Mother wouldn't have sold our jewelry to Darlene Schiller. She would have packed her off to Harry Winston. Or let her circle, like a vulture, around Northbie's or Sotheby's."

"Same story for Josie Frankenberg and Muddy Mari Schlieffen. Off with you to Winston or Buccelatti."

"She handpicked our clients as carefully as she designed her jewelry."

"That was Mother. One lousy businesswoman. She didn't give a tinker's damn for who would cough up the top dollar," Marcus said with something akin to awe. "She would only sell to collectors who loved the work for its beauty." He looked hard at Cella. "You ought to try Zen breathing for relaxation. I wish I had some chocolate bars to give you. Chocolate is a relaxant."

"Nothing will improve my disposition when I think of our clients. I can hear their voices. 'I need something for the beach and I do adore this ruby toe ring. But do you think it's really me?' Or, 'I was thinking about earrings with sapphires. Antique, of course. But definitely sapphires. It brings out the blue in my contact lenses.' Or—and this was a whopper— 'What I'd like is something in the Borgia tradition. Lucretia Borgia. You know what I mean—a poison ring.' And the guy hasn't even married the rich bitch yet."

"Wasn't it Judith Townley who wanted something special—a choker of pearls and golden Roman coins to wear for jogging?" Marcus asked as he scrambled to his feet.

"Tennis, not jogging. She wanted to change her approach to the game. Clothes, jewelry, backhand."

"I guess life isn't all roses on the right side of the tracks. But count your blessings, Cella. Father isn't all wrong. As they say on Wall Street, what good is happiness? It can't buy money." He kissed her cheek. "I'll call you in a day or two." He waved good-bye as he ambled from the room.

Cella remained cross-legged on the hassock, sipping her brandy and remembering her beloved and lost mother. Spina had been the finest creator of antique and ancient gold jewelry in the world. Her work was so perfect that no one—neither scholars nor antiquaries, not archaeologists or art historians—ever questioned the truth of the jewelry. It was ancient. It was exquisite. It belonged to the past. Even as her mother did. Cella had always taken pride in the wonderful creations. In her mother's genius. It reaffirmed what the world had long forgotten: the beauty and vitality of the Etruscan life.

Cella took a deep breath. It had never occurred to Marcus to use a word like *forgery* when their mother was alive. But he used it now. Was it true? Was the work her father and she did forgeries? Cella finished her brandy in one swallow. Then she sat absolutely still, eyes closed, her head tilted to one side, holding her breath, waiting, listening, visualizing her mother, trying to remember her mother's final words. If only she could remember what her mother had said, she would know if Marcus was right.

Then slowly she felt it happening. The mists parted and the sun broke through on the shores of memory. The color of each moment of their last months together became sharp and clear. She was barely out of girlhood, and her mother had begun teaching her the beauty and wonder of the world that was lost. It was a time of magic. Her mother's magic. A time that had never come again.

PART TWO

1976
ANCIENT WAYS

Chapter Two

Cella had been looking forward to today for a month. At Christmas, among many other presents, her parents had given both Marcus and her an ancient coin. Marcus had received a Carthaginian coin with the head of Hannibal on one side. And she was given a coin issued by Mark Antony; on it was the head of Cleopatra, the only woman in the ancient world ever to appear on a coin. It was Cella's opinion that if the face on the coin bore any resemblance to the real woman, then the only explanation for Cleopatra's celebrity was her talent for pleasing men in bed. Examining the coin under a magnifying glass convinced Cella that Shakespeare, and Shaw and legend, had vastly overrated the Egyptian queen. Cleopatra hardly looked like a woman for whom one would toss away Rome. And if one came right down to it, history justified Cella's view of Cleopatra. In her parents' large collection was a Roman coin that commemorated the defeat of Mark Antony and Cleopatra. It was inscribed with the words AEGYPT CAPTA: Egypt captured. As every student of ancient history learned, the woman did not even have the sense to hold on to Egypt, let alone conquer Rome.

But the coins were more than gifts. Spina Taggard suggested that her children create something beautiful with the coins. And show their father and her their creations in a month. What followed was very much in character for both Cella and Marcus.

Cella took some gold from her mother's workroom in their home in Sands Point, gold that Spina sometimes used for repair work on their less precious pieces—the ancient pieces were never touched—and made a U-shaped channel to fit around the coin. Then she threaded a gold chain through the loop and attached seed pearls to either side of the chain. The result was a charming necklace such as a child of three thousand years ago might have worn.

Marcus' conception of beauty was something else entirely. He bargained with the clerk in the rare-coins shop on West Fifty-seventh Street and left whistling, with a check for a substantial sum of money in his wallet. His next stop was Farrel & Fenway, a Wall Street brokerage house, where he opened an account. He then proceeded to speculate with his newly acquired wealth, buying two thousand shares of Alpha-Beta stock, a computer company he had read about in one of the investment advisory services to which he subscribed. They said the new issue was ''hot.'' At seventy-five cents a share, the stock was a steal.

When the time came to show what they'd done with their coins, Marcus was so full of himself he had to show his work first. He pulled his Alpha-Beta stock certificate out of a manila envelope and flourished it before his mother. He then opened the previous day's *Wall Street Journal* to the page listing over-the-counter stocks and proudly pointed out that in only a month Alpha-Beta had tripled in price. The stock he bought was now worth three times the value of the coin. ''What can be more beautiful than that?'' he said. ''Tripling your money in only a month?''

''Quadrupling your money,'' Spina responded.

''You're right. Quadrupling it. Making a hundred times your money. You do understand, Mother,'' Marcus enthused.

''And more money. And still more money. And more. And more. And more.'' Spina stopped and smiled.

''Yes! More, more, more!''

''And will you ever dance for joy, Marcus?''

''I'm dancing now. Making money is my dance of joy.''

Spina looked deeply at Marcus, a strange look. Cella saw pity and great sadness at the bottom of it.

''So you choose to be poor all your life?'' their mother asked.

Marcus grew pale. When his eyes met his mother's, he was seized with a great fright. It was not what his mother had said about his love of money. It was a dark, ancient fear entering the room. Only after a long silence did he take the stock certificate and slip it back into the envelope. Then he folded up the newspaper. ''I'm sorry I disappointed you,'' he said at last. ''It's the way I am.''

''You will kiss the feet of many fools,'' Spina said softly. She looked at her two children. They were truly good-looking people. Marcus was almost too handsome and Cella was a beauty. Both were well above average height and harmoniously built. Both had long, slim hands and thick eyelashes and white, even teeth, a wide span between their eyebrows, and narrow hips; both of them were light and graceful in their movements. Their eyelids lay loosely over their eyes, casting a shadow that gave a rare limpidity and depth to their glances. There could be no mistaking that they were brother and sister. But they could not have been more different in temperament.

Turning from Marcus, Spina studied Cella, her expression changing, becoming less stern. Slowly she smiled, and Cella, tilting her head slightly, smiled in a return of love. It was then that one received from their faces the key to understanding the particular type of beauty of the Vilanova-Taggard family. It gave out the truth frankly and simply. Each was an Etruscan face that looked as if it could not know guilt; a face that, without warning, might suddenly reveal the bewitching, enigmatic smile first seen by archaeologists in the tombs of ancient Etruria. It came easily with joy or with pride, but never with guilt.

A thin, delicate laugh rose in Spina's throat as she looked at Marcus again. "The heart, the heart. That which brings us all our joy. And all our sorrows." She turned back to Cella. "What have you done, my young one?"

Cella drew a deep breath and then handed her mother a velvet-lined box. Spina opened it and studied the necklace. Finally she leaned over and kissed her daughter lightly on the forehead. "Are you pleased with it?" she asked.

"No," Cella answered in a clear voice. "It isn't good enough."

"It's beautiful," Marcus said.

Cella stood immobile, lost in thought. "Marcus," she said at last, "it isn't helpful to be applauded for being second-rate."

"But it's beautiful," Marcus insisted.

"Is it, Mother?" Cella asked.

Spina put her arms around her daughter. "You did your best. For my sake."

"No. For my own sake," Cella replied. "And it isn't good enough."

Her mother lifted up Cella's hands, looked at them and smiled. "Your hands have a life of their own, my daughter. But they have no discipline yet. Your hands will learn. They have the 'gift.' Someday they will please you."

Cella's heart grew light. She would consider her life filled to the brim if someday she were half as talented as her mother at creating jewelry that mirrored the art of the lost worlds.

* * *

That summer, as usual, Spina and Sebastian Taggard and their two children vacationed in Spina Taggard's ancestral home in Tuscany: the Villa Taraquin, outside Carrara. Marcus was bored during the time spent away from Manhattan, but Cella loved the old villa built into the side of a rocky hill. It seemed to her that each summer the hills and valleys, woods and villages, that encircled the house were like old friends she came to know better and better. They were all part of her childhood, her slow blossoming into young womanhood. The names of the places were as familiar as her own, and she never forgot how the streams ran and the narrow roads turned, and what the signs of the changing seasons were, and how the people on the farms were related to one another. She felt more at home in the old villa than she did in any other house. There was much power in those remembered things.

Every time they returned, she felt that she entered a world that contained a greater richness of life; a more vivid multiplicity of color and melody in the house and the garden and the surrounding countryside. Life was everywhere—laughter and talking, gossip and disputes, hushed lovemaking at night. The full sweetness of life was here in the alternation of work and play, sunlight and starlight. It was as though the whole solar system revolved around them.

One morning in early August the sky was high and blue. On the rim of the horizon, large gray clouds which might bring on rain and thunder tomorrow towered up. A little stream hurried noisily from under a thicket, through the dark foliage, and the sparklings of sunlight dropped into it like a drizzle of gold.

Sebastian had been called to London on business, and while they waited for his return, Cella's mother suggested a picnic. They would make their regular pilgrimage to the resting place of their ancestors. Cella was ready for this suggestion as a field plowed and seeded is prepared for the spring rains, but Marcus was not interested. He had done this many times before and preferred reading the European edition of *The Herald Tribune* and two business magazines that had just arrived, a week late, from the States.

Cella's mother had Celeste, their cook and housekeeper, pack a picnic lunch in a wicker basket: a bottle of Soave Bolla, half a loaf of Italian bread, cheese, salami, olives and grapes. Enough for a picnic on the hillside, where they would rest before completing their pilgrimage.

Cella and her mother spread their lunch on a flat rock in a

clearing on the hillside quite hidden from view, high above the summer landscape that lay calm and golden below. They had reached the clearing by an all-but-overgrown path that wound in and around and up the slope between the underbrush and rocks. The woods just to the west were a deep green—a summer vault—and where the beams of sun filtered through the leaves, it became luminous and filled with a verdant richness. From time to time a flight of wood pigeons rose from its green depths and circled the sky. Spina watched them intently. It was like praying in a cathedral, Cella thought. She had seen her mother like this before. It was praying and more than prayer. It was an act of divination. Her mother was "seeing." After some minutes, Spina blinked, shook her head as though waking from sleep and, in a change of mood, remarked to Cella, "Walking on city streets quickly makes me weary. But walking in the fields or climbing up a hillside refreshes me. Don't you prefer the earth underfoot to a sidewalk, Cella?"

"I like them both, Mother," Cella said. "Sidewalks and fields. Maybe fields and hills a bit more."

"You are a twentieth-century child," Spina said. And then, with an appraising glance, she continued. "But you are also my daughter and you belong to the past." She seemed like a connoisseur standing in her wine cellar, evaluating a particular vintage, and Cella held a candle high so her mother would more easily be able to read the label.

The clearing was surrounded by many boulders, large and small, scattered this way and that, as though tossed there in random play by a giant hand. Except for the smooth, flat rock on which they placed their basket, the uneven terrain was not one to invite picnickers. And yet the twisted path that they had followed to reach this sunny spot seemed almost as though it were meant to unite the rocky hillside with the open country below. Then the path stopped as if in fear of giving away a secret.

"What are you thinking, Mother?" Cella asked when they had finished their lunch and sipped the last drop of wine.

"Of the past." Spina sighed. "Of the grandeur and beauty and joy that they knew. It all seems to be disappearing from the earth. So many men and women—the rich as well as the poor—live and die in narrow, dingy cellars."

Cella's long fingers played with her dark hair. "In the summer, my dreams are wonderful. They must be of the past. My mind becomes full of scenes such as I've never seen in the world of today. Wild lands—mountains and valleys—run down to meet the blue sea. Strange animals appear. And the people I meet—magnificently dressed or all but naked—fight with spears and shields or dance wildly, embracing each other.'' She laughed. ''When I'm dead they can write on my gravestone, 'Her days may have been gray, but her nights were glorious.' ''

''You dream of the past,'' Spina said softly. ''Why shouldn't you? We bear old names. Vilanova. Taggard—out of Tages. These names are as old as the fields and trees around us. Older. They've been known to the people, to this country, for centuries and centuries. Thousands of years.'' Spina spoke very slowly as though revealing a hidden passion. ''Remember, my daughter, we are of the Etruscan line. Out ancestors brought joy and dancing and music to this land when Rome was a collection of mud huts. Be proud of your heritage. Remember what it has created. It is our blood running warm in the veins of the Latins that gave them their great tradition of beauty. Of art. Of music. This is the reason that the 'gift' of beauty has been put into our hands, yours and mine. Our dead have put their trust in us. To keep their vision alive.''

Cella's eyes glowed with delight. ''What a splendid world to put into our care.'' She looked at her mother expectantly. ''Isn't it time to pay our respects?''

''Yes.'' Spina gave Cella a loving look. ''It is time to pay homage. I'm glad you're impatient.''

Leaving the remains of their picnic tucked in the basket, the two women rose and picked their way toward a flat slab resting against the upward slope of the hillside. When they came within touching distance, each positioned herself against one side. Placing their hands on the stone, using every ounce of strength in their bodies, together they pushed. But nothing happened.

''Wait a moment, Mother,'' Cella said, breathing hard.

''Are you giving up so soon?'' Spina asked.

''Giving up?'' A strong sense of pride ran through Cella's body. ''Of course not. I just wanted to catch my breath.'' Bracing herself, she pushed against the stone as if her life depended on the act. Actually, what was most important in her life did. She was so intent that she did not notice her mother standing, silently watching, doing nothing. The stone slid slowly to the left, moving on invisible bronze hinges. As it turned, it became apparent the stone was a portal to another world; and when it opened, they seemed to hear the music of double flutes and a hundred little voices that whispered and laughed and sang and called out from somewhere below the earth. Cella turned to look at her mother and realized that she had been standing back.

A great light passed over Cella's face. "The portal opened for me," she said.

Spina's pride in her daughter shone through her dark eyes. "I waited to see if you could pass through alone. If they would welcome you. They have done that. Now come. To the Tomb of the Lioness. Our ancestress." Taking a small flashlight from a pocket in her skirt, she stepped in front of Cella and moved forward into the darkness of the buried cavern. Cella hurried after her mother. The ancient world called.

It was too dark for Cella to see the huge chamber that lay hidden beneath the mountain. But every fiber of her being could feel it. The room had a life of its own that was part of the past. Its breath met them on the threshold. There were stone steps leading down, and as the two women slowly descended, the air around them grew colder. Yet Cella felt comfortable and refreshed and happy. This was the sepulcher of the Taggard family, and the stone steps were worn by the passage of thousands of feet ever since they were first carved more than twenty-five hundred years ago.

Down, down, down they went into the darkness, with Spina's flashlight showing the way. There was no other light, and yet as Cella's eyes grew accustomed to the blackness, it seemed that the room glowed with its own radiance. She could see everything in the chamber and she wondered, as she always did, how it was possible that she could see so easily. Was what she saw real or imagined? But when her mother's flashlight happened to shine on an object or a wall at which she was staring, it revealed exactly what she saw without the added illumination. When they reached the bottom of the steps, they looked around, each feeling the deep ecstasy of having this old and magical world opened again to them. Here everything had a deeper meaning for the heart. Here the mother and daughter, hand in hand, could pay homage to the old, wise gods.

The sepulchral chamber was in an excellent state of preservation, and Cella saw clearly the vividly colored paintings everywhere. The ceiling was covered with paintings of circles, ivy leaves and small flowers. The walls were painted from top to bottom with hedonistic scenes of men and women banqueting, scenes of naked men and women dancing. On a stone altar, a powerful man with seven golden antlers that extended from his head made love to a young woman, nude except for a gold chased necklace and golden armlets that had been wrought in the form of snakes. On the lid of the sarcophagus, set on a platform in the center of the chamber, were two faces sculpted in bronze relief, faces of a man and a woman smiling at each other. That half-amused, enigmatic Etruscan smile. Cella marveled at how much her mother resembled the woman—the woman who was her own ancestor of thousands of years ago. Then, glancing around the chamber, she was again enraptured and transported by the wonders it contained. This tomb, hacked out of stone for eternity, was furnished with everything that its makers might need in the afterlife. Pots and pans for cooking, painted ceramic vases, single and double flutes, expertly crafted bronze armor and weapons and, of course, exquisite gold and silver jewelry that their owners would need for ornamenting themselves in the other world. Everything was a testimony to beauty, to the joy of living, to a distinctive civilization. What joy in the face of death! Cella found herself staring with delight at her mother.

"It's beyond words," she said, her eyes blurring as if filled with tears.

"And it is all true. And it is yours," Spina said gently, seeing the glow in Cella's face. She waited for a while in silence before saying, "Now we must go."

"I know." Cella suddenly felt the cold.

"But you can come back," Spina said. "Remember that. You can always come back."

Cella followed her mother to the foot of the steps; in the dark that was light enough, she looked back at the chamber and listened once more to the music and the whisper of voices. Yes, she thought, I can always come back. Always.

Holding hands, the mother and daughter silently walked up the steps, at peace with their loved ones.

Above ground, Cella was surprised to see the changes that had taken place. The high sky had paled as if bleached. The clouds which had appeared white now floated like slate-colored clots. The sun was close to setting. They had been in the chamber of their ancestors far longer than she had realized. Overhead, the pigeons were flying again, and Spina's face grew solemn.

"Is it an omen, Mother?" Cella asked.

"Yes," her mother said quietly.

Cella hesitated to ask further questions. She helped her mother pack the picnic basket as best she could, making certain they left behind no trace of their visit. Everything must look as it had when they arrived: virginal, untouched by human beings, a neglected patch of accidentally clear earth in the midst of a disorderly array of stones.

They picked their way rapidly down the path, and when they reached the flat, curving road that led to the villa, Spina began to walk at an extremely rapid pace. "We must get home quickly," she explained. "A danger threatens. I cannot 'see' what it is, but I must be there."

Marcus had seen them coming along the road and ran down the steps of the villa to meet them. "Mother, what took you so long? You've been gone for hours. Something has happened."

"I know." Spina spoke very slowly. "What exactly is it?" she asked as she hurried into the great hall of the villa.

"Father is at the airport in Genoa. He telephoned an hour ago. The airport is a wreck. The plane Father was on was blown up."

"Oh, my God!" Cella cried.

"It's all right. He wasn't hurt. Nobody was hurt. It happened after everyone had disembarked. The bomb was in a suitcase that was still on the plane. They think it was supposed to explode while the plane was in midair, between Milan and Genoa, but something went wrong with the timing mechanism."

For an instant Spina went so deadly white that Cella thought she might faint. She asked, trying to reassure her mother, "You're certain Father is all right, Marcus?"

"He's okay. He wants Mother to pick him up at the Marguerita Ristorante in Genoa. He can't rent a car because the place is in an uproar."

"I'll go now," Spina said, glancing rapidly from her daughter to her son. "Have Ettore put gas in the Alfa."

"I'll go with you," Marcus said.

"So will I," said Cella.

"No. You will both remain here." Her statement was a command. "I will go alone."

Never afterward could Cella explain why those words seemed to express a delicate choice between life and death. Nor why she felt that at that one moment, if she could have found the right words, she might have stopped the workings of fate. But the look on her mother's face struck her dumb.

Spina turned on her heel and walked toward the great door of the house. Antonio, an old servant, opened it for her, and the menace of the summer twilight struck Cella anew. As she watched her mother walk through the doorway, she accepted that everything was out of her hands. Her mother had nothing more to do here. It was time for her to leave.

Cella and Marcus tried to play boccie on the hard, packed dirt rectangle set aside for the game. It was no fun. So they sat on the terrace and ate some fruit and drank some wine and listened for the sound of a car in the driveway. Cella's body felt chilled and she put on socks to protect her feet from the cold marble. Genoa was little more than an hour away. Cella's hearing had become abnormally acute and she could hear many distant sounds: a cart rolling along the road, a dog barking, a baby crying. But no sound of a car. It seemed to Cella that hours and hours had passed before the telephone rang. Antonio said it was Mr. Taggard. He wanted to speak to them. Cella raced to the phone ahead of Marcus and picked it up. When he tried to grab it from her, she kicked him.

"Father!" Cella was almost too excited to be coherent. "Is Mother there?"

"No." Sebastian sounded irritated. "Didn't Marcus give her my message?"

"She left hours ago. In the Alfa. To pick you up." Cella had to keep kicking and punching at Marcus, who was trying to yank the phone away from her.

There was a long silence on the other end of the line. When he spoke, Sebastian's voice was slightly hoarse. "I'll try to find a taxi to drive me out to the villa. If I can, I'll leave a message for your mother at the *ristorante* that she should return home."

He rang off immediately, and Cella knew that he had done this because he didn't want to answer any questions.

"Give me the phone, Cella. Give it to me!" Marcus pulled it out of her unresisting hands. "Father, I gave Mother your message. The Marguerita Ristorante and everything," he shouted into the dead phone. "Father? Father?" Marcus slowly replaced the phone. "Father hung up," he said in a puzzled voice.

"He's going to try to find a taxi."

"Where's Mother?"

A terrible panic swept over Cella, but all she could do was shrug her shoulders. The brother and sister had nothing to say because they had too much to say. Something was wrong. Cella felt that the burden of whatever had happened was upon her shoulders. The responsibility for not stopping her mother was hers, and her guilt set her to pacing around the room.

"She 'saw' something. I know it. I should have stopped her," Cella whispered.

"What you should do is stop it now. Just cut it out. I don't want to hear about Mother's 'seeing.' I don't know if she really 'sees.' And neither do you."

"She does. I know it."

"And do you 'see'?" Marcus asked sarcastically.

"I wish I did."

"You can wish all you want, but you don't. So you don't know anything about it. Or what Mother does or doesn't do. So knock off the gloom-and-doom routine. Every time you go to the Tomb of the Lioness you fill up with all that old mystic garbage."

"It's not garbage. It's real."

"Maybe yes, maybe no. But right now it makes no difference. So quit behaving like a nut. Mother probably got a flat tire."

An hour later their father arrived with his cousin, Victor Vilanova, and Victor's young nephew, Anton Vilanova. They'd bumped into each other in Genoa in the restaurant.

"Has your mother telephoned?" were Sebastian's first words on entering the house.

"No," said Marcus.

Cella kissed Anton lightly on the cheek. Anton and she had grown up together, and had spent many hours trying to work out how closely related they actually were. The summer before last they'd decided that they were fifth cousins. "Not so close that we can't be lovers," Anton had said, only half teasing. And Cella had answered, "When I'm older, we will be lovers." Also only half teasing. Despite her grave concern for her mother, Cella felt a little of the familiar lifting of her spirits that being with Anton always gave her.

Sebastian went to the liquor cabinet and poured himself a stiff scotch. He offered one to Victor, who nodded, and to Anton, who declined. Outside, the sky had darkened and the heavy clouds blotted out the stars. The warm summer day had become a cool evening. The marble terrace was wet with moisture. A single bird, and then another, started singing high up in the trees in the garden. It seemed strange to Cella that in the midst of so much beauty, death should be in the air. She no longer believed that her mother had avoided it. Or that she had expected to avoid it.

By the time the telephone rang, Marcus was dozing, Cella's hands were held tight by Anton's, Sebastian was woozy from too many scotches and no food, while Victor was still sipping his first. The telephone rang three times before Sebastian an-

swered it. It was the police. The news was as bad as Cella
had expected.

"Tell me, what is it?" Sebastian was unaware of how
strained he sounded.

"Who are you?" asked the policeman, wanting to be careful.

"I'm Sebastian Taggard, Rufio. For God's sake, you know
me."

"Aaah, Commendatore Taggard. I have sad news indeed.
Suo moglie, Signora Taggard, is in the hospital."

"Then she's alive!" Sebastian almost shouted with relief,
his body straightening.

"Sì. Mi dispiace molto, Commendatore. It was an automobile accident. Two drivers with two large trailer trucks.
They fight for position on that narrow, winding road—you
know which one I mean—along the coast between Genoa and
La Spezia."

"Yes, I know. What happened?" Sebastian's initial exu-
berance changed to fear.

"One trucker, he tries to pass the other on a blind curve.
So he has a head-on collision with Signora Taggard's car. Her
condition is not good."

"Oh, my God!" Sebastian's body sagged again.

"The trucker, he has minor injuries . . ."

"Minor injuries!" Sebastian exclaimed.

"Yes. I am sorry about la Signora Taggard. You come to
the hospital in Genoa now."

Sebastian slammed down the telephone. "Spina is in the
hospital in Genoa. Let's go."

When Sebastian and the family arrived at the hospital, the
nurse at the reception desk looked at their strained faces and
estimated their capacity for truth. She decided to let the doctor do it.

"Dr. Lollini will be with you shortly. Take a seat in the
waiting room, please."

Dr. Lollini did not arrive shortly. The long evening
stretched on and on. Sebastian spoke to the nurse three times.
Victor spoke to her twice. Cella, Marcus and Anton remained
slumped on the bench like puppets whose strings have been
cut.

Hours later—they'd lost count of the time—a young man in
a white coat entered the waiting room, glanced around and
walked toward them.

"Are you the Taggard family?"

Sebastian stood up and took a deep breath. "We are. I'm Sebastian Taggard. Your patient is my wife."

"And I'm her cousin," Victor said, standing up beside him. "How is she?"

"Sono Dottore Lollini. She's been in a coma. Her head has sustained serious injuries."

Sebastian gestured helplessly, his face ashen.

"A coma? Will she live?" Cella asked through numb lips.

"Who are you?" the doctor asked.

"I'm her daughter. Will she live?"

"And I'm her son," Marcus said.

"We don't know. She's just come out of the coma, but we don't know for how long." The doctor paused and then gently continued. "I have to tell you there is a strong possibility that she will die."

Sebastian put his face in his hands. When he looked up, his face was no longer that of the internationally known art collector and dealer. It was the face of a very young, vulnerable man. "Can we see her?" he asked without force, a pleading note in his voice.

The doctor frowned. "Not yet. Not all of you. But she has asked to see her daughter." He glanced at Cella.

Cella groped for words. She had been trying to fit what had happened into some sort of understanding and found herself unable to do so.

"What about me?" Marcus sounded angry.

"She said her daughter," the doctor repeated.

"Can we see her later?" Sebastian asked anxiously.

"I don't know," the doctor replied. Then, looking again at Cella, he said, "Please come with me."

Cella followed the doctor down a long corridor that she never saw and into an elevator that took them to another floor, the number of which she did not notice. She saw nothing except the back of the doctor. But when she entered the room where her mother was lying in bed, she began to tremble.

Spina waited for the doctor to leave before beginning to speak. Cella listened to her mother's words and spoke words in response, but as the mists of death slowly closed around Spina, Cella's mind first blurred and then obliterated everything that was said. She didn't know how long she sat at her mother's bedside before she realized that Spina no longer spoke and that the hand she was clutching was lifeless. Cella studied her mother, desperately trying to memorize forever her face. She didn't close her eyes when the tears streamed down her cheeks, because she had to absorb every detail; this

was the face she had to remember all her life. Spina had
closed her eyes and accepted death, smiling. It was the same
ancient, familiar smile as on the carved faces in the Tomb of
the Lioness. Cella bent down and touched her lips to her
mother's forehead, a kiss of farewell and safe passage. She
gazed for a moment longer and knew, with comforting fore-
sight, how little of the face she would forget in the years to
come. She then covered her mother's face with the white
sheet.

When Cella returned to where her family was waiting, no
one had to ask what had happened. There was a wordless
communication between Cella and her father and brother and
the Vilanovas that told everyone that Spina was dead. Only
Sebastian needed something more.

He held Cella close and asked, "What did she say? Before
she died?"

Cella swallowed hard. She raised her hands in helpless
confusion. "I . . . er . . . I . . . I don't know," she stam-
mered, and her face mirrored the muddle in her brain.

Sebastian stepped back a pace and studied his daughter.
Then he gently cradled her cheeks in his two hands. He could
feel the rapid beat of the pulse in her temple pounding against
the tips of his fingers. He wrapped his arms around her again,
holding her close. "It's all right, my child," he said. "When
the time comes for you to remember, you will remember
everything. Until then . . ." He left the thought unfinished.

Cella could only nod. She was certain her mother's dying
words were very important, and she hoped her father was
right—that when the time came, she would remember everything.

PART THREE

1989
THE HOUSE OF UNI

Chapter Three

In this age of media hype, it was hard for Frank Ford to believe that an establishment catering to the rich and the very rich would actually be so difficult to find. Especially a store that flourished in the East Sixties between Madison and Park, a neighborhood that proudly proclaimed its wealth. Feeling like a damn fool, he paced the street twice, squinting hard, looking for the building, and still did not find it. Then, abruptly, he saw the shop and forgave himself for having missed it. No canopy. No storefront displaying expensive merchandise. Nothing enticing to catch the eye of the passerby. And definitely nothing to stop the Rolls-Royce rich without prior knowledge of the place. The only evidence of the shop's existence was a tiny window display on the ground floor of the building. The gray stone town house was set back about fifteen feet from the sidewalk and protected by a high, wrought-iron fence which made the window even more difficult to spot. The entrance to the three-story building was next to the window. He knew from the information furnished him that embedded in that lustrous mahogany door was a sheet of half-inch bulletproof steel. He opened the gate, and as he walked toward the door, he saw, just to the left, a small white Carrara-marble plaque inscribed with hieroglyphics and, below the hieroglyphics, the word UNI. This was The House of Uni.

To see what was on display required close examination. Then all one saw was a simple bronze choker ringed with bronze drops designed to move with a woman's neck. It was neither gaudy nor glittery enough to attract the hungry eyes of vandals. But those who knew recognized it for what it was: a rare piece from the time of Ur, at least four thousand years old. And they knew that its price—though it was neither golden nor jeweled—was considerably higher than an ordinary piece of twentieth-century jewelry that required diamonds to establish its value for everyone.

Cella had watched the thin, balding, bearded young man through the one-way mirror of the window display. She smiled as he slouched up and down the street. His deeply lined face with its high cheekbones and cleft chin suggested an artist rather than a journalist. But as journalists go, he seemed surprisingly unobservant. Or he should have his horn-rimmed glasses checked. He'd passed by the shop twice and missed it twice. Perversely, Cella was pleased. That was as it should be. At The House of Uni no one was ever admitted without an appointment. Collectors and dealers knew where to find them. So did the museum world. Strangers, like Ford, had to have an introduction. The House of Uni operated under the same principles as had the House of Morgan when old J.P. was alive. "If they don't know where I am, I don't want to do business with them."

The bell sounded a soft, fluting note, and Juliana, the quasi-store manager, a distant cousin via marriage and hand-picked by Spina, raised her eyes from a Greek earring she'd been cleaning. Sebastian and a client, Buffy Rutledge, were examining a gold cross set with enamel, pearls and sapphires, vintage 800 A.D., said to have belonged to Charlemagne. Buffy's father, a man who owned blocks of Manhattan real estate, had long ago changed his name from Rubini to Rutledge. He had, more recently, changed his religious convictions. Since his remarriage he claimed to be an atheist. Sebastian watched Buffy with patient, practiced sympathy. Despite the young woman's desire to please her father—he wouldn't blink at a diamond bracelet—Buffy also wanted to please herself. And her dead mother. Sebastian had his money on Buffy. When the chimes fluted again, he glanced up to signal Cella, but she was already walking toward the door.

For all its hidden weight, the door opened easily on silent, well-oiled hinges. Frank Ford's face was full of professional good will. Then his mouth fell open as he stared at the young woman. He had thought of antiques dealers as gray-haired and dowdy—almost as ancient as the pieces they sold—and was not ready for so much beauty. There were her large violet eyes, and the paleness of her skin accenting the gleam of the blackness of her hair. But there was more. He saw a face with the strange, haunting beauty such as ancient sculptors had captured. He knew that generous, sensuous mouth. He had seen her Etruscan ancestors in art books containing photographs of their work. And when she smiled, he knew that bemused smile; it exiled the grim facts of today and carried him to another time, somehow more joyous and sunlit.

"I'm Cella Taggard," she said. "And you?"

The name itself, Cella, rang a bell. Gaia Caecilla, an echo of the Etruscan world with its gods and goddesses. Seconds passed. They stared at each other, both smiling; he in rapt appreciation, she with courtesy.

"I'm Frank Ford," he finally said. "From *The Washington Post*. We made an appointment on the telephone."

"Of course."

"As I told you, I'm getting married. Dr. Lord suggested I consider purchasing an antique wedding ring for my wife. He said that The House of Uni has the best selection."

"We do. Come with me."

He followed her into the shop, and as they moved quietly through the softly lit room, Buffy glanced at the visitor. She couldn't place him. If she didn't know him, he wasn't worth knowing. She turned back to her meditation on her father, the cross and his newly acquired atheism.

Sebastian quickly appraised the young man Lawrence Lord had sent. And dismissed him. What had Lawrence been thinking of? He turned his attention back to Buffy Rutledge. He would reassure and encourage her. The gold-and-jeweled cross was not religious. It was history.

Frank Ford followed Cella through the shop, his eyes growing large. Every inch of the artfully crowded floor contained an astonishing range of antiquities, from a five-thousand-year-old Egyptian pendant to an ankle band set with rubies from India, a mere six centuries old. Frank Ford kept trying to look blasé, but the gold necklaces, pendants, adornments of all kinds, jewelry such as he'd never before seen, made his head spin. My God! he thought. What am I doing here? I can't afford any of this. But he couldn't help stopping to examine a splendid emerald ring set in the form of a snake.

"Is this for sale?" he asked Cella.

"Everything you see is for sale. Our private collection is not on exhibition."

"I don't suppose I could afford it," he murmured.

"It's very old—the second century B.C.—and very expensive," Cella said tentatively. "But you have good taste. Emeralds were believed by the Romans to have a calming effect on the personality of the wearer. So if you want your bride to be calm . . ."

"I'm the scion of an Old American family of dirt farmers.

My bride will live with her quiet desperation." Ford's voice was slightly choked.

"Ah." It had taken Cella only seconds to realize that, despite Lawrence Lord's recommendation, Frank Ford was not a customer for The House of Uni. She quickly led him to the back of the shop—away from impossible temptations—and touched a spot on the dark brown, velvet-covered wall. A hidden door slid sideways, and she ushered Ford into a small, elegantly appointed chamber. Cella seated herself in one of the leather chairs and gestured Frank Ford toward the chair beside her. "Here we have privacy and can speak more freely about what you have in mind. And how much you expect to pay for the ring."

"Oh, well . . ." Frank Ford shrugged his shoulders. Something had occurred to him that—temporarily at least—seemed more important than buying a ring. "What are those hieroglyphics on the plaque next to the front door?" he asked. "Etruscan?"

"Yes. They say, 'The House of . . .' "

Ford finished her sentence. "The House of Uni. I know. But how do you know those hieroglyphics stand for those words? The Etruscan language has never been deciphered. The inscriptions that were found resemble the Greek. They can be read and pronounced, but nobody knows what the words mean. No bilingual text like that on the Rosetta Stone has ever turned up."

"My family is of Etruscan descent. My family knows many things that the modern world has lost." Cella spoke quietly, her eyes wide and candid.

Ford's eyebrows shot up. "Miss Taggard, the Smithsonian Institute would pay a fortune for information on that language!"

"The Smithsonian will have to find out in their own way. It's not my place to tell them."

"Why not?"

"It's forbidden by our religion."

"That's off the wall."

"Why off the wall?" There was a pause as Cella sat poised, far too poised for Frank Ford's comfort. "You don't think Shia Muslim women are off the wall because they wear veils. Or the King of Morocco was off the wall for having a harem. Or the Orthodox Jews who eat only kosher meat. So why is the Etruscan vow of secrecy off the wall?"

"You're right. I don't mean to be a boor, but you see, I've always been interested in ancient history. It was my major at

Georgetown.'' He gave her a look of approval. ''What little I know of the Etruscans I admire. Life-loving. Joyous. Incredibly creative. And their women! Real late-night types. They shocked the hell out of the Roman matrons.'' He chuckled. ''It was a lot freer society than the Greek or the Roman.'' His face slowly reddened and he gave a nervous twist to his tie.

At that moment Juliana popped her head in the door. ''Darlene Schiller is here, Cella. She flew up from Washington to see your father. He wants you to join them.''

''I'll be with them in a minute.''

''Is that Darlene Schiller, the wife of Herman Schiller, the White House Chief of Staff? I've met her several times. There's a rumor in Washington that she has the only mirrored Jacuzzi east of Marin County.'' Frank Ford wiped his glasses as though the steam coming from Darlene's mirrored Jacuzzi had suddenly fogged them.

''It is Mrs. Schiller. She's a client. Originally recommended by Dr. Lord. As you were. Before I forget, be sure to give him my regards. He's an old family friend. I saw him just the other day, when he returned from his trip to the coast.''

''I didn't realize he was an old friend. Or that he'd been to the coast.''

Cella raised her eyebrows. ''He's updating his book on art in America. Checking small museums around the country. He does it regularly. The book is a bible for art dealers.''

''He never mentioned the book to me, and we had lunch twice in Washington last month. I thought he spent the winter in New York and London.''

Cella gave Ford a shrewd, steady look. ''Perhaps there are two Dr. Lords in the world. Yours and mine. I have the feeling that your Dr. Lord is not Dr. Lawrence Lord, Gulbanian professor of art history at Harvard?''

''No. I don't know Dr. Lawrence Lord. I was sent here by his son, Dr. Jason Lord. The archiometrist—the specialist in art forgeries. He paid you a great compliment.'' Ford became obsequious. ''Dr. Lord said that in the world of art—a world full of frauds, forgeries, hoaxes—the Taggards were among those rare dealers in the antiquities whose clients have never required his services. He would guarantee that any ring I bought here was genuine.''

Two faint lines appeared between Cella's eyebrows. ''Did I say something wrong?'' Ford asked. ''I thought you knew Dr. Jason Lord recommended me.''

"It doesn't make any difference." Cella gave him another of her special smiles. It would have taken a far keener observer than Frank Ford to see the use she was making of his information. "About the ring you want for your bride . . ."

Ford suddenly remembered his reason for being there. "My bride? Yeah. I think Dr. Lord made a mistake. I don't know what the hell he was thinking of." Ford laughed uneasily.

"I have a suggestion that might interest you. And it's quite reasonable."

"You'll put the snake ring with the emerald in a Cracker Jack box?"

"Not exactly. I want to show you . . . well, you'll see. Follow me." She rose and moved toward the door.

Cella led Ford through the main part of the shop, passing Sebastian, who was trapped in discussion with a remarkably shapely sliver of a blond vampire, all teeth and talons and rounded bottom and jutting bosom. Her mink-lined raincoat was tossed over her shoulder and she was standing, legs apart, in her Calvin Klein dress, a pair of chinchilla-cuffed boots lying beside her stockinged feet: Darlene Schiller of the mirrored Jacuzzi fame. Frank Ford decided that she was one of the advantages of working in Washington. Providing one could take advantage of the advantage.

"Hello, Cella, you dear thing," Darlene called out. "I need your help. Your father is giving me a pain in the you-know-what." Then she noticed Ford. "Frank Ford," she murmured. "How nice."

"I'll be back in a minute, Dolly," Cella said without stopping.

Ford grinned. "Mrs. Schiller," he said and continued after Cella, who led him to a small alcove off the center of the gallery. Here, too, the lights were subdued, but instead of the hazy, soft gleaming gold of the main shop, this lighting seemed more silvery, like moonlight seen through a mist.

"This is where I display my own work," Cella said over her shoulder. "The pieces are called Cella Classics. They're contemporary interpretations of antique and ancient jewelry." She looked at Ford pleasantly. "I could show you some wedding rings. My versions of beautiful rings from civilizations of the past."

"I could never afford one," Ford said sadly.

"I think you might afford something. I created this line for people who can't spend as much as some of our customers. Let me show you the rings." She pulled out a jewelry tray from beneath the semicircular counter and placed it in front of Ford. The tray contained rings of all kinds. Some set with precious stones. Some not. There were ring brooches made of silver engraved with various designs, ring brooches made of gold in the shape of a heart, a gold-and-enamel ring set with opals and a pearl at the center that opened to reveal a heart. Frank Ford picked it up gingerly.

"This is beautiful," he said in a hushed tone.

"That's a copy of a sixteenth-century German wedding ring. It might be a little too expensive for you. Five thousand dollars."

"Only five thousand dollars for something this beautiful?" Ford laughed weakly. "That's probably nothing compared to the price of the goodies in the rest of the shop. How come you're giving it away?"

"We're not giving it away. It's not an authentic piece of ancient jewelry. It's one of my creations. For my work, the prices are . . ." She hesitated, searching for just the right word. "The prices are reasonable."

Ford replaced the German ring and picked up another. A gold ring decorated with a scene depicting Leda and the swan. "Is this reasonable?"

"Not reasonable enough. My version of a Greek ring. Fourth century B.C. Thirty-five hundred dollars." Frank Ford winced. "But how about this?" Cella selected a plain gold ring made of two divisible hoops of gold with motifs of hands painted in enamel. When the rings were united, the two hands interlocked. "I think this is quite lovely and appropriate. It's an exact copy of a fourteenth-century Italian wedding ring. And it might suit your wallet as well as your bride." Cella's eyes were clear as a child's and full of pleasure.

Frank Ford put the rings cautiously in the palm of his hand. "They're wonderful. How much?"

"Six hundred dollars."

"Even more wonderful. What if they don't fit?"

"I'll give you a guard ring."

"Sold! Amy will be ecstatic. A semi-authentic antique. She loves that kind of thing. Do you take MasterCard?"

Cella suppressed her laughter. "Sorry. MasterCard won't do. Nor will Visa, Diner's Club or the platinum version of the American Express Card."

"Then how do I pay for it?" Frank Ford was flustered. This was a different world. A place where credit cards weren't accepted.

"If you don't happen to have a check on you, you can send us one when you get back to Washington. The House of Uni does accept checks." She paused. "Of course, there are those who carry considerable amounts of cash with them."

"And they usually have bodyguards with bent noses." Ford shook his head. "You'd trust me to send you a check? You barely know me."

Cella gave him a sideways, mischievous look. "I know you, Mr. Frank Ford. You're a distinguished journalist who writes for *The Washington Post*. And how could I not trust a man who was recommended by Dr. Jason Lord?"

"That's damn decent of you. I'll tell him about these wonderful rings of yours. They're so beautiful and they look so old, you could probably sell them as antiques. For a lot of money. But you don't. That's the kind of honesty that Dr. Lord is committed to. He's really bugged when it comes to fakes and forgeries in the art world. I'll describe your work to him as authentic copies."

" 'Authentic copies.' What a charming way of putting it. I'm confident Dr. Lord will appreciate your description too." She spoke with an irony that Frank Ford missed. "Now if you'll excuse me, I must see my father and your friend Mrs. Schiller. Juliana will be here in a minute to wrap your gift." She gave him another of her special smiles. "I enjoyed our conversation."

The first words Cella heard as she approached her father and Darlene Schiller were, "Sebastian, you are being unreasonable. If you persist in being obstinate, I'll take you off Herman's birthday party list. The President and Honey will be there. Everyone will be there. Top Washington and international people. Lots of distinguished titles. Even one old Washington family who lived in Georgetown before Georgetown existed." She smiled winningly. "I have the invitations in my purse. But I'll only give one to Cella. And you can sit home and twiddle your twiddle-dee-dee." Darlene was now furious. "You'll sell that Aphrodite necklace to someone. Why not me?"

"How do you know we have it?" Cella asked casually.

"Don't you play an innocent Botticelli angel with me, Cella Taggard. I told your father I was plugged into the Northbie's modem auction when you bought it. I took the Louis Sixteenth commode. You outbid me for the necklace. You paid one million three. I'll give you one and a half million for it."

"Darlene, please!" Sebastian enjoyed giving the impression he was harassed.

"Don't 'Darlene, please' me!" She flourished a jeweled

hand. "The only time Herman is truly motivated to be generous is on his birthday. He worries about aging. If I don't buy the necklace now, I'll have to wait another year, for his lordship's fiftieth birthday. By then some ghastly slut will have bought it." She gave Sebastian a seductive glance. "Sebastian, please. Please! Please! At least I'm a classy slut. I'll pay two million. That'll give you a handsome profit, and it's my birthday present."

"I thought it was Herman's birthday," Cella said.

"It is. As I explained, Herman always gives me a very special present on his birthday."

"And what do you give him?" Cella asked, trying to distract her.

"That's a good question." Darlene gave Cella a wickedly female, conspiratorial look. "I want a gold-handled chariot whip. I imagine you must have something like that somewhere in inventory. The gold handle, I mean. Something Ben Hur or such Roman types would have used. It should be Roman and at least B.C. The leather must be shiny, slick and new. So one can flick it neatly off the shoulders. And other places when one is . . . er . . . playing. Herman does like to play." She patted Sebastian on the behind. "So you will find me a golden handle and have a whip attached. Stop trying to distract me, Cella." She rummaged in her bag. "Look here, Sebastian. Here are the two birthday party invitations," she said as she held up two envelopes. Then, very slowly and deliberately, she handed one to Cella. "This is for you, Cella, my love. But none for you, Sebastian. Unless you get some sense into your head." She put the other invitation back in her bag and drew in a hissing breath. "Sebastian, I mean it. I want that necklace. For my birthday present."

Although Sebastian was normally infinitely patient with clients, Darlene Schiller was starting to irritate him. "We do have the necklace," he admitted. "But someone has put in an offer ahead of you."

Darlene stared at Sebastian with thoughtful calculation. Then she leaned over and kissed him forcefully, almost antagonistically, on the mouth. Automatically, he returned her kiss with enthusiasm. "Isn't it a pity that Herman is so disgustingly rich?" she said, catching her breath.

Sebastian dropped his hands. "What money has joined together, no man can put asunder."

"No man," Darlene agreed. She took the second invitation from her bag. "And this is for you, Sebastian, you bastard, even though you don't deserve it. I don't for one moment believe you have another buyer." She slipped on her mink-lined raincoat and started pulling on her chinchilla-cuffed boots. As she leaned against the counter, she saw Frank Ford coming out of the Cella Classics section.

"Frank," Darlene called out, "what in heaven's name are you doing here? Did some little old auntie in running sneakers die and leave you big bucks?"

"No such luck." Ford grinned. "But Miss Taggard helped me select one of her own creations—an authentic copy—for my fiancée."

"How divine. Why don't we fly back to D.C. together?"

"Why don't we?"

Darlene finished adjusting the fur cuff on one of her boots and straightened up. "You know," she whispered to Sebastian and Cella, "there are fifteen thousand journalists in Washington. And only about thirty worth having to dinner. He's one. What a nice piece of luck." She patted her hair and then brought her face up close to Sebastian's. "Do you really have a better offer?"

"That's what I said."

Darlene's eyes flashed. "And I said I don't believe you. Bring the necklace to the party. I'll be expecting it." Darlene brushed her lips against Cella's cheek and flounced off.

Sebastian and Cella watched Darlene advance on Frank Ford like some seductive bird of prey. They left the shop, arm in arm.

Cella shrugged indulgently. "Little Dolly Drop Drawers does like her own way."

"So do most of our clients. Buffy bought the cross."

"I thought she would. What will Daddy say?"

"Daddy will find a reason for letting her keep it. What did that young man buy? One of your charming lost leaders?" He couldn't keep the scorn out of his voice.

"A wedding ring. For a whopping six hundred dollars. As you would say—and he agreed—practically a giveaway. He called it an 'authentic copy.' Wonderful phrase." Cella's smile was too guileless. "Makes me want to throw up. I'm the talented designer of extraordinary jewelry. Not antique or ancient, of course. That would be fraud. But of 'authentic copies.' " There was an abrupt drop in her voice, like a reflex to a general fatigue. "Father, Frank Ford was not sent by Dr. Lawrence Lord."

"When he telephoned, he said that Lawrence Lord suggested he stop in and look at some rings."

"Not exactly. He said Dr. Lord suggested he stop in and look at some rings."

"So?"

"There are two Dr. Lords."

"Two?" Sebastian gazed at Cella with sudden gravity. "You mean it wasn't Lawrence? It was Dr. Jason Lord who suggested Ford stop in?"

"That's what I mean. Ford tells me Jason Lord admires our reputation for integrity. Do I look green?"

The impact of Cella's words winded Sebastian, but he made a quick recovery. "You're overly concerned."

"Jason Lord is not like his father. Lawrence Lord sends us clients. Lawrence Lord gets five percent commission. Lawrence Lord is a civilized man, cooperative and accommodating." Cella was severely composed. "Jason Lord is another animal entirely. Everyone tells me he is obsessive about truth in art. He prefers a plastic cup to an exquisite twelfth-century golden chalice. At least he can prove the plastic cup is authentic plastic, while the chalice may not be authentic anything."

"Nothing that we've sold has ever been questioned. I think he sent Ford for the reason Ford gave—our reputation." Sebastian was trying to ease his own anxiety as much as comfort Cella.

"Dammit! He sent that reporter because he's interested in us."

"What if he is? Many people are interested in us."

"Dr. Jason Lord is dangerous. Probably the foremost art sleuth in the world." Cella gave Sebastian a measured look. "Why do you think he's suddenly interested in us?"

"Marina?"

"Marina."

Sebastian momentarily closed his eyes, as if to blot out his daughter's meaning. "You're borrowing trouble."

Cella did not raise her voice, but her anger was evident. "With all the women who dog your footsteps, baying at your heels, calling you at every hour of the day and night, here, in Rome, in Athens, in London, why in heaven's name did you pick Marina?"

"If you'll think back, you introduced us. And why should it matter to Jason Lord that I see her?"

"How do I know? I thought I'd discovered another client for The House of Uni, not another woman for my father, and not the mother of the famous archiometrist. Lawrence Lord I understand. He's worked with us for years. Without a peep out of Jason Lord. I'm positive Lord knows nothing of his father's business arrangement with us. But the art world is a cesspool of gossip. No sooner do you regularly bed Marina Lord—several of your neglected ladies have kept me posted— than Dr. Jason Lord sends us Frank Ford. It's too coincidental to be a coincidence."

"I did forget about the curious Jason Lord."

"What does she say about him?"

"She hasn't mentioned him."

"Marina Lord says nothing about her son? Nothing about his work? You don't think that's strange? Don't you think he's chosen an odd profession, when his mother inherited millions along with a first-rate art collection and his father is a professor of art history at Harvard?"

"I think it's logical. He's working in the field of art."

"On whose side? From his reputation, it wouldn't surprise me if one day he challenged one of his father's art appraisals. Or told Marina her paintings were all fakes."

"Stop looking under Freudian rocks." Sebastian strained to remain calm.

"Father, I do think it would be wiser if you saw less of her, just for safety's sake. You shouldn't stop completely after Ford's visit. That would make Jason Lord more suspicious."

"I don't like your tone," Sebastian flared. "You will treat me with proper respect. I know what I am doing. Rich women spend money. And money calls to money, like moose to moose. Marina is one of the herd. Marina brings friends. Friends bring friends."

"Business contacts, connections, I understand. All I care is that you keep your sex life separate from The House of Uni."

At that moment, the front-door chimes rang. Relieved at the interruption, Sebastian answered the door himself. He smiled, said, "Welcome," and stepped aside to let Anton Vilanova enter the shop.

Over the years, Anton had grown into an elegant rapier of a man: tall, wide-shouldered with a lean, muscular, whip-cordlike body, blue-black hair like Cella's, a long, aristocratic face and a smile that forever marked his ancestry. He walked directly to Cella and pulled her to him.

"I was up all night on the plane thinking what it would be like kissing you," he said.

Slowly Cella relaxed as they stood with their bodies melting together, feeling the other's breathing and communicating a wordless secret, half of which each of them possessed. A long, tender minute passed and then Cella raised her eyes. "This is Wednesday. You're three days early."

"I couldn't keep away. I missed you. I used some business here as an excuse to myself to return sooner. So we could have a very long weekend together."

"Ah! Such devotion. Did you run into a sudden shortage of actresses on the Via Veneto? More famine than feasting on this trip?" Cella smiled knowingly. "Are we spending the weekend at Sands Point, Father?" she asked without looking at Sebastian.

"You know we are. We have a great deal of work to do."

"All right. I'll settle for a short weekend," Anton said with genuine impatience.

"Let's negotiate. We'll have dinner tonight and tomorrow night. I'll come back early Sunday and we'll have a little playtime before we go to the Artists and Models Ball together."

"Does dinner tonight and tomorrow night include breakfast?"

"As always."

"Done."

Huddled in Anton's Aston Martin, Cella bowed her head. Anton parted the curtain of hair that veiled her face. As he raised her chin, he saw her face was set.

"Darling, what is it? What's happened?" All the love and concern he felt for Cella was apparent in his voice.

"My father happened. He's a family problem. Or a curse."

"Let me try to help," Anton said quietly. "Do you love me, Gaia Caecilla?"

"I love you, Tinia." It was their ritual god-and-goddess game, remembered from their childhood years. "I'm glad you're home."

"So am I. You will tell me what this is all about soon?"

"By the dawn's early light." She looked at Anton, and her world seemed to be reinvented. Anton had once told her that there was more to the family than even The House of Uni, than her father's money lust and the threat of Jason Lord. There had been her mother. There was Anton. There were Taggards and Vilanovas who had lived and died, loving and trusting each other, for millennia. She laid her head against Anton's shoulder, and the wind coming off the East River blew the hair back from her face. "Maybe we'll skip dinner," she murmured.

Chapter Four

Dr. Lawrence Lord loved intrigue. He loved it almost as much as he loved larceny. Fortunately, the two loves were born to coexist peacefully. His enjoyment of intrigue had been developed in his early youth, when he skillfully manipulated his father against his mother, thus managing to have one or the other satisfy his every demand. His taste for larceny, coming a little later in life, was a natural extension of his taste for intrigue. He approached larceny in much the same manner that he approached his studies of a school of painting: with discipline, research and an attention to facts. He concluded that larceny required imagination, invention, and, for success, cool nerves and charm. In fact, the higher the stakes, the cooler the nerves, and the more charm necessary. The practice of these talents served him well in his illustrious career in the art world. For, outside of politics, which Lawrence felt to be too open to media curiosity, there is no other occupation—not medicine, law, science or even banking—in which intrigue, larceny and charm are at such a premium and can be so profitable with almost no risk from the law.

Once having been anointed with tenure as the Gulbanian professor of art history at Harvard—and having rapidly recovered from the unexpected divorce by his wife, Marina— it was inevitable that Lord should look around for ways to exploit his exalted position. Ways, that is, beyond collecting the five percent commission from The House of Uni for sending them wealthy clients. Ways beyond building a valuable art collection for doing nothing more than accepting fine paintings as gifts from grateful painters in return for a glowing review by Lord in the press, or in one of his many books.

What occurred to him was a scheme so well conceived that it could easily be mistaken for generosity of spirit. He made himself available as consultant to a few dozen small, American museums located all around the country. Museums that were both shakily financed and even shakier in their convictions when it came to their collections. They knew that Manhattan—Soho, Madison Avenue, the Met and MOMA—was the art center of the country. And they were five hundred or a thousand or two thousand miles away. So, trustingly, these small museums depended on Dr. Lord to keep them apprised of current trends, and to appraise at a fair price a painting that a trustee or the curator had decided was merely taking up wall space. And subsequently, to find them a more appropriate painting—also at a fair price—to fill in the empty wall space and round out their eternally imperfect collections.

The good Dr. Lawrence Lord did all this for a fee so minuscule his work could be considered a charitable act. He did it for the sake of art; to broaden the vision of the surrounding communities that they might come to see art as one of the supreme pleasures of life, as natural as sunlight.

So it was on a warm April day that Dr. Lord was wandering through the carpeted corridors of a small museum in Orange County, California. Accompanied by Roger Rubins, the curator, on one side and by Ann Crowell, a trustee of the museum, on the other side. As they walked they chatted, and as they chatted, Lawrence Lord was charming. It was difficult for him to be anything else. One could never believe anything but the best of him. His perfectly tailored, light gray, tropical worsted suit and conservatively striped tie were in keeping with his eminent position. At the same time, his manner was that of a romantic Italian. His voice was a rich tenor, and he used his hands gracefully in elegant, refined gestures. He stopped for a moment to study a painting that Ann Crowell had magnanimously donated to the museum. She'd painted the seascape herself.

"It stands up very well. Very well," Lord murmured softly.

"I think so too," said Ann, with her double chin, her curling gray hair and her platinum-and-diamond pin all bobbing up and down in agreement. Her husband, a builder worth many millions, had donated the money needed to add a wing to the museum, and Ann had very definite opinions about all things pertaining to art.

"Ann is weary of the Hathaway," remarked Rubins, who was six feet tall but stooped so much that one had the impression he was a short man. His eyes rolled constantly as if he were in perpetual surprise. His self-effacement was marred only when he spoke and the words filed out in a nasal New York accent. "Ann feels American primitives are passé."

"Oh?" said Lawrence Lord. "Rufus Hathaway?"

"I find him boring. Childish," Ann said authoritatively. "I'm not one of those insecure people who believe that collecting art that is less than fifty years old is risky."

"How refreshing." Lord was approval incarnate.

"What I would like is perhaps an Abstract Expressionist. Maybe a Motherwell if we could afford it. Or a Lynde Bayles. I do think the idea of rubber poured on the floor is splendid. Innovative."

"It is interesting," Lord said.

"Or Bruce Marden with his wax and oil. That sounds appealing," she continued. "Or Ken Noland—I have always liked stripes on canvas. If he's not too expensive."

"I think I know exactly the kind of painting you want." Lord smiled at Ann, showing his warm, obliging nature. "And I think I might have a buyer for the Hathaway."

"There are two Hathaways, not one," said Rubins.

"Two? Really? Well, I believe I can manage that."

"Oh, Lawrence!" chirped Ann. "You dear man. How wonderful! They're part of that atrocious collection old Mrs. Jensen bequeathed to the museum. Since her grandfather built the original building, we had to accept it."

"Of course you did," said Lawrence Lord. "And on my next visit you must show me more of her atrocities."

"Do you really want to see them?" Rubins asked.

"Why not? If I can be of some help in clearing out the debris from this delightful museum, why shouldn't I be?"

"You are too kind, Lawrence," Ann said.

"And the Hathaways? You believe you can dispose of them?" Rubins rolled his eyes. "You mean somebody actually would buy a Rufus Hathaway? I agree with Ann. I think American primitives are depressing. And boring."

"I understand your view. But there are many unsophisticated eyes who find them sympathetic." Lawrence had the sincerity of the pure in heart.

"I suppose. How much do you think you could get for the two?" Rubins asked, a disarming innocence in his manner, as if money mattered not at all.

"Perhaps—now, I say perhaps—twenty thousand dollars."

"Is that all?" Rubins asked.

"We'll take it," said Ann Crowell. "Don't quibble, Roger. Twenty thousand for both is quite enough for those impossible pieces."

"I'll make it up to you another time," Lord said, eyeing Rubins, and they both understood what he meant. The disarming innocence of Rubins' manner had nothing to do with his instinct for turning a dollar. Lord knew he would have to dispose of one of Rubins' own paintings from his truly terrible collection. But the price from the resale of the Hathaways would leave room for that too.

"It would be wonderful if you could find something for us by the beginning of December," Ann chirped away hopefully. "I'm giving a large party then, and it would be such fun to have a first showing of whatever you find above the mantelpiece. Or on the floor. What do you say, Lawrence?"

"I'll find a painting for you, my dear. Rest assured."

Ann giggled. "You know, I'd really like something funky. Art doesn't have to be beautiful, does it? Art can be ugly—don't you think?"

"Dear Ann, what a profound perception," Lawrence Lord said reverently. "Consider El Greco."

"El Greco! All that wonderful distortion," Ann said, clapping her hands. Then she arched her eyebrows coyly at Lord. "Now I must run, Lawrence, dear. But I'll see you tonight at our little soiree. It's in your honor, so don't forget to bring a bathing suit. We plan to have dinner served in the large Jacuzzi."

"Come, I'll show you the Hathaways," Rubins said.

In his hotel room, Dr. Lawrence Lord put in a long-distance call to New York. When he reached his party, he started to laugh. The man he was calling recognized the laugh and waited patiently for Lord to subside.

"Do you know what I've just laid my hands on?" Lord asked.

"An undiscovered Rembrandt for two thousand dollars," said the voice at the other end.

"Not quite. A Rufus Hathaway. Not one, but two. At twenty thousand for both."

"Hathaway? The American primitive?"

"The same. You'll buy them next week. Have the Luxembourg Corporation set up an account in the name of Weintraub. Or Beckett. Or anyone we've never used before with them," Lawrence said. "You know, Ann Crowell is quite marvelous. She finds Hathaway boring. We should be able to sell them to Toby Phipps in Brandywine for . . ."

"For double?"

"For five times the twenty thousand. For each. Toby has the money, and I've sold him other paintings. We have an understanding. Of sorts."

"And what does Mrs. Crowell want to replace Hatha-way?"

"Something funky. Her word, not mine," Lord said. "After all, art can be ugly. Talk to you next week from Indiana." He hung up.

Chapter Five

The subbasement of the rambling Sands Point home of the Taggard family was temperature- and humidity-controlled, the air comfortable with just the proper amount of moisture; similar to the weather in Tuscany on a warm spring day in the twentieth century. And, undoubtedly, similar to a warm spring day in Etruria in 500 B.C. On the clock of time, civilizations change far more quickly than climates.

Cella and Sebastian sat on wooden work benches on opposite sides of a long, highly polished oak table. The table was strewn with the tools of the ancient trade of jewelry making—an anvil, two hammers, two wooden pincers, engraving tools, flint knives and the like. Sheets of pure yellow gold were· laid out on vellum. Earlier in the afternoon, Cella, dressed in jeans and a blue denim shirt, had been working on a feathery gold-and-ruby Persian anklet. Out of various soft felt pouches, she had spilled on the table sapphires, emeralds, alexandrite, rubies and pearls of various sizes and minutely examined them. Later, when she was helping Sebastian in his work on a pair of golden Langobardic earrings, she had opened a sizable velvet-lined case containing garnets, turquoise and opals. They had settled on pearls and opals as a compromise. At least pearls and opals were occasionally used; though Langobardic earrings, in the sixth and seventh centuries were most often simply gold with colored glass beads. But The House of Uni clients would not appreciate glass beads, authentic or not.

Having finished her anklet plus helping Sebastian with one of the earrings, Cella scooped up the jewels to return them to the vault. Sebastian was still engrossed in work on the other earring, soldering its gold wire loop to the base of the disk from which the pendant was hung.

Cella closed the closet-sized wall safe—steel and concrete buried within the ordinary bricks—and thoughtfully watched her father for a moment. He worked much more slowly and with less confidence than she did. But the finished piece was always perfect.

"Father, I'm through," she said. "The earring is on the table. I'm going upstairs to change."

Sebastian grunted and glanced up. "Where is the earring?"

"In front of your nose."

Sebastian's eyes ran over the table and saw the Langobardic earring where Cella had placed it. "Hmm. Very good," he said and gazed at her for a second. "You do have the instinct. Your work is so beautiful, you should be proud. But you haven't been yourself lately. Why? Have you been having those dreams again? Revelations and visions?"

"You want to know about my revelations?" Cella smiled as she spoke, reaching over to lay a finger on his lips. "I'll give you the answer the oracle at Babylon gave to Alexander the Great. 'Gaze into my eyes and you will know everything. Everything to know is there. But as you gaze you must not think of the left eye of a lion. To think of the right eye is dangerous enough. But to think of the left eye is damnation.' " She drew back her hand and started to laugh.

Sebastian smiled in spite of himself, then shook his head impatiently. "I'm sorry I asked." He turned back to his work.

When she reached her rooms, Cella considered the relief of a bath. Tonight she and Anton were going to the Artists and Models Ball. It should be fun and wild and crazy. It always was. She sighed. When he was near, other men seemed dull. The thought made her frown. Had she succumbed to the American obsession with fidelity? No! Anton was a trusted and loving constant in a world that had grown more unpredictable.

Unwillingly, she gazed at the television set on its small wheeled table near the window. She glanced at her watch, hoping it would be too late to catch the show. It wasn't. The program had been on for only ten minutes and was scheduled to run for a half hour. Why did she have to watch it anyway? Why upset herself with such nonsense? Suppose she hadn't noticed the announcement in the Arts and Leisure section when she was skimming *The New York Times* over breakfast? Suppose she hadn't known anything about it? She closed her eyes; it was no good. She did know about it.

Reluctantly, she flipped the television set on, spun the dial to the public television channel and sat down cross-legged on the floor. Okay, she thought, let's beat the devil. She stopped herself. Why did she think of him as a devil?

"She's so lovely she looks almost magical." The young blond interviewer was staring at the marble figurine of a beautiful naked woman which had been placed on the table in front of her and her guest. "What did she symbolize?"

The man smiled engagingly. "She is lovely. But her meaning is a mystery."

"Maybe some kind of fertility goddess?"

"Or a virginity spirit. All we know is that she was a major divinity."

"Don't you have any writings—um—diaries or journals or . . . ? Oh, I know, parchment scrolls or clay tablets to tell you about her?" The interviewer laughed at herself for not being able to rattle off the terms.

"We have nothing. Actually, the figurine is very ancient. And very rare. One of the earliest examples of Greek art." The man studied the idol. "And Cycladic maidens—especially those carved in marble like this one—are especially rare."

"If I wanted to buy one, how much would it cost?"

"When these figurines first started circulating in the art market in the sixties, they fetched around thirty thousand dollars. But with inflation and the increased interest in this kind of 'find,' today the price would be much higher."

"Thirty thousand will do, thank you. I could never justify it on my expense account."

"If this were a genuine Cycladian maiden, it would be worth every penny."

"You mean this is a fake? This lovely figurine isn't authentic?"

"Yes. What you are looking at is an excellent forgery. This Cycladian maiden does not come from the Cycladic Islands. She comes from a workshop which we believe is located somewhere in Marseilles. But no one knows exactly where in Marseilles. One of my clients, who paid a fortune for the idol, lent it to me for this program."

Cella caught her breath as she studied the man who was speaking. Although it was hard to tell on television, Dr. Jason Lord appeared to be well over six feet tall, with the bone structure and muscles of a professional football player. He had hair that looked sun-bleached, which he wore combed straight back from a wide, high forehead, and strong, almost too-perfect features. Except for one curious note. Resting on the bridge of his nose was a pair of small, round glasses with wire templates—as unflattering a pair of glasses as could be imagined. Cella decided they were deliberately chosen to play down his striking good looks. For with it all, he had an air of quiet confidence, seeming to look at the world with a mild irony. It struck her that it was as if the best qualities of Lawrence Lord had been sifted through a mesh, leaving only those elements necessary for a finely developed precision of mind, body and spirit.

"But it's so beautiful," said the interviewer with real unhappiness.

"Most forgeries are. They have to be. What never ceases to astonish me," Dr. Jason Lord said with some amusement, "is the gullibility of the art buyer. Though I published my report on the Cycladic idols years ago, many that were originally bought are still being displayed as authentic."

"I guess most people are not sophisticated art collectors."

Lord shook his head. "On the contrary, it's the sophisticated art collectors who are proudest of them. I see the idols everywhere. In Philadelphia, Boston, New York, San Francisco. In major museums and important private collections. In the hands of reputable art dealers. And should I make any comment, the owner is offended. They always insist my report referred to other Cycladic maidens—never theirs." He smiled. "And they will not permit me to examine their idols. They cost too much to begin with, and they'd rather not know if they happen to be forgeries."

"Did you actually prove this idol is a fake?"

"I did. Much to my client's distress."

"Was it hard to prove?"

"It took time. To prove a work of art—a painting, a piece of jewelry, an idol, for instance—is a fake is as painstaking a business as a police detective solving a murder . . . when the killer is a brilliant criminal and there are no eyewitnesses to the crime."

"How do you find the evidence of crime?" the young woman asked, laughing. "You can't look for fingerprints or murder weapons."

"No. Playing Sherlock Holmes with art treasures requires the use of the latest technologies and the most sophisticated tools. For example, I used emission spectroscopy to determine the composition of the Cycladic idol. It can detect the presence of suspicious properties that would be inappropriate for the age and the place where the figurine was discovered. I also used X-ray diffraction and microscopy, two other valuable techniques, for analyzing exactly what elements are present in compounds. In the case of this idol, the patina on the statue consists of calcium sulfate—or gypsum. The presence of gypsum would not, in itself, be proof of forgery." He paused and looked closely at the interviewer. "That is, it wouldn't be proof if the ground or surface water on the Cyclades Islands had a high calcium sulfate content. But it doesn't."

"You're sure?"

"Positive. There's data on the composition of the island water from an American project designed to improve irrigation. There is no water source on the islands with enough sulfur to cause gypsum to form. Not now. Not ever. Yet the patina on this idol—and on many others like it—consists of gypsum."

Jason Lord looked pleased with himself. It was apparent to Cella that he saw himself as a man with a mission, and he enjoyed proving that the Cycladic maiden was a fake. She wondered what was driving him.

"What a pity. It's so beautiful."

"It's too beautiful. Besides the gypsum in the patina, there's the business of the spotless purity of the marble. In theory, this figurine has laid in the soil of the humid Cyclades for forty or fifty centuries."

"That long?"

"That long. Remember, they're examples of the earliest Greek art. If they were in the soil for four thousand years, they should have spots. Spots caused by the iron in the soil. When iron rusts, it forms spots on marble. But the forged idols, like this one, have no spots. They are clean as a whistle." He laughed, but there was no humor in his laughter. "Perhaps they would have sold for less if they had unsightly spots?"

Cella glanced at her dressing table, on which a Cycladian maiden stood. It had the appropriate spots, Cella noted with appreciation. Probably Anton had bought the original from Uncle Victor. But, dammit, why did Uncle Victor permit his studio to ignore the spots in the copies? Cella frowned. Perhaps the reason was exactly as Lord claimed. The art market preferred spot-free idols. She just wished Jason Lord had never seen a Cycladian maiden. Damn! Damn! Damn!

"Dr. Lord," simpered the blond interviewer, "I can see that detecting an art forgery is no simple matter. Your work is fascinating."

"It is to me. Art forgery is as old as art itself. And keeping up with the counterfeiters is difficult. They're as clever as we

are. We publicize the results of our investigations to inform
the world, and unfortunately, we inform the counterfeiters
too. They can read. And believe me, they do. They bone up
on our latest techniques by reading our scientific papers. They
know more than the curators and collectors.'' For an instant,
his natural arrogance was apparent. ''Our best hope is the
sloppiness of the forgers, not the brains of the buyers. The
key question always is: How much trouble and expense does
the forger want to go to to fool us?'' '

''Are you saying that if they make the effort they have a
good chance of escaping detection?'' the blond girl asked,
wide-eyed.

''That is exactly what I'm saying. If they make the effort
and make no stupid mistakes . . .'' He smiled at the girl, and
Cella could see the interviewer react to Jason Lord's overwhelming masculinity. ''But not all are perfectionists. For
instance, take antique gold jewelry. There's an explosion in
this market. Because, today, the countries of origin prohibit
the export of antiquities, genuine pieces of Greek, Etruscan
and early Roman work are at a premium. For instance, look
at these.'' The camera moved back to reveal two velvet boxes
on the table next to the Cycladic maiden. He opened them
carefully. In one box was a gold griffin pin set with emeralds
in a border of intertwined flowers; in the other was a broach
with a gold-and-jeweled satyr's head.

Though neither piece was the work of The House of Uni,
Cella felt a shiver of fear. Her conviction was growing that
Jason Lord was a problem that would not go away.

''Oh! They're exquisite!'' the interviewer exclaimed.

''Exquisite. Except one is authentic and one is a forgery.''

''I don't think I'd really care,'' said the interviewer. ''I'd
like to own either.''

''You'd care about the price. The authentic pin costs considerably more than the forgery,'' said Lord.

''Well, then, yes, I'd care,'' agreed the interviewer.

''Can you guess which is the fake?'' Lord asked.

The interviewer picked up first one piece of jewelry and
then the other. She examined each of them minutely, then
shook her head. ''They're both so beautiful. Each in its own
way. Is there something wrong with one of them? Is it the
gold or the jewels?''

''That's a good guess,'' said Lord approvingly. ''It's the
gold.''

The girl studied the gold again. ''It was only a guess. One
of them isn't really gold?''

"No. Nothing that crude. They're both gold. But X-ray fluorescence spectrometry of both pieces showed that the gold in the broach on the left with the satyr's head is about three thousand years old. The gold in the forged griffin pin on the right is about a hundred years old. That gold shows traces of impurities that genuine ancient gold jewelry doesn't have. But besides the use of modern gold, the emeralds in the griffin pin have been faceted—or cut. Until the fifteenth century, stones were only polished, never cut."

"But they're both gold," the girl insisted.

"People who buy ancient jewelry are not buying gold. They're buying antiquity. Buying mankind's past . . ."

Cella switched off the television set and stared at the darkened screen with stony eyes. There was something strange about the charming, magnetic Jason Lord, an oddness about the man that had nothing to do with his work as an art sleuth. The art world was full of experts devoted to exposing frauds. And always had been. One of them, Charlie Lashfeld, was an old friend. But Jason Lord was different. All the professionals she knew were genuinely upset when they had to tell a client that a beautiful work of art on which the client had spent a fortune was a fake. She had a strong hunch that Lord was unhappy when something he tested turned out to be genuine and he couldn't denounce it. She wondered how he'd react if he tested something made by The House of Uni and all his mind-boggling testing techniques—microscopy, spectrophotometry, X-ray diffraction, chromatography, dilatometry—she could name a few technologies that Lord hadn't gone into on the program—turned up nothing. Would he give up on The House of Uni? Or would he redouble his efforts? She didn't know.

She stood up and stretched, feeling stiff with tension. She barely had time for a shower, but there was something she must do first. Stepping quietly from her bedroom, she entered her study to gaze at a small alcove at the far end of the room. A thick curtain hid the dark interior, but Cella knew what she would see when she drew the curtain aside. As in the Tomb of the Lioness, the dark would be light enough.

She walked toward it slowly, feeling rather than seeing the glow of tapers around the altar in the alcove. The shrine had been created by her mother. After Spina's death, she had changed it to match the shrine she sometimes saw in her dreams. When she entered, there was still the flickering of the candles that she had set around the altar when she arrived at the house; each starry candle was a reminder of the ancient world and her mother.

Within the depths of the alcove were small, carved clay figures of hunters, warriors, dancers, leopards, lions, stags and other creatures—some half human, half beast. The flickering light revealed an enormous wine bowl wreathed with ivy painted on the center of the back wall, flanked on either side by naked dancers exuberantly whirling among flying dolphins. In the center of the alcove was a stone altar, and on the altar stood the figure of a beautiful woman sculpted in terra cotta.

To the uninformed, it might have been simply another of the antiquities the Taggard family collected. Cella knew better. It was the only existing replica of the mother goddess, Uni. When her own mother had died, it had been passed on to her. As it had been passed along for countless generations to certain women of the clan. In the candlelight, it looked huge, and she sank to her knees before the goddess, as Spina had done before her in times of perplexity.

At such times Spina would take her dilemma into the mystic silence, bow her head and remain passive. As a child, listening at the entrance to the alcove, Cella had never heard voices. But Cella was convinced that not once in the many years that her mother had knelt at the altar—with her questions and doubts—had she ever been disappointed by the goddess.

This miracle, if that was what it was, had never happened to Cella. In the beginning, when she had first dared to speak to the goddess—in words or in her mind—she had received no answer. So, after many disappointments, she said nothing, asked nothing, simply knelt in meditation. But this evening she approached the shrine with a feeling of great awe, expecting for the first time to receive a sign.

And as she knelt, Cella began to sense a power, felt herself growing stronger as the power flooded through her body, filling her with the holy presence. It seemed that the sound of many flutes was in the air, and all her ancestors, all those who had ever knelt before the goddess, were gathered here at this moment beyond time. A radiance filled the alcove, and Cella closed her eyes as the ancient world came alive for her. How long she knelt in supplication she did not know, but when she opened her eyes, she felt as if she'd been dreaming. She stared in wonderment at the terra cotta figure of the goddess. Had anything actually taken place? Had her mother's time of magic really come again?

Slowly, she rose from her knees. One by one, she blew out each candle, and without a further glance at the beautiful figure on the altar, she left the shrine. She walked to her study window and gazed out at Long Island Sound. The waves and the sky were turning the evening rose, and there were only the remnants of the glorious golden-red sunset that had flamed across the heavens. She vowed she would do her best to defend The House of Uni from Jason Lord. The high goddess would give her the strength.

Chapter Six

Anton Vilanova removed the painting from its wooden crate and held it at arm's length as he studied it. The painting had been delivered to his penthouse condominium on Friday morning, two days ago—registered and insured—but he had only just found the time to uncrate it. It was as fine a piece of work as he'd expected from his associate's description. The man had a fine eye for paintings and a barracudalike appetite for money. With a typical show of cheap generosity, he had agreed that Anton need only pay double the cost of the painting, rather than the five times he would have asked from Toby Phipps. Mentally, Anton shrugged. He had far more money than he could spend. And he'd learned early that the bazaar mentality was ageless and raceless—the bargaining back and forth was practiced today even as in his ancestors' time. You give a little, you get a little. His partner wanted money, and he wanted the painting. So he'd pay the two dollars, as the old joke went.

He scanned the walls, wondering where to hang his acquisition. The walls were already overcrowded. Unable to decide, he leaned the painting against the couch and strolled into his bedroom to get ready. Cella would be arriving at seven.

He showered and slipped on a beige silk bathrobe. Then he put a record on his phonograph: Spanish sardanas arranged and conducted by Pablo Casals and played by Spanish pipes. The pipes had a strange, haunting sound that caressed his spirit. He poured himself a small glass of La Ina sherry and looked again at the painting leaning against the couch. Shaking his head bemusedly, he went out onto his terrace to wait for Cella and gaze at the skyscrapers surrounding him. With their lighted windows appearing to be multifaceted eyes, they seemed like huge animals that had reared up on their hind legs—and you didn't know if they meant to play with you or devour you. This was the splendid and politely ruthless twentieth-century world he had been born into, similar to and yet so different from the openly savage, wilder and yet more joyous world of his earliest ancestors. The lost world Cella's mother had taught her to love.

In today's world, the rules of behavior were carefully spelled out; rules of right and wrong, of good and bad. Anton had gotten the message when he was quite young. A man who knew his way around could ignore the rules—not openly—but could ignore them under the guise of conforming. As long as one didn't get caught with the proverbial "smoking gun," one was welcome everywhere. The "best people" invited scoundrels to dinner, to play tennis and golf, to cruises on their yachts. In fact, he often thought the world turned on the judicious breaking of the rules.

Anton sipped his sherry, thinking about Cella and the dilemma she faced. During their nights together, he had listened as she poured out her confusion over Sebastian. Was the way he ran The House of Uni right, with his monomaniacal concentration on profits? Sebastian was the capitalist incarnate. Anton had sympathized, but her talk sounded achingly naive. Privately, he blamed Spina for her daughter's illusions. For Spina, the passion for ancient Etruria had the quality of religious fervor. But Cella wasn't Spina, and now she stood with one foot in today's world and the other in the past.

He thought of Cella's lovely face. How similar it was to Spina's. Was it Spina's fault? Spina had done no more than she'd been taught by her own mother. What it came down to was Lucca. If only there hadn't been a Lucca, Anton thought grimly. Until Lucca, the family had been celebrated by the aristocrats of Italy as brilliantly talented goldsmiths and jewelry designers. But their jewelry had always been of the period in which they lived. Until Lucca. Quite by accident, Lucca had discovered the ancient family tomb with its fabulous secret vault stocked ceiling-high with the gold and jewels that the earliest members of the family had used in their work.

His musing was interrupted by the ringing of the telephone. He picked up the extension on the terrace. "Hello," he said.

"Did the painting arrive?" the voice on the other end asked.

"Friday. Thanks."

"Did you deposit the check?"

"Friday. But if I hadn't deposited it Friday, I would Monday morning."

"Good. So much for that." There was a click as the caller hung up.

Anton put the receiver down, a look of disgust tightening his mouth. He went inside, poured himself a second sherry. His mind veered back to Cella's family. With Lucca's find, their luck had run out. Lucca, being Lucca, with her sense of personal destiny and pride in her family history, had seen the discovery as an omen—and Etruscans were famous for the reading of omens. She had believed it was a command from the old gods to restore the beauty of lost Etruria through the medium of their jewelry, long ago prized as sacred offerings to the gods.

It was Lucca who had despised Mussolini and bullied her family into leaving Italy. Here in Manhattan, with Spina, she had established The House of Uni. It had never occurred to either woman that the jewelry they created were forgeries. Each had had a saint's capacity for faith and the arrogance of innocence. What they had done was right. It was the spirit of Etruria, of the pagan world, called back into a time without a soul. It was not to be questioned.

When he heard Cella's key in the door, he sighed deeply to rid his mind of the not-too-pleasant thoughts. There was Cella and he smiled with pleasure at seeing her. Her trenchcoat hung from her shoulders like a cape, and she was wearing Levi's, a work shirt and scuffed sneakers on sockless feet. But, incongruously, dangling from her ears were delicate golden-and-jeweled basket earrings.

"Since you have a key to my door," he said, laughing, "we should be married in the American way. The doorman probably thinks you're my unfaithful wife. Here today, not here tomorrow."

"Believe me, the doorman only thinks of who tips and who doesn't." She stood in the doorway and tilted her head back and forth so that the earrings swung gaily with her movements. "What do you think of them?"

"Exquisite."

"What period?"

"A.D. fifth century or so. Langobardic."

"You're overeducated."

"Did you make them this weekend?"

"Father made them. I helped."

"He's doing fewer Etruscan and Greco-Roman things."

"He's broadening the line," Cella said in a low voice. She

slipped past him into the living room, dropping her coat on the chair. "You started ahead of me. I'd like a glass of something too."

He followed her into the living room, enjoying the sway of her hips. "Vodka?"

"Perfect."

While he was at the bar, Cella stood before the recently uncrated painting, rocking back and forth on her heels.

"What do you think of it?" Anton asked, handing her the drink.

"I like it very much. A nonangelic painting of a child is always interesting."

"What's the school?"

"American primitive."

"And the painter?"

Cella hesitated. "Grant Wood?"

"Close. Rufus Hathaway."

"I should have guessed."

"He's not that easy. Besides, your specialty is ancient and antique jewelry. And those earrings are beautiful, but they won't go with the costume I've had made for you for the ball."

"Darling, gold goes with anything," Cella said, parodying the mashed-potato accent of a New York socialite. "Anyway, I promised Father I'd wear them."

"To show them off in case there's a buyer hanging around in the cast of thousands." Anton relaxed in a comfortable chair.

"In case . . ." Cella sashayed toward him in a comically overdone sexy strut.

"Come here, my lovely." He placed his drink on a side table and beckoned with his hands.

"No," she said, standing still and facing him. "Did you pick up my costume? If it's perfect I'll reward you."

"It's perfect. You'll win a prize."

"A Jezebel with her nipples peeping out. I hope Louise cut the décolletage properly. She's a marvelous dressmaker but a bit of a prude."

"That's not the costume."

"What do you mean? I told Louise exactly what I wanted."

"Yes, you did. But I never cared for Jezebel. Then I had a stroke of genius on the plane to Paris. I telephoned your Louise when I landed. The costume you now have is perfect for the ball. You know the theme."

"The American Sinerama. Americans are fixated on sin. What have you done without my consent, you bastard?"

"You'll go as a Puritan to the Artists and Models Ball." Anton chuckled at the startled look on Cella's face.

"Me? A Puritan? Never!" Cella took a deep swallow of vodka. "Really, Anton . . ."

"This is an Etruscan-type Puritan. You wear a Puritan cap and blouse, black with a starched white collar. And a transparent gauze skirt."

"It gets better. And underneath the skirt? Me? Just me?"

"Not quite. Under the skirt you wear a chastity belt. More or less the real thing. It hooks in back."

"I love it," she said, laughing. "And you? What are you going as?"

"An American painter. Black tie, white ruffled shirt, tuxedo jacket, blue jeans and sneakers."

"That's not original with you."

"No, darling, it's original with painters. Anyway, I'm not in the competition for a prize. Now will you come here?"

"Mmm . . ." she said.

She put her drink beside his and knelt between his knees. Her hands slid around his neck and she reached up to him. "Glad to see me?" she murmured, nuzzling her face into his neck. Suddenly she stopped and raised her eyes. "Don't start anything you can't finish, sir."

"I can finish," he promised as his arms circled her waist.

The grand ballroom of the Waldorf Astoria was lit up like a street festival with strings of dazzling colored bulbs crisscrossing the ceiling. Numerous spinning prismatic lights were hanging from three sides of the balcony. There were tables and chairs set around a large dance floor, and a stage with a full dance band took up the far end of the room. Steps led from either side of the stage to the floor. Under the balcony, stalls offered hot dogs, bagels and lox, tacos, chili, egg rolls and pasta as well as multinational beer, wine, hard liquor and champagne. Across the ballroom from the stage there was a stage flat of a brothel with a red light over the front door. Two girls in skintight, micro-mini red dresses walked back and forth in front of the door, swinging their purses, and naked girls sat in the windows; it took a sharp eye to recognize that the naked girls were really department-store mannequins.

Anton noticed that the press was everywhere, but as the press was in costume—and many blatantly sexual—the press was muzzled. This was the kind of party that never got news coverage. It amused him that a conspiracy of silence on sexual matters typified the American way of corruption; the American press reserved its headlines for financial scandals. Money mattered. While in England, financial corruption took a backseat to sexual transgressions. In London, this ball would make headlines in all the tabloids.

It was the vivid commotion that attracted Anton and Cella to the ball. It pleased them that it wasn't black tie and formal. The seminude Indian brave doing an obscene version of a ceremonial dance complete with bumps and grinds and a huge, fake phallus that he offered to watchers was more amusing than shocking. The girl portraying the first American flag—wearing a red G-string with a blue square and thirteen white stars painted on her bare chest, using her nipples as two of the stars—was rather clever. The transvestite, looking like Jacqueline Onassis kissing Lizzie Borden, was appropriate. And it was all part and parcel of the tongue-in-cheek attack on the "sacred cows" of society, always the underlying theme of these balls.

To Cella, the sights and sounds were an intoxicant. She inhaled the scent of perfumes, sweat and different foods. In her ears was the din of laughter and voices. The music, with its sudden bursts of drums and the twang of electric guitars, drowned out the notes of the fife and drum symbolizing the Spirit of '76. She loosened her hand from Anton's to let the sway of the crowd carry her where it would. She stopped in front of a soapbox to watch a man in a white sequined suit, wearing a blue ribbon and reading *Presidential Candidate,* do a conjuring act by pulling scarves out of his sleeves while exhorting his listeners to vote for him because he would provide free circumcision.

A few couples were dancing as best they could, never allowing their bodies to touch since that might spoil their costumes. Abruptly Cella was dragged into the heart of the throng of dancers by a man wearing nothing but bumper stickers printed with slogans like "Dancers Do It in Eight Counts" and "My Other Car Is a Rolls." Where did she know him from?

"This is practically a family reunion," he whispered.

"Marcus! What are you doing here?"

"Giving free rein to the creative side of my nature. That's some costume! It's responsible for more erections than the whorehouse or the flag girl."

"Thank you, dear brother," she said as they whirled around the floor.

"I also like the earrings. Inappropriate with the costume, but good display for sale. Yes?"

"Yes."

"A recent acquisition?" he asked, smiling.

"Quite recent. Why?"

"I might have a buyer." When Cella raised her eyebrows in a question mark, he said solemnly, "Me."

"You? For a woman?"

"Of course a woman. I haven't had an operation. She adores antiques."

"Can you afford to be a customer?"

"I'm about to make a killing on a new issue. How about a discount for a member of the family?"

"No discounts. Besides, the Contessa Orsini would love them."

"Cella, she hasn't a sou—"

At that moment Lawrence Lord, smiling warmly, dressed in white tie and tails, cut in.

"Hello, sir," Marcus said affably. As he walked away, he called over his shoulder, "Cella, skip the discount."

"How are you, my dear?" Lord asked as they moved to the music. He made no comment on her costume.

"Wonderful. I always enjoy the hullabaloo."

"I do too." He kept his eyes fixed on her eyes, and his voice sounded as if it had been dipped in honey. "Though sometimes I feel I'm a little antique for this playpen."

"Lawrence, you're fishing for compliments. There isn't a woman here who wouldn't want you on her charm bracelet," Cella said smoothly as she followed him in a cross between a waltz and a fox trot.

"Your earrings are lovely. Langobardic?"

"Yes." As Cella expected, he'd noticed the earrings, not her costume. She'd been waiting to see if he would mention them. "You recognized the basket?"

"Of course. It's typical. A recent acquisition?"

Cella marveled at how thoroughly Lord had done his homework. She wondered if he kept tabs on every item in the shop. They'd have to be more careful in the future when he was around. "No, we've had them in inventory for years. Picked them up in an estate sale in Tuscany."

"Which estate? I keep close track of all important estate sales."

"I'm not sure. It wasn't an important sale." She hesitated

as though trying to recall exactly where they had found the earrings. "I'm sorry. I really don't remember, but among the paperweights and music boxes, we found these earrings. One never knows what a family will own."

"Never! I might have a buyer."

"I have one too," Cella said, her expression unchanged. "Actually, I have two. The Contessa Orsini has been begging us for a pair of earrings like these. She's almost the reason we took them out of the vault."

"Delightful woman, but she'll never pay what they're worth."

"So I've been told. But Mother and she were close friends. I know she'll cherish them."

"You're too sentimental, Cella. I'm sure Sebastian would see it my way," Lawrence remarked sagely. "I'm thinking of someone who could become a steady customer. And will pay top dollar."

They stared at each other for a moment.

"Who did you have in mind?" Cella asked.

"Business secret. Let me borrow them for a very short time, and if I don't make the sale, you can always offer them to the contessa."

"For how long do you want them?"

"Not long, Cella." He was prepared to sound offended. "Haven't I always been a staunch supporter of The House of Uni?"

"At what price?"

"Around one hundred and fifty thousand."

"You win," said Cella, removing the earrings as she danced. She dropped them, almost reluctantly, into Lawrence Lord's outstretched palm.

At that point a gray-haired Statue of Liberty wearing dark glasses cut in.

"Good evening, Sebastian. Cella and I have been doing a little business. Where's Marina?"

"Catting around." Lord ambled off, and Sebastian turned to Cella. "He took the earrings," he said as he swept her away.

"Gobbled them up," she replied. "As you expected."

"As we both expected." He gave her a benign smile. "You never disappoint me."

"I'm not sure I take that as a compliment." Then, seeing his frown, she glanced at his draped figure and laughed. "Father, I never thought you were the type for such a costume.

It just proves that anyone is capable of anything. And men are rarely what they seem.''

"Marina picked the costume. Don't you like it?''

"It's in keeping. Where is the popular lady?''

"Drifting. You advised me to disengage myself, so I'm doing my best, though she does cling. By the way, tonight she mentioned Jason. En passant.''

"What did she say?''

"It's not what she said, it's how she said it. She said she's very fond of her son. But I have the impression he troubles her, and they don't see much of each other.''

"Why?''

Before Sebastian could answer, a pint-sized, underweight and balding man with glasses, wearing a football player's uniform with the green-and-white colors of the New York Jets, cut in and whirled Cella away. She'd catch up with her father later and learn more.

Everything settled down to a mind-numbing chaos of people, lights, color, music as the momentum of the ball gathered speed. For an instant, Cella's stomach tightened because George Washington—in a full-dress military coat, a white wig, wooden teeth and jockey shorts—was watching her. His eyes ran over her like a swab, from her face down her throat, passed over her starched blouse, pausing to take in the transparent skirt and her nakedness beneath it, except for the chastity belt. Then he stared with concentration at her long, strong legs, clearly visible through the skirt. Cella felt alone and on trial. Her heart beat faster. She was certain the man was Jason Lord. But that was impossible. He was known to be a solitary man who never went to parties and whose only hobby was playing chess. In a gesture of defiance, she spun about, giving him a good view of her bare buttocks. When she turned back, meaning to go over and say, "I saw you on television earlier this evening," Washington had vanished. Now she'd never find out if he was Jason Lord.

As she whirled around the floor with Miles Standish in ballet tights, she caught sight of a woman wearing a mask of J. Paul Getty, with her pants down, stretched across the knees of a West Point cadet—could it be Peter Petty? Yes. It was Peter Petty, and he was spanking his grandfather's rival rhythmically to the beat of the drum while the girl went through a make-believe struggle. The crowd closed around Cella, and she saw no more.

Later, after entering the ladies' room, Cella opened the door to a booth and closed it quickly. But not before she had seen a woman who might be Josie Frankenberg costumed as an 1890s policeman—with her pants around her ankles—moving a rubber truncheon shaped like a penis in and out of herself. She'd barely recovered from her shock when she felt a gentle hand patting her behind.

"Not tonight," she said in a bored voice without bothering to turn around. "This is my month for men."

"You look luscious, Cella. Good enough to eat. That's the trouble with that obscenity you're wearing between your legs. It's impossible to eat you."

Although the woman's face was covered by a dead-white mask and she wore a wig and an ankle-length cape, there was no mistaking Darlene Schiller's voice. "It comes off when I feel in the mood for a nibble," Cella said.

Darlene laughed. "We have so much in common. We don't use the salad fork for dessert and we know the difference between 'dining out' and 'eating someone out.' "

Half amused, half irritated at the intimacy of the remark, Cella changed the subject. "Since we're sisters under the skin, let's see the costume you're hiding with that silly cape."

"No way."

"You can trust me."

"I trust no one who says 'trust me.' Let alone those who don't. But be patient, and you'll see me at my glorious best." She suddenly shifted gears and her eyes glittered behind the oval eye openings of her mask. "About the Aphrodite. I want it. I don't suppose you would like to make a little wager?"

"Can I trust you?"

Darlene gave her a shrewd look. "I suppose I deserved that. Don't trust me—trust yourself. If you win first prize in the contest for the most original costume, I'll give you the two million I'm ready to pay for the necklace. But if I win first prize, you give me the necklace for free."

Cella couldn't help laughing. "Two million dollars on a costume? Dolly, you're too much. No, I don't trust myself or you that much. Besides, you can see almost all of me, but I've no idea what you've got on. Or don't have on. I don't like the odds. Take it up with my father. You and he have even more in common. Maybe you can persuade him to trust you."

"What a splendid suggestion! Herman and the President are busy this week solving the Central American disasters, so I've the time and the inclination to be persuasive. I must find him. I have an itch for the Aphrodite that he ought to scratch."

"Do that. I'm panting to see how it comes out," Cella said. If Darlene thought for one moment that a sexual itch could compete with Sebastian's itch for money, she didn't know her man.

"You're too pleased," Darlene said. "You don't believe he'll scratch."

"I think you're a well-matched pair."

"We are indeed, darling. Any way you slice it, I'll come out ahead. If he doesn't satisfy one itch, he'll satisfy the other. A talented scratcher is pure bliss for someone with a chronic itch like me." Darlene gave Cella a second, more intimate pat and strolled toward the door.

Cella revised upward her opinion of Darlene Schiller. It was no accident that little Dolly Drop Drawers was probably the country's most successful whore. Win, lose or draw, Dolly enjoyed her work.

Punctually at one, the band played the theme song of the American Beauty Contest while a girl in a string bikini with a wobbly soprano sang, "Here she comes, Miss America . . ."

Anton appeared and separated Cella from a fat man with spindly legs dressed in a very abbreviated Mafioso costume consisting of a black coat, white-on-white shirt, white tie, red flower and little else. He led her to a line forming to the right of the stage. The male judges, in white tie and tails, and the female judges, in evening gowns, were already seated on what looked like a large vegetable crate. Lawrence Lord acted as master of ceremonies, explaining to the crowd what each costume was supposed to represent. One by one, the women marched up to the stage, paraded to the center, stopped in front of the judges and did a slow, 360-degree turn so that the judges could get a good look at their entire costume—or lack of costume. The crowd enthusiastically applauded each contestant.

Cella, more drunk on excitement than on liquor, turned seductively in front of the judges. She thought she'd received the loudest burst of applause. She then waited with the rest of the contestants as Darlene—still covered from head to foot by her cape, mask and wig—sauntered slowly across the stage. As Darlene approached the place where she was to stop and pose for the judges, she tossed her wig at the audience. At first glance, it appeared that Darlene had shaved her head and covered it with a white powder. But when Cella looked more closely, she was able to make out the edges of a tightly fitted white skullcap. Still covered by her cape, Darlene reached the center of the stage. With a huge flourish, she flung the cape back, allowing it to fall to the floor. The applause and shouts of approval were deafening. Darlene was stark naked, her pubic hair shaved and her entire body covered with a white powder that matched her mask and skullcap. Extending out from her vagina was a green stem that reached up, up, up—held to her body by some kind of paste—until it ended between her full breasts in a huge red rose. She was the American Beauty Rose. Cella admitted to herself that Dolly's costume was by far the most original and most daring.

After a brief consultation with the judges, Lawrence Lord made the announcement of the winner. "The first prize of fifty Susan B. Anthony dollars goes to our American Beauty Rose. Will the winner please step forward to receive her prize?"

Darlene did a series of bumps and grinds as she crossed the stage. When Lord dropped the pile of coins into her hands, she looked puzzled for a moment as to where to put the money. Then, with a broad grin, she took one coin and slipped it into her vagina. "Fertilizer to make America's roses grow," she called out in a loud voice. The audience went wild, and when she threw the remaining forty-nine coins to the onlookers, there was a scramble for the dollars.

Lord's voice boomed over the babble of voices and laughter. "The second prize of Twenty-five Susan B. Anthony dollars goes to our American Puritan. Will our American Puritan please step up and receive her award?"

Everyone cheered as Cella accepted her coins. She had a similar problem as Darlene—what to do with the money—and there was no way she could possibly top Darlene's performance. But she was going to give it a damn good try. She placed three coins inside her chastity belt. As the onlookers laughed, she proclaimed, "A small additional award for the man who liberates the American Puritan." She then tossed the remaining coins to the raucous crowd.

Lord handed out the third, fourth and fifth prizes, which finally came down to "twofers" to a Broadway show that had closed a month earlier.

Cella caught a glimpse of Sebastian and Darlene—covered again by her cape—moving toward a side door. A man covered with firecrackers—the Fourth of July—and a woman dressed as a 1920s flapper, her hair full of sequins, hurried past them on their way to the exit.

"Marina!" Cella called, recognizing the flapper.

"Cella! Have you seen Sebastian?" Marina asked.

Cella shook her head, and Marina gave a careless backward wave as she vanished with her man for the night. Although he was costumed as a firecracker, Cella identified him as Phillip Mckay, curator of the ancient treasures section of the Metropolitan Museum. Mckay was an old and dear friend of hers and had been Marina's lover before she and Sebastian became a number. Maybe, Cella hoped, Marina and Phillip would get back together again and she'd drop Sebastian.

Little parties were greeting each other and leaving together. Out of nowhere Anton appeared. "Let's dance," he said. They joined what remained of the dancers in the center of the dance floor. Their blood pulsed to the beat of the drums. Then, as if by common consent, without either saying a word, they stopped, went to the cloakroom, picked up their capes and left the ball. They rode uptown in a cab, holding each other close.

"Where are the earrings?" he whispered. "I know you didn't lose them."

"I did, in a way. I gave them to Lawrence Lord. He has the kind of customer Father prefers."

"Mmm," said Anton. "Do you still give him two percent?"

"Five percent now." Though the night was warm, Cella shivered slightly under her cape.

"What's the matter, dear?"

"I was thinking of my father. Anton, I think you should take me home."

He held her protectively. "I think not. I think you'll feel better at my place. Your home away from home. Take a deep breath and stop thinking of him. Think of me."

"Do you want some champagne?" Anton asked, once they were in the apartment. He reached for her cloak, but Cella said she felt cold and kept it on her shoulders.

"Stop thinking of Sebastian."

"I wasn't. I was remembering what Marcus said the other evening. It was quite unpleasant. And now there's Jason Lord. Did I tell you I saw him on public television before we returned to the city?" she asked, pacing restlessly around the room.

"No, you forgot to mention that." Anton noticed her restless movements and the almost feverish brightness of her face. "You're letting Jason Lord upset you because what he does jibes with what Marcus said. But Marcus is not Lord," Anton insisted. "You've heard his song and dance before. And he's family. He can be trusted."

"You're right. But Jason Lord is hard to ignore. According to Father, he even troubles his own mother," she said softly.

"Why?"

"I don't know. Father mentioned it when we danced."

Anton had his own opinion of the Lords—father and son. But the best he could do for Cella now was to make light of everything.

"It's all very interesting. But not for tonight. Let me give you a brandy to warm you. After that I have other ideas." As he poured them each a snifter, Anton considered that perhaps the time had come to make Cella see the truth. That Marcus was right. What The House of Uni did today was not an offering to the old gods, but simply wonderful forgeries. Then he asked himself a question: Weren't their forgeries in keeping with the way of today's world, which he privately saw as a gigantic rip-off? One maintained one's sanity by not taking it seriously, laughing at the self-righteous thievery of so-called respectable citizens, all the way to the bank. And the pious Dr. Jason Lord too. Something of a fanatic, Jason Lord. What were his hidden lusts? There had to be something in it for him. Fanatics had a way of saying one thing, doing another and wanting to do something else entirely. Anton glanced at Cella, now huddled on the couch, and decided the truth could wait.

"You'll be warmer after you drink this. Now take off that chastity belt. You're not a Puritan."

Cella stood up and unhooked the belt, her fingers trembling. The three coins fell, unnoticed, to the thick carpet. Then she slipped out of her entire costume and wrapped herself loosely in her cloak. Anton handed her the snifter of brandy and removed his jacket, tie and shirt. His upper body gleamed in the soft light of the apartment, his tight blue jeans emphasizing his lean hips, the length of his legs. Cella's silky, shining black hair fell to her shoulders, her pale skin golden in the light. At the opening of her cloak, Anton could see the sensuous line of her breast, the throb of a pulse in her throat.

"Finish your brandy," he said, and when she did, he put the two empty glasses on the floor. He reached for her as her cloak slipped to the floor and all the pent-up passion of the evening flowed through his body. Linked together, they moved toward a closed door off the living room.

Anton pushed the door open. When they stepped inside, it was as though they had stepped into another world.

"I love it here," Cella whispered.

"So do I. My personal homage to the old gods."

The walls of what Anton and Cella called the room of Tinia, in homage to the Etruscan god of life, were covered with paintings, reproductions of the walls of an ancient Etruscan tomb. Men and women dancing, feasting, reveling. The floor was carpeted with a handwoven rug that looked like leaves. A golden light came from some invisible fixture in a ceiling that seemed overhung with the branches of trees.

"Now you must dance for me a true welcome dance. Remember, I'm a warrior returning from battle," Anton said.

"I'll dance for you and for the great god Tinia." There was neither guile nor premeditation as she put his hand to her breast. "Feel how my heart is pounding."

He teased her nipples with tantalizing skill. "I accept the offering with love."

Cella glanced at a castanet that lay on the floor next to a golden flute.

"It's been waiting for you." Anton's voice was low.

Cella picked up the castanet with one hand and held up her other hand, with fingers forked. Her eyes were closed and her excitement mounted as she began to dance in the way her mother had taught her, the way she danced only for Anton. And while she moved in erotic abandonment, Anton played a strange, sensuous melody on the flute. Then, still playing the flute, he danced with her as their ancestors had danced thousands of years ago. Time stood still and the music grew wilder. Until, at some inner signal, Anton tossed the flute into the air and Cella dropped the castanet to the floor. Only the sound of their rapid breathing filled the room. Their dancing reached a fever pitch. As if an invisible burning glass had been playing on them, they caught fire and sank to the floor, each knowing what to do with the other's body to arouse the greatest ardor.

"I never can get enough of you," Anton whispered as his fingers explored every inch of her nakedness.

Sensations she had forgotten were possible surged through Cella as she reached heights of pleasure she only dimly remembered from dreams. I can never get enough of you, she echoed in her mind. No man but Anton could so play on her passion. Her hands, her tongue, her entire body, responded with reckless abandon. Incited by her lustfulness, his pulse racing as fast as hers, Anton plunged his hard sex deep within her. A primitive wildness rippled through Cella's body and a low moan escaped her lips. Tremors spread through her, blurring her mind, and unknowingly, she cried out, half sob, half laughter, from the overflow of joy.

Much later she lay weak and spent with the wonder of this timeless world of the senses, a world that she entered only in her dreams or with Anton.

Chapter Seven

Dr. Jason Lord's office was Scandinavian modern and totally impersonal. His marble slab of a desk was almost bare. On it were a telephone, a tape recorder and a single pile of papers set at precisely right angles to the corner of the desk. He was in shirtsleeves, dictating the results of his latest investigation of two Greco-Etruscan pins into the tape recorder. The tapes would later be transcribed by his secretary, Emory Portland, also a would-be actor. Emory knew nothing about ancient art and cared less, but he could type professionally and had a flair for punctuation and spelling. When Jason finished dictating, he leaned back in his chair and gazed reflectively at the two Tiffany boxes on his desk. Each contained a piece of jewelry that did not come from Tiffany.

Jason Lord was a rara avis in the world of art. He was scrupulously ethical. If he had unpleasant news to report to a client, he did his best to be gentle. To be kind. But it took an effort. There was another side to Jason Lord, a Dorian Gray portrait of the man that hung in a tightly locked closet of his mind.

This afternoon, the cool, detached, cerebral Dr. Lord, as seen by the world, waited with amusement for Anthony Hadley. Anthony and Amanda Hadley were born-rich, twenty-year-old twins who had nothing in common, except for the fortune they'd inherited from their dead mother, Gretchen Therese von Wittenstein zu Wittenstein Hadley. The late baroness had insisted on skiing the highest slopes of Davos despite the avalanche warnings. Anthony claimed that he felt like a pauper because their trusts were tied up until they were thirty. The only thing of value that their mother forgot to tie up was the Hadley collection. Gretchen Hadley had been an important collector of beautiful and rare antique and ancient jewelry—the Hadley collection was celebrated.

The twins had inherited the collection jointly. It meant

nothing to Anthony, who was interested in collecting Formula 1 racing cars, not bracelets. It meant everything to Amanda, who could wear the jewelry and also be admired as a patron of the arts. So Anthony had concocted a scheme to dupe his sister and had approached Jason for advice.

Jason glanced at the digital clock on his desk and grew impatient with Anthony's tardiness. He had been due at four o'clock. It was now four-ten. Promptly at four-fifteen, Amanda—not Anthony—Hadley was ushered into his office. A moment later the telephone rang. Jason picked up the intercom. "Hold all calls," he said to his secretary and hung up as he watched Amanda slink toward him.

Amanda was short rather than small, and hovered dangerously between being pleasingly plump and unpleasantly fat. Her hair was black and cut to fashion; her clothes were too stylish, her eyes too roguish, her smile too seductive. Men constantly told her she was sexy and she believed them. She did her utmost, under all circumstances, to give the impression of sensuality. Her efforts were wasted on Jason.

"Jason, darling," she trilled. "My double-crossing twin, Anthony, has been trysting with you."

"Anthony and I had a business meeting," Jason admitted amiably. "I assume he mentioned it to you."

"Mentioned it, indeed. Hell, no!" Amanda bubbled gaily. "I have the s.o.b. by the short hairs. The rat had one of Momma's very special, very precious pieces of jewelry copied by some corrupt Roman faker. Didn't he?"

"Yes," Jason admitted.

"The gold griffin, Greco-Etruscan dress pin decorated with a border of intertwined flowers. Fifth century B.C. Yes?"

"Yes."

"Yes, yes, yes. I found the bill from the Italian forger in his bureau. I regularly check his bureau for evidence as to how he's wasting his time and our money." She clicked her tongue against her teeth. "And I threatened to denounce him to the district attorney for grand larceny. He wanted to sell the authentic and substitute the forgery. He asked you to test both of them to see if the fake had too many flaws. Anything I'd spot."

"That was what he had in mind," Jason said, smiling, waiting to see if he were next in line for threats.

"There's nothing funny about your twin brother trying to rob you blind," Amanda said with spirit. "After I threatened him sufficiently, and thoroughly terrorized him, we had a sensible talk." She regarded Jason with eyes that were surprisingly shrewd. Then she opened the two Tiffany boxes on his desk and studied the pins. "Aren't they lovely?" she cooed. "Like two peas in a pod. I can't tell them apart."

"Without the proper technical equipment, it is difficult."

"You agree the forgery is a good job?"

"Highly professional."

"I'm glad at least Anthony picked a talented forger. But then, I would expect him to show a little of the Hadley brains." She gave Jason a long look, expecting agreement, but Jason said nothing. So Amanda continued. "My con-artist twin gave me the most divine idea. You see, our grandfather conned the public and made two fortunes. It runs in the family."

"I see." Jason listened, showing proper respect for Amanda's con-artist grandfather.

"No, you don't see. You're not a Hadley." Amanda dropped her voice to a seductive whisper. "Why don't we have the entire collection duplicated? Who would know the difference if we sold anything? Except professionals like you. I could still wear one or two pieces whenever I chose, and Anthony and I would have money to spend."

"You mean from selling the originals?" Jason asked.

"Naturally the originals. What do you take me for? A common con-artist?" She tossed her head indignantly. "But there's this divine seven-thirty-seven jet—it's been totally remodeled by one of those men who publish sexy magazines—that our dumb trustees won't let me buy." She considered the pins. "We might keep some of the original jewelry. But there are well over fifty pieces in the collection. If we sold just half, we'd have enough money to live comfortably until we get our trusts."

Jason thought about their Park Avenue duplex, their chalet in St. Moritz, their house in Hobbe Sound—away from the riffraff of Palm Beach. He also thought, What an unappetizing young woman.

Amanda looked at Jason full of good will. "What do you think of the idea?"

"It's interesting."

"It's brilliant. It'll spare me all sorts of penny-pinching," Amanda enthused. "The first piece we'll sell is the Greco-Etruscan pin Anthony brought you. You've examined both. You know which one is authentic. How much do you think I can get for it?"

"You do mean the one from your mother's collection, not the recent Italian copy?" Jason said very carefully.

"Yes, the original." Amanda smiled warmly.

"About ten thousand dollars." Jason was enjoying himself even more than he'd expected."

"Ten thousand dollars? For an authentic Greco-Etruscan pin from the fifth century B.C. ?" The girl flushed with anger. "Apparently you don't understand what's happened to the market for ancient jewelry. It's gone wild—through the ceiling. There's so little authentic stuff around anymore. And the countries where such jewelry is found are no longer permitting exports. Except under rather slippery circumstances."

"You mean crooked circumstances?"

"Something like that."

"I'm aware." Jason sounded slightly bored. "Ten thousand dollars would be a good price for the pin."

"You're out of your fucking mind! For an authentic—"

"The pin is not authentic."

"It is!" Amanda shouted.

"It isn't." Jason smiled.

Amanda was temporarily silent. "You examined the wrong pin," she said at last.

"I examined both pins. Ran extensive tests," Jason said gently. His somber expression completely masked the sexual pleasure that he felt in his groin. "Frankly, I was surprised. The gold in your mother's pin is mid-nineteenth century. The pin is perhaps one hundred twenty years old. Technically an antique. But only technically. And definitely not a piece of genuine ancient jewelry. As far as the other is concerned, the gold is quite recent." He chuckled. "Could be dental gold. The pin is worth a few thousand dollars. Though they are both excellent forgeries, the one from your mother's collection does show more knowledge of the ancient world."

With a violent spurt of energy, Amanda slammed the boxes shut and dropped them into her Bendel shopping bag. She was halfway out the door when she turned to glare at Jason.

"You're to say nothing about this!"

Jason nodded. "Of course not. Unless I hear that you've offered the pin for sale as a piece of genuine ancient jewelry. In any case, my secretary will send you my bill."

Amanda had disappeared through the door when Emory Portland entered with three pink telephone message slips, which he handed to Jason.

"Anything pressing?" Jason asked.

"Dr. Lawrence Lord wants you to call back as soon as you're free."

"My fath—? Dr. Lord? Anything else?"

"Mrs. Todhunter Clark wants to set up an appointment. And the PBC is interested in your appearing again."

"Thank you," Jason said, and Portland padded out of the office, as silent as a cat.

Jason placed the three messages on his desk. The only one that seriously interested him was the one from his father. He leaned back again in his chair, wondering what his father wanted, wondering when he would call him back.

Dr. Lawrence Lord leaned back in the chair behind his desk in his office at the Fogg Museum at Harvard. His body movements were reminiscent of the way Jason Lord slouched in his chair. Lord glanced at Jason's telephone number in his appointment book and thought about his son. He hadn't seen him in months. Was it worthwhile contacting him at all? Why the devil was Jason taking so long to call back? Lawrence Lord admitted to himself, half wistfully, that he had never understood his son. Their relationship had been merely a fact that they'd both acknowledged. Perhaps the trouble was that Jason was too much his mother's son. Jason and Marina had been as thick as thieves, until suddenly they weren't. It had happened almost simultaneously with her decision to get divorced. There were times when he thought it was Jason who had divorced both of them. As he recalled Jason's behavior during Marina's and his last months together, Lawrence shook his head. His son was a very strange young man.

At eighteen, Jason Lord knew he was going to become an architect. Actually, it was Marina's suggestion. The two of them went on junkets together, driving around New England. Marina explained they were looking at old houses and studying the evolution of the saltbox, investigating land sites and working out the kind of houses that would be suitable for each site. Sometimes it would be dark by the time they returned home, and dinner had long ago been served. Lawrence would come out of his study to greet them, feeling a pang of envy at their windblown faces, their happy air of play. He couldn't stop a hot flush of resentment which he recognized as jealousy of his son.

One day Jason invited his visiting professor from Heidelberg, a young man named Hans Etzel, to dine. Etzel was invited three more times. The fourth dinner was not quite the success of the previous visits. Lawrence did not feel like talking about paintings, and Jason had nothing to say about architecture. Hans and Marina tried to keep the conversation alive, talking about buildings with glass skins, post and beam construction, the Bauhaus school. Throughout the evening Marina squirmed about in her chair, her glance remaining fixed on Hans, dismissing the presence of her husband and son with an occasional irritated, back-of-the-hand nod.

Then Hans had some kind of an accident—Lawrence studiously avoided listening to any gossip as to exactly what had happened—and much to his relief, the man stopped coming to dinner. Eventually the semester ended. Etzel returned to Germany and the Lord family settled into their summer routine at Nantucket. Except that it was like hearing the sound of far-off thunder and waiting for the storm to hit. Marina was always in a mood, sarcastic or silent, biting or cold.

She had lost interest in making love. There were a variety of excuses: a headache, her period, exhaustion. Lawrence wondered why. As far as she knew, he'd accepted her affair with Etzel and not asked for a divorce. Why wouldn't she accept that her affair had ended and the marriage survived? Meanwhile, Jason watched his mother at the dinner table, his eyes dark with hurt and reproach. Often Lawrence wondered what Jason was thinking. He had the curious feeling that Jason knew something he didn't.

One afternoon in the long, cold summer, Lawrence returned from his usual walk along the beach to find Marina packing her bags. She was flying to Manhattan that night and on to Mexico to get a divorce. It was too ridiculous. "Why?" Lawrence asked. Marina would barely speak to him. The reasonable being in Lawrence could not accept it. But the ridiculous had become reality.

After Marina returned from Mexico, she moved to Manhattan, leaving Jason to continue his studies at Harvard and live in the house in Cambridge with his father. But Marina was the thread that connected Lawrence and Jason, and the thread had snapped. Jason dropped the idea of becoming an architect and turned to the study of archiometry. That was another conundrum. Archiometry, of all things. Lawrence finally accepted that he could not pretend nothing had changed when everything had changed. And Jason's choice of a new career was simply another example. In his junior year at Harvard, giving no reason, Jason packed a flight bag and moved out of the house. When he was settled, he sent for the rest of his things. After that, Lawrence and his son did not speak for several years.

* * *

Lawrence Lord glanced at his appointment book again. Perhaps telephoning Jason had been a mistake. He had thought that asking his help might be the start of something resembling a father-son relationship between them, as well as accomplishing certain practical ends. These days, he admitted to himself without a qualm that enlightened self-interest was his guiding principle. His instinct for larceny told him that there were more ways to profit from the Taggard connection than he had yet considered. And that was where Jason came in. So where the hell was he? Lawrence almost reached for the telephone to call him again, but restrained himself. Precisely at that point the telephone rang. It was his son. A meeting was arranged for the following Monday afternoon between the two Drs. Lord.

As he walked down Greene Street toward the renovated loft building where he was to meet Jason, Lawrence Lord considered his son's selection of a Soho loft for his office to be a rather canny piece of self-promotion. The office, which was also part of his living quarters, was not where most of his research was carried on. That was done in laboratories attached to MIT. But the virtue of an office in the center of the art world gave his work a certain glamour by association. Jason had set their appointment for five, and promptly at five, Lawrence Lord was shown in by Jason's secretary. Jason looked up from the first pages of the report on the Hadley pins that his secretary had transcribed earlier. He eyed his father with the suspicious eye of a Presbyterian minister in a home for unwed mothers.

"Hello, Father," he said. "Now what can I do for you? I don't drink and I don't smoke, or I'd offer you something."

Lawrence smiled at the self-righteous remark. He'd had sufficient dealings with his son to know that any indication of discomfort would be a mistake. "The sun is not yet over the yardarm, so I can skip the scotch. And I brought my own cigarettes." He took a pack of Gauloises from his pocket and lit one. "You don't mind?"

"They're your lungs. Is this purely a social call?"

"It's a mix. Next time we can do our business over lunch."

"I never go to business lunches. You know that," Jason said crisply.

"Sorry. I'd forgotten. Then we'll have dinner. And talk."

"About what?"

"These." Lawrence took a small velvet box from his pocket and placed it on the desk. Jason looked at Lawrence briefly, his face expressionless. Then his eyes traveled to the box.

"Open it," Lawrence suggested.

Jason opened the box and glanced back at Lawrence Lord. "Langobardic earrings," he said matter-of-factly. "Rather good examples of the type."

"Aren't they," Lawrence Lord said, smiling. He was pleased with his decision to show the earrings to his son. "Would you mind authenticating them?"

"Where did you get them?"

"The House of Uni."

A slow smile lit Jason's face. He leaned back and said, half to himself, "The House of Uni?" There was an edge to his voice as he added, "I'll put them through their paces for you. It'll take about ten days." He stared at his father. "When I'm finished, I'll call you and, as you suggested, we can talk."

Dr. Lawrence Lord left his son's office feeling rather pleased with himself. It was probably the worst mistake he'd ever made.

PART FOUR

THE SACRIFICE

Chapter Eight

The smallish, unobtrusive, middle-aged man sat on a kitchen chair in a spick-and-span kitchen in Astoria, Queens. He wore a clean but rumpled bathrobe, socks and slippers, and a black yarmulke that was pinned to a fringe of gray hair. He claimed that he wore the yarmulke not for religious reasons but to keep the drafts off his almost bald head and protect him from catching a cold. His wife, Sophie, insisted that he would wear the yarmulke in the shower, if possible. His suits were brown, black and gray—worn with color-coordinated yarmulkes. Over Sophie's strong objections, sometimes he would go to bed wearing one.

Everything about him was self-effacing—his size, his pallid complexion, the quiet, gentle manner you were certain went with the face. Everything was ordinary and totally deceptive. Except for his hands. His hands were exceptional: large, bony and strong. They were the hands of a mechanic or an electrician or a plumber. One of those invisible, competent people summoned in time of an emergency to repair some breakdown of efficiency, someone who fixed things. In a way that was exactly what Ben Stein did. He fixed things.

Now he studied the rough sketch of another pair of hands, the hands of Grimling Gibbons in the frontispiece of the book that lay open on the kitchen table. The sketch had been done by one of Gibbons' pupils. The hands were remarkable. Strong and bony, like Ben's, and something else—what? Imaginative, Ben decided. That's what they were. The hands had imagination. And even though they were attached to Gibbons' arms, as he saw from the sketch in which the sleeves were rolled up, the hands had a life of their own. They were thinking hands, dreaming hands, visionary hands. No wonder Gibbons had been royal master carver to the crown of England, one of the great artists of Western civilization. His wood carvings were historic. As well they should be. Ben would have liked to take some lessons from him. What a pity he died almost three hundred years ago.

Ben studied his own hands as if he had a searchlight in his eyes. Good enough for all the things hands were supposed to do. Very handy hands. But he suspected they had no imagination. No vision. They grew hot and perspired when he worked, and sometimes he lost his grip on the limewood when he was too deeply immersed in a piece. The carving he did was good, but Gibbons could have taught him a thing or two. Ben glanced at the eight pawns he'd already carved. Eight two-inch-high Cycladian maidens. Actually, he was rather proud of them. There were eight more to do—those he would do in ebony—then he'd have his sixteen pawns. Half of the thirty-two pieces he needed for his new chess set. The curves of the maidens could have been more delicate, the lines of the legs more disciplined. It wasn't the fault of the limewood, the wood was strong yet soft, and close-grained, so it could be worked across or against the grain, lending itself to any desired shape. No, it wasn't the wood; it was his hands. They didn't know enough. That was why one or two of the maidens looked ever so slightly clumsy. Flaws and all, Ben Stein decided that his work would do. No one would notice except Jason Lord.

The telephone rang and he clenched his hands together helplessly. He closed his eyes and an image appeared on his inner lids: himself bending over an inert body. Blood still oozing from a dozen wounds. Blood soaking into bed sheets, a towel turning the water in the bathtub red. Sights he wouldn't let himself think about. Playtime was over, and he picked up the phone. His hands did that very well.

"Ben Stein here," he said.

"Hello, Ben. This is Reilly."

"Sergeant," Ben said resignedly, as though life had worn down his powers of resistance.

"I hope I'm not disturbing your creative inspiration."

"Not at all," Ben said calmly, not seeming to notice the wisecrack. "Actually, I've been doing my tax returns."

"You mean you haven't been whittling a morning glory? Or a seashell? Or horse radish leaves?"

"Nope. My tax returns," he repeated with an air of mild obstinacy. "Maybe tomorrow I'll start an altarpiece. Now what can I do for the Sixty-sixth Street precinct that I haven't already done?"

"Meet me at the Metropolitan Museum of Art. In front of

the entrance at the top of the Fifth Avenue steps. Be there in a half hour.''

"Okay." In spite of his preoccupation with the Cycladian pawns, Stein began to feel the familiar tingling of the challenge. "Who got murdered this time? Queen Nefertiti?"

"Close, but no cigar. Would you believe King Tut?"

Sergeant Reilly hung up, and Stein stared for a moment at the telephone. Only his eyes gave evidence of his growing excitement. He shuffled toward his bedroom and changed from his bathrobe into a rumpled brown suit that fitted him much like his bathrobe. After he knotted his tie, he substituted a brown yarmulke for his black one and fastened it with two brown bobby pins. Although his suit was unpressed and several sizes too large, Lieutenant Ben Stein of the New York City police, permanently attached to homicide, would never be caught dead using black bobby pins with a brown yarmulke.

At forty-five, Tobias Phipps was a clean-cut, blond all-American type, with a ravishing smile, bright brown eyes and the ego of a peacock. Though a reasonable six feet three inches in height, he weighed an unreasonable three hundred pounds. For a man of his weight and girth, he was astonishingly light on his feet. And as further proof that he was every inch an original, he detested health foods, exercise, fiber diets. To the bewilderment of three cardiologists, his annual medical checkup proved that his arteries remained stubbornly whistle-clean. There is no accounting for genes.

Next to art—paintings in particular—Phipps adored food. Gourmet food, that is. And he adored New York because New York was for him the center of the universe of food. As far as Toby was concerned, Paris in the spring, all of France for that matter, was good enough for Cole Porter, the tourists and the French. "But for the serious gourmand, there is no place like Manhattan," he was in the habit of saying to Lawrence Lord. "When I go abroad, I never travel without a case of Talbot 1949. You can't predict how good a restaurant's wine list is going to be. And even if the menu is interesting, it's merely an imitation of the best cuisine in New York. After all, the money is here, so why not the chefs?"

Though Toby, as he liked his friends to call him, was an entertaining dinner companion, Lawrence had come to dread his visits to Manhattan. Toby expected to be wined and dined and feted at the very best restaurants. Anything less would have been an insult. Since Tobias Phipps was the curator of a small but exceptionally well funded Maryland museum whose trustees included members of the Du Pont family, Lawrence had no choice but to do the decent thing. As a curator, Toby was worth his weight in gold.

Toby had been a hard nut to crack. The hardest. The difficulty was he had a mind of his own. Along with his highly developed palate went a discouragingly thorough education in art, as well as a shrewd eye when it came to judging a painting. Unlike many other curators around the country, Toby politely refused to bow his head and bend his knee to Lawrence Lord's authority. He bought nothing on faith. He would not accept a painting on consignment—even though it could be returned to the seller if it did not come up to his standard or the trustees objected. Toby refused to waste his time. He insisted on examining a painting before he made the purchase. With the tiresome result that, Lawrence being unable to persuade him to accept anything sight unseen, greed had finally overcome his caution.

Since the Maryland museum could afford the very best, he risked inviting Toby to New York. They paid a visit to the Morgan Manhattan warehouse, where the Luxembourg Corporation stored its always changing inventory of paintings. Lawrence never mentioned the corporation. He simply explained to Toby that the space he rented in the warehouse was the most efficient way to adequately service the many museums that depended on his judgment as a consultant. Since what one museum wished to sell, another wanted to buy to round out its collection. Lawrence made it absolutely clear that he received no financial reward for the altruistic service he performed. The fees the museums paid him as a consultant covered the warehouse storage costs for the paintings.

Toby was enchanted with a portrait of a young woman by the underrated Danish painter Christen Kobke. Toby did have an eye, Lawrence told himself, for aesthetic value and investment growth. An eye quite as acute as his own. Toby made a commitment to buy the painting for thirty thousand, ten thousand more than Lawrence had expected. Afterward they went to a lavish dinner. For Lawrence, it was the best of times. The worst of times came the next morning.

It was over his morning coffee that it dawned on him exactly what a hell he'd brought down on himself. Toby liked to preen, to show special knowledge, and it was entirely possible he would tell people about the variety of paintings stored in the Morgan Manhattan warehouse, and about the paintings that, with his acute artistic perception, he'd purchased through

his dear friend Lawrence. And as Toby chatted on, some
dealer, a critic, a crawling creature of the night with a suspicious mind and a taste for detective-story chicanery, might
start having thoughts about Lawrence's rented space in the
Morgan Manhattan warehouse and why he would need such
a large inventory of paintings. The idea made Lawrence Lord
want to throw up.

As time passed and Toby's visits became increasingly frequent and increasingly lucrative, Lawrence grew increasingly
wretched every time Toby's limousine—courtesy of the museum—arrived in Manhattan. But Toby was a natural for the
remaining Rufus Hathaway, so, like it or not, on a Wednesday in late April, Lawrence invited him to New York.

At Lawrence's suggestion, Toby arrived in time for lunch.
It was Lawrence's idea that a sumptuous lunch, followed by
a stroll in the park, should prepare Toby nicely for a visit to
the warehouse to see the Hathaway. And while viewing it,
Toby would have in the forefront of his mind the thought that
he still had a superb dinner to anticipate.

Lawrence breathed freely at lunchtime. The Grill Room of
The Four Seasons was usually not a hangout for artists or
museum curators or art dealers, or for the art world in general. Later, at the warehouse, Toby pronounced the Rufus
Hathaway "a find." He would tell Lawrence at dinner exactly
how much he would pay for it. He would pay handsomely,
but Toby insisted there be no haggling. He was not an Ar-
menian rug dealer.

The evenings Lawrence spent dining with Toby were agonizing. They required the strategic planning of an Israeli rescue mission.

He had precise arrangements to make, and to make them
he needed as much advance information as possible. In preparation for Toby's visits, Lawrence kept a constantly updated
list of the best restaurants in Manhattan: the Quilted Giraffe,
Lutèce, Chanterelle, La Côte Basque, Hatsuhana, La Tulipe,
Le Cirque, La Grenouille, Le Cygne, The Four Seasons dining room, and so on and so forth. But that was only the
beginning. Along with the restaurants, he kept scrupulous
track of which nights the maître d' considered his restaurant's
most popular. Those nights Lawrence avoided the restaurant
like the plague. If Toby were visiting Manhattan on a Monday, and Monday was the Big Night at Le Cirque, then Lawrence would reserve a quiet table for two for Monday at the
Quilted Giraffe, where the Big Night was Thursday. Optimis-
tically, he hoped that the worst that might happen was that

they'd be seated next to a politician or a television talk-show host.

This Wednesday evening they were dining at Le Bernardin, an off night at the popular restaurant. They arrived at eight and were escorted to a good table a comfortable distance from the entry. Lawrence felt moderately at ease. Art patrons, being dedicated to conspicuous consumption, preferred to spend their money on the "on" nights. His hand holding the wineglass was steady as a rock, his conversational tone composed. Toby wouldn't have noticed if Lawrence were having a heart attack. He was concentrated on a loin of baby rabbit stuffed with foie gras, with a thyme-flavored sauce, accompanied by asparagus and a delicate potato tart. Meanwhile Lawrence contented himself with keeping a watchful eye on the door and nibbling at a grilled sea bass covered with a light tomato sauce. Between them, they consumed two bottles of wine—a Château Carbonnieux '81, a flavorful dry white Graves, and a Château Leoville Las Cases '62, a mature red from the Médoc. It was a splendid meal, and although the check would easily pay a month's rent plus utilities for a studio apartment on the Upper West Side of Manhattan, it was worth every penny. Lawrence waited until Toby had finished off the dinner with a slice of mocha mousse studded with fruit and bathed in two sauces, a crème anglaise and a raspberry puree, followed by an orange soufflé served with a glass of Grand Marnier, before mentioning the Rufus Hathaway.

As Toby finished the last drop of Grand Marnier, Lawrence said, "So you like the Hathaway?"

"Mmm. Very good. Better than good. Excellent. I like it very much," Toby said, belching contentedly.

"How do you think the trustees will like it?"

"They'll like it very much. Yes, very much. They tend to like what I like." His eyes twinkled roguishly. "When one is as wealthy as my trustees, one becomes accustomed to being taken care of. Advised. By authorities, of course. As their artistic authority, I am confident I can convince them that we need the Hathaway to fill a particular gap in our collection." He continued smiling innocently enough. "But we won't pay more than seventy-five thousand."

Lawrence looked thoughtful, though he was mentally dancing in the streets. "I'll see if I can convince Hammerschmidt," he said. "He expected at least one hundred thousand." Lawrence hoped the figure didn't sound as ridiculous to Toby as it did to his own ears.

"All right, tell Mr. Hammerschmidt I'll go to eighty," Toby said without a blink, ignoring his earlier claim that he would never haggle. "But not a penny more."

"I'll do my best. In fact"—Lawrence stroked his chin as thoughtfully, as though he was about to take a risk—"I'll speak for Hammerschmidt. The man is unfamiliar with the market for art, since he never sells anything and wouldn't sell this if his wife hadn't sold their condo in Arizona where it was hanging. I say done! Eighty it is. For the Rufus Hathaway."

"Fine," said Toby with an expansive wave of his hand that made heads turn and Lawrence mentally cringe. "Now we need more espresso. And a little brandy. Courvoisier. Or, if the cellar has it, a Napoleon. Either way, a cognac, don't you think? To celebrate?"

Lawrence longed to leave, but he was buoyed up by a wonderful exhilaration. Eighty thousand was less than he'd hoped for, but one mustn't be too greedy.

"Lawrence! Darling! How divine to see you," a familiar voice caroled. "Isn't it terrible about Phillip?"

There she was, striding toward him, wearing a strapless red satin gown reminiscent of the fifties, pointed-toed red satin shoes with stiletto heels and a small black satin hat with a veil. At the sight of her, Lawrence felt sick. It was Darlene Schiller, on the arm of a young man with cinematic good looks—a minor rock star who recently had cut a narrow swath through the New York saloon circuit. He was wearing a T-shirt and scuffy jeans. Full of hometown charm. Joy to the world, Lawrence thought venomously. At the moment the young hustler's name escaped him. Huckleberry. Or Web Foot. Or something equally tasteless. He probably sang and chewed on a cocaine-laced straw at the same time. Why would anyone over fifteen care to be seen with him? Except Darlene Schiller, who had the glands of an adolescent boy.

"Phillip who? Isn't what terrible?" Lawrence asked calmly.

"You mean you haven't heard?"

"Haven't heard what?"

"Of course. How could you? Warm and cozy and well fed in this blissful place. You haven't been near a news broadcast in hours.'"

"Sometimes in days. Darlene, what are you talking about?"

"Phillip Mckay, dearest." Darlene, who never missed a trick, was now eyeing Toby.

"What should I have heard?" Lawrence asked, wishing a trapdoor would open and Darlene would drop through it.

"Phillip was murdered. Last night. The cleaning woman found him in his office—dead! I heard it on the radio while I was dressing." Darlene's voice changed to an intimate murmur as she focused her attention completely on Toby. "Don't I know your friend, Lawrence?"

"You do, Mrs. Schiller. I'm Toby Phipps." Toby smiled expansively. "We met at lunch at Amy's."

"Oh! How could I have forgotten? We discussed Amy's splendid needlework."

"You said your mama had a genius for altar pillows."

"She did. An absolute genius." Darlene gave Toby a smile full of white teeth and animation. Then she gazed at Lawrence with pretended petulance. "You never told me that you knew Tobias Phipps. Or Amy Du Pont. If I'd known Toby was going to be in New York, we could all have dined *intime* at my pied-à-terre. I have a modest duplex on Park." Darlene sparkled at Toby.

"Next time I schedule a trip to New York, I'll insist Lawrence tell you," Toby said genially.

Lawrence nodded, unable to speak and thankful that he was seated, because he felt weak in the knees. His head was throbbing mercilessly and he only hoped that no sweat had broken out on his face. When the police asked him where he'd been last night, what would he tell them?

"Lawrence, you must stop hoarding such a treasure as Toby. Amy tells me she absolutely depends on him for every single art purchase she makes."

The boy rock singer was growing bored. "Baby, I'm hungry. We eat now, or I find a McDonald's and another broad."

"Your gallantry is touching." Darlene smiled at her rock star, then glanced slyly at Toby. "He's a luxury when I feel like indulging myself. We all have our little excesses. Don't we, Lawrence? At any rate, bye-bye for now, Tobias." She waved as she sashayed off, pulling the young man after her. "Don't forget, we must be in touch the next time you're in New York." She paused and turned back to Lawrence, her face filled with counterfeit grief. "Oh, my dear, whatever shall we do without Phillip?" And again she continued on her way.

Lawrence was almost too exhausted to speak. Between Toby, Darlene and the prospect of the police, it was all too much.

"The body of that boy is an icon," Toby remarked with yearning. "Do you think she would invite him to dinner with us?"

Now Lawrence could feel the sweat on his brow. "It's possible, but," he said with a lift of one eyebrow and a nervous bravado that was slightly off key, "her cook is a disaster. A true disaster."

"What a pity," Toby said glumly. "So is Amy's cook. And Amy's palate."

"That's unfortunate," Lawrence said cautiously. Abruptly he sensed something not quite right. Toby had never said anything critical about Amy Du Pont before.

"You don't know the half of it. I dine with Amy at least twice a week. One night we'll start with canned vichyssoise. Then Rock Cornish game hen. With green peas. The next evening it's chicken Kiev. With green peas. Two nights a week I have dinner with Elizabeth and Steven. Steven is Amy's brother. Elizabeth prefers to start with a canned jellied madrilene soup. And for her main course she frequently relies on beef Wellington, which is Steven's favorite dish since it was his father's favorite dish. Elizabeth varies the beef Wellington with beef stew. That was her father's favorite dish. Now it's her favorite dish."

"That sounds rather dull," Lawrence murmured.

" 'Dull' is an understatement," said Toby. "There is nothing basically wrong with any of those dishes, but after a while the little unmanageable birds, the fillet in its skin of burned crust and the stew with its base of canned beef consommé and no wine are a bit horrid."

"I can imagine," Lawrence said. The drift of the conversation was making him nervous.

"You can't possibly imagine. It's sheer hell. Fortunately, the portions are small. Very small. The Family believes large portions are vulgar."

"A minor blessing," Lawrence Lord commiserated, searching Toby's face intently for a purpose.

"Too minor. That doesn't end it. For special occasions like an engagement party or a gala buffet for an anniversary, you would think they'd show some imagination. No, there is no enlargement of horizon. No reach. If you study the buffet table you will see crackers, lots of crackers, everything from Carr's water biscuits to Triscuits and Fritos. You can also count on there being bottled Vienna sausages or anything that can be served on a toothpick and dipped into a communal mustard bowl. There may or may not be frozen mini-pizza, but you can depend on celery hearts, deviled eggs, cocktail onions, smoked oysters on Melba rounds and waterlogged lobster with Hellmann's mayonnaise. That's what I said, Hellmann's mayonnaise! They do not believe in Beluga caviar. Or pâté. Fresh baby eels or a really fine cheese such as Pyrenees is out of the question. In fact, not even a Roquefort or an old Camembert is ever seen. Anything that does not come in a can or a frozen-food package is beyond them.''

"I never knew," Lawrence said.

"How could you? I try not to complain. But the Family—and their friends too—tends to live very low on the hog.''

"How do you bear it?" Lawrence surveyed Toby's huge body in awe, checking his desire to ask what he was driving at.

Toby played with his coffee spoon. "Sometimes I drive to Washington to have a second dinner. Then, too, I have a painter friend''—he smiled as if it were some private joke only he could appreciate—"who has taken up cooking quite seriously. A second profession. He accommodates me and I accommodate him. The museum bought two of his better paintings.''

"I see." Lawrence was beginning to see a great deal.

"I know the Hathaway is just a wee bit high, though quality does count," Toby said amiably. "And I am sure you have other such prizes in inventory." He paused to give emphasis to the word *inventory,* then dismissed it with a shrug, trying to look a little embarrassed. "I don't mean actually in inventory. I mean quality paintings that you might find for me from collectors or museums wishing to dispose of them. Paintings to fill in gaps, as the Hathaway does. Or paintings to replace those I might want to dispose of. Possibly with your assistance.''

Lawrence understood the implication. He read it in the glitter of Toby's eyes. He understood that Toby understood, and he did not answer but instead waited for a definite demand. He did some rapid mental calculations as to how big a kickback Toby would ask for. And how much the Luxembourg Corporation could afford. Or did Toby have a few paintings in his personal collection that he wanted to sell at a profit?

Tobias Phipps gave him a long, steady look, took a sip of his espresso and said in a soft voice, "I suggest that we may have to discuss art and the artistic marketplace more regularly than we have in the past. Once every few months isn't enough. You must invite me to dine in Manhattan and talk business—let's say twice a month.''

"I understand," said Lawrence, the essence of reasonableness, but he didn't understand at all. "And . . . ?" He was waiting for the second shoe to drop.

"And you pick the restaurants. I'll come up early. So we can have lunch and dinner together. I'll usually bring a special friend along for dinner. Lunch and a visit to the Morgan Manhattan warehouse we'll do together. But there will be three for dinner."

"And . . . ?" Lawrence pressed on.

"And what?" Toby started to laugh.

"And what else do you want?"

"That's all."

"That's all?" Lawrence said it almost to himself.

"Yes, that is all. Oh, Lawrence, for heaven's sake! Are you thinking of money? Don't be silly. That would be criminal, and furthermore, money's not my greed. I've more than I need right now."

Lawrence tried hard to conceal his astonishment. "I understand."

"You don't. But you don't have to. Different people have different greeds. I am a Phipps. I have a substantial inheritance. You must know Amy and Steve are my cousins on my mother's side. Why else would I put up with their abominable cooking if family ties didn't obligate me to?"

"That's true," Lawrence said, feeling as if nothing more could surprise him.

"I can do nothing about their cooking. But I can save them from their equally abominable taste in art. It's my contribution to the Family heritage. Now let's have the brandy, shall we?" he remarked cheerfully. "I need something to help me forget tomorrow evening. Tomorrow I dine with Hazel Reynolds. She's a third cousin, so I only have dinner there occasionally. But since I'm a desired guest, in my honor there will be half-raw roast beef with overdone Yorkshire pudding. Plus green peas. The Family adores green peas."

After dinner Lawrence and Toby strolled slowly up Madison Avenue to the Hotel Plaza Athenée. The night air was refreshing and Lawrence thought what a profitable evening it had been. And of equally profitable evenings to come.

After saying good night to Toby in front of the hotel, he waited a long five minutes. Then he entered the lobby and looked for a public telephone booth. He dialed his son. The telephone rang ten times while Lawrence's frown grew deeper. It wasn't like Jason not to be home at this hour. Ten-thirty was late for him. Lawrence dialed again, thinking he might have dialed the wrong number, but again there was no

answer. He hung up and left the hotel. By the time he reached
his apartment, he decided it was too late to call. Even if Jason
had finally arrived home, to call so late would give his request
undue importance. He'd wait until morning.

For once he was glad to have bumped into Darlene Schil-
ler. Or he would not have known about Phillip. My God!
Phillip Mckay murdered! He felt a chill of apprehension.
Their meeting yesterday at five was the last appointment on
Phillip's schedule. He'd left him in his office, very much alive.

As an old, dear friend of Phillip's who was, perhaps, the
last person to have seen him alive—except for the murderer—
he would be questioned by the police. Where had he gone
and what had he done after leaving Phillip? He had an alibi,
but he didn't dare use it. He'd gone to the Morgan Manhattan
to check on the Rufus Hathaway. He'd wanted to make sure
it was ready for Toby's inspection. Then, on a fatherly impulse, he thought of calling Jason and asking him to join him
for dinner. He dismissed the impulse quickly as sentimental
and instead stopped for a bite at a nondescript cafe. He was
in bed by nine-thirty. Now he wished he'd acted on his impulse to call his son. The beat of Lawrence's heart quickened
at the possibility that the subject of the warehouse might come
up. If it did and the police started digging into Morgan Manhattan records, the existence of the Luxembourg Corporation
would come to light. That mustn't happen. The police must
not learn about his visit to the warehouse. Or the space he
rented there. If he were connected in any way to the Luxembourg Corporation, it would destroy him.

Chapter Nine

Cella sat on a hassock in the library of the Taggard home, sipping a martini, her eyes glued to the television screen.

". . . neighbors still find it hard to believe that Mrs. Vincent Murray III will be arraigned at the Larchmont police station on Wednesday. The alleged charge is shoplifting." The television announcer's voice became hypersincere. "It is now alleged that Mrs. Vincent Murray III is responsible for the disappearance from local boutique shops of thousands of dollars of merchandise. Mrs. Murray, one of the wealthiest women in Larchmont, is known for her high standard of morality."

"Cella, what has come over you in the past few weeks with this appetite for petty criminality?" Sebastian said as he entered the library.

Cella started guiltily for an instant. "I'm studying the modern criminal mentality." She smiled quickly, as if smiles were out of season. "I want to understand it."

"I don't know what there is to understand. It simply confirms my faith in the depravity of human nature."

"I like your commonsense appraisal."

"I'm a realist. But I admit I don't understand you."

Cella glanced at her father, her eyes filled with some mysterious purpose that seemed to puzzle her as much as him. At last she said, "I don't understand myself, if it comes to that."

". . . and it appears alarmingly evident," the newscaster continued, "that Patrolman Claude Harrison-Smyth was implicated in the dog kidnapping—or dognapping—that has been occurring in the silk-stocking district between Madison and Park avenues in the Sixties . . ."

"Will you please turn off that ridiculous program so we can have our drinks in peace? You can turn it on again at seven o'clock, when the world news comes on."

117

"You are interfering with my education." Cella rose to her knees and reached for the television switch, but her hand froze as the announcer's voice suddenly brimmed with a new spurt of energy.

". . . about midnight last night, the cleaning woman, Mrs. Etta Pivovarski, entered the office of Dr. Phillip Mckay, the world-renowned curator of classical art at the Metropolitan Museum of Art. She found Dr. Mckay lying in a pool of blood on the floor. It is the coroner's opinion that the death occurred sometime between ten and eleven last night. Dr. Mckay was apparently bludgeoned to death with a five-thousand-year-old marble idol. The idol is a twelve-inch-high figure of a nude woman dating back to the most ancient years of Greek art. It is called a Cycladian maiden. Phillip Mckay's alleged murder is already sending shock waves through the art world . . ."

"Phillip McKay!" Sebastian gasped.

"Phillip! Good Lord!" Cella slumped back in a sudden collapse.

The picture on the set changed from a head shot of the TV anchorman to the entrance of the Metropolitan Museum of Art, where a small man, wearing a too-large brown suit and a brown yarmulke, was being harangued by a group of reporters.

"Lieutenant Stein," a young, pretty, blond woman called out, "what can you tell us about Dr. Mckay's murder?"

The lieutenant replied, "Nothing. It's too soon."

An older man with a puffy face and slicked-back black hair brandished a microphone in front of the officer's face. "Was anything stolen from the museum?"

"It's too soon to know. We're waiting for an inventory report."

Another man shoved his microphone in front of the lieutenant. "Was the museum broken into? Or was it an inside job?"

"We don't know. It's too soon to tell."

"What do you know, Lieutenant?"

"Nothing. Only that it is alleged that Dr. Phillip Mckay died from an alleged blow on the head." The lieutenant smiled. "You can say we're rounding up the usual suspects. That's it!"

The camera cut back to the anchorman in the studio.

"You've just heard the famous homicide detective, Lieutenant Benjamin Stein, state that the police are baffled. However, those of us who have followed the long career of

Lieutenant Stein know that he is always baffled—it's always too soon to say—until five minutes before the alleged guilty party is arrested. But while we wait for Lieutenant Stein to pull his usual rabbit out of the hat, our roving reporter, Gabriella Press, has obtained an interview with the world-renowned authority on ancient art, Dr. Jason Lord. Dr. Lord has made a particular study of the Cycladian maiden that is alleged to be the murder weapon.''

Jason Lord appeared on the screen, seated in a chair. His expression was solemn, as befitted the occasion. The TV reporter facing him was unique in an industry that hired female reporters more for their looks than for their journalism abilities. She was short, heavy-bodied, and her untouched gray hair was only slightly longer than most men's hair. Occasionally the television lighting reflected off her thick-lensed glasses.

"Well, well, well. We now have Dr. Jason Lord," Sebastian said with impatience. "The world-renowned authority."

Gabriella Press began. "It is my understanding, Dr. Lord, that you have some strong opinions about the possible murderer of Phillip Mckay, the celebrated authority on antiquities."

"Let me correct you, please," Lord said. "There is a misconception here. I have a strong opinion about what might have prompted the murder. But as to who the actual killer is"—Jason Lord smiled—"as Lieutenant Stein has said, it's too soon.''

"I see. But you do have a suspicion as to the motive."

"Of course he has a suspicion. He makes a living out of his suspicions. Accurate or not," Sebastian said under his breath.

"A strong suspicion," Jason Lord said.

"Would you tell our television audience what you suspect?" There was a thin coating of skepticism in Gabriella Press' voice.

"Yes. But only because I believe what I have to say will be a public service. I think this tragedy might serve as a warning to all those interested in collecting art." As he spoke, Jason Lord removed his round, rimless spectacles. He stared directly into the camera. Cella could detect nothing nearsighted or squinty in his look, which confirmed her original opinion that Jason Lord used the old-fashioned glasses as some kind of disguise, not because he needed them. "I am speaking of any purchases of paintings, furniture, sculptings, jewelry, coins. The list is endless.''

"You mean, all art buyers beware?" Gabriella Press asked.

"Exactly," Jason said. "Naïveté can be very expensive. And it's found in the highest circles of art sophistication, as well as among amateur collectors. About a week ago Phillip Mckay and I had a discussion about the authenticity of the four Cycladian maidens the museum has had on display for almost two decades. It has taken me time, but I am now convinced that the maidens are fakes. Exquisite fakes, but fakes nonetheless. The Metropolitan was duped. I offered my evidence to Dr. Mckay and have been waiting to hear from him."

As she watched Jason Lord's face, it occurred to Cella that although his words expressed concern about the naïveté of art collectors, his expression was a taunt to the entire human race. He was a man who would enjoy exploiting the weaknesses of others.

"What evidence did you present to Mr. Mckay that this was the case?"

"The idols themselves. The marble was too spotlessly pure. Perfect. Theoretically, they had lain in the soil of the humid Cycladic islands for almost five thousand years, yet they showed no sign of exposure to the soil."

"I saw him on public television last Sunday," Cella said. "I could give you his song and dance word for word."

"Why didn't you tell me?" Sebastian asked.

"I didn't think you'd care. And you believe I'm on a witch hunt where he's concerned," Cella answered indignantly.

"All right. I want to hear the rest of this."

". . . and I confirmed that the idol Dr. Mckay gave me to work with contained suspicious elements"—Lord had the tone and manner of a prosecutor—"that are quite inappropriate for the alleged age of the figurines and the place where they were theoretically discovered. They had to be fakes."

A hand reached over Cella's head and switched off the television set. Cella glanced up in surprise.

"Anton! I didn't hear you come in. Isn't it terrible?"

"Phillip's death? Yes. I heard about it on the radio in the cab coming over. Lord is having a field day. He should pick up some business from the publicity."

"Turn it on again, Cella. I think we ought to hear the rest of what he says," Sebastian said firmly.

"He sets my teeth on edge," Anton insisted. He went to the liquor cabinet and poured himself a stiff scotch. Then he settled himself on the floor beside Cella. "Self-righteous s.o.b., full of fire and brimstone. How did he ever miss the pulpit?''

"He didn't. He's on one now," Cella said impatiently. "But Father's right, dear. We might as well hear his sermon."

"Why?"

"We'll learn what he told the police."

"Turn on the set," Sebastian insisted.

Cella reached up and switched it on. ". . . I am convinced that whoever sold the Metropolitan the figurines knew they were frauds. They were purchased many years ago, and according to Phillip Mckay, the records of sale were lost or mislaid. Still, Dr. Mckay did remember who the dealer was, but he refused to give me the man's name. However, he promised me he would contact the dealer and discuss the matter. If the figurines proved to be copies, he wanted the museum to be completely reimbursed. There are substantial sums involved. Hundreds of thousands of dollars."

"Look at the bastard, agonizing with integrity," Anton said with disgust. "It's his stigmata."

". . . and the dealer," Jason continued, "is someone who, I suspect, has a fine reputation in the art world." He paused to give emphasis to his next words. "At any rate, I think Dr. Mckay did contact whoever it was who sold the figurines to the Met, and I believe it was the dealer who murdered him."

Again Anton reached over and switched off the television set. This time Cella, Anton and Sebastian sat for a moment without talking.

Then Sebastian said, "Victor?"

Anton did not answer; his eyes were withdrawn. At last Cella said in a quiet, unhurried tone, "Dearest, you look as if you've contracted some exotic disease."

"I have. Jason Lord. I'd better call Air France and see if I can get a seat on the Concorde tomorrow morning."

"You're flying to Paris tomorrow? There goes our weekend. When will you be back?" Cella asked.

"About a week. After I see Uncle Victor, I might as well go on to Hungary. A month ago Victor mentioned a panel of Saint Peter he thought worth looking at."

"I'll go with you after dinner and help you pack," Cella said.

"Thank you."

"You're welcome."

Cella grew thoughtful, as in the back of her mind she began to sort things out. The Cycladian maidens. Jason Lord had explained on the public television program why they were fakes. He had said they were made in a workshop in Marseilles. Uncle Victor had many artist friends in Marseilles. She remembered glancing with affection at her own Cycladian idol—the rust spotting had made her smile. Now she had a question and even as she raised it, she already knew the answer.

"Anton, did the idol you gave me for my twenty-fifth birthday come from Uncle Victor's studio?"

Anton sounded weary. "Not from the studio. From Uncle Victor himself. The only reason he sold it to me was because it was for you. Family. You wouldn't understand it. He didn't believe an ordinary collector would appreciate its flaws."

"It was the original?" She was amazed at how calmly she spoke the words.

"Yes. The one the studio copied. I assumed you knew that."

"I did, but I didn't think about it." For a moment she was at a loss. "The sooner you go to Paris the better."

"I know," Anton said. "But you seem upset, Cella. Why?"

Sebastian interrupted. "Why don't you telephone Victor tonight? The telephone is faster than the Concorde."

"I'd rather a face-to-face conversation."

"Then I'll telephone him later. And prepare him."

"Do that," Anton replied, still gazing at Cella in puzzlement. "You haven't answered my question. Why are you upset over this Lord thing?"

"I'm very upset about Phillip's murder. You know how good a friend he was. But it's more than that. I don't know what, exactly." Cella leaned over and lightly kissed Anton on the lips, then stared over his head for a minute. One way or another, she had to ask the next question, though again she knew the answer. But it would be a relief to get it out in the open. "I know Victor commissioned the figurines, but did he kill Phillip?"

"For God's sake! Why should he? Not only is it not in his nature, but he called me from Paris on another matter about ten last night. He was an ocean away when the murder occurred." Anton sounded impatient. "Furthermore, Jason Lord can't be thinking of Victor Vilanova. He knows my uncle is too old and too wise to waste his time killing anyone over a business disagreement. Murder is for passion. There was nothing at risk with Phillip that money wouldn't buy. That prick Lord is doing something that I don't understand. But I've got to talk to Uncle Victor and work out how he handles the authorities, should Lord suggest they contact him.''

''I suppose so. It's interesting. The figurines are exquisite. Much as I love the original, I would have had no objection to owning a copy. Those rust spots are like teenage pimples.'' Cella half smiled.

''Which was why Victor wanted them spotless. Collectors of ancient art are filled with admiration for antiquity, but not for the wrinkles, the moles, the pockmarks of time that go with the aging process,'' Anton said dryly.

Cella nodded her head slowly, a faintly ironic look on her face. She could see Victor's point. In some strange way, it seemed to her that the allegedly false Cycladian maidens had something in common with Mrs. Vincent Murray III and her alleged shoplifting.

Chapter Ten

Lawrence Lord was unable to reach his son until Friday morning. Emory buzzed Jason on the intercom and said his father was on the line again. Jason Lord almost said, "Tell him I'm still out," then changed his mind. He would not like his father to know how much his new effort to stay in touch bored his son. Reluctantly he picked up the telephone.

"Good morning, Father," Jason said. "What can I do for you?"

Lawrence Lord's voice was calm, even hearty. "Good morning, Jason. How are you?"

"I'm fine. And I repeat, what can I do for you? If this is a business call, the tests on the Langobardic earrings are not quite complete. I was up at MIT yesterday double-checking the data. I caught the four-thirty shuttle back. I'll have the report ready by the end of next week."

"So that's where you were. I tried to reach you all day. I'm not calling about the earrings. When you're satisfied with the report, you'll inform me. I've something else on my mind. You could do me a favor."

"If I can, I will."

"It's a rather sticky business . . ." Lawrence paused.

"Yes?" Jason listened more intently.

"By the way, were you in on Tuesday evening? I almost called you to ask if you'd join me for dinner."

"Sorry. You wouldn't have reached me. I play chess on Tuesdays."

"Wednesdays, too?"

"Sometimes. What has that got to do with the favor you want?"

"Then you haven't heard? On television or the radio or seen it in the *Times?*"

"Heard what? Seen what?" Jason sounded impatient.

There was again a silence at the other end of the line. After a moment Lawrence Lord spoke soberly. "That Phillip Mckay was murdered."

"I know about it. As a matter of fact, I was contacted by the police yesterday because of the murder weapon used. I gather you missed the news on NBC. They interviewed me last night."

"Did they? I'm sorry, I did miss it."

"They wanted to know if I saw a connection between the murder weapon—the Cycladian idol—and the possible murderer."

"Do you?"

"Yes, but it would be difficult to prove. At any rate, what favor would you like?"

"Well, the fact is I need a beard."

"A beard?"

"A slang expression. I'll explain. Tuesday night, the night Phillip was murdered, I was, shall we say, almost caught in flagrante delicto."

"What are you talking about?"

"About romance. I was spending the evening with a happily married woman whose husband was happily, supposedly, out of town. But he arrived home unexpectedly, and I had to leave quickly by the service entrance."

"So?"

"I was Phillip's last scheduled appointment the night he was murdered. The police are bound to question me. If I have to tell the truth about where I was later that evening, it will cause a number of very nice people considerable unhappiness."

"You need an alibi."

"Precisely. I need an alibi. That's where the favor comes in."

"I'm to be your alibi."

"It would help." There was a note of pleading in Lawrence's voice. "If you agreed that we were having dinner together Tuesday evening . . ."

"Yes . . ." Lawrence couldn't see the curious upscrewing of Jason's lips as he smiled. "All right, I'll be your beard. Your alibi. On Tuesday night we were having roast beef and Yorkshire pudding."

"A gourmet delight," Lawrence said, and now he too smiled.

They judiciously worked out the details of their dinner together—the time, the place, the wine, the entire menu, the coffee, the conversation. When it was over, Lawrence thanked Jason profusely and said good-bye.

After Jason hung up, he sat at his desk, as motionless as a statue, staring thoughtfully at the telephone. When he finally stirred, his movements were abrupt, almost uncoordinated. He told himself there was no reason for further postponement. Now was the time to call. His skin felt hot as he picked up the telephone receiver, but his blue eyes were cool and his expression ambiguous.

The woman's voice that answered was warm and deeply sensual. "Hello?"

"Mother—Marina—this is Jason."

"Jason! My dear! How wonderful to hear from you."

"It's been too long. But I wish the circumstances for my calling were happier."

Marina Lord sighed bleakly. "You mean Phillip's death?"

"Yes, it was awful. But what can I say?" he asked hesitantly, searching his way through this familiar purgatory.

"Nothing. Then this is a condolence call?"

To his dismay, Jason noted that he was sweating profusely, and he patted his forehead with his handkerchief as he spoke. "Yes and no. It is a condolence call—I know how much Phillip meant to you."

"He was the very best of friends."

Jason looked confused at her use of the word *friend*. He then said, "It must have been a terrible shock."

"Terrible." Marina and Jason remained silent for a moment, allied, it might seem, in mutual sympathy. "Strange, your calling now. I was thinking of calling you."

With the atrocious swiftness with which the human heart can attack the human brain, Jason had to struggle to control his voice. Somehow he managed to ask with casual politeness, "You were going to call me?" His lungs felt shallow, and before he could continue he had to take a deep breath. "About what?"

"Something's come up. It's been coming up for a long time and now I mean to face it. Phillip's death brought it all into focus. I think you could help me, if you would. Straighten things out. Break the jinx. If that's what it is."

"Anything. Anything at all, Mother," he said almost humbly. "If it's in my power . . ."

"Well, to be quite frank, you're the only one who can help."

"If I can, I will. You can count on me."

"Perhaps if we had lunch . . . ?"

"Yes, lunch. That was my second reason for calling. Or possibly dinner?" He stopped himself, embarrassed by his eagerness, and backed off rapidly. "Lunch would be fine. I'm glad you're not in mourning."

Marina spoke in a gentle, low voice. "No, dear. What mattered deeply between Phillip and me had unfortunately flickered out. Let's say I fell out of love. And in love with somebody else. I regret Phillip, I grieve for him, but I am not in mourning."

Jason felt unexpectedly abashed and was relieved his mother couldn't see his face. Stretching his shoulders as though his muscles had stiffened, he said offhandedly, "Last time we spoke you mentioned marriage to Phillip. I thought by now the date and place would be settled. I've been watching the mail for an invitation to the wedding and wondering what kind of present to get the bride who has everything."

"You can still think about a wedding and wedding presents. There is a man who has become very important to me."

"Who?" Jason asked, courting martyrdom.

"That's what I want to talk to you about at lunch."

"How does next Friday look?"

"Friday? Friday I'm flying to L.A., then driving to Santa Barbara for your cousin Sheri's wedding. You were invited too, but I didn't think you'd want to . . ."

"You thought quite correctly. Sheri from Santa Barbara? Tan skin. A thin, elongated body. Shoulders stooped to minimize her height. She has a huge appetite and plays hard tennis. The simplicity of her brain fascinates me. Also, her mother is a gorgon."

"Jason! My sister, Lila, is not a gorgon," Marina objected, laughing.

"If you can't make it Friday, how about Thursday?"

"No. Friday is fine. My plane doesn't leave until four."

"Friday it is, then," Jason said too quickly. "I know a charming restaurant in Soho. Or would you rather have lunch uptown? Would that be more convenient?"

"If we lunch early enough, Soho is fine," Marina said promptly. "But I always get lost there. Why don't I pick you up at your office rather than meet you at the restaurant?"

"Fine. I'll expect you at twelve-thirty?"

"Twelve-thirty it is." They hung up simultaneously, as if in an effort to escape each other.

Jason sat silently, staring into space. Two parents, two favors in one week. That must be some kind of record, he thought. Then his mind swarmed with visual images of his mother—her sensuous face, her generous mouth, her eyes that promised. He clutched at memories with the fright and clarity he always felt when thinking of her. And as always they unsettled him, haunted him, calling to his buried self, the self he alone knew existed.

He walked slowly to his library. He knew he was about to engage in the forbidden, or the forbidden was about to engage him. Yet there was no debate within him about the right or the wrong of his actions. Quietly he closed the library door.

The room was lined with shelves of books from floor to ceiling. Books on all forms of art—paintings and prints from all cultures and periods, jewelry, sculpture, furniture and more; books on art history and, of course, technical books on archiometry. Jason walked to the library steps that stood against the north wall where the scientific books lined the shelves. He rolled the ladder to the section on the history of medieval art, climbed the three steps and easily reached up to the top shelf. Next to a history of Madonna paintings was a large vellum book entitled *Mater Semper Est.* With the book in hand, he descended the ladder and moved to a round mahogany table in the center of the library. He sat in the one Queen Anne chair facing the table, for a long minute doing nothing. Anyone watching him could not be certain if he was awake or asleep with his eyes open. Finally he unhooked the clasp that held the book closed.

As he opened the cover, it became apparent the book was not a book but a box. For many minutes Jason stared at the contents, inhaling the fragrance of Shalimar that drifted up from its interior. With deft fingers, he lifted out a pair of delicate, scented lace panties, apricot in color, and laid them reverently on the table. After that, one dainty satin mule, and then a shimmery silk chemise that filled his senses with the perfume. His mind was inflamed with erotic images. Finally, he took out a small, five-ounce bottle of Shalimar, which he occasionally used to sprinkle on the items. Jason's heart was beating in a strange, excited way as he studied his treasure trove. He put out his hand and touched the panties with trembling fingers. Then the satin mule, the silk chemise. He held the slipper in his hand, aware of a stirring in his loins as he remembered the flash of an ankle, the arch of an instep. He put the mule down and picked up the chemise, bringing it close to his cheek. It seemed to him still warm, as though a woman had recently taken it off. As the warmth ran through his blood, memory overwhelmed him. And with memory came a sick dull aching in his heart as he slipped into another world. . . .

He was a child again at Marina's heels. And she was always picking him up, hugging and kissing him. Sometimes in the morning he would climb into her bed, and she would hold him close against her firm white breasts, welcoming him with her warm body. Her long dark hair, hanging forward, caressed his face. She would be wearing a silken nightgown that did not interfere with his feeling the soft roundness of her body; in fact, the flimsy protection of the nightgown only added to his childlike excitement. About her neck she always wore two necklaces, one of them beautiful amber beads. She would smile at him, a loving smile, and Jason would feel a strange new excitement between his legs that he didn't understand.

Sometimes they lay as close as lovers. Marina crooned softly to her young son, stroking his hair and quieting him, but when his father was there in the bed, he would reach over, angry and jealous, and take Jason into his arms. In Lawrence's arms Jason felt peculiar and alien, as if the time he had spent in his mother's arms had changed him, made him somehow less Lawrence's son. Without understanding the reason, Jason could feel his father's anger in the tension of his arms.

What he did not know as a child was that Lawrence resented his son. He complained that Marina coddled Jason too much. That she preferred Jason to him. And this was a truth that Marina seldom faced. For Marina fondled Jason with more pleasure than she showed when holding Lawrence. Her son was so bright and golden, so muscular and noisy, it was like handling a puppy. Lawrence was long-boned and lean. His elbows and shoulders were spears sticking into her body.

When Lawrence was away on a speaking tour, his absence gave Marina an excuse to have Jason sleep in the same bed with her every night. It was a time Jason always looked forward to. He loved to bury his head deep in his mother's bosom and breathe the perfume between her breasts.

One night, although Lawrence was away, Marina went to bed without taking her son with her. Thinking about her beauty, Jason couldn't sleep. Finally, he got up out of his bed and walked barefoot down the corridor to his mother's room. Exultant yet terrified, he tiptoed into her bedroom. Since his father was away, he knew his mother would be sleeping alone in the huge bed.

When he opened the door and stared around the room, he didn't feel like an intruder, but like someone who has come to worship at a shrine. His mother's sheets were pale lavender, her favorite color. She was sleeping with the curtains open, and the moon filled the room with a soft silvery light. Stealthily, Jason approached the bed and stood on tiptoe looking at her. Her dark hair lay across the pillow; her breathing was regular and soft; one arm lay across the covers. Jason stared at the silky tanned skin. Her arms and shoulders were bare except for the very thin straps of a nightgown. He knew the kind she was wearing. She always wore the same nightgowns in summer. She called them shorties.

He wished he were a grown-up man. Like his father. So he could sit down on the bed the way his father did. Swing his legs under the sheets and lie down beside her and press his body against hers. The way he'd seen his father do.

But he couldn't. He was too small. Too young. Unless she helped him. But she was asleep.

Now, his hands shaking, he felt for the sheet and stealthily drew the covers back. The curves of his mother's body were bathed in the moonlight. There were shadows under her breasts, one had slipped out of the nightgown, and the nightgown itself had slid up around her waist, revealing the milky skin of her soft belly and the crisp, curly dark hair between her thighs. Small Jason shuddered at the sight of her with an ecstasy of spirit. He didn't want to wake her, he just wanted to be close to her. To feel warm and happy.

Somehow he managed to climb into the bed without waking her. He lay next to her for a long time, very frightened, but feeling that his body was burning with a strange new fire. He loved to be in bed with her, and it was even better now that she was asleep. Though he didn't know why. Until he did something he'd never done before. Without knowing what he was doing, he bent his head, pressing his lips against her naked breast. She stirred a little as if she were about to wake up; then she lay still again.

Her movements startled and frightened him, but excited him even more. He wanted to kiss her again. The scent of her body was so sweet he felt he could never get enough of touching her. He hesitated; then he licked the nipple of her breast. The way he had done when he was a baby. He was sure he remembered sucking her breast for milk. So why not suck the nipple now? Its softness hardened and she moaned softly in her sleep. He stopped instantly, terrified that she would wake up. She didn't.

Feeling bolder, he gently touched the tangled, curly hair at the bottom of her belly with the tips of his fingers. When he did this, she moved slightly, her breasts brushing against his cheek. He felt a tingling, confused feeling in his groin, and when he rubbed himself gently against her thigh, the feeling got stronger. He wanted her to awaken and stroke him there, but somehow he knew that couldn't happen. He wanted to lick the hair too and kiss her breasts again, but he didn't dare. Suppose she woke up?

Jason lay back, his mind spinning, holding his breath. He did not move a muscle for fear that he would wake her. He lay still for a long time, afraid to do anything more. At last he slept curled against her body.

Afterward he was never sure how long the dream had lasted. Because afterward he was sure it must have been a dream. The kissing of her breasts and the licking of her nipples—it had to be a dream, even though he wanted to do it all the time.

Jason Lord became aware of a tapping sound. The tapping seemed to come from another world. Abruptly he realized that it did. Someone was tapping on the library door. His mind cleared and he reentered the present.

"Yes?" he called out.

"Mrs. Hancock is here, Mr. Lord," Emory responded.

"I'll be right there," Jason said as he replaced the chemise, the mule, the lace panties and the small bottle of perfume in the book box. "I've been reviewing the work done on the Caesars."

"Certainly, Mr. Lord."

"She brought the thing with her?" Jason said in a loud voice as he ascended the ladder and put the book box back in its place.

"Yes. It's in a blood-red velvet case."

"The Julius Caesar dagger is in a blood-red velvet box. How appropriate. His blood itself would be more convincing," Jason said. "If we could prove it was his."

"She brought with her the invoice and documentation from the dealer in Rome, detailing the proof that it was the dagger Brutus used."

"Not the one Cassius or Cato or maybe the ghost of Augustus used." Jason descended the ladder, smiling, but it was a smile of distaste. "Pure fake," he murmured as he opened the door to the here and now.

Jason was seated at his desk a week later, trying to concentrate on his notes on the Brutus dagger, when Emory announced the arrival of Marina Lord.

"Send her in," he said with more gruffness than he intended, and scrutinized his notes, trying to look like an industrious scholar ant and not a man who had been seething with impatience. As usual, Marina was late.

He could smell the fragrance of Shalimar even before he raised his eyes and saw her enter the office, half smiling, without any haste or embarrassment, refastening a bracelet about her wrist where the clasp had unexpectedly opened. As always, Jason couldn't help staring at her. She looked to him a trifle too thin, worn, a little older than he remembered. But the mysterious authority of beauty and sensuality was still about her. It was there in the sureness of the lift of her head; in the movement of her eyes, which, without being theatrical, struck him as wise and full of conscious power. He had to stop himself from becoming furious at what had gone into the making of those knowing eyes. This was Marina, the mother he knew. Even the simplicity and warmth in her manner, the straightforwardness and frankness that were so highly appealing, were pure deception. More than anyone, he understood how full her nature was with the twists and seductions of instinctive guile.

"I appreciate your promptness," Jason said with a nod.

"You're being chivalrous. I know I am quite late." She glanced around the office approvingly. "Again I congratulate you, Jason. Your office is as effective as a painting by Mondrian. The later period. A clean, clear statement. No waste, no clutter, no needless luxury—truly monastic in its dedication."

"I'm not sure I take that as a compliment."

"It is. It has an austere excellence. Your mother did not raise you to be a clod."

"My mother raised me to see things as they are," Jason said quietly.

"Then I have reason to congratulate myself."

For an instant Jason had nothing to say. "I made a reservation at The Painted Word," he offered at last. "A sunny quiet little place at the top of a loft on Hudson Street. You can have a cold gazpacho soup, several dozen mussels and a cold salad of marinated cod, tomatoes and other vegetables. And conversation until we're talked out."

"How well you know my tastes." Marina gazed indulgently at her son. "A luncheon of appetizers. Actually, my life seems to be based on appetizers. No main courses."

"You'll tell me about it. But first, if you'll excuse me a moment, I'll go wash up." Once in his bathroom, he studied his face in the medicine cabinet mirror. What he saw relieved him. The face in the mirror showed nothing of the self-pitying boy or wretchedly anxious lover; it was the steady, controlled face of a man with many things on his mind. It would do.

While he was gone Marina inspected his desk. Briefly she scanned the notes on the Brutus dagger and grinned. Jason could always be caustic. Then she noticed a black velvet jewel box and opened it. A pair of exquisite earrings gleamed in the light. She couldn't resist trying them on.

When Jason returned, wearing his jacket, she tilted her head from side to side, the earrings swinging back and forth the way they had when Cella wore them.

"How do they look?"

"Wonderful. On you."

"Are they authentic?" Marina asked, taking one earring off and examining it in her hand.

"They are. I've run all the tests and they are what they appear to be. Langobardic earrings. A.D. fifth century. Northern Italy."

"Who wanted them authenticated? Anyone I know?"

A faintly amused smile crossed Jason's face. "You know my client list is confidential."

"Sorry," Marina said. "I forgot."

"Come, I want to hear all about you. Tell me how I can help lift the jinx from your life."

The restaurant in the loft overlooked the Hudson River. It was bare and cool, and the tables were covered with coarse checkered tablecloths. Jason and Marina lunched slowly and meditatively, with mute intervals between rushes of small talk.

Marina sipped her white wine. It helped her feel relaxed. Since her divorce she was always tense with her son, though she hardly understood why. She lifted the glass again, her ringed fingers sparkling as brightly as the wine.

As for Jason, what he had to say couldn't be said; what he was there for was to see her, to be with her and to listen to her, not missing a word of what she might tell him. All week the thought of her had run through him like fire, but now that she was seated opposite him, he was afraid to do or say anything that might disturb the delicate balance of her good will. He was aware that she thought him "strange," and probably he was. That made no difference as long as she was happy to see him.

Jason broke one of their long dialogues of silence by remarking, "Remember all the picnic expeditions we used to take when I was going to be an architect?" His voice was full of nostalgia and shyness. Whenever they were together, he felt like a boy on his first date, crippled by secret desire.

"I remember," she said, leaning on the table, her chin resting on her clasped hands. "They were so wonderful, those afternoons. You would have made a fine architect."

"We'll never know," he said and after a just perceptible pause asked, "But what is it, Mother, aside from the pleasure of my company? What can I do to help you so that 'no spirit dare stir abroad, the nights are wholesome . . . no planets strike . . . nor witch hath power to charm. So hallowed and so gracious is your time.' "

"Oh, Jason, you always understood me so well. Lawrence thought my superstitions silly. You didn't." She reached across the table and for a moment squeezed his hand in affection. Her face clouded as she continued. "Something is happening—has been happening—and I don't know what to do about it," she said in a low voice. Unexpectedly, tears came into her eyes. "For the first time I'm starting to be afraid."

"Afraid of what?"

"Of something." She was casting about for words. "Of the fates. Of God. Of destiny. I don't know."

Jason's eyes darkened. "I can hear Father saying it's your 'cafeteria mysticism.' But what brings it up now?"

"I hate to use the word *omens*. So let's say I have a feeling of warnings. Phillip's murder—his death—seems part of a pattern. Does that sound melodramatic? Ridiculous?"

"I can't judge. What kind of a pattern?"

Her paleness turned to a fugitive flush. "There was Andrew. Andrew Henderson."

"A great man and a terrible tragedy." Jason studied his mother's face. "A loss for you. And for the world."

"He was out of his mind to drive in that freak snowstorm. I begged him to wait for me in Bordeaux. But, like a child, he insisted he must meet me in Barcelona."

"Andrew wanted to be married in Barcelona," Jason said.

"Yes, but the car . . ."

"Went through a fence into a ravine."

"I loved him so much."

"I know that, Mother."

The change in expression on Marina's face was her only comment. Her look passed from sorrow to absolute distress.

"But Andrew wasn't my first sinister experience. There was Hans."

Jason had known for the last few moments that the words were coming, but when they came they sent the blood rushing to his temples.

"Hans. My tutor in architecture. You were going to leave Father to marry him." Jason gazed at her with anguish.

"Not to marry him. To live with him. He was my escape hatch from marriage. A marriage that was a silly young girl's mistake." Her lips stiffened with the effort she was making to speak calmly. "Hans was brutally attacked by someone. The doctors were under strict orders not to tell me what actually happened to him."

"It was shocking."

"He wouldn't see me when I tried to visit him at the hospital. He insisted Lawrence had something to do with it. Hired someone to hurt him," Marina said tightly, her voice showing the strain. "I told Hans that violence wasn't in Lawrence's nature, but he didn't believe me. I think he was convinced that if I left Lawrence and lived with him, Lawrence would have him murdered. So instead he left me."

"As I remember it, he was offered a post in Heidelberg at the end of the term. Hans was a fool. You were right about Father."

"I know. I was never in love with Lawrence, but I understand him. Probably too well." Marina went on speaking softly, her eyes fixed on the tablecloth. "And now three men who loved me are gone. Hans refused to see me, even after I divorced Lawrence. And Andrew and Phillip are dead."

Jason raised his eyebrows inquiringly. "Where do I fit in? What can I do?"

"You can help me break the jinx." Their eyes met and she gave him a small smile. "I'm in love. More than I ever thought possible. I think perhaps loving is as necessary for me as breathing. And I feel if at last I can remarry, the jinx will be lifted."

Jason was silent, and he stayed absolutely still until he could no longer stand it, until he felt he might suffocate. "Who is the lucky man?" he asked.

He saw a flush creep up his mother's face. She sat upright, facing him with smiling dignity. "Sebastian. Sebastian Taggard. He loves me too."

He'd half expected the answer. "Taggard? Of The House of Uni?"

"Yes. You know him, Jason. We want to be married."

"You're very much in love with him?"

"As much as I ever loved Phillip—or Andrew. More. As much as a woman can love a man."

Jason's voice was dry and measured despite the fever of his thoughts. "It's really a romance?"

"The romance of romances."

"I'm glad for you, Mother."

"I'm glad for myself. I've felt so alone. With Sebastian I feel safe and cared for."

Looking into his mother's gray eyes, Jason had a new and unexpected feeling. He was alarmed at the possibility that he might come to hate her. "Sebastian Taggard and I are not exactly friends. But since you love him and he loves you, I don't see why my help is needed. Unless there is some particular wedding present you would like?"

"I need help with Cella. She objects to Sebastian's seeing me. As for our marrying, she'll never agree."

"Cella Taggard? His daughter?"

"Yes."

Sebastian Taggard, Jason thought. Once he'd started hearing the rumors about Sebastian and his mother, an instinctive warning signal clicked on in his brain. But this was far more than he'd expected.

"Isn't Sebastian a grown man?" Jason asked with mild irony. "Does he need his daughter's permission to marry?"

"Those people are not quite like us, Jason. Our ancestry is English. The Taggards are of Etruscan descent. Etruscans live in very tightly knit family groups. I don't understand their family relationships, but if Cella continues to object, Sebastian won't marry me."

Jason glanced around the restaurant with a sense of utter exhaustion. He felt as though he'd been struggling for hours up the face of a steep, rocky precipice. "I don't understand any of this. Why does she object?" Marina brooded silently for so long, staring out the window, that he repeated the question. "Why?"

"Her reason is you."

"Me?" Jason stared at her. "I don't know the woman."

"She knows all about you. Sebastian said Cella claims that you think an authentic plastic cup is more beautiful than a Cellini. You would have to test and retest a Cellini to prove it was an authentic Cellini. You're blind to its beauty. Beauty is meaningless to you. Your idea of truth is not beauty. Your idea of truth is plastic. She doesn't want you in the family."

For an instant Jason felt a strong inhibition against saying anything. Then he answered quietly, "But I love beauty. In all its forms. What I am against is fakery. Counterfeits. Frauds."

"And so is Cella. She agrees with that. But she says you are like a religious fanatic. You leave nothing open to question. You sound like the voice from the burning bush."

Jason laughed. "That's true enough. I burn with indignation at lying cheats."

Marina lifted her thin black eyebrows. "You know; dear, you are sometimes overzealous. Look at the posture you took about the Cycladian maidens. I watched you pontificate on television the other evening. When Sebastian and I discussed it, we both felt you'd carried your theoretical suspicions too far."

"I don't believe I went half far enough."

"That's what Cella means. You know how murky the field of authentication is. Take Spiro Lenos. A recognized expert in the field of Greek antiquities. He says the idols are authentic."

"Lenos is wrong."

"Jason, you are not the only living authority. Stop behaving as if you are."

Jason's smile never reached his eyes. "I often think I am the only living authority."

"That's exactly what I mean. What Cella means. You must stop talking that way."

For an instant Jason was tongue-tied. He could not bear the thought that a barrier was rising between them. "All right. Why don't you tell Taggard—and for that matter, Cella—that among all the dealers in antiquities in the world, I regard The House of Uni as one of the very few dealers who are beyond reproach. I have never had occasion to question a single piece of jewelry that they sell."

"Is that true, Jason?"

"Yes, Mother." For a man of Jason's usually resourceful nature, it would have been difficult for him to look more defenseless. "Remember the Langobardic earrings that you tried on in my office? If they had come from The House of Uni, I would probably have refused to test them. It would have been pointless."

"You mean that?"

"I mean it."

Marina lifted her head high, like a beautiful woman challenging a roomful of rivals. "I will tell Cella what you've said. That will make everything so much easier between us."

Jason would have laughed if anyone had told him that in this meeting with his mother he would lie in his teeth to play the part of Cupid. But he was in no mood for laughing.

"I'm glad I could be useful," he said, nodding soberly. "Keep me informed of your wedding plans."

They left the restaurant in seeming harmony, Jason smothering his sense of outrage. As he watched Marina enter a cab, he thought with self-disgust, It's not love that is blind. It's jealousy.

Chapter Eleven

The library in the Taggards' Sands Point home had an ancient, mossy smell: the smell of an old church where services have not been held for centuries, where grass grows around the flagstone walk leading to the front door and ivy tendrils creep to the multimullioned windows. Even in warm weather when the windows were open, the breeze that drifted into the room did not disturb its aura. The perfume from the carefully tended rose garden, and the heady fragrance from the wide green lawns, became part of the unchanging air. Although the small, white-capped waves in Long Island Sound were clearly visible from the windows and sprayed houseward, carrying the unique odor of the marshes, the salty, pungent smell evaporated in the library, becoming one with the books, the high, white scrolled ceiling and the bleached oak paneling. When one was in the room, one wouldn't know the Sound was anywhere within miles. It was a peaceful room, a room for meditation.

But on this Saturday afternoon Cella could not settle into the peace the room offered. She couldn't control her mind. Phillip Mckay had been brutally murdered, and she was unable to stop remembering the many rich hours she'd spent with him. He had been a true friend, not a "Gorgeous." A man with whom she'd had lunches, dinners, evenings at the theater, the opera, the ballet. They had frequently attended art auctions together. She was going to miss him terribly. Why? she asked herself over and over again. Why would anyone want to kill Phillip? And why use that particular statue? Uneasy, she sipped tea from a large Rosenthal china cup and watched Sebastian as he sorted the accumulation of his personal mail that had been delivered while they were in New York City. His expression continually changed as he riffled through the envelopes, frowning at one, smiling at another, dismissing the next with no expression.

"Here's a note from Marina," he said, looking up from a piece of mauve stationery. His face was full of animation, and a spot of color appeared on his cheekbones. "She had to fly to Santa Barbara for a wedding. She says she has something important to tell us." His eyes, fixed on Cella's face, were a curious mixture of pleading and arrogance. "That we'll be pleased with her news."

"I can hardly wait. Maybe she's discovered another Aphrodite necklace in a Santa Barbara attic." Cella forced an artificial smile, but Sebastian wasn't amused. She added lamely, "I wonder what her news is."

At that moment their plump Italian housekeeper, Celeste, appeared with a teak tray. On the tray were a cup and saucer and a circular Chinese charm plate holding pieces of golden-yellow Chinese fruit cut in slices that formed a star. She placed the tray on the marble coffee table.

"Master Marcus is here," Celeste announced. "He is in *il gabinetto.*"

"I am out of *il gabinetto,* Celeste," Marcus said, saunter-ing into the room. He wore a beautifully tailored, double-breasted, doeskin flannel blazer with bits of ivory in place of the usual brass buttons. His beige cavalry twill slacks had a knife-sharp crease. But his pin-striped silk shirt was open at the collar, he needed a shave and his black hair fell forward over his forehead. "Shame on you, Celeste," he said. "I told you I wanted to surprise them."

"I bring them your present. I cut it up as you ask," Celeste said sternly. Her nose pointed toward the ceiling as she ex-ited, deliberately ignoring Marcus.

"Carambola, isn't it, Marcus?" Cella asked, reaching for a slice of fruit.

"I come bearing gifts," Marcus said.

Cella smiled. "Mmm . . . this is good." She chewed on the sweet, juicy fruit. "Taste it, Father."

Sebastian reached for a star-shaped slice. "Pleasant. Chi-nese carambola. Unusually succulent and juicy. Where did you get it, Marcus?"

"It's not Chinese. The seeds came from Thailand. Sweeter than the Chinese variety. I picked it up in Florida. They're growing them like oranges. I could have bought the fruit at Dean and DeLuca, but I was coming here from La Guardia, so I took some with me on the plane."

Sebastian took another slice. "Cella, when we get back to town, call and order a dozen."

"You like it, Father, don't you?" Marcus was openly

pleased with himself. "And so does the rest of the world. It's selling like egg rolls in Chinese restaurants. Only one of my many astute investments." Marcus seated himself next to Cella and poured himself a cup of tea. "But I did think of my family first. I pleaded with you, I begged you to put a few dollars into Rare Fruits and Vegetables, Limited. I damn near got down on my knees . . ."

"Unless rare fruits are on a plate, they don't interest me," Sebastian said as he returned to sorting his mail.

For an instant Marcus was deflated; then he hurried on with an explosion of nervous energy. "You're wrong. America is discovering haute cuisine. Rare Fruits specializes in—"

"If I remember correctly," Cella interrupted, "the prospectus said they would be shipping carambola, monstera deliciosa, atemoya, fiddleheads, wampee. And yes, we have no bananas." She was trying to distract her brother's attention from their father. She understood how much Marcus wanted Sebastian's approval, and it pained her that his efforts were so useless. Sebastian could be unbelievably stubborn.

"That's the ticket. No bananas. No oranges. No apples, Father. Only rare fruits." He gave Cella a lofty, sideways look. "Tease me all you like, but you should have followed my advice. I invited the family in when the stock was selling for three dollars a share." Marcus paused for dramatic effect, giving Cella another brief, impudent glance. "You'd have tripled your money. Fiddleheads, Radicchio, and Wampee Limited is now selling for nine. And that's not wampum!"

"Oh, Marcus," Cella groaned. "That's awful!"

"Sorry. But you deserved it. You could have made a bundle, Father."

"Are you staying for the weekend, Marcus?" Sebastian asked without looking up.

"No. This is an eat-and-run visit. But I have another succulent piece of information for you."

"So do I. For you," Sebastian said. His expression was mildly disapproving. "Five boxes of shoes arrived for you from London. From John Lobb Limited, bootmaker by appointment to Her Majesty Elizabeth the Second. How much did they cost you?" He shook his head. "Don't tell me. At least a thousand a pair."

"Two thousand. Not including hand-carved shoe trees."

"For a young man in your position, I find John Lobb shoes an outrageous extravagance."

"They were made exactly to my measure. From leather I personally selected," Marcus said cheerily.

"Wall Street is changing you. You seem to have no respect for money."

"Are you suggesting that I've been tainted by the rich, glitzy people I associate with?" Marcus said. "Really, Father, I'm only following in your footsteps."

"Why didn't you have them sent to your own apartment?" Cella asked. "Then Father wouldn't have a clue to how you squander your money."

"Because Lobb takes six months for delivery. And in the crazy business I'm in, I spend as much time out of New York as I do in town. I couldn't be sure when the shoes would arrive, and sad but true"—he lowered his voice—"I don't trust my doorman."

"So you dropped in to see if your shoes had come?" Sebastian poured himself more tea. "You could have telephoned and asked."

"I dropped in, as you say, out of sheer family loyalty. My aim is to add to your wealth."

"Not another stock," Sebastian said with some exasperation.

"You'll love this offering, Father. It could have been made with you in mind. I'm buying it for all my customers. I've bought a bundle myself." His enthusiasm grew higher. "But let's look to the future. There's this small company, also in Florida, that has stumbled on the alchemist's dream."

"A fruit company that turns orange peels to gold? Must I listen?" Sebastian said.

"It will be criminal for a man devoted to jewelry to ignore this blessing. This small company, Minnerex, located in Tallahassee, Florida, is high—very high—technology. They've come up with—well, in a way, it is like the alchemist's dream. It boggles the mind. Listen!" Marcus lowered his voice again. "They've discovered a way to harden carbon to the point where it is . . ."

"Let me guess," Cella said sweetly. "Almost as hard as a diamond."

"Not 'almost as hard.' *Just* as hard as a diamond!" Marcus enthused. "Jewel thieves will have schizophrenic breakdowns. Minnerex was the major reason I was in Florida. To check for myself. I wanted to see samples, and I did. After all, I am a Taggard, and you must admit I do have an educated eye," Marcus said. "My firm is taking the company public at twenty-five dollars a share. Now's the time to buy in. And buy in big. Get in on the ground floor."

"Excuse me, Marcus. I have to do a little more work,"

Sebastian said, gathering together his mail as if his son had not spoken. "I've gotten an idea for the Astarte. I want to sketch it while it's still fresh in my mind."

"Do you have to start now?" Cella asked. "It's almost four-thirty."

"I want to," Sebastian said, looking at his hands, and then at Cella. "I'll do a rough sketch now. It will give me a head start. We'll see how it strikes you. You might have some interesting ideas. You always do." He picked up his mail and rose to his feet, ready to leave.

Marcus frowned, an odd, half-angry expression on his face. "Please sit down, Father. You won't buy any Minnerex stock. Okay. I was a fool to think you might. But I have one thing more to say. And I might as well get it over with."

"What is it, Marcus?" The strain in his son's voice caught Sebastian's attention. Reluctantly he sat down.

Marcus said nothing.

"Well?" Sebastian waited.

He was searching for the right words, Cella realized.

"It's this way . . ." Marcus hesitated.

"What way?" Cella encouraged him gently.

"I'm fully invested . . ."

"But you need more money?" Cella guessed.

"Yes, I need more money," Marcus said, a rush of color on his face.

For a moment no one helped him.

"To buy more Minnerex stock," Cella said with surprised disbelief.

"Why do I feel guilty? It's diamonds they're selling, not porno videotapes." Marcus' gaze settled on his father. "Yes, I want to buy more Minnerex. I'm into the big money game. But to make big money you need big money."

"And you would like me to make you a loan?" Sebastian asked in a neutral voice.

"In a manner of speaking. Not a loan exactly."

Again there was a silence. At last Sebastian spoke. "No, Marcus, I will not lend you any money. I will not encourage your investing in some harebrained speculation."

"I'm not asking for a loan," Marcus said with injured virtue. "I want you to give me my own money." He turned the full intensity of his need on Sebastian.

It was Sebastian's turn to be at sea. "I wasn't aware that I had control of your holdings."

"You do. You control my interest in The House of Uni. According to last year's profit and loss statement, the shop netted over five million, after taxes and the huge salaries and expense accounts you give yourselves. Given a price/earnings ratio of, let's say, conservatively, ten, The House of Uni is worth at least fifty million dollars. Mother left all of us shares. You own fifty percent. Cella and I, twenty-five percent each.''

"If you say so."

"I do. I say more than that."

"What do you have in mind?" Sebastian was very pale, but there was no way to tell whether it was because of anger or the effect of the light in the room.

"I want what is mine, Father."

Sebastian chose first to look at the floor. Then he glanced at Marcus, as if surprised that there should be any question regarding his son's rights. "As you should," he said. "And what is yours is quite substantial."

"It was."

"Was? Come, Marcus. I don't understand. You can't have spent it all—even the way *you* spend money. When you left the family business for Wall Street—against my wishes, but I did nothing to stop you—you took the cash and the stocks and bonds your mother had left you. It was quite a substantial sum."

"Adequate, as sums go."

"It was several million dollars. And like everyone who has enough, you want more."

"I learned from you, Father. With the exception of Cella, this is a greedy family."

Sebastian seemed not to have heard. "If I remember correctly, that barely adequate sum bought you a partnership in the brokerage house. A duplex on Sutton Place. An apartment in Paris. A thirty-five-foot sloop. A number of impractical cars at outrageous prices . . ."

"Please, Father. I'm getting the message," Marcus said politely. "I've been well provided for. But I need more."

"I'm getting the message too."

"So where do I go for money?" Marcus paused to catch his breath. "To you. To my family. As I said, Cella and I both own a quarter of The House of Uni. I would like to sell you my share. I figure it's worth about twelve million."

Cella was speechless. So was Sebastian, this time without calculation.

When Cella found her voice she managed to say, "You can't do this, Marcus. It's your heritage."

"Yours. Not mine." Marcus was defiant. "We live in two different worlds. You're still caught up in this forging of ancient knickknacks. At least on Wall Street what you call scams—"

"Stop it, Marcus! How dare you talk that way about our work? About our mother's work?" Cella was shocked at her brother's lack of respect.

"Okay. I'm sorry I spilled diet cola on your altar. You have your gods and I have mine." He grinned. "Or shall we say scams?"

"We are not running a scam," Cella said with icy formality. "We are giving back to the world the lost beauty of the ancients."

"There is no arguing with religious fanatics," Marcus said with resignation. "Let's drop the philosophy. Just buy me out."

"There is no arguing with naïveté, either," Sebastian said. "But I am your father, and I won't let you pauperize yourself by selling—even to us—your most valuable asset."

"And according to Mother's will, I can't sell the stock outside the family."

"Quite so."

"Damn it, Father, you won't help your own son!"

"No! I will not help you be a bigger damn fool than usual!" Sebastian paused, struggling to keep his voice flat despite his outrage. "You will have to make do, Marcus. Maybe you could return your John Lobb shoes." Sebastian stood up and walked toward the library door. "Cella, when you weary of having Marcus weep on your shoulder, I'll see you downstairs in the workroom."

For a second the room was silent. "Go ahead, Cella," Marcus said. "You might as well."

Cella made a small sound of unhappy confusion that Sebastian caught. He stopped, turned and looked at his children with infinite sadness. Then, with a visible effort, he tore himself from the room.

When they were alone Cella said, "You're right about one thing. I don't believe in what you're doing on the Street. Or in your Minnerex stock."

"But you do believe in Uni."

"Yes. I believe in Uni. And in Tages, too. Remember Tages. The great god who gave our family its name."

"I've heard that song before."

"You haven't really heard it. Dammit, Marcus, how cliché American can you get? You want to be the boy wonder of Wall Street."

Marcus shrugged sadly. "In for a penny, in for a pound."

"What will you do?"

Marcus' eyes were shrewd and piercing. "I'll think of something."

Cella couldn't help smiling. "You never give up, do you?"

"No. Do you?"

"No," Cella said, matching his tone. "You'll come home one day. You will!" But in the meantime, Cella knew that all she could do was watch and wait and pray that her brother's greed didn't get him into too much trouble. If it did, she would hope and pray that the family could get him out of it.

PART FIVE

THE GODDESS OF LOVE

Chapter Twelve

Few countries ever charmed Anton as much as Hungary. The feeling of crossing into another world was almost tangible—the language, food, faces, the "socialist" political system, differed so markedly from the ways of Western Europe. The country too had always proved a treasure trove for the Vilanova family, and in his childhood Anton had often visited it with his father. It was a place where they could pick up incredible "finds" from bakers, teachers, singers, aristocrats. "Finds" from a variety of cultures. The Hungarians had lived for a thousand years, under a series of foreign occupations. The past of Hungary was not simply in the cobbled streets and the houses on Buda's Castle Hill in Budapest. It was hidden under trapdoors, in closets, even in cemeteries, all over the country. The Hungarians realized that their history, though painful, was precious, and they knew how to barter with their prizes of their past. It was only because of years of friendship with these sturdy, irrepressible people that the Vilanovas had the right introductions. They were the keepers of the secrets of many families, and when someone for whatever reason wanted to sell a prize of the past, it was the Vilanovas who were usually contacted. It was these kind of "finds" that had helped build the Vilanova Trust.

In keeping with this tradition, Victor was contacted by a barber who owned an authentic Saint Peter panel. Having seen it, Anton decided it was well worth the price. And since he was in Hungary he thought it time to look up old family friends and perhaps discover other such prizes. He found more than he had expected. Families were eager for money. And after a coded telephone discussion with Victor, he anticipated returning to villages, paying for and picking up his "finds." Then catching the flight back to Paris to deposit his booty with Victor. The trip had been far more profitable and hectic than he'd counted on, and before completing his business, he felt he could use a little rest.

He chose the Gellart, one of the great spas of Budapest, at which to revive. He was there now. After undressing and handing his clothes to an attendant in the baths, Anton slipped on paper slippers and a faded terry-cloth robe still smelling of chlorine. He slopped into the mosaic-and-majolica-tiled room where radioactive mineral-water baths bubbled and steamed. Theoretically, these waters could cure everything from *A* for arthritis to *V* for Vincent's infection. Anton would settle for simple relaxation. He scrutinized the faces of the men splashing about in the waters, not actually expecting to know anyone.

It surprised him when he heard a cheery "Hello" from a voice he knew only too well. There was Maurice Wheelock lying naked on his towel bathrobe, his feet dangling in the steaming waters of the enormous bath.

"Maurice! What are you doing here?" Anton said, squatting down beside him.

"Frankly, I could stay here forever. It's so soothing. I can see why the ancient Romans took the cure here. A marvelous place to discuss politics. There's something reassuring about taking a dip together. A naked man can't hide a knife." He grinned. "And what are you doing here?"

"I usually stop in here before I return home."

"Leaving so soon? What a pity. I just arrived."

"On a tour of duty?"

"Heavens, no! I am taking a world-class vacation," Maurice remarked genially. "There are ski slopes, the horse country, Gypsy music. Potato bread filled with slabs of freshly roasted goose liver. And the women." Maurice placed the tips of his fingers to his mouth and blew a kiss into the air.

Anton shifted to a more comfortable seated position. "You've covered most of the highlights, but somehow you managed to omit the museums. The fact that Hungary has more museums per one thousand citizens than any country in the world is of no interest to you?" Anton raised his eyebrows. "Sorry, I forgot. You're on vacation. Not scouting for Northbie's."

"Me, scouting?" Maurice was the picture of offended innocence. "Absolutely not."

"Of course, with American dollars there's no end to what you might pick up here," Anton remarked casually.

"My dear Anton, you know as well as I do that foreign

currency may not be exchanged with Hungarian citizens. It's against the law."

"True, this being an Iron Curtain country," Anton said with mock resignation.

"It would be tempting fate."

"Exactly."

"One could disappear forever if one is discovered exchanging a few dollars on the black market—let alone using dollars to bribe an avaricious museum curator. Although he might have a really magnificent marble Greek kouros. Which no one appreciates." With the splashing of water all around and the hum of voices, there was little possibility of Maurice's being overheard, but out of habit he lowered his voice. "I hear Peter Petty purchased a Greek kouros for seven million dollars. My source tells me it was smuggled out of an Iron Curtain country. I must admit Petty's range of interest is improving." Maurice licked his lips. "But no, I wouldn't consider looking for anything here." He then asked with deceptive straightness, "And while we're on the subject of the charms of Hungary, what are you doing in this land of pleasure and semipious Communists? France. Italy. England. Those are your usual stomping grounds—or is this a stop on the way to Istanbul?"

"Istanbul?" Maurice did not notice Anton's slight intake of breath or the dilation of his nostrils. "Why would I go to Istanbul?"

"You mean you haven't heard?"

"Heard what?"

"Good Lord!" Maurice chortled. "It's a first. The first secret in the history of the New York art world. Amazing! It runs contrary to nature—like water running uphill."

"I appear to be missing something."

"You are, my dear chap. And it's such a hoot. If it weren't serious it would make a Keystone Cops comedy. Pity I can't tell you. We could have a juicy gossip." He yawned lazily.

"I'm addicted to juicy gossip. You can tell me," Anton said, full of good will.

"Sorry. My lips are sealed."

"From me? Your old chum? Come on, Maurice."

Maurice was clearly tempted. It was not often he had an opportunity to lord it over Anton Vilanova. "You see, you're related to the interested parties."

Anton's eyes were suddenly alive with predatory intelligence. "Which of my many relatives come to mind, Maurice?"

"Forget it. I've already said too much." Maurice dismissed it all with a wave of his hand. "Now excuse me a moment. I need to dunk."

He slid into the water, and Anton had no choice but to do the same. Eventually Maurice climbed out, shook himself and sank down onto his robe again. He caroled to Anton, who was still in the water, "As I asked before, why are you here?"

Anton pursed his lips and climbed out of the bath, sinking down lazily beside Maurice. "Well, Paris was my first stop, but I love Budapest. And I thought I'd get a little skiing in before I went home."

"Isn't Budapest a bit out of the way?"

"Hungary has so much to offer."

"Doesn't it," Maurice said, smiling impishly. "And how is your uncle Victor? Has he anything for Northbie's? I could give him a look-see on my way home."

"Drop in, by all means," Anton said. "Uncle Victor always enjoys your visits." Clearly Victor and Istanbul weren't connected. Thank God for small favors.

"I suffer for the poor chap. He must be having a hemorrhage with Jason Lord holding forth on Cycladian idols. It was before my time, but I think poor Phillip Mckay—God rest his soul—bought the idol from Victor."

Anton looked puzzled. "That's a curious idea. I think not. Uncle Victor would have spoken up. He takes great pride in what he sells. He knows the provenance of every item down to the B.C. years, if necessary."

"The soul of integrity, of course. Anyway, I would personally like to hang that sanctimonious Dr. Jason Lord by his balls." Maurice was genuinely irate. "He gives the art world a bad name. The madman actually suggested Northbie's put him under contract as a consultant. What a black eye that would give us professionally. Hiring a consultant who specializes in discovering fakes. As if we're incompetents who can't judge what we sell."

"Think of him as Saint Jason. His voices tell him to 'cleanse the world.' "

"And collect his reward on earth, not in heaven."

"Of course, anything one picked up here could easily stand the challenge of our purified Dr. Lord."

"You mean you've seen a few things?"

Deftly Anton began to lay out the bait. "I'm sure you realize that not only the curators but the butchers, the bakers, the Gypsy violinists all crave American dollars. Consider a family with some rare treasure—an icon, a fifth-century il-luminated Book of Hours, a triptych—who knows?''

"I know there are homes with hidden trapdoors, but one has to be able to find them.''

"And be able to grease the hinges.'' Anton smiled.

"American dollars,'' Maurice said dryly. "There are so many uses for American dollars.''

"Countless. If one knows how to spend them.''

"You surprise me, Anton.'' Maurice gave him a searching look. "Offer a private family dollars? For a national treasure? The Hungarians cherish their treasures more than their children. And they love their children very much.''

"You misunderstand me. Not a national treasure. A family heirloom.''

Maurice sat up straighter. "You mean something the Haps-burgs and the Commies overlooked?''

"Something they missed.''

"The government takes a very dim view of anyone filching its treasures. But family heirlooms,'' Maurice said thought-fully. "That does give one another perspective.''

"Especially heirlooms the government has never seen. Take the Gothic altarpiece I happened to see at a friend's house in Balatonfoldovar . . .''

"Where is Balatonfoldovar?'' Maurice's eyes blazed.

"Maurice, you shock me. If that altarpiece is what I think it is, it is a national treasure.''

The first trace of an East Bronx nasal twang crept into Maurice's English public-school accent. "Listen, buddy, we've just agreed it's a family heirloom. I want to examine the altarpiece. Northbie's will split the proceeds with you.''

Anton rambled on blithely. "I did see a panel of Saint Peter, strongly reminiscent of the work of Carlo Crevelli, in the bedroom of a baker's house in Tihany. And a wonderful icon in a child's room in Gyor.''

"We have come to a meeting of the minds, Anton. I'll make you a trade. You know this country better than I. Take me to the altarpiece.''

Maurice had swallowed the bait. Now the fun would begin. "I thought you were on a world-class vacation.''

"Don't be ridiculous! Take me to everything you've seen.'' Maurice's tone became honeyed. "And we'll split the pro-ceeds. No, you'll get the lion's share. On my word of honor.''

"We do have a great deal in common.''

"A community of interests, you might say.'' Maurice's face remained expressionless. But he had the firm impression that they had struck a bargain. "All I have to know are the addresses. And you must provide the introductions."

"Agreed. Now, what about Istanbul?" Anton said offhandedly.

Maurice's mouth flew open. "You bastard! You led me on!"

"I did not. Everything I described is there for the taking."

"At a price."

"What price? As I understand it, the treasures of Istanbul have become bedroom gossip."

"Northbie's would never forgive me."

"They'll forgive and forget quickly enough when you bring back the heirlooms. In fact, there is nothing to forget. Why shouldn't I know? The art world has no secrets."

"All right." Maurice glanced furtively over his shoulder and then to his right and left. "I must talk softly."

"You think Christie's is listening?"

"Anything is possible." Maurice started to chuckle in spite of himself. "It's about the Aphrodite necklace. And the Taggards."

"The Aphrodite? What about it? Is it a fake?"

"Don't be an ass. The Aphrodite is too authentic if anything," Maurice murmured fervently. "The necklace reached Northbie's via a seller of impeccable credentials who had fallen on hard times. The man he had purchased the necklace from had the same experience. Originally, the necklace was given by Stavros Livanos as a wedding gift to his daughter—when she married Aristotle Onassis. An unfortunate choice of husband, as it turned out. And an example of the checkered history of the necklace in the modern world. It has an impeccable provenance, but the luck it brings is questionable. In fact, the piece has a rather sinister romantic history."

"Why?"

"We are speaking about Aphrodite, the goddess of love. There is always something sinister about love." Maurice again looked around the huge room suspiciously. The nearest patron was a plump man flapping around in the middle of the bath. "Everyone who has owned the necklace has been ground to dust—by crimes of the heart. You have heard of the excavations at Geyre in Turkey?" Maurice asked in a stage whisper.

"Yes . . ." Anton frowned as he scrambled to recall what he'd heard. "They have something to do with Aphrodisias."

"Nosy archaeologists discovered a great sanctuary and temple of the goddess there."

"Fine. But what has that to do with the Taggards?"

"They bought the Aphrodite necklace."

"So?"

"So the necklace, it seems, was stolen from the Geyre site. The city of Venus Aphrodite."

"This isn't the first time an ancient temple or tomb was looted. It's been happening for thousands of years. Why all the fuss? The Aphrodite is a rare piece of ancient jewelry, but it's not as if someone made off with the gold sarcophagus of King Tut."

"There are people to whom the Aphrodite is more priceless than Tut's gold. If it were simply another piece of ancient jewelry . . ." Maurice paused for effect. "But it isn't."

"If it isn't, what is it?"

"You won't believe this."

"Try me."

"According to Abdul Hamid . . ." As Maurice whispered the name he glanced fearfully around the room, missing the flash of recognition in Anton's eyes. "He's the Turkish Minister of Archaeology and Culture, and he claims that the necklace is the original necklace—I repeat his words 'original necklace'—of the divinity who founded the cult of Aphrodite. It belonged to the goddess Aphrodite, no less." Maurice sputtered with laughter. "Can you imagine! That idiot actually believes there was an Aphrodite. And that what Northbie's sold the Taggards was the necklace the goddess wore."

Anton didn't laugh. His family lines were too ancient, his heritage too buried in the mists of the past, for him to take lightly what Maurice saw as ridiculous. There undoubtedly had been a real Uni. Even as there had been a real Jesus Christ. A real Moses. A real Muhammad. Why not a real Aphrodite? "The necklace is a sacred relic," he said after a moment.

"Sacred, my ass. The CIA, the FBI and all the other crazies, like assassins and other well-meaning types, are now in the act. The Turkish nose is out of joint, and since Turkey is a member of NATO, the President wants peace in the family. And no dillydallying about returning the necklace."

"Then why doesn't Northbie's buy it back from the Taggards and return it to Abdul Hamid? You did say that was his name?"

"We can't. That would be admitting guilt by association," Maurice said firmly. "For public consumption, Northbie's insists it is not Aphrodite's necklace. It's a fine piece of ancient jewelry from the cult of Aphrodite. We wouldn't have touched it if we thought for a moment it was a sacred relic."

Anton knew what he had to do. And there was no room for mistakes. "I think I had better tell Sebastian and Cella."

"The sooner the better. Suggest to the Taggards that they dispose of the necklace as quickly as possible. It isn't safe for them to own it. They should sell it now for as much as possible. Set the price by what Abdul Hamid will pay."

"Which is—?"

"Abdul Hamid has offered ten million American dollars to any true believer who returns the necklace to him. Ten million dollars," Maurice said with awe. "Need I tell you how many people are eager to filch it?"

"The Taggards could sell the necklace to Abdul Hamid," Anton said.

"Never! Abdul Hamid claims that infidels stole the necklace. Infidels sold it. Infidels bought it. Infidels auctioned it. He will not pay money to an infidel. To do so would contaminate the necklace. It may be exchanged only with love and respect. With a true believer. In short, keep the money in the family," Maurice remarked shrewdly. "An old Eastern custom, Turkish kickbacks."

"But Aphrodite wasn't a Muslim goddess. She was a pagan Greek goddess." Anton's tone was deceptively naive.

"Don't talk logic to me. He'd call that Western hypocrisy. Aphrodite belongs to Turkey. The temple was found near Izmir." Maurice began to chuckle again. "It's staggering! That clown will pay ten million dollars for the jewels of a mythical goddess."

"Where do I find this Abdul Hamid?" Anton asked with an expectant expression. Listening to his own voice, he silently approved. He sounded as if he really didn't know.

"In Istanbul, old chum. Now, don't be a fool. You can't strike a deal. To begin with, you're an infidel."

"Not so much an infidel as you think," Anton said softly.

Maurice gave him a long, hard look. "If you go looking for Abdul Hamid, you'll be walking into the lion's den."

"I'll chance it," Anton said, playing the heroic fool.

"*Vaya con Dios.* Or the Hungarian equivalent. But before you go, you owe me one. I would like—"

"The names and addresses of the families with the altarpiece, the icon and Saint Peter," Anton finished his sentence for him. "Where are you staying?"

"The Dana Continental."

"The information will be waiting for you at the desk of your hotel with a note introducing you to each family." Anton stood up, wrapping his robe tightly around him.

Watching Anton leave, Maurice was certain the names of the families would be at his hotel desk as Anton had promised. He trusted the man. And that was unusual. That anyone in the art world should trust anyone else was as rare as a necklace belonging to the goddess Aphrodite. Maurice began to chuckle.

Anton spent the morning in his hotel room at the Budapest Hilton, packing, and on the telephone to Paris, Rome and Genoa. In a short time he found what he was looking for: a discreet introduction from a cousin to Abdul Hamid who, he learned, among other things was distantly related. But what Turk wasn't? He debated calling Cella, but decided to wait. There was still time.

Chapter Thirteen

As rapidly as traffic would permit, Anton drove his rented Mercedes along E5, the superhighway crossing the Greek border at Ipsala. Since he was not pressed for time, he entered the old town though the Topkapi Gate, doing his best to keep his purpose for coming to Turkey out of his mind, and to concentrate on the sights and the smells; as always, there was something indescribably haunting about Istanbul. In the old town he followed Millet Caddesi to Aksaray Square and zigzagged his way to the Istanbul bypass, the only bridge in the world that connected two continents—Europe and Asia—and more than a few centuries. Spanning the Halic, or the golden Horn—the deep inlet that separated the old town with its flavor of medieval Constantinople from the new town with its faceless modern suburbs spreading along the shores of the Black Sea—the bridge offered a view that was a spectacular study in contrasts. It stopped Anton from thinking too much. Almost too soon he arrived at the Buyukdere Caddesi exit and drove to his hotel in the new town.

When he registered at the Etap Marmara, the only five-star hotel in Istanbul, he found a letter from Abdul Hamid waiting for him at the desk. It had not been typed by a secretary. Abdul's handwriting seemed to give off the heavy, musky scent of the writer himself. It also conveyed loudly the honor that Abdul was bestowing by writing to him, personally, in his almost indecipherable English scrawl. He begged a thousand pardons, but he had to change their appointment from lunch that day to lunch tomorrow. But not in Istanbul. Anton should meet him at his office in Izmir. The address was included. And directions. As an old friend of the Vilanova family, Abdul was certain Anton would understand that he was a very busy man. Anton had expected some such change. To be unpredictable was Abdul's specialty.

* * *

158

After unpacking and changing into a sport shirt, jacket and slacks, Anton decided that he would stroll round the old town to see how much or how little had changed. Anything he could do to stop his mind from chasing itself in circles would be useful. Later he would lunch at Delfino's, if it were still there, opposite the Blue Mosque. The dishes were Turkish, simple and particularly good. He was leaving his room when the telephone rang. Abdul Hamid? he thought. Changing plans again? He almost didn't pick up the phone and then thought better of it. "Hello?" he said. "Anton Vilanova here."

"Anton, dear boy, what a pleasure to find you in."

"Who is . . . ?" Anton started to ask, then answered himself before the voice could. "Tobias Phipps. Are you in Turkey too?"

"If I'm not, we are both suffering from a folie à deux. But that usually happens to lovers. Since that isn't possible, given your narrow view of the sexes, we must be in Istanbul," Toby said genially.

"How did you know I was here?"

"I passed you in the lobby on the way to my room. You were too distracted to notice me. Or anyone. You disappeared into the elevator before I could catch you."

"Are you here on business or for pleasure?"

"Emory's business, which I thought would be my pleasure. But he is a genuine, card-carrying provincial. Not only can he not talk intelligently about art, I'm not sure he can read without moving his lips. If he weren't so beautiful—but he is." Toby paused for breath. "Do you know, last night we had dinner at Abdullah's. You know Abdullah's?"

"Everyone knows Abdullah's."

"And I had midye dolmasi."

"Stuffed mussels." Anton was familiar with Toby's obsession with food. "Who is Emory? I don't usually forget friends."

"You may have met him and don't remember. You haven't an eye for male beauty. Emory Portland, from Portland. Where else? He's Dr. Jason Lord's secretary. Actor incognito. He works for Lord to pay the rent. When I don't."

Anton was suddenly interested. "What is he doing here?"

"Acting as courier for the eminent doctor."

"If he's checking the humidity, it's not the same as in the Cyclades Islands."

"Don't remind me. I bought one of those idols for the museum collection. Fortunately, Amy never watches the

nightly news. Or reads anything but the society pages of the
Times. What a nuisance if she'd ever heard Jason Lord running off at the mouth about the idols,'' Toby said heatedly.
''Anyway, the good doctor sent Emory to pick up a jewel-
handled dagger from the Topkapi Museum on Friday. Belonged to a sultan of the House of Osman. Someone at the
museum wants the eminent Dr. Lord to vet the dagger. What
are you doing here?''

''A little pleasure, a little business.''

''Super! Why don't we join forces in matters of pleasure?''

''You'll be bored silly. I was going to take a sightseeing
stroll in the old town to see what is and what isn't still old.''

''A marvelous idea. Emory will finish breakfast shortly.
We can ramble together. I am trying to give the dear boy an
education. Expose him to more of life than he sees on *L.A.
Law.*''

''All right. I'll meet you both in the lobby in fifteen minutes,'' Anton said. It was always possible that knowing Jason
Lord's secretary might have its uses someday.

''Istanbul has about four hundred fifty mosques, each with
one to four minarets. Only the Blue Mosque has six.'' Toby
was trying hard to keep Emory amused.

''Should I applaud, stamp my feet and yell bravo?'' Emory
asked peevishly. ''No, I will not drink that water,'' he said,
pushing away the urn of water and the hand of the Turk holding the small ceramic cup.

''It is good for the health of your body and soul,'' Toby
said indulgently.

''It's full of typhoid and cholera germs. Every germ that
ever lived since Adam left the Garden of Eden is in that water.'' Emory started toward the courtyard.

''Take off your shoes!'' Anton called after him.

''And walk in my socks? You crazy, man!''

''If you won't take off your shoes, put those slippers over
them, or we won't be allowed in the mosque,'' Anton said
sternly.

''Please, Emory. When in Istanbul, we do as they do,''
Toby pleaded.

With an irate grimace, Emory kicked off his loafers. ''What
an insane religion. The things backward people believe.''

''This is not a backward civilization. It's one of the oldest
in the world. And the custom of taking off shoes when entering a holy place has nothing to do with religion. It has to do

with cleanliness. A praying Arab touches the ground with his head,'' Anton explained, trying to keep his temper.

"These are Gucci loafers,'' Emory said. "You are quite sure some praying Arab with a clean head won't have a yen for my loafers and see them as a gift from Allah? It is Allah, isn't it?''

" 'There is no God but Allah, and Muhammad is his Prophet,' '' Toby said in an exalted tone. "And if your loafers rise to heaven, I'll buy you another pair.''

"Thank you and fuck you,'' Emory said, entering the courtyard in his socks.

Anton and Toby followed Emory into the vast courtyard. They gazed in wonder at the color of the glazed blue tile of the mosque shining in the daylight, and the glowing blue-tinged colors flooding through the hundreds of stained-glass windows. "Awesome,'' Toby said in a hushed voice.

"The people too,'' Anton murmured, his eyes ranging over the mass of people kneeling or prostrate on prayer rugs.

"Why are we whispering?'' Emory whispered. "Why am I whispering?'' he repeated in a full voice.

"Shh!'' Toby said in a low voice.

"Shh yourself. I was set for a massage, but you insisted on my coming. To broaden my vision. I've more vision than you think. Dr. Lord has taught me a thing or two. Dealers will pay a fancy buck for authentic prayer rugs. Like those. They're worth more than those scummy characters praying on them. I could make a fortune if—''

"Emory, the sheer beauty of your soul astounds me,'' Toby said between his teeth.

"Unless you stop talking, we should leave,'' Anton said quietly.

"Fine. Now that I've seen the celebrated Blue Mosque and my spirits are uplifted, let's split.''

Toby looked at Anton apologetically. "I'm sorry,'' he murmured. "I knew what Emory was the minute I met him. Those classically chiseled features conceal the King of the Pig People. But how could I fight it? Beauty isn't everything—it's the only thing.''

"What does he do for Jason Lord?''

"Not much. Corrects Lord's spelling and punctuation. To my amazement, Emory can spell and punctuate and type. His letters are never marred by white-out. When he wants to flagellate me, he tells me how beautiful Jason Lord is.''

By the time they reached Emory, he had slipped on his loafers and was ready to go.

"Anywhere but another mosque," he said.

"At St. Sophia you can leave your shoes on. It's not really a mosque, it's a museum. We even have to buy tickets. Like at Disneyland," Toby said eagerly.

"Maybe they sell popcorn," Anton added.

"One more mosque and it's back to the hotel and a massage," Emory said. "By the way, where are we going for lunch?"

"There are many places in the old town."

"I want a steak and mushrooms. I'll even settle for a hamburger. I can't stand fried eggplant . . ."

"You make life in Turkey difficult," Anton said dryly.

"I am sick to death of Turkey. So sick, I may not even be able to eat turkey at Thanksgiving."

And so the afternoon went.

The evening was an improvement, mainly because it ended early. And at ten o'clock the next morning, Anton took the forty-five-minute flight from Istanbul to Izmir. If the visit had been for less troubling reasons, Anton would have looked forward to seeing the great Anatolian coast again.

For the better part of three thousand years, Izmir—or Smyrna, as the Greeks called it—had been a great cosmopolitan city, the center of classical Ionia, the place where Oriental, Greek and Roman culture had collided and colluded. The goldsmiths of Etruria had grown rich trading with relatives living in Lydia. Lydia, the land of Midas where the rivers ran gold and silver, the ancient land that the Etruscans called their first home.

Now Lydia was gone, and what was Izmir today? The third largest city in Turkey; so modern that its newness made it a cliché. The large apartment houses and office buildings, painted white or pastel, were architecturally ordinary and devoid of both a past and a future. The town of Izmir lacked the character of ancient Smyrna that had vanished in the flames of the First World War.

Anton remembered a family story. How his father, Oliver Vilanova, the head of the family, had notified all the relatives living in Smyrna to return to Tuscany, or they would be trapped in the ancient conflict between the Greeks and the Turks, who both claimed ownership of Smyrna. Most of the Vilanova family took the warning. They pulled up stakes and moved to Italy. When a bloody struggle between the Greeks and the Turks began, those who remained were not heard from again.

Anton gave his family history another few seconds of reverie, then put it away as of no further use. The attitude of the Turks toward the Greeks was unimportant, except as it affected the present. He had an appointment in an hour with Abdul Hamid. Old friend of the family? Or new enemy? How could one know? All too often people switched sides—for ideology, for convenience—for survival.

As Anton changed his clothes in his hotel room, he wondered what Abdul looked liked today. He hadn't seen him in more than thirty years, but he remembered well the small man who had visited the Vilanova villa in Siena when he was a child. Abdul Hamid had held himself straight, dressed in a dark suit, and to Anton's already old, wise eyes, he had given off the aromatic air of a pious fraud. Anton remembered Abdul Hamid's voice as if it were yesterday.

"I have come across something you will admire. A delicate faïence figurine in gold." Very carefully Abdul opened a long velvet box and removed a small statuette of a woman. She had huge, bare breasts and was wearing a tiered skirt with a wide belt. In each hand she held two snakes.

"The snake goddess," Anton's father said with interest. "Very beautiful."

"Isn't she."

"Knossos," his father said.

"Originally. More than three thousand years ago. I bought it from a Turkish banking family in need of liras," Abdul said as he looked up from beneath his long black lashes, while a secretive smile played at the corners of his mouth. "I thought it would be ideal for your shop. Your clientele. I can make you a very nice price."

For many years, the Vilanovas and Abdul Hamid had enjoyed a golden age of friendship—a business partnership of sorts that was highly lucrative to both, with Abdul providing artifacts that were ideal for the Vilanova clientele. Until one day Abdul paid a social call to explain his plans for the future.

"I have had the good fortune to make a certain amount of money. I have purchased several houses; I own a Rolls-Royce and a chauffeur, several other cars, several servants. I have several wives and my daughters go to the best boarding schools in Switzerland. My two sons are successful engineers. I consider the rest of my life my own. So I am retiring."

And retire he did. For a time he vanished from the world of art dealing and art collecting, regaining visibility when he became the minister of archaeology and culture for Turkey. Which proved that in Turkey, as elsewhere, a rich man could be successful in politics.

When Anton entered Abdul Hamid's office, what struck him first was that although the man was at least seventy, he seemed not to have aged. It was the Abdul Hamid whom he remembered from childhood. He gave Anton a welcoming smile.

"Anton Vilanova! What a pleasure to see you again."

"It's been a long time."

"True, but I never forget a face." His English was as flawless as ever. But then he had always spoken a great many languages perfectly. It was part of his talent.

"Abdul Bey," Anton said with mild irony, "the last time we met I was about five or six. These days I shave. I trust I've changed somewhat."

"You have the Vilanova face. Your father's face. Your grandfather's." He licked his lips like a cat savoring cream. "And I had your photograph wired to me by your cousin Virgil."

How in character, Anton thought. Abdul never took unnecessary risks. "I thought you might want it. I prepared him for your request."

"A Vilanova to the bone!" Abdul laughed. Always the Turkish gentleman, he was the personification of elegance in his light gray suit and vest. With the gracious manner of an old-style diplomat, he stood up, walked around the desk and grasped Anton's hand and arm warmly, as though he were a long-lost old friend, all the while making polite, meaningless noises of welcome.

"What would you like? Tea? A cup of Turkish coffee? Make yourself at home. Be comfortable." He extended his hand toward a chair.

"Nothing, thank you," Anton said, glancing briefly around the room. Except for the exquisite Tabriz carpet flung over tiled floors, and the tiles themselves, it could have been an office in any Western country. The view from the long row of windows had its own individuality. If there were still beauty in the town of Izmir, it lay in the curving bay beyond the office window, in the moving greens and blues of the water, and in the *imbat*, the breeze that churned the waves as they broke against the wharf.

"Very well. What can I do for you? Would you like a

guided tour of the region? The archaeological sites are well worth seeing.''

"As a matter of fact, I'm here to talk about a site. The famous site at Aphrodisias,'' Anton said, letting the silence claim them both.

"Ah, yes. At Geyre.'' Abdul's expression became serious and cool. Collected, contained, he sat with his elbows resting on the desk, brows knit, eyes half hidden by the still-long lashes, slowly rubbing the palms of his hands together. "What about the site?'' he asked without looking at Anton.

"A great sanctuary and temple of Aphrodite were discovered there.''

"This time the foundations got their money's worth. The scholars actually did as well as a shepherd might do.''

"A necklace was stolen from the temple site. Perhaps from an underground tomb.''

"The looting and pilfering of ancient temples and tombs are as old as mankind itself,'' Abdul noted without expression.

"This was a more grandiose looting. A unique piece of ancient jewelry.''

"All ancient jewelry is unique. Jewelry, gold and silver ornaments or weapons, anything that shines is the first thing that grave robbers take. I'm surprised there is still anything precious left for today's thief,'' Abdul said good-humoredly.

"True. But this was—what shall I call it?—a burglar's bonanza. A genuinely impressive theft. It was not simply a piece of valuable ancient jewelry that was stolen. It was a necklace of golden pomegranates, pearls and . . .''

"Anton, dear boy, necklaces have always been in demand by grave robbers. Usually they are gold-encrusted with jewels.''

"This one had more to offer than its gold and jewels.''

"You make it sound interesting.''

"It was a necklace from the cult of the goddess Aphrodite.''

"Was it really?'' Abdul said, as if he merely wanted to get it all clear in his mind. "I know of three such necklaces in private collections today. Earlier thieves got them first. I would like to have them returned to Turkey, but it is impossible. To reclaim them would cost more than I'm willing to pay.''

"This one is more precious than any of those. Rumor claims it was the necklace of the goddess herself. The goddess Aphrodite,'' Anton said very quietly.

Abdul Hamid glanced up. With his left hand he rubbed the side of his face like a schoolboy pretending to think. "Do you believe it?" he asked.

"What do you believe?"

At the question, Abdul put a forefinger to his lips. "How would you like to take a drive out to the site? There you will see what is worth believing."

"To Geyre?"

"To Aphrodisias. Come." He stood up. "As the son of an old friend, you should see some of our remarkable country-side."

Taking his cue from Abdul, Anton rose. "A fine idea. I'd been planning to go there after I left you."

Abdul had a Jaguar XJ12 waiting at the curb with a driver in the front seat. This surprised Anton. How could they talk with the driver present? He paused on the steps. "Abdul Bey, I understand the need for protection. But the driver . . . ?"

"Kamil has been my bodyguard for twenty-seven years. He cannot speak English. He cannot understand English. He has carefully avoided learning English because he knows it would disturb me."

"You have more faith in Kamil than I have."

"I have no faith in anyone. His brother-in-law, Melik, also works for me, as a gardener. He is jealous of Kamil. In truth, he hates him. Kamil knows very well that if Melik ever found out that he was studying English—and how could Melik not find out, since the family lives together in one house?—Melik would tell me. I would then have Kamil's tongue cut out. And he would have nothing to say. Ever."

Anton gazed at Abdul: so elegant, so businesslike, so willing to maim and mutilate. Truly a man of culture.

"Any more questions?" Abdul asked with a charming smile.

Abdul prepared for the two-hour trip by stopping at an open-air market in the center of Izmir and having Kamil shop. The driver returned with a well-stocked wicker basket of dates, figs, apricots, olives, sesame-sprinkled bread and bottled, ice-cold mineral water. Then they headed south from Izmir through miles of Anatolia's most fertile valley. The two-lane blacktop road stretched before them—sometimes flat, sometimes winding up and down hills—through grape vineyards, olive groves, orchards thick with fig, apricot and orange trees. Now and then a farmhouse appeared. But hardly a farmhouse in the American sense. Small, usually white with a low-hanging roof, occasionally quite new, but always constructed low to the ground, safer in this earthquake-prone country. Once they passed the ruins of a house that might have been a thousand years old. Anton almost choked on the date pit as the car swerved at the last moment to avoid hitting a seminaked child leading a goat in the middle of the road.

As they drove through the countryside with its ancient history, it amused Anton to pull an apricot from a plastic bag within the plastic-lined wicker basket. How typical of Turkey. Twentieth-century plastic among ruins and relics of thousands of years. The very old and the very new, under one sun.

"Is it true?" Anton asked, his eyes fixed on the countryside, thinking it wiser to avoid Abdul's gaze.

"Is what true?"

"Is it the necklace of the goddess?"

"How should I know?" Abdul appeared surprised at being pressed.

"Yes," Anton said quite gently. "How would anybody actually know? It's impossible to track down the truth of such a story. Three thousand years have passed. Perhaps the truth is the least important thing. What is more interesting about this story," he continued, smiling as he spoke, "is that the word is out that you have offered ten million dollars for the return of the necklace."

"Fantastic stories always circulate in the art world. Everything changes. Everything is the same," Abdul purred as he leaned back against the cushions, nibbling on a fig. His eyes had closed as though to better enjoy the taste of the fruit. Watching him, one might think he had come simply to get out of the office and picnic. But, given his man, Anton knew better.

The miles of vineyards and orchards were pleasantly soothing, and Anton almost fell asleep. Then his attention was suddenly aroused when he spotted on a distant ridge the agora, theater and gymnasium of an ancient Greek town.

"That's Tralles, isn't it?" Anton said, hoping to provoke Abdul into talking. "Wasn't it a Hellenistic center of art?"

"So the archaeologists tell me," Abdul said sourly. "We have more ancient Greek sites in Anatolia than the Greeks have in Greece."

"Including the sanctuary and temple of Venus Aphrodite."

"Yes," said Abdul, without moving an eyelash.

"But you won't say if the story is true or false?" Anton asked, as though their conversation about the necklace had never ended. As, in reality, it hadn't.

"What I will say is that the story is being circulated by the Greek infidels. The government in Athens wants to possess the necklace and claim it belonged to the goddess. It makes her that much more their own. Those swine!" This time Abdul's malice was evident. "Look at what is ours. The ancient towns. Temples. Theaters. And the Greeks claim to be the cradle of Western civilization! Pah!"

Anton said nothing more, feeling it was wiser to wait until they arrived at the site. Abdul's acrimony toward the Greeks could put him in a mood that might not be favorable for Anton's purpose.

Nothing had prepared Anton for the archaeological richness of the ancient city of Aphrodisias, so strange yet so familiar. He wished Cella could see it. Abdul and he strolled through the hippodrome where, almost three thousand years ago, thirty thousand spectators had watched athletic events and gladiator-and-animal combats. They walked softly as though not to disturb the dead, exploring the ancient theater with its marble tiers, its stage, its seats. Nearby were the baths with what must have been luxurious dressing rooms. The effect was staggering and had for the spiritual ear something like an echo of far, faint singing.

"Those people knew how to enjoy life," Anton remarked as he and Abdul walked on.

"They took their pleasures seriously. Few Westerners today understand the high level of joy they achieved." Abdul appraised Anton guardedly. "Let us see our reason for being here—the temple itself."

Abdul led the way through the poplar groves until they reached a place where marble columns seemed to grow out of the ground. They paused and stood silently before fourteen battered Ionic columns that, like wounded sentinels, had remained stubbornly erect through thousands of years of earthquakes, storms, tempests and changing cultures.

"There it is. Look at them—so harmonious, so pure in line, they might almost float. It's what they've discovered so far of the temple of Aphrodite."

"Built around the first century B.C.," Anton said.

"Yes. The temple is very old. Its purpose is ever young. It was meant to celebrate the rites of the great goddess of love and fertility." Abdul's tone was reverent. "Those haphazard trenches, scattered rocks and blocks were once an incredible shrine where the people worshipped her and performed the sacred rites of Aphrodite. But now they can find her only by digging through rubble. Time and earthquakes take their toll." Abdul sighed.

"War takes a bigger one."

"So it does. Even the inner sanctum of the temple, where the image of the goddess was kept, was desecrated."

"Vandals?"

"Looters. Or fanatics who hated what she stood for." Abdul smiled suddenly. "But Aphrodite still lives. By great good fortune, fragments of a colossal marble statue of the goddess were found close by some years ago."

"The holy statue of the goddess herself?"

"No, but one belonging to the shrine. The holy image of Aphrodite was undoubtedly made of more precious materials than marble. And covered with gems."

"And wearing a necklace."

Abdul's voice was both gentle and fervent as he ignored the remark. "Here one can almost feel her presence."

"What about the shrines of Aphrodite on Cyprus?"

"The Greeks! Always the Greeks! They would like to claim Cyprus as the origin of Aphrodite. But even they admit that the first Neolithic settlers came from western Asia, bringing with them the mother goddess whom we know as Aphrodite. Those dancing people passed this way first. And many settled here. Perhaps others did go on to Cyprus," Abdul admitted resentfully. "But here the great goddess rests. Forever! The Greeks know it too. That is why they make so much fuss about the Aphrodite necklace."

At last Anton's patience had been rewarded. "You mean the necklace that Northbie's auctioned?"

"Bah! Northbie's! Infidel scum! They will sell anything if the money is enough." Abdul started to pace around the temple grounds.

"If they thought the necklace they auctioned was actually Aphrodite's, it would have brought in millions more. They say it wasn't." Anton sounded brisk, even impatient. "Was it?"

"It may be. It may not be." Abdul stopped and gazed at Anton, his eyes quiet, like a pointer's. "Why do you ask?"

"Only that would explain why you are offering ten million dollars for its return."

"What could that mean to you? Unless you know who bought it?"

Anton pretended embarrassment at being caught off guard. "If I don't know, I might ferret out who does. There is always a finder's fee in these matters."

"I will not allow the Greek swine to have the necklace," Abdul said as though he hadn't heard Anton's words. "When they burned Izmir they burned my mother, my father, my sisters."

There was a silence and Anton waited. At last he said, "I understand your personal feelings. And, too," he added after a slight hesitation, "it may be that the necklace actually did belong to the goddess herself. If it did, you have a very sound reason for offering ten million for its return."

Abdul made a face of disgust. "You keep talking about this ten million dollars! Who says so? Gossip! The art world dines on gossip."

"For the sake of discussion, let's pretend you did make the offer," Anton said, with nothing but deference in his tone. "What troubles me is I don't understand why. This site is too recent. That necklace was known about long before the temple was discovered. It first came into view when Stavros Livanos bought it as a wedding present from a private collector in Switzerland. The provenance is impeccable."

"The Greek! His way of doing business. He gave it to his daughter on her marriage to Onassis. A dangerous gift when not given in love, but to cement a business deal—then Aphrodite grows angry."

"You know its history."

"I know its history," Abdul said, pleased with himself. "The private collector was my cousin in Switzerland. We sold Livanos the necklace. For one hundred thousand dollars." He laughed unexpectedly. "That was before inflation."

"Where did you get the necklace?"

"I found it in the tomb here."

Anton's head was reeling, but he managed to sound remarkably rational. "You found the Aphrodite necklace?"

With a quaint pout of professional vanity, Abdul conceded the point. "You are aware of my history. Long before Dr. Erim discovered Aphrodisias, my cousin and I had—to use the Western word—looted the sanctuary of Aphrodite." For an instant a shadow of guilt crossed his face. "When I was a very young man and very eager for wealth, before I understood the reasons for keeping national treasures at home, I found the necklace and a few other exquisite pieces buried here at the temple. It was in the tomb of Aphrodite herself, far down a shaft in a silent, splendid place where she still sleeps. This they have not discovered yet."

"You actually found the tomb of the goddess!" Anton said in amazement.

"I found many things. In the sacred tomb." He smiled the old, secretive smile and sat down on a marble rock. "Anton, son of my dear late friend Oliver, who sold your father the snake queen of Knossos? Who sold him the headdresses worn by the women of Sumer, found in the royal cemeteries of Ur? Four thousand years old. The beaded-and-gold wreaths with exquisite gold, leafy pendants and lapis-and-carnelian centers." Abdul's eyes were alive with excitement.

"You did," Anton said, also seated on a rock, trying to guess where Abdul was leading.

"Yes, I, Abdul Hamid. I did. I made him a king among art dealers. I made him a rich man. I made his son, you, a rich man. I helped your family build the Vilanova Trust. But your father was not my only customer. By no means. Now I will tell you a family secret. Because your people are Etruscans, an ancient race. Etruscans are from Lydia. Lydia in Turkey. Some ancestor of yours may have been an ancestor of mine. In a way, you are one of us, yes?"

"It is possible," Anton agreed, feeling Abdul's eyes boring into him, all the way to the next dark turning.

"You are as Oriental as I am. Which to a Western mind means devious." His face shone with amusement. "Where did you think I got the treasures I sold your father?"

Anton had long ago developed the art of deliberately misunderstanding. "I believe you once mentioned a Turkish banking family in need of funds. People like that."

"Your father never told you the truth?"

"My father never discussed your sources with me."

"Your father was always a wise man. You were too young to understand," Abdul said with approval. "Sometimes I would acquire something precious from a private owner. But more often I would acquire something precious from the dead."

"The dead?"

"Yes. The dead dispose of their possessions willingly. They give with a generous hand."

Anton pursed his lips and frowned as if to say he was trying to understand.

"Listen. My family was once in trade, as the English call it. We found and sold art. Not paintings but mementos of civilizations. Pottery, headgear, weapons, jewelry, anything of beauty one might find in an ancient tomb or a temple."

He paused, searching for the right phrase. "Or to use your crude Western words, we have been grave robbers. Looters."

"Not my words. Yours," Anton murmured.

"They apply. To common thieves. But my family was respectful. We were artists too. We took only the best, and we were never greedy. We never destroyed a piece for the sake of the gold or the silver or the jewels. We admired and revered the creativity of the past and sold it to buyers of taste. Appreciation. And, of course, wealth."

Anton nodded. He did not say that he had always suspected as much.

"So now you know more about Abdul Hamid. As I know more about you." His glance was sensitive and seemed to signal friendship. "Anton, tell me, do you happen to know who now owns the necklace?"

"Would you pay the buyer ten million dollars for it?"

There was a sudden emptying of Abdul's eyes. "What kind of fool do you take me for?"

"Not a fool. The Minister of Culture and Archaeology of Turkey. Who wants the necklace of the goddess returned."

"Very deeply. And a reward of ten million is a fine way to start a worldwide search."

Choosing his words with extreme care, Anton asked, "You mean it has all been publicity, no substance?"

"Publicity, yes. That's all. Why should I pay an infidel for something that already belongs to Turkey?" His manner became noticeably defensive. "Even if I wanted to, I could not pay that much."

"You want someone to return a necklace that cost millions of dollars for nothing? For the sake of Turkey?"

"I cannot pay the ten million dollars. It would be the end of my career. And I do not have to pay ten million dollars. There are scoundrels who will find the necklace for me. And take pennies in return." He paused, smiled and then continued conversationally. "So tell me, my boy, who purchased the necklace?"

Anton got to his feet. "Perhaps Athens would pay more than publicity for the necklace of Aphrodite. What do you think?"

"It would be wiser to tell me who bought it."

"It would be wise if you would reconsider your offer," Anton said. "Assuming I can find out who has the necklace. And you must remember, whoever it is, he, or she, did pay a pretty penny for it."

Abruptly Abdul's mood changed. Again he entered into the

spirit of good fellowship. "I am not an unreasonable man. You've known me for a lifetime, and I have always believed that everyone should make a little something. Ten million is too much. Far too much." He rose to his feet. "But you make a point. They did pay money. And I do not cheat friends. I will pay what they paid. No more. No less. Tell them."

"I'm sure the necklace can be sold for more than they paid."

"I'm sure. But let me warn you that there are fanatics who will stop at nothing to regain the necklace for Turkey. With or without my encouragement."

"You mean they would try to steal it?" Anton asked.

"They will do what they believe they have to do." Abdul gave Anton a mocking smile. "But as for me, I shall try to be as generous as I can. If not as generous as the dead, at least generous. I have always liked the Taggards. Like you, they are one of us. Etruscans. And Spina was never greedy. But Sebastian, I don't know. I hear he is greedy. I hope not."

It came as no surprise to Anton that Abdul Hamid had known from the start who had bought the Aphrodite necklace.

When Anton boarded Flight 707 at Yesilkoy Airport in Istanbul, he was weary and worried. He was not at all sure that the price Abdul had ultimately offered would sit well with Sebastian. As he fastened his seat belt, he hoped the seat next to him would remain empty. It didn't. Just before the plane doors were shut, Toby Phipps lumbered aboard, handed the stewardess his raincoat and sat beside Anton.

"Toby!" Anton said.

"Anton!" Toby said.

"As we began our trip we end it. Together." Anton looked at Toby. The man's appearance shocked him. For all his huge size, Toby Phipps always made a point of being well groomed and immaculately dressed. Even dashing, in a lumbering way. Now his eyes were bloodshot, he was unshaven, his shirt was open at the collar and his beige covert cloth suit needed pressing badly.

"Not quite," said Toby mournfully. "Emory has left me high and dry."

"A spat?"

"He's with a ridiculous Arab boy," Toby said almost through tears. "Emory likes them young and untouched. He is such a fool. That little boy is older than Topkapi."

"You're too good for him, Toby. He'll regret it when he comes home with syphilis. He'll want you to take him back," Anton said.

"I know it. And that's the hell. I will take him back."

"Emory will soon be home. He had only the Topkapi people to see. I don't believe Dr. Jason Lord is generous to a fault. He won't pay for an extended vacation with a street child."

"Dr. Jason Lord, the s.o.b., is paying for Emory's trip to Izmir. We were supposed to go together and explore the ancient ruins. Now he'll take that child. Perhaps get him there at half fare."

"Izmir? What has Lord got to do with Izmir?" Suddenly Toby's love life was no longer a sad joke.

"I have no idea. Emory has an appointment with some Turk named Hamid."

"About what?"

"He doesn't tell me everything. In fact, he usually tells me nothing."

Later, even after numerous scotches, Anton maintained an awesome sobriety. He had a terrible hunch time was beginning to run out and asked himself again if he shouldn't have called to warn Cella. And again he decided that he'd been right to wait. It would only alarm her. Better to tell her in person. Together they'd convince Sebastian to accept Abdul Hamid's offer.

PART SIX

THE WRATH OF THE GODS

Chapter Fourteen

"The two tiny silver cylinders—they're really scrolls—were discovered in a burial cave overlooking the Valley of Hinnom, in Jerusalem. They predate the Dead Sea Scrolls by more than four hundred years," the small man said reflectively. Although the gray yarmulke he wore was attached to his hair by two gray bobby pins, the stiff wind gave him some concern, and as he tightened the bobby pins, he remarked, "They were made in either the late seventh or early sixth century B.C." His precise choice of words contrasted with his classic Brooklyn accent.

"My God! What a find!" Cella blinked and reached in her purse for her handkerchief. She was seated on a wooden bench, listening with more than her ears, and the late April wind whistling down Fifth Avenue was making her eyes tear. She hoped she sounded properly impressed, which she was. And calm, which she wasn't.

"They were an important discovery. The scrolls are so tiny they could easily have been overlooked. The larger is one inch in width and unrolls to a length of three-point-eight inches. The smaller is a half-inch wide and unrolls to one and a half inches."

"Finger size."

"The smaller is pinkie size."

"What genuis!" Cella's voice was full of real awe and false composure. "Imagine a silversmith hammering silver so thin."

"The scroll itself is as thin as a hair. The silver plaques on the scrolls are thinner."

"Amazing," Cella murmured in a hushed voice. "The plaques were inscribed with a Hebrew prayer?"

"The oldest biblical inscriptions ever found."

"That ancient. Truly a remarkable discovery," Cella said with a professional air.

"It was. Originally the silver scrolls were tightly rolled into thin, hollow tubes so that they could be threaded and worn."

"I know just how—as an amulet on a chain around the neck." Cella sighed with admiration. "What incredible craftsmanship."

"And reassuring for the wearer," the small man said.

"Yes. To carry the blessing of your God with you wherever you go," Cella said reverently. "I only wish . . ." But she could no longer keep up the game. Under any other circumstances, her interest in the scrolls would have been intensely real, but here and now it was no longer possible for her to pretend. Before she could blurt out her feelings, a small white puppy leaped onto her lap.

"What the devil!" Ben Stein said.

A small boy stood panting in front of her. "Sorry, miss," he said, grabbing the dog and picking up his leash. "I hope he didn't pee on you. He isn't toilet-trained yet."

Cella looked at the lap of her mink coat. "I'm still dry, thank you."

"You're luckier than my mother," the boy said as the puppy ran off with the boy holding on grimly to his leash.

Ben Stein shook his head and grimaced. "When I telephoned and suggested we meet on a park bench in front of the Metropolitan Museum of Art, I thought we'd have more privacy than if I stopped off at your shop. I didn't want to bump into any of your clients. Including your friend Dr. Lawrence Lord." Abruptly his face crinkled into a smile. "But I didn't expect you to be assaulted by a Samoyed puppy. Maybe the Sixty-sixth Street precinct would have been a better choice."

"I didn't think you asked to see me to discuss ancient artifacts," Cella said, carefully watching the little man. "How do you know Lawrence Lord is a family friend?"

"When I'm working on a case, I make it my business to know who knows who."

Lieutenant Ben Stein had made a strong impression on Cella when she'd seen him on television. He'd called her the day before to set up their meeting, and her original reaction to the man was reinforced the moment they met. He gave her the feeling of a precocious, prematurely aged boy who, she suspected, might be far more perceptive than even very bright men. During the brief time they'd been talking, she could feel beneath his agreeable manner a kind of dangerous waiting, like that of a fine, razor-sharp blade, carefully sheathed but ready should the occasion arise.

"I believe we're here because you wanted to talk to me about something other than ancient scrolls," Cella remarked warily.

"I'd say that's half the case. It's always interesting to have an intelligent conversation with someone who knows about something other than murder."

"Like Phillip Mckay's murder. That's the real reason you wanted to see me?"

"It's real enough."

"How did you know we were friends?"

"The name Cella Taggard often appears in his appointment book. You saw him two weeks ago."

"Three o'clock on Tuesday, March twenty-second. We have a Byzantine pendant he was interested in."

"You'd make a good detective with a memory like that." His tone was friendly, but his face was impenetrable.

"Phillip was a family friend and on occasion we did business with him. As you probably observed, in the art world, friends and business mingle." She felt as though she'd stepped into a searchlight. His eyes were clear, intent, and missed nothing. "Are we suspects—my father and I?"

"The case is in the early stage. It's a long tunnel. As of this moment there are no suspects. And, conversely, everyone is suspect. That's why I'm here."

"You're going to ask me what I was doing the night Phillip was killed. Do I have an alibi? That's the standard procedure, isn't it?"

"I suppose so," Ben Stein admitted. "But it's not the way I work."

"Then why did you want to talk to me?"

"I'm taking an opinion poll," he remarked amiably.

There was a wary pause, but his quiet voice, his gentle manner, peeled away her caution. "What do you want to know?" she asked.

"Who hated Mckay?"

"Hated him? No one hated Phillip. Why should anyone?"

"I don't know why. Yet. But someone did. Whoever it was killed him."

"Dr. Jason Lord was interviewed on television. He said it was a crime of greed."

"I know Jason Lord, and I know what he said," Ben Stein remarked. "I wish he'd stick to things he understands. Like art."

"You don't think the motive was greed? Or, rather, a mixture of greed and fear? Fear of exposure as a dealer in fakes, and greed for the money that comes from the sales?" A gust of wind made Cella feel cold, and she tried to sink deeper into her fur.

Except for a ritual touching of his yarmulke to make sure it was still in place, Ben Stein seemed impervious to the weather. "A person will kill for greed. What causes the greed—desire for wealth, or power, or celebrity—is of little consequence unless it's the immediate motive. This murder was not caused by greed for money. Or by fear of the possible consequences of discovery of fraudulent sales. This was a crime of passion." His brown eyes were very still.

"Greed as a passion?"

"No. Greed is a cool passion. This one was searing hot," Ben Stein explained. "The murder was too violent. Greed is cooler. Self-contained. Often skillful. Usually calculated. No, it wasn't greed because of fear of exposure. This was a killing of fury. Rage. Hate. The head was bashed beyond recognition. The idol on the floor was covered with blood. That much violence was not required to dispose of one fragile human being named Phillip Mckay." The small man paused, studying Cella. He said, "Give me an educated guess. Mckay was your friend. Who might have hated him?"

"I really can't think of anyone."

"Please think harder," Lieutenant Stein said, standing up. "I'll be in touch." He started to walk away, then turned around. "Incidentally, think along sexual lines. Sexual jealousy. Many scholars believe the Cycladian idols had sexual meanings." He paused and glanced at the sky. "Yes, very definitely a crime of passion."

"At last you're here," Marina called out as Cella entered The House of Uni.

"I'm here," Cella said. "Hello, Marina. Any calls for me, Juliana?" she asked.

Juliana consulted her pad. "Billy Gorgeous called. He said you'd know the name." Juliana suppressed a smile. "He has tickets for *Otello* with the new baritone, Apollo Granforte, and wanted to make sure you were still on for tonight. He left his telephone number."

Cella considered the offer as she slipped off her coat. "Why not? Call him back and suggest he come by at seven-thirty. We'll eat after the opera."

"Let's see. A Wayne Somebody also called. He said he's 'Gorgeous.' He wanted to know about tomorrow night."

"That's a strange coincidence," Marina said. "Are they brothers?"

"Under the skin. Tell him to call tomorrow. Who else?"

Juliana drew closer and whispered in a voice only Cella could hear, "Mrs. Schiller has telephoned three times. She wanted to speak either to you or to Sebastian."

Cella raised a quizzical eyebrow. "I'll call her."

"No. She said, 'Don't call me. I'll call you.' Really!"

"It's her chorus-girl humor."

"I've been waiting for you for ages," Marina said, sparkling. "If I didn't know better I'd think you were avoiding me." Turned out with grace and taste in a rich maroon suede pantsuit, white ruffled silk shirt, and maroon string bow tie, she leaned against a counter.

"I'm sorry. I didn't know you were waiting. But here I am. And at your disposal." Cella half smiled.

The smile irritated Marina. It was a sign of the younger woman's deep confidence, which worried instead of soothed her.

"Come," Cella said, "we'll talk in my office." She walked toward the rear of the store, Marina keeping pace with her. "Isn't my father here?"

"Juliana told me he's with a Mrs. Grundy," Marina said. She added quickly, "I've something marvelous to tell you."

Cella refused to ask her what, and instead fastened her attention on Mrs. Grundy. "I wonder what Mrs. G. has in mind? Buying or selling? A cheery soul. Owns one of the finest private collections of first-century to fifth-century jewelry in the world. And she won't give or sell a pearl to the Met. Hates all museums. Claims if she ever dies she'll consider taking everything with her."

Cella's amusement with Isabelle Grundy struck Marina as excessive, if not evasive. Cella wished to avoid hearing the reason for her visit. Well, she wouldn't permit it. "Forget Mrs. Grundy, Cella. I have something to tell you. Something marvelous."

Cella felt a need to be intensely still. "Sit down, Marina," she said, indicating a chair. "Tell me everything."

"I wanted to speak to both of you in person." Marina hesitated, then blurted out, "But to you in particular."

Cella waited for her to go on, with an uneasy impatience that she hoped didn't show. "Why? Am I that important?"

"You are. It's . . ." There was another moment of hesitation, during which it seemed to Cella that Marina wanted to say one thing but decided instead on another. "I had lunch with my son, Jason, before I left for Santa Barbara."

"That's nice." Cella seated herself behind her desk. "I gather you don't see him very often."

"Not often enough. He is my son, but sometimes . . ."

Cella waited again.

Marina's sparkle dimmed a trifle as she continued. "We haven't always understood each other. He was bitter about my divorcing Lawrence."

"And now he isn't?"

"No. He's finally matured. He's a different man."

"I'm glad you feel he's matured. But I'm not sure what that has to do with me. Or with us." Cella wished Marina would stop talking about Jason.

"He's always objected to my remarrying."

"I didn't know." Cella's heart had begun to beat to the rhythm of suspense.

"He has." Marina was filled with excitement. "But he no longer objects."

"And you're thinking of remarrying?" Cella asked brightly.

"Sebastian and I have talked about it."

"Oh?" The unthinkable had come up, and the women sat quietly for a long moment, face-to-face.

"Sebastian told me that you object to our marriage. Primarily because of Jason." Marina's face changed color. "I can understand that. He has been difficult. But he's different now."

Cella shrank from using words that combined Marina's future with her own. Finally she cautiously asked, "He gave you permission to marry my father?"

"In a way." Marina hesitated once again, still searching for the proper posture. "He told me how much he respects The House of Uni."

Cella thought about this. First Frank Ford and now Marina. Bringing with them regards from the celebrated Dr. Jason Lord. His great respect. His unquestioning approval. What the hell was Lord doing? She would have to see him for herself as soon as possible. "That's nice to know," she said. "Your son usually makes a point of showing his lack of respect. Especially for art dealers."

"That's Jason's work," Marina said defensively. "But please believe me, he speaks very highly of The House of Uni. Of you and Sebastian."

"It's nice to have the approval of the esteemed Dr. Lord,"

Cella remarked, relieved to be able to say something that was natural and true.

"Someday you may even see him as a kind of brother. You have no reason at all to dislike him. I saw proof."

Cella was silent as she drowned in waves of anxiety. "What kind of proof?" she finally asked, thinking it a safe question.

"He has a client who brought in a pair of Langobardic earrings for testing. I saw them on his desk while I was waiting in his office. They're beautiful. I tried them on," Marina ran on happily. "While we were at lunch we talked about them. And do you know what Jason said?"

"Tell me," Cella replied pleasantly.

"He said if they'd been purchased at The House of Uni, he wouldn't have wasted his time testing them. That's how highly he regards you. And the exquisite ancient jewelry you sell."

Cella looked vague, innocent, beautiful, as Marina merged with Frank Ford. "That's your marvelous news?"

"Yes! It should make you think better of him."

Cella asked herself if she was afraid. If she was, she must smother her fear. "Think better of him, and look forward to your marriage to my father?"

Marina gave a light laugh. "That would seem to follow."

Cella wanted to be straightforward, but it wasn't possible. "Why my father? You might marry anyone, now that Jason approves of your remarrying."

"I suppose I might—if I wanted anyone else. But I don't."

"Anyone else for what, Marina?" Sebastian asked as he stood in the doorway of Cella's office.

Marina gave him a startled look, hurried to his side and, raising her head, kissed him quickly. First on the cheek, then on the lips. "Sebastian! How wonderful!" she said, stepping back.

Sebastian smiled at her, at what he saw: a tall, beautiful, elegant woman who had for him an echo of the same appeal that Spina had once had. But for entirely different reasons. As a man who had known many women, he was pleased that he only had to appear for her to make him feel in the "right." Marina asked nothing from him, beyond his presence. She had learned how to efface herself in the ways only certain clever European women knew. And the world's great courtesans. It was a rare talent. One that Spina had lacked. Spina had been independent. She had assumed equality; the right to make her own decisions freely; to be with whom she chose, when she chose. In Spina's blood had run the ways of her heritage—of the ancient, strong-willed Etruscan women. In

Marina, for the first time in his life, Sebastian discovered a warm, beautiful woman for whom he came first; his pleasure, his happiness, was what mattered.

"When did you get back?" he asked, putting his hands on Marina's arms and looking her up and down.

"Late last night. Too late to call you." Marina was gay again. This time it was spontaneous and rang true. "You promised to take me out for dinner my first evening home."

"I'm a man of my word. What time shall I call for you?"

"I'll be ready by seven."

"I'll be there at six."

"Do that," Marina said, leaning over and kissing him again on the lips. Then she moved quickly toward the door.

"Wait!" Sebastian called out. "What's your news? And what were you two conspiring about?"

"Cella will tell you about it," Marina said. "You'll be pleased. And if you want more details, I'll fill you in later."

Sebastian watched Marina leave; then he turned to Cella, who gave her father a brilliant, congenial, lying smile. "We've been having a quiet womanly gossip. How was Mrs. G.?"

"Mrs. G. wants to buy the gold turtle pin we showed her last October. What were you and Marina talking about?"

"Her news, as she said. Which is that her son, the esteemed Dr. Jason Lord, has nothing but the highest respect for The House of Uni," Cella said dryly. "He approves of you and me. He approves of Marina's marriage to you. He approves and approves and approves."

"I see."

"The hell you do. You don't begin to see."

"You just said that Marina said Jason Lord has nothing but respect. I told you not to be concerned."

"What else did you tell me? That I was on a witch hunt?"

"Those could have been my words."

Sebastian looked at Cella and saw two solemn eyes searching for an answer to a question.

"All right. Let's have it. What am I missing?"

Cella struggled to maintain her inner balance. She must not show anger. "I am not going to give you maxims to live by," she said as gently as she could. "I am only going to tell you the case as it stands. On what Marina bases her belief that Dr. Jason Lord has such a glorious opinion of us."

"I'm listening."

"A client asked him to examine a pair of gold, Italian earrings, vintage A.D. sixth century. Marina saw them on his desk when she picked him up for lunch. He told her if they'd come from The House of Uni, he would have refused to test them. He trusts us so implicitly.''

"That's a sign of good will,'' Sebastian said with a flicker of bravado.

"Is it? They were Langobardic earrings.''

Sebastian gave Cella a long look. At last he said wearily, "You will agree that there are more than one pair of Langobardic earrings in the world?''

"Our life doesn't permit me to accept that much coincidence.''

Sebastian wasn't ready to surrender. "All right. Suppose Lawrence did bring them to Jason Lord to examine? That doesn't mean that Lawrence told him where he got them.''

"I suppose it doesn't. But it's hard for me to believe that Jason Lord doesn't know.'' Cella's love for her father was a weight within her.

"If Lawrence did take the Langobardic earrings to his son, the question is—why?'' Sebastian said uneasily. "What's that bastard up to?''

"What Lawrence Lord is up to is only half the question. The other half is what Jason Lord is up to. Suppose he didn't tell Marina the whole truth?''

Sebastian managed a grim laugh. "All right. Tell me exactly what you want me to do.''

"Marina says you've talked about getting married.''

"We have, and we'll go on talking. Until we know more about Dr. Jason Lord. Is that satisfactory?'' Sebastian asked. "I'll tell her you'd like to meet him yourself.''

Cella gave her father a curious look. He'd come to the same place as she had. "Do that. Just don't let her try to set it up.''

At that moment Juliana appeared at the door of Cella's office. "Sebastian, Darlene Schiller is on the line for you. She sounds a bit hysterical.''

"That's not unusual. All right, tell her I'll be there in a moment.'' He said to Cella, "This shouldn't take long.''

"Take it on my phone. She called several times earlier when I was out with Lieutenant Stein.''

"I forgot you had an appointment with him. Will he want to see me? Are we suspects?''

"He may want to see you, but I don't think we're suspects. At least no more than anyone else. He has a theory about Phillip's murder that's a bit unnerving. I'll tell you about it after Darlene.'' Cella pressed one of the buttons on her telephone and handed the receiver to Sebastian.

"Darlene, how are you?" From the enthusiasm in Sebastian's voice, it was impossible for anyone to know his stomach was churning and that dealing with Darlene Schiller at that moment strained all his reserves of charm and flattery. "Slow down, my dear . . . Mmm . . . Yes, dear girl, I do hear you . . . Mmm . . . All right, Darlene . . . Yes, I do understand. Your point is well taken. But I must discuss it with Cella . . . No. I cannot have an answer for you today . . . Of course I'm sorry, but Cella isn't here at the moment. She's on her way to Paris . . . That's right, Paris. Something came up . . . I don't know why Juliana didn't mention it. Cella won't be back until the end of the week . . . That's right. I'll speak to her and try to have an answer for you next Monday. I can promise that . . . Good-bye." Slowly he hung up the receiver. "She's offering three and a half million for the Aphrodite."

"Good God! Why?"

"I don't know. I haven't had a chance to tell you, but she called yesterday and offered three million then."

Cella gave her father a bewildered look. She had the strange feeling that their life was like an electric cable buried beneath the ground which had abruptly snapped, plunging them both into darkness. Why hadn't he had a chance to tell her about Darlene's offer? And why was she now supposedly on her way to Paris?

"I have the strong impression you don't want to sell Darlene the Aphrodite," she said, trying to sound casual.

"Not yet. If ever. I'll need it when I work on the Astarte. And while we're on the subject, frankly, Cella, so far you've come up with no ideas. At the risk of repeating myself, I ask, what's got into you lately?"

"Nothing, Father. Fatigue. I had to finish the Egyptian scarab bracelet. I'll do better this weekend," she said earnestly. "I have had some ideas."

"I'm glad to hear that," Sebastian said. "Now tell me about Lieutenant Stein."

An immense weariness possessed Cella. But sleep would not come. Billy Gorgeous had turned out to be a bore, and she had sent him home without the reward he'd expected. She had felt so exhausted that she thought she would go to sleep immediately. But the instant she had lain down, every nerve in her body had started into vivid wakefulness. Jason Lord cast a sinister and dangerous shadow across her future. She was unable to stop her mind from playing with all kinds of menacing possibilities.

She switched on her bedside lamp. She would read, as she often did when the world gave her no peace. She picked up Spina's book *The Enigmatic Etruscans*, needing to escape to the ancient world that she understood more instinctively than she did the world of today. She opened the book to the page with the bookmark.

"Livy, the Roman historian, wrote that a few generations earlier Roman boys studied the Etruscan literature as conscientiously as they later did the Greek. . . .

". . . the Romans borrowed and learned much from their Etruscan teachers. The Roman toga originated as the Etruscan ceremonial garment; the official robe of Etruscan rulers was purple, a color which is still an emblem of royalty. Romans inherited the gladiatorial shows from the Etruscans. Rome even copied the Etruscan military formation for the Roman legion . . ."

As always, reading about her ancestors worked as a tranquilizer. Without her being aware of it, her quivering nerves slowly quieted down. Her eyes closed, and the book slipped against her body as she fell into a deep sleep.

Sometime later Cella unwillingly opened her eyes. The telephone was ringing. It was three-fifteen in the morning. What idiot had gotten hold of her private number? Suddenly her face was radiant. Anton! She reached for the telephone, and her hand froze in midair. It wasn't her private line that was ringing; it was the line that connected directly to the local police station. She picked up the receiver as gingerly as if it were alive.

"Hello," she said.

"Sorry to wake you, Miss Taggard," a strange man's voice said. "This is Sergeant Reilly of the Sixty-sixth Street precinct."

"What is it? My father?"

"No, nothing like that. Someone tried to break into your shop, The House of Uni."

"Damn!"

"Fortunately, you have a highly sophisticated alarm system. The bars came down and almost trapped the thief. A fragment of cloth was caught by the bars. Also, the alarm worked perfectly and alerted us."

"Thank heaven for that. But no one has ever tried to rob the shop before."

"There's a first time for everything. Officer Max Browsky

will be around in the morning to inspect the premises more closely.''

"Are you sure the shop wasn't entered?''

"Absolutely positive, Miss Taggard. I'm sorry to have woken you, but I wanted you to know what happened. There'll be a patrolman on duty in front of the shop for the rest of the night.''

"Thank you, Sergeant Reilly.''

"Part of the job, Miss Taggard.''

"Good night,'' Cella said, staring at the ceiling as she hung up. An attempted robbery? My God! What next?

Sergeant Peter Reilly hung up the telephone and studied the report the patrolman had handed him. This late at night it was relatively quiet in Manhattan's East Sixties. He glanced up from the report. "Too bad the bars didn't spear the slime-ball.'' He held up a fragment of cloth. "This all you got?''

Officer Max Browsky nodded. He was five years on the force, tall, good-looking, and still had as trim a waistline as when he'd played basketball for Clinton High School. He'd graduated at the top of his class at the police academy—an ideal example of the new breed of New York City police-man—and it was only a matter of time before he'd be pro-moted to sergeant, then lieutenant. If he kept his nose clean and didn't get too greedy with the precinct "black book,'' he might make captain one day.

"Looks like it came from a cheap raincoat. Maybe foreign. I checked the premises very carefully,'' Browsky said. "No one got in.''

Sergeant Reilly, a twenty-five-year veteran and forty pounds overweight, rubbed his chin thoughtfully. "Call Lieutenant Ben Stein at homicide in the morning. Give him a complete report. And the evidence. The lab'll give him an analysis of the material.''

"You think Stein expected something like this?''

"How the hell do I know? That son of a bitch doesn't tell us a fucking thing until he wants us to make an arrest. That's all he thinks we're good for. Snap a choke hold on some poor asshole, read him his Miranda rights and toss him in the slammer.'' The sergeant's eyes narrowed. "But he had to have something in mind when he told us to keep him in-formed on the Taggards and their shop. My hunch is it's something to do with the murder of that art type. What was his name?''

"Mckay. Phillip Mckay. You think the Taggards're suspects?" Browsky asked.

"I don't know. I'm only a fat precinct sergeant. Stein's covering all bases. Maybe they're a base. And what Stein needs we give him." Reilly glared at the officer. "Any more brilliant questions, Officer Browsky?"

Chapter Fifteen

After five rings the telephone was finally answered.

"I'd like to speak to Dr. Lord."

"Dr. Lord is with a client. He'll be free at three. Who shall I say called?"

"Dr. Lawrence Lord."

"Oh, yes." The temp giggled nervously. "You're his father. Emory told me. He said he had an appointment with you at four-thirty. Not Emory. I mean Dr. Jason Lord."

"He does."

"Your name is written in Dr. Lord's appointment book. Dr. Lawrence Lord. It says so right here."

The girl sounded like the village idiot. "Fine," Lawrence said. "I'll be there at four-thirty."

"Yes, sir, I'll tell Dr. Lord."

"By the way, where is Emory?"

"In Istanbul. Isn't that cool? I'm only here because Emory asked me to sit in for him," the temp said heroically. "But I've got a part in an Off-Off Broadway production that goes into rehearsal tomorrow. So Emory had better be back by tomorrow, or he'll have to get a new secretary. I mean Dr. Lord will. Not Emory."

He couldn't do any worse, Lawrence thought. "I see your point. Good-bye." He hung up the phone, chuckling at the vision of his fastidious-to-a-fault son coping, day after day, with an Off-Off-Broadway actress who probably came to work in torn jeans and a man's T-shirt.

He glanced at his watch. Four o'clock. He was meeting Peter Petty at The House of Uni at five-thirty. The Taggards had agreed to see them after closing time so they could be certain of privacy. He was pleased with himself for having picked up Peter Petty as a new client. After that it was easy to convince Peter that a collection of antique jewelry was vital to a world-class museum like The Petty. With the Petty Museum as a client, the Luxembourg Corporation should prove even more lucrative in the future. Peter would pay prices that ordinary museums would gag on. If things went on in this way, Lawrence might consider dropping some of his smaller clients. And buying a flat in the East Seventies. More appropriate for a man in his position. Lawrence glanced in the foyer mirror and ran a comb through his hair, still thinking about Peter Petty.

He glanced again at his watch. He'd given himself plenty of time to get to Jason's office, even if the traffic was back-to-back hearses. He started toward the front door of his apartment and stopped. Suddenly uneasy, he turned and walked quickly to his desk. He stared at the telephone answering machine, rewound the tape and replayed it, listening intently to his messages for the second time. Five messages. The only one of importance was from Jason. There was no word from the police. He wished they would call. Waiting made him nervous. Then he shrugged, brushing aside the anxiety. He had a perfect alibi. Why borrow trouble?

As Lawrence left the apartment, he felt an excitement building within him. What were the results of Jason's tests on the earrings? That could be another coup.

Jason Lord was standing looking out the office window when Lawrence entered.

"Sit down," he said without turning.

Lawrence sat down in the chair opposite Jason's desk. "How are you, Jason?"

"The same, Father." He turned and seated himself behind his desk. He reached into the top drawer of the desk and pulled out a velvet box. "Here are the Langobardic earrings." He handed the box to his father.

Lawrence opened the box. The earrings gleamed up at him, delicate, graceful. "They are quite lovely, no matter what the results of your tests."

Jason's face was neutral. "The earrings are authentic," he said.

Lawrence looked up at Jason, his smile steadfast. "The gold? The craftsmanship?"

"The gold is almost pure, but alloyed with a small quantity of silver. Not enough to affect the color or the malleability. I believe it came from mines in Asia Minor. Possibly Turkey. The artistry is perfect. The technique for making and soldering the gold wire baskets is of the type associated with the Langobard goldsmiths. Exquisitely done. Nothing is mechanical. I know of only three other comparable examples of Langobardic earrings. Two are in Italy. One pair was donated to the Met. Your friend is lucky to have found them. They're very rare.''

''That's good news. My friend will be delighted.''

''Even if you're not,'' Jason said with a taunting grin.

''But I am. Whenever my famous son puts his stamp of approval on a piece of ancient jewelry, I'm delighted.''

Jason gave him a curious look, then asked, ''To whom do I send my bill?''

''To me. You know my Manhattan address,'' Lawrence snapped. He closed the box containing the earrings.

''To you? Why are you picking up the tab?''

''Do you mean, why did I have you test the earrings?''

''Yes. I thought your friend was the Doubting Thomas, and that you believed the Taggards to be above suspicion,'' Jason said wryly.

''I do. But like all of us, they can make mistakes. I wanted to be sure. These earrings are expensive. And the buyer is a good friend.''

''Sparing yourself a crisis of conscience, just in case. . . .''

Lawrence looked warily at Jason. ''You might say that. Why are you asking these questions?''

''Idle curiosity,'' Jason said. ''Oh! One more thing. Speaking of questions, Lieutenant Ben Stein questioned me yesterday.''

Lawrence felt his heartbeat quicken. ''You told him you had dinner with me the night Mckay was killed,'' Lawrence said as he dropped the jewelry box into his briefcase.

''He didn't ask me what I was doing that fatal night. He'd heard of my report on television and seemed interested in why I had such a strong conviction about fraud as the motive for Mckay's murder. I talked and he listened. He's good at listening.''

''You sound as if you know him.''

''We play chess together at the Seventy-second Street chess club. Usually he beats me. He said the case had a quirky coincidence. Ben likes to carve his own chess pieces, and he's just started a set using the Cycladian maiden as a pawn.''

Lawrence let out his breath. ''Your friendship should either put us above or under suspicion.''

''It will have no effect, either way. I doubt that Ben Stein would let his feelings for me, if he has any, get in the way of his job.''

''Does he have any suspects?''

"I don't know. But he does have truckloads of false confessions. Every crazy in town is confessing."

"I haven't been contacted yet."

"You will be. Ben Stein never overlooks any possibility," Jason said in the kindliest tone imaginable.

"Thank you for warning me," Lawrence said.

Cella glanced up from her calculator printout and saw Juliana and Lawrence Lord standing at the door to the Clients' Room. Juliana gestured to Lord to enter, shaking her head with disbelief as she glanced at the teak table. Then she hand-signaled Cella that she was leaving for the day. Cella nodded as she watched Lawrence take in the scene before him. If he were not so expert at concealing his reactions, his expression would have matched Juliana's. She could almost hear his gasp of inner shock at the sight before him. The proceeds of a billionaire's spending spree. If Peter Regis Petty was nothing else, he was a billionaire.

At the moment, the oblong teak "show" table in the center of the Clients' Room looked as though a king—or at least a Saudi prince, before the oil glut broke the price of OPEC oil—had come to buy presents for his court. Normally a pair of earrings might have rested on the black silk cloth, one bracelet, perhaps a single ring, or a solitary necklace, a piece or two, at the most, of glittering jewelry that a customer was conscientiously considering, calculating the beauty of the jewelry versus its cost. That was under normal circumstances. But nothing was normal with Peter Regis Petty. For Peter, the display was incredibly lavish.

Arranged on the show table were a gold mesh necklace set with emeralds and pearls; lavish pendant earrings hung with dancing sirens; a pair of gold-and-silver serpentine arm bracelets; a golden ring sparkling with sapphires embossed with a woman's head. And more. Much, much more. More earrings. More rings. Necklaces. Hair combs. Belts. The table was laden with the loot of ancient civilizations. So many pieces one could hardly see the black silk.

Cella watched, half amused, as Lawrence mentally totaled the huge commission he'd earned. Full of eagerness, Peter had arrived a half hour before Lawrence and in only thirty minutes had made a valiant effort to buy out the shop. And her father, full of spurious geniality, was paying court to the Big Spender.

It gave her a bad taste. Cella was normally a reasonable woman, an open-minded person who accepted people for what they appeared to be. But she had watched Peter Petty in mute amazement. Even for Petty, he had gone too far. From the minute he'd entered the shop he seemed determined, without discrimination, to buy everything in sight.

"Hello," she heard Lawrence say. "Sorry I missed the grand opening."

Peter, full of high spirits, answered, "You're just what I needed for a pick-me-up. Isn't this white-gold collar magnificent? Look at the engraving. Who would believe that barbarians could do such remarkable work?" Peter held up the golden neck ornament. "It's a Bronze Age piece, isn't it? From Portugal?"

"If by 'barbarians' you mean they were uncivilized, those people could give lessons in civilization to all of us," Cella said with impatience.

"Sorry, ma'am," Peter said politely, rocking back and forth on his heels, admiring his purchases. "I wasn't serious. Anyway, I'm taking it."

"You've passed the seven-million-dollar mark, Mr. Petty," Cella pointed out.

"I know," Peter answered brightly. "I inherited my grandfather's knack for adding and subtracting columns of figures in my head. And this is only the beginning. I haven't seen anything yet that I didn't like. Now, you just keep showing me your best pieces. There were a couple of things in the shop that caught my eye before you hustled me in here," Peter said as he strode toward the door leading into the shop, Sebastian baying at his heels. As he passed Lawrence he grinned and said, "You really hit the jackpot."

"I'm glad you're pleased," Lawrence said, watching Peter move between the display cases. When he glanced at Cella, he found she was staring at him.

"I don't know how to thank you for sending us Peter Petty," she said.

"Do I detect a note of sarcasm in your tone?"

"He has one redeeming social value," she said. "The Petty Museum."

"He does have the Petty Museum," Lawrence said softly. "Why do you dislike him?"

"I neither like him nor dislike him. He's a wonderful example of what used to be called Japanese ingenuity. If you can't make something yourself, steal it. In Petty's case, buy it. And keep on buying it. It's only the museum that makes his grabbiness bearable. At least the people who visit the

Petty Museum will enjoy the beauty of the ancient world," Cella said with a shrug.

Lawrence observed the cool detachment of the slender, graceful young woman. Petty's money didn't interest her. In a way, it put her off. "You underestimate Peter's taste," he said,

"He really has a fine and sensitive nature?"

"I'd put it slightly differently," Lawrence said. "I believe he thinks of himself as a Renaissance man."

"He is. A twentieth-century American version. He presumes there are no limits to what his money can buy." Cella looked closely at Lawrence. "Now, why do I have the impression that you have something on your mind?"

"I do," Lawrence said, oozing sincerity from every pore. "Reluctantly, I'm returning the earrings you lent me. My friend says they're exquisite, but she feels that drop earrings are wrong for her face. You know how women are." He opened his briefcase, took out the velvet box and handed it to Cella.

Cella opened the box and smiled at the earrings glowing in the soft light. They were as lovely as she remembered. "The Langobardic earrings."

"I am sorry to have wasted your time."

"Don't worry. They're just right for the contessa's face."

"I've a better idea. Peter will be miffed if you stop him from buying. So make a good-will gesture. Show him the Langobardic earrings. Ask an outrageous price. He'll believe they're even more special than they are. And you'll satisfy him and your father."

"And you."

Lawrence chuckled. "Well, yes, there is me to consider. My commission."

Cella's eyes meeting Lawrence's were clear and candid. "Which reminds me, did Dr. Jason Lord approve of the earrings?"

"Jason?" Suddenly Lawrence was all bells and whistles and screeching, screaming jolts, like a fast-moving train that was sharply braked. "What would Jason have to do with the earrings?"

"Ordinarily, nothing. But it occurred to me you might have suggested he vet them."

"Why would I do that? They're perfect. The gold is almost pure except for the smallest amount of silver that doesn't affect the color in the least. The artistry is perfect. Even the technique for making and soldering the gold wire baskets is of the type associated with the Langobard goldsmiths. Why would they need testing?''

"I have no idea," Cella said sweetly. She then added, "I had no idea you were such an authority on Langobardic earrings. I'm impressed. You sound like one of our friends, 'Pico' Cellini or Garsen Walsh. Or even your own son."

Lawrence blanched and looked around the room, anywhere except at Cella. He cursed himself. What an asinine blunder, to mouth the same words Jason had used.

"Probably I shouldn't be so impressed. You are an acknowledged authority on all periods of painting. Why not antique jewelry?" Cella noted his embarrassed confusion and smiled thinly. "Did I say something wrong? I seem to have disturbed you."

"I'm no authority, Cella. I simply read up on everything," Lawrence said too quickly. He hated being out of his depth.

"I admire how you keep up on things. You're a very well informed man, Lawrence. Another Renaissance man." Cella's smile didn't change, and before Lawrence could say anything, she left the room.

Peter Petty and Sebastian were standing beside a glass case.

"There! That's it! That's it! That's one of the pieces I missed," Peter said, pointing to a glass case in which a glorious gold-and-jeweled triple diadem was displayed on a white silk cloth in isolated splendor.

"What is it?" Peter asked. "It's fantastic!"

"It's believed to be a queen's headdress," Cella said, joining them. "Though it could have belonged to any woman of high birth."

"It's magnificent. There are jewels I don't recognize—not the emeralds and sapphires. What are they?"

"Exotic gems. Lapis lazuli, white opals, cornelians, agate and chalcedony. In modern terms, they're semiprecious stones," Sebastian said. "But the ancients adored them."

"They're beautiful," Peter said. "How old is it?"

"It comes from the city of Ur," Cella said quietly.

"Where?"

"You haven't heard of the city of Ur?"

"No. Sorry, I haven't."

"It's the same Ur of the Chaldees that's mentioned in the Bible," Cella said.

"I've never done much Bible reading. My mother did it for the whole family. But that doesn't mean I don't respect the good book. If this city is mentioned in the Bible, I'll take their word that it was quite a place," Peter said, full of good humor.

"The biblical scholars will appreciate your confidence. At any rate, the necklace comes from Ur. It is very old."

"How old?"

"The dating is around 2500 B.C.," Cella said. "That's about forty-five hundred years ago."

"How much is it?"

"It's not for sale," Cella answered.

"Cella!" Sebastian sputtered with astonishment.

"It isn't," Cella said with a cool smile. "Nor is anything else in the shop. Listen to me carefully, Mr. Peter Regis Petty. You are not Sears Roebuck, and we are not a wholly owned subsidiary that exists for the sole purpose of supplying you with automobile tires and batteries."

"Cella!" Sebastian almost shouted.

"I mean it, Father. Mr. Petty has bought quite enough for today."

"I'm sorry if I've offended you." Peter Petty had long ago accepted that there were paintings in the world that were simply not for sale—not to him or to anyone else—at any price. But that a piece of art should exist that was clearly for sale, but not for sale to him, put him off his stride.

"You haven't offended me. You forgot that we are collectors and dealers in ancient jewelry. Our inventory is limited by what we find in private collections, at auctions and from other dealers or sources that we alone have. It takes decades of constantly foraging the world to accumulate a collection of the caliber of The House of Uni. And to maintain it."

"I didn't think of that."

"You don't have to. I do. This is not costume jewelry. We can't call the factory in Hoboken and order two dozen rings, a half-dozen necklaces, some earrings, some brooches. And we do have other customers to consider."

Sebastian hovered over Cella like a storm cloud. "You're embarrassing Mr. Petty, Cella."

"I don't think so. Mr. Petty is a Renaissance man. One of the last of a dying breed. You're not embarrassed, are you, Peter? You do understand?" Cella smiled at Peter Petty as only she could smile, and placed the box with the Langobardic earrings on the counter.

Peter was winded. The rules had suddenly changed. No one had ever refused his money. His face mirrored his confusion. From the time he'd reached puberty, the most ravishing creatures in the world—of both sexes—had offered themselves for his amusement. Women of all ages, races, colors—daughters, mothers, wives—women proud of their undeniable appeal, were eager to please him in any way he might wish. Usually he wanted little from them. Women were not his passion. Art was. Until Cella smiled at him.

She engulfed him. She could no more be ignored than the tides could ignore the moon. How splendid she was! More splendid than even the most glorious jewelry in the store. Her beauty had the irresistible appeal of great art. But Cella was living flesh and blood. Catching his breath, Peter knew he wanted her more than he had ever wanted anything in his entire life. A series of wild possibilities quickly passed through his mind. Buy The House of Uni. No! Cella's father—he'd known greedy men like Sebastian from childhood—would leap at his offer. But not Cella. She wouldn't agree at any price. Worse, she'd be offended. Offer her the position of director of the Petty Museum. No! She'd never accept the position. And wouldn't thank him for offering it. He had to think of something, do something. Name the— He stopped himself. Yes! She might like that.

"I do see what you mean," he said. He was not the grandson of Rex Regis Petty for nothing. Cella had called him a Renaissance man. The least he could do was behave as he imagined such a man might. "I know you have other customers to consider. But you are aware I'm not buying for my personal collection. I'm buying your beautiful jewelry for the Petty Museum."

"That's why I agreed to sell you as much as we have. But the world is larger than the Petty Museum. There are other museums as well."

"The Getty?" Peter pounced.

"Other museums," Cella repeated.

Lawrence had been standing in the doorway listening to the dialogue. Now he said, almost admiringly, "You have very high principles, Cella."

"Only a few. But those I have are engraved in old gold."

"Just show Peter the Langobardic earrings and we'll call it a day," he said.

Cella and Lawrence exchanged glances like crossed swords. Then Lawrence deliberately winked.

In spite of herself, Cella couldn't help laughing.

"I like your laugh," Peter murmured. "It sounds like water in a mountain stream."

Lawrence, ever the diplomat, interrupted before anyone could react to Peter's surprising compliment. "Peter, in that box are a pair of stunning Langobardic earrings. There are only three other pairs like it in the world. They are very rare. If Cella permits you to see them, and you like them, that should do it for today. We have other dealers to see.''

Peter Petty thought this over, and in the light of his strange new emotions, he decided Lawrence was right. There was always another day for buying. And another reason to see Cella Taggard. "Agreed," he said, his eyes fixed on Cella.

Cella responded to Peter Petty's blatant admiration by opening the box. Peter leaned over and studied the Langobardic earrings. He glowered. He pursed his lips. He grunted. Squinted. Sebastian scowled.

"How much?" Peter asked.

Before Cella could answer, Lawrence intervened. "A half million.''

"For a pair of earrings?" Peter raised his eyebrows. It was the first time he'd questioned a price since he arrived, but his inherited shrewdness had come into play. Instinctively he knew it was wiser from now on to allow Lawrence to convince him of the value of the earrings. Cella would respect him more if he were difficult than if he followed his natural inclination and said, "Magnificent! I'll take them.''

"I told you they are very rare, very special," Lawrence said. "J.P. Morgan had one of the better examples. Almost as fine as these. He donated them to the Metropolitan.''

"Ah, J.P. and the Met. I'd be in good company," said Peter. "How old are they?''

"A.D. fifth century," Sebastian said.

"Sold," said Peter, glancing at Cella for approval. Although she didn't know it, he had bought the very rare, very special earrings for her. When the time was right, he'd give them to her.

That settled, Peter said, "Miss Taggard . . . may I call you Cella?" At her nod, he said, "Cella!" The awe in his voice made her name sound almost holy. He bit his lower lip to keep from saying more. There was an awkward pause before he continued. "Cella, Mr. Taggard, I would like you both to come to the gala I'm giving in September to celebrate the opening of a new wing in the Petty Museum. I think you'll be pleased with what I'm doing.''

"A gala, Peter? You never mentioned this," Lawrence interrupted nervously.

"I don't tell you everything, Lawrence. Any more than you tell me everything," Peter said, still looking at Cella. "I'm making up the Class A invitation list now. There'll be several hundred people. And for those who don't have their own planes, the museum will supply Lear jets. Will you come? Please?''

"Of course," Sebastian said smoothly. "We'd be honored to attend such an important event."

"That's wonderful! The wing will have two parts. You see, I'm putting together a collection of ancient Aegean artifacts and art. It's art even older than Protoattic pieces.''

"Good Lord! Older than Protoattic. That's the rarest of the rare. Where did you find the pieces?" Lawrence asked.

"I have my sources, Lawrence." Petty was enjoying Lord's discomfort.

"What have you bought?"

"I'm not saying. But the wing will be dedicated to ancient Hellenistic art and ancient jewelry." Peter gave Cella a sunny smile. "I can't thank you enough. This jewelry and my Aegean collection will make the Petty Museum a force to be reckoned with in the art world. Would you be kind enough to have the jewelry packaged and waiting for me? The Brinks' people and I will pick it up Friday, before I fly back to Dallas. I'm staying at The Helmsley Palace. If you'll leave word for me there as to the exact cost of my purchases, I'll have the museum's bank prepare a cashier's check.''

After much handshaking and good will, Peter sauntered toward the door. Lawrence watched him go, a look of consternation on his face.

"Peter, we're seeing Schmirderer tomorrow," he suddenly called out. "Remember—old and exotic watches. At eleven.''

Peter nodded. "I remember," he said and opened the door.

"Peter?" Lawrence called again.

"Yes?"

"Oh—nothing," Lawrence said.

Peter gazed at Lawrence. "Did I forget something? Oh! I did. I'm sorry, Lawrence. Yes, you are on the guest list too." With that he left the store.

Cella smothered her laughter. Peter Regis Petty was not quite the domesticated little lamb tied up with pink ribbons that Lawrence had described.

"He wasn't here a full hour, and he spent close to seven million dollars," Sebastian said with a glaze over his eyes.

Lawrence Lord glowed. "And he'll be back for more.''

"And more," Cella said.

"Why not?" Lord's manner became looser, more confiding. "You can space him out over the years. The shop will make a tremendous amount of money.''

"It's nice, the way you have our best interests at heart," Cella said.

"Why not? If you make money, I make money. And, Cella, one way or another, the Petty Museum will benefit. I've got to run. I have to catch the shuttle for Boston. I'm giving a lecture tomorrow at Harvard." He smiled and shook his head ruefully. "A lot of work for a few thousand dollars." He sighed. "But it makes other miracles possible. Like Peter Regis Petty. Sebastian, I'll be by Friday afternoon for my commission. And I trust you. I don't need a cashier's check. Good-bye, Cella." Lawrence waved a mock salute as he left the shop.

The moment the door clicked shut, Sebastian said reverently, "This is by far the biggest single day in the history of The House of Uni. Peter Petty's account alone could carry the shop."

Cella spun about, her face flushed with fury. "Forget Petty! He's just rich. That bastard Lawrence did take the earrings to Jason Lord."

"How can you be sure?"

"He gave me a description of how the earrings were made. He told me the gold contained a small amount of silver. The technique for making and soldering the gold wire was of the type associated with the Langobard goldsmiths. He said—"

"That's enough. Why did he do it?"

"I don't know. He's up to something. I don't know what, but we'll find out soon enough. And whatever it is, I have a nasty feeling we won't like it."

Since her mother's death, Sebastian was acknowledged as the head of the family. It was up to him to guide them, to say how they should handle the threat from either Lawrence or Jason Lord. If a threat existed. She waited, her attention fixed on her father. But as the moments passed, the frozen expression on his face told her that now, in this matter, he was baffled. Actually frightened. Cella took a deep breath. It was up to her. She'd been ducking the responsibility for too long. She knew Lawrence Lord, and until now, she had thought she understood the man. But Jason Lord was a mystery. As soon as possible she must meet the eminent doctor. Once she did, she would trust her instincts to judge how dangerous he was to the family. Was he lurking in the shadows, waiting to pounce? Or was he merely another denizen of the art world running his own private scam? She had a strong sense of foreboding that time was running out. Whatever she did had to be done soon.

════ Chapter Sixteen ════

The VIP parking lot at the Metropolitan Museum of Art was choked with limousines: Rolls-Royces, stretch Cadillacs and even a few vintage Mercedes 600s. As usual, the Angels were prompt. As usual, Cella was late. It had completely slipped her mind that today was the day when the Angels of the Arts previewed their most recent donations to the Metropolitan. She must have a mental block against going to the meetings. She walked quickly through the spacious lobby of the Met, down the hall, turned right and headed toward the special room reserved for the meetings of the Angels. She would slip in unobtrusively. Contrary to most of the Angels, she was not inclined to make an entrance.

The Angels were truly Olympian in their outlook. Exclusive yet democratic. They accepted as members women of humble origin who had made fortunes in the cosmetic, fashion and perfume industries or women who had the intelligence and luck to marry multimillionaires. But a countess who was a second cousin—once removed—of Queen Elizabeth II of England had been expelled after six months for not paying her dues. At that, the dues were more the queen's style. It cost a cool hundred thousand to become an Angel of the Arts, and the annual dues were twenty-four thousand. Despite the high initiation fee and dues, membership in the Angels, which was restricted to one hundred well-heeled women, had a waiting list that stretched from Manhattan to the moon. Only death or the surrender of a New York City address created a vacancy.

Cella tiptoed into the hushed room, seating herself on a vacant sofa against the rear wall. The meeting was drawing to a close. The funds for the acquisitions now on view had come from the annual dues, plus gifts—mostly donations from foundations controlled by the families of Angel members.

202

There were ancient Hellenistic pottery, the bust of a Roman emperor, a kouros, a Minoan fresco, and five inspired pieces of ancient jewelry. One of them, a golden glove, brought a mist to Cella's eyes.

Cella surveyed the groups of Saint Laurents, Lagerfelds, Valentinos, Geoffrey Beenes, Armanis, Ungaros, Montanas—the list read like a Who's Who of *Women's Wear Daily*—that were gazing in rapt attention at Charles Grimm while he held forth on the pieces that surrounded him on the small, raised platform. Cella wondered if the women actually heard a word Charles said as they sneaked sideways glances at one another's shoulder lines and waistlines, buttons, embroidery and seams, estimating how high was their high style.

"We're not simply a collection of paintings," Charles was saying. "The Metropolitan has eighteen departments, millions of visitors annually, hundreds of employees. We're an encyclopedic institution, a national museum containing the cultural history of the world. That's why the antiquities section requires expansion . . ."

"You mean you could use more money, Dr. Grimm?" an Ungaro asked.

"Yes, my dear Mrs. Levin. Which is why I am eternally grateful to you, and all the Angels of the Arts, for your generous donations to the antiquities wing," Charles said earnestly. "With your help we have been able to add to our collection. Pottery. Weaponry. Vessels of all kinds. Jewelry. Kouros . . ."

"What are kouros?" a Lagerfeld tweeted from a deep chair near the platform.

The cognoscenti laughed indulgently. This Lagerfeld regularly put her foot in her mouth. But since her husband, the demolitions tycoon, had practically endowed an entire wing, Lagerfeld's foot was considered Cinderella size.

"Kouros is sculpture, madam," Charles said briskly. He indicated a small, graceful male musician carved in marble and blowing a double flute, standing on a table on the platform. "This is a kouros. From the island of Keros. About twenty-five hundred B.C. We were able to purchase it with your recent donation." He fumbled, "I mean the donation of the Angels of the Arts."

Cella's eyes gleamed with amusement. It wasn't a Cycladian maiden, but it was another of Victor's triumphs.

There were oohs and aahs as the Angels of the Arts, moving as one woman, leaned forward to see what was in the glass étagère behind Charles. The glass case was on wheels, and Charles pushed it forward.

"Look at that glove," a Montana gasped. "Did we buy that?"

"No, madam. That would have cost considerably more than even your generous donations permitted. It was donated to the museum by the de Rochmont foundation."

The Saint Laurent who represented the de Rochmont foundation beamed.

The golden glove was indeed extraordinary. It was made of gold mesh, held at the wrist by a chain circlet and clasped over the fingers by four golden rings, one for every finger except the thumb.

"We believe it was part of the dowry of a princess," Charles said, glowing with pride.

"I wish my father had seen it," murmured a Valentino. "Those old kings sure knew how to treat their kids."

"Ladies," Charles said, "if you'd like to study more closely the splendid works your generous donations have added to the antiquities section, please come to the platform. Otherwise we can adjourn for the day."

The chairs were pushed back, and here and there women rose to their feet, some moving to the platform to study the jewelry.

"Cella, darling, I adore your outfit," an Armani said, drifting over. "Where did you assemble it?"

"Do you mean my skirt and sweater?"

"Yes. And how clever of you to wear an alpaca coat. So much smarter than reversible sable. You look very English village." She arched one eyebrow. "You sly thing. Everything English is 'in.' "

"Darling!" said an Ungaro, grasping Armani by the arm. "Are you coming to the Carlisle for lunch?"

"You joining us, Cella?"

"Sorry. It's back to the shop for me. I'm a working stiff."

"Some working stiff," the Armani teased. "The other day Juliana showed me that gold chain you're wearing. It's from Babylonia—1000 B.C. A mere quarter of a million." The Armani sashayed off.

Cella glanced at the Angels chirping at each other in the aisle and milling around the étagère. There were too many women obstructing her view of the golden glove, but in her mind she saw it clearly, perfectly.

Suddenly she was jolted out of her reverie by a dear, familiar voice. She glanced around the room, then at the doorway and gasped. There was Anton, signaling her. She rose from her seat and hurried toward the door.

"Anton! You're home!" Cella said as their fingers entwined, her heart pounding unreasonably. Then she stepped back to study him, as though to reassure herself it was really him. Every detail of his appearance leaped out at her. His straight black hair, his thick, slightly Satanic eyebrows, his brilliant dark eyes that took in everything. How wonderful he looked! So darkly handsome and so much his own man.

"How did you know I was here? Who let you in? You hardly look like an Angel." She glanced at the Burberry trenchcoat worn over his shoulders like a cape, his Irish wool sweater, brown twill pants, Wallaby desert boots.

"Juliana told me you were here. The door was open so I walked in. No one said, 'Boo.' "

Cella glanced around the almost empty room. There were still a few Angels chattering in the aisle and oohing around the étagère. Charles Grimm was enthusiastically lecturing a silky, sexy red Ralph Lauren suit, who returned the compliment by flirting outrageously.

"The Angels donated the queen's golden glove to the museum," she whispered to Anton as they stepped out of the meeting room.

"Ah. The daughter of the Baroness de Rochmont," he said, gripping her arm and edging her along.

Cella's eyes filled with love for him. "You remember everything."

"If it concerns you, I do."

"It was the de Rochmont foundation," Cella said.

"Your mother created the glove especially for the Metropolitan. She always wanted them to have it."

"But the de Rochmonts offered Sebastian more."

"Yes, but now the Met does have it. The wheels of the gods grind slowly," Anton said as they walked through the museum. "Would you like lunch? A walk in the park? Or love in the afternoon?"

He stared at her as if he hadn't seen her for years. She stared back and her mouth went dry as he bent his head toward hers. His tongue slid past her lips to touch hers, and for an instant the blood rushing through her made her dizzy. Her body swayed, arching against him, feeling his excitement as intense as her own. Abruptly she pulled back, extricating herself from his arms. She gazed up at him. "Anton," she whispered, shaking her head to clear it. She reached up to touch his sensual lips with two fingers. "I'm so glad to see you."

"And I you. That's why I suggested love in the afternoon."

"I can't. Sebastian may be practicing that art form with little Dolly Drop Drawers. She's in town and they were lunching together. Until he returns, the shop is in my care." Cella paused. "You have no idea how much has happened in the short time you've been away. And how much I missed having you to talk to."

"Only to talk to?"

"Only for everything. But we do have to talk."

"Did you miss me more than usual?" Anton probed as they continued to pace through the museum.

Cella smiled almost shyly. "It seems so." And in fact it was so. In the last year her feeling for Anton had grown even deeper. He was now so much a part of her that she felt only half alive without him.

Their fingers tightened. "I have things to tell you too," Anton said soberly. "But maybe it's better if you begin first."

"Things about Paris? I know you saw Victor. I called him, but I missed you. He said you'd already left for Budapest."

"I saw Uncle Victor and we worked everything out. And I did go on to Budapest. That was the easy part."

"I tried to reach you at the Budapest Hilton, but they said you'd checked out. Victor didn't know where you'd gone. Where did you go?" Cella felt a spurt of ridiculous jealousy.

"To Istanbul."

"Istanbul? Why? What's in Istanbul for you? Besides the Blue Mosque?"

"I didn't go for me. I went for you. But that comes later. First tell me what's happened here."

Cella's eyes searched his face as though they were alone, not standing in the middle of a jostling crowd of people. She had known Anton all her life, but he never ceased to surprise her. Yet he was absolutely dependable in every circumstance. God! How she needed him now!

"It's hard to know where to begin," she said.

Anton saw that her face was pale and her violet eyes had darkened with anxiety.

"Begin at the beginning. What's troubling you?"

Cella took a deep breath and plunged in. By a chain of unlikely connections, she explained, she was now living with a horde of dark question marks hovering over her. She spoke quickly and resolutely, filling him in on her meeting with Ben

Stein, on the entire Lord family—Lawrence, Jason and Marina—on their involvement with the Langobardic earrings.

Anton's face was inscrutable as he listened quietly. When she seemed to have finished, he said, "That's quite a bit of news. Is there anything else?"

Cella stared at him, then shook herself. "Oh, yes. I almost forgot. There's been so much to tell. You know we keep a very low profile. But a week ago today, the first time in the history of The House of Uni, someone tried to break into the shop. There was an attempted robbery." They were standing on the wide steps of the Met now, and the wind whipped around Cella's legs and tugged her hair.

Anton's eyes were fixed on her face, his interest fully engaged. "That's the second thing you've told me that I truly don't like."

"What was the first?"

"Jason Lord. You're right. His good will is too blatant. Sebastian's an idiot for having started up with Marina."

"And he won't stop. Do you think Jason Lord had something to do with the attempted break-in?"

Anton waited until they had crossed Fifth Avenue and were striding toward Madison Avenue before he answered her. "No. He's certainly tested the Langobardic earrings. But I'm sure the attempted break-in leads to Istanbul. I didn't think it would happen so soon."

Cella turned to him. "What are you talking about?"

"Abdul Hamid. I went to Istanbul to meet with him."

"Abdul Hamid? I remember that name." Cella stared at Anton, startled. "Our families did business with him—didn't they?"

"Our families made him so rich he's no longer in business. He's Turkey's minister of culture and archaeology."

Cella swallowed. "My God! Our Abdul Hamid, minister of culture? Why were you seeing him?"

"The Aphrodite necklace that you bought at Northbie's auction."

Cella felt the tension flowing through her body. She tightened her grip on Anton's arm, waiting for the bombshell to explode.

"Hamid claims it's the necklace that belonged to the woman who was actually the goddess Aphrodite." Anton then went on to recount in detail everything that had happened on his trip abroad, from his meeting with Maurice Wheelock in Budapest to his flight back with Toby Phipps.

Cella listened, occasionally giving Anton a sideways

glance. Otherwise her face remained quiet. She waited until he finished, then asked, "Are you sure you don't think Jason Lord is connected in some way? To the Aphrodite? To the attempted break-in?"

"I'm sure. Don't be misled because his secretary had a meeting with Abdul the day I left Istanbul." Anton's face was pale. "Dr. Jason Lord is dangerous, but attempted robbery isn't his style. He has other fish to fry."

"Then whose style is it?"

"Abdul was not always as public-spirited as he's become since he's grown rich," Anton remarked cynically. "Now he's concerned with Turkey's prestige, with Turkey taking its high place as the cradle of Western civilization. Above that of Greece. So the Aphrodite necklace has political as well as cultural significance." Anton stopped and looked down at Cella. "Somehow he found out that The House of Uni bought the necklace at Northbie's auction, and . . ."

"Who told him?"

"Dearest, as Maurice Wheelock so aptly said, there are no secrets in the art world. It could have been anyone. Even one of your Angels. Americans and Europeans are not the only members. If I remember, there are two Saudi princesses. There may even be a Turkish relative of Abdul's among them."

Cella nodded. "And Abdul would like the necklace back."

"He'd like it back so much that he mentioned en passant that if Sebastian proved too unreasonable, an attempt might be made—nothing that he'd have anything to do with, of course. Naturally not. But some rabid Turkish nationalist might try to steal it."

"And attempt a break-in of the shop," Cella said in a low voice. "So Abdul was behind that." She frowned. "How could he be so foolish? The shop is as difficult to break into as Fort Knox."

"Abdul isn't foolish. Let us say he's giving warning," Anton said grimly. "Believe me, if he puts his mind to it, he can think of far more effective ways of regaining the necklace than what strikes me as a makeshift attempted break-in. And with it all, Abdul will still keep his hands clean."

Cella took this in. "I think we'd better talk to Sebastian. With luck, he may simply have had lunch with Dolly. And no more. If so, he'll be back at the shop."

When Cella and Anton arrived at The House of Uni, Sebastian was there busily taking stock inventory.

"Anton! Juliana told me you'd returned. I'm delighted you're back. It should do wonders for Cella's insomnia." Sebastian smiled at Anton. Then, bubbling with good spirits, he turned to Cella. "I have some fascinating news for you. I'm seeing Darlene tonight for dinner. Lunch was too hurried—she had a fitting appointment at Bergdorf's. We had no time to talk. But tonight we'll have all night to talk."

"Talk about what?" Cella asked.

"About the Aphrodite necklace. What else?"

Cella hoped she maintained a neutral expression. "How much did she offer this time?"

"You won't believe it." Sebastian paused for dramatic effect, then remarked almost casually, "Four million dollars."

There was silence in the shop. At last Cella said, with the same offhand casualness, "Where's Juliana?"

"Delivering some earrings," Sebastian answered peevishly. "Didn't you hear what I said?"

"Yes. Dolly Drop Drawers offered four million dollars for the Aphrodite necklace. So? The offer is academic."

"Four million dollars is never academic."

"Well, for one thing, I thought you did not intend to sell the necklace until the Astarte was completed. Or am I wrong?"

"No. Darlene's offer adds to my commitment to the Astarte. I think the longer she has to wait for the Aphrodite, the more she'll offer. It's a pleasure to watch the number in front of all those zeros rise." Sebastian chuckled. "It is a tempting offer, though."

"Tempting or not, you can't sell the Aphrodite to her," Cella said evenly. "Not now. Not ever."

"What are you talking about?" Sebastian demanded. "If I choose to, I can sell it to Mrs. Grundy."

"You can't. Anton has something to tell you."

For the second time that day, Anton told the story of his experience in Budapest and later in Istanbul. Unlike Cella, who had listened without the flicker of an eyelash, Sebastian could not hide the twitching of his muscles in a spurt of anger, or his indignation in the pulling on his hair and the movements of his hands. Twice Cella had to restrain him from interrupting.

When Anton came to the end of his story, he summed up its consequences. "Since Abdul has offered a substantial reward for the return of the Aphrodite necklace, it's now a field day for lunatics. Every crazy, every assassin, with or without a cause, will be looking for it. And the reward. To say nothing of the Turkish secret service. And Turkish chauvinists. Who, as Abdul suggested, would not stop at stealing. Or worse.''

''You mean it was Abdul's people who tried to break into the shop?'' Sebastian asked uneasily.

''I can't prove it and he'd deny it, but I think that's the case. I don't believe he expected to succeed this time. But he wants you to know he means business. I think it's essential you meet with him. Strike a bargain and get rid of the Aphrodite as soon as possible,'' Anton said firmly.

''You said he is offering ten million dollars?'' Sebastian asked. ''That's a nice price.''

Anton corrected him. ''I said that was the price he mentioned to start the publicity rolling. The actual price must be negotiated. Abdul knows what you paid Northbie's. He'll permit a reasonable profit.''

Sebastian's laugh had an edge to it. ''Very generous. Well, you can tell him, 'Thanks, but no thanks.' ''

''Father—stop it!'' Cella said sharply. ''Abdul Hamid is not Darlene Schiller. You can't play footsies with him. And to ignore him is to ask for trouble.''

''I don't think so. With the worldwide publicity that seems to be coming—and that Abdul brought on himself by offering ten million—if he tries to pull anything, he'll have television coverage from here to Istanbul. As for us, we'll sell the Aphrodite for an astronomical price—when we're good and ready. Darlene herself could go to ten. And, by association, the Astarte will not do badly either. Another version of the goddess, another ten million.'' He glanced at his watch. ''I have to change for the evening. Cella, will you close the shop? I told Juliana to go home after making the delivery.'' Ignoring Cella's protest, Sebastian hurried through the door in the rear of the store that led to the private staircase to their apartment.

''Sebastian's greed is becoming dangerous,'' Anton said. ''He completely underestimates the man.''

''I know. All we need are a few more attempted break-ins. And the subsequent publicity. Heaven knows what else Abdul might come up with.''

''There is always kidnapping.''

''Abdul wouldn't! He's an old family friend.''

''*Was* an old family friend. Now he's Minister of Culture, et cetera. He's the same. But he's different.''

Cella took a deep breath. ''Between Abdul Hamid and Dr. Jason Lord, I am leading a full, rich life.'' She glanced at her watch. "Darling, I must close up shop now. He's expecting me at five."

"Who's expecting you at five?"

"The eminent Dr. Jason Lord."

"You're seeing Lord? Why?" Anton was obviously concerned. "I told you not to worry about Emory's visit to Abdul. I have a hunch about that. Once the Aphrodite began to gain celebrity, I believe Lord sent Emory to check its authenticity. The Cycladic idols were my first clue. He's scratching around for something to smear the reputation of the Vilanovas. Or the Taggards."

"You are following in my footsteps," Cella said bitterly.

"Then relax. No matter what Lord hoped for, Emory brought him back no satisfaction. Abdul will swear in blood that the necklace is the real thing."

"I'm thankful for small blessings. But the Aphrodite was not my reason for wanting to see him. I made the appointment last week after listening to Marina's sermon on how much he admires us. I want to estimate for myself how much of a threat—or not—he is to the family. That is, if Sebastian actually marries Marina. His admiration gives me the jitters. Like you, I think he's after blood. Our blood."

"I'll go with you."

"No. That would make him suspicious."

Anton's mouth tightened. "I don't like it. And you can't keep that appointment. Darling, I just got home. I thought . . ."

"You thought rightly. I'll come straight to your apartment after I see him. And then I'll welcome you properly. With all the ancient rites of our people."

"After seeing Jason Lord?" He shook his head. "You'll be in no mood to give an Etruscan welcome."

Cella molded herself to Anton's body. "With you, my darling, I'm always in the mood."

Chapter Seventeen

Cella sat on the edge of her seat in the immaculate reception room of Dr. Jason Lord's office. The walls, wooden floor and ceiling of the office were painted a spotless hospital white. Except for several small, hard, leather-covered couches and a few very simply framed photographs of ancient artifacts, the area was bare, almost spartan. From under half-closed eyes Cella watched the man she assumed was Emory Portland as he typed. Remembering Anton's report of Toby's infatuation, she wasn't surprised at what she saw. Emory was elegantly small-boned, with narrow shoulders, thin wrists and delicate hands. He had the perfectly proportioned limpid features and the gentle expression of a Raphael madonna. But beneath the deceptive exterior Cella sensed a tough, heartless man who had learned his "street smarts" the hard way—and survived. Poor elephantine Toby, she mused. So rich, so worldly, so spoiled, so silly to fall in love with the likes of Emory.

But what did having Emory say about Jason Lord, about his own capacity for deception? It said that he had selected his secretary with calculated shrewdness. Here was the perfect intermediary for Jason when he either was too busy or felt his own presence would be intrusive. Emory was so unlike Jason, so appealing and seemingly guileless. He could ask all kinds of leading questions without seeming to probe. Of course, to Abdul Hamid, the "pretty boy" would be entirely transparent. But not many had Abdul's canniness. The more Cella watched Emory, the less she relished the interview ahead.

The intercom on his desk lit up and without stopping typing he said, "Dr. Lord will see you now. Through that door." He motioned with his head toward a clean white trimless door that Cella had thought was a wall panel.

When she entered, Jason Lord stood up and came around

his desk with his hand outstretched to welcome her. At the sight of him, Cella was again struck by his physical presence. He was as he had seemed on television. Very tall, inches over six feet, probably as tall as Anton, but with the huge, powerful body she associated with professional athletes. Although he wore a button-down white shirt and a tie, she could see the hard muscles running from his neck to his shoulders. He was a man to reckon with, all sinewy strength, exuding a potential for passion and—was it menace or simply her overwrought imagination? His golden hair was tangled, almost as though he'd forgotten to comb it that morning. His features were rugged and arresting, not the pale cloistered look one expected of an intellectual. To her amazement, Cella found that for an instant she was unwilling to look away. His wide mouth was lifted in a tantalizing smile, so bold, so provocative, it almost made her flinch. He wasn't wearing his camouflage glasses, and she felt herself being appraised by quick, intelligent eyes; strange eyes that sparked blue flames and blue ice. Yet for all his dazzling masculinity, Cella sensed an austerity and aloofness in the man, a brooding darkness that made her wary. The charm of his smile seemed a shade too practiced to be natural.

"Miss Taggard," he said. "At last we meet."

"Hello, Dr. Lord." Cella gave him an incandescent smile. "Yes, I think it's high time we met."

Jason stood as though rooted to the spot. He seemed to be searching for appropriate words, then stepped back, suddenly unwilling to continue the close contact for too long. "Please sit down," he said, nodding toward the twin Barcelona chairs facing his desk. "And call me Jason."

He returned to his own chair behind the desk, relieved to put his desk between them. The impact he felt at the first sight of Cella had hit him in the pit of his stomach, and the shock had sped down to his legs. He was so conscious of her femaleness that he was alarmed.

Cella lowered herself into the chair and crossed her legs, her skirt rising a shade above her knees. "And you must call me Cella," she said.

"Agreed, Cella," he said, surprised that his voice sounded normal and steady.

Cella glanced around the office, admiring its austere yet elegant modernity. "My compliments. Along with your professional interest in the ancient world, you also have an eye for the finest in modern furniture."

Jason cleared his throat. "Originally I studied to be an architect. The International School."

Cella gave him a puzzled look. "That's a long way from archiometry."

"I know. I changed my mind," Jason said, wondering why he'd mentioned his early dream. He arched a blond eyebrow and his expression became questioning. "Why are you staring at me?"

"I could say the same for you. You're not quite what I expected—although I did see you on television."

"You're not what I expected either."

"Worse or better or merely different?"

"Infinitely better."

"You too. Good!" Without her being aware of it, her smile became easier, almost intimate. "We start on a better footing. Though I don't know how it could be much better than it was. We've been told—my father and I—that you have very nice things to say about The House of Uni. Praise coming from someone with your high reputation is a real compliment. Like you, we're aware that art fraud is as old as art itself. It's a pleasure for us to know that you acknowledge our standard of ethics is as high as your own."

"It is," Jason said. "I've respected your dedication for a long time. The items of jewelry you sell are among the very few pieces I regard as above question."

"That's why I'm here. I wanted to say thank you."

"No need. It's only what I know to be true." Jason studied Cella with undisguised admiration. "Corruption is so widespread. Art is the new stock market, the place to make a killing. Inevitably art and big money fall into each other's arms. That's why the atmosphere today is ripe for an explosion of forgers and charlatans panting to satisfy the buy orders of the rich."

"Proving that the law of supply and demand is in good working order. The demand for ancient art has far outstripped the supply, so forgers work overtime."

"Time and a half. And double time on Sundays."

"Only the other day I heard that a new workshop in Cyprus is turning out ancient gold amulets, pendants, rings—dating back to 1000 B.C.," Cella remarked, laughter playing around her eyes.

Jason grinned. "I heard the same story. As Barnum said, there's a sucker born every minute. And today the boom in suckers is in the art market." He shook his head with amused superiority. "Did you know that a high-tech silver factory on

Rhodes is making early Christian silver? Presumably from the third and fourth centuries. Cups, rings, church jewelry and the like.''

"I missed that one. Today's forgers are very ambitious.'' To her surprise, Cella was enjoying gossiping with Jason. "The art world. It's the best show in town if you know where to look.''

"Quite so. The shams and chicanery would be pure comedy if the results weren't so disastrous.''

Cella's smile acknowleged their rapport. It was going better than she dared to hope. The sinister Dr. Jason Lord was perhaps not so sinister. But then she felt a tensing in her body, knowing full well what she had shied away from; how she had sidestepped the real reason she wanted to meet Jason Lord. She could no longer avoid it.

"By the way," she said, "I wonder if you can answer a question people often ask me.''

"I'll try." Jason's eyes focused on her expectantly, kindly.

"If a forgery fools everyone—even the experts—why isn't it as valid as the work it pretends to be?''

A sternness crept into Jason's face. When he spoke his voice was no longer warm. "Personally, I do not believe that important art frauds can go undetected forever. I'll give you an example. Take the Cycladian maidens. I spoke about them on television, as you know.''

"It was fascinating," Cella said, thinking of the Langobardic earrings and that she must tread carefully. They had struck a cordial note and she wanted to keep it that way.

"You know my opinion of the Cycladian maidens," Jason said, looking at her reflectively. "The darlings of museums and the monied collectors. Those statues were universally accepted as genuine for some twenty-odd years." He slapped the desk with a heavy hand to punctuate his point. "Now the farce is ending. When I finish, no respectable collector or museum will dare show them. Unless they plan an exhibition of frauds. Admittedly the Cycladian maidens are exceptionally well executed frauds. But they are frauds.''

"One of those statues was used to kill Phillip Mckay," Cella said quietly.

"I've a theory about that too." Jason's tone grew harsher. "Phillip was a good man. It's a pity. But I have every confidence in Lieutenant Stein, the detective in charge of the investigation. I know the man. He'll catch the murderer. And when he does, I will denounce him.''

Cella felt as though she were stepping sideways through a

narrow pass. "I agree that in this case the fraud was detectable." Cella's tone of voice became diplomatic. "But there's something else to consider. Think of the beauty of the statues. Viewing them has given thousands of people great pleasure for many years."

"A spurious pleasure. I believe art collecting is akin to a love affair. The pleasure one gets from art is like the pleasure a man gets from a woman he loves. But when the art you love is a fraud, it's like discovering that your love has been unfaithful." He paused. "What remains is sordid, not beautiful." As Jason talked his voice grew still harsher and more intense. He placed both hands flat on the desk and held them rigidly in place. "In the end the lie destroys the love, and the beauty grows ugly. A piece of fraudulent art is simply another kind of cheating on one's love."

Cella's perplexity flashed across her face. The idea of fidelity was not one that the Etruscans were attuned to. "You think of forgery as the equivalent of a lover's infidelity?"

"I do."

Cella was quiet for a moment, making minute adjustments in her own thinking. Recently she'd been sifting through a whole range of new and possessive feelings about Anton which made her impatient with herself. At last she said, half mockingly, "Sometimes I feel that the goddess of love has a penchant for fraud. Isn't so much of what we love dressed up by our own imagination, by our illusions? And if we find on occasion that what we invented isn't true, how can we complain? Truth is for physicists. Mathematicians. But dreams, illusion, beauty—wouldn't you say they belong to the realm of poets? Of artists?" Her expression was obliging, the look of someone who understands. "And of lovers?"

Jason's voice took on unexpected animation; there was vigor and meaning in his tone, as though he'd given the subject a great deal of thought. "All right. Let's go back to your original question. Suppose a fake can be so good it is beyond detection. You asked what difference does that make."

"Yes. Suppose the fraud is so good it's never discovered, not even by the most sophisticated technology." Cella met Jason's eyes, blue and icy, increasing her sense of disquiet and foreboding. "Consider the possibility that a forger might possess immense technical skill, erudition and a feeling for the time in which the work was created. Then detection becomes virtually impossible. In that case, if it's beautiful, why isn't it true?"

Jason watched Cella, a small, tolerant smile on his lips.

"Your point is well taken. I agree that a great forgery may be beautiful and true to itself in its beauty. But it's the lie a forgery tells us about our humanness which concerns me." His tone was as serious as his face had become. "For me, it comes down to the value of truth in every sphere of life. In art. In science. In living. Fraudulent art is a lie about our past. Think of Troy in flames—the topless towers of Ilium burning for Helen. Think of Iphigenia sacrificed by her father to the winds. Of Euripides eaten by dogs. Of the pirates of Mycenae who laughed when they killed and looted the towns of women, horses and sheep. Think of fearless kings. Vengeful daughters. Tragic queens. What has come out of all this human striving? And suffering? Daring philosophy. Splendid art. Majestic poetry. Nothing less than the civilization of half the world."

"It is called the Heroic Age," Cella said softly.

"And it was heroic." Jason's eyes flickered. "How can even a genius re-create the spirit of that time? A time known only by hearsay."

Cella felt the atmosphere growing strained, but her urge to continue was too strong to resist. "If one understood the age and the people, why would it be false?"

"How can one understand what one hasn't lived? How can anyone today who lives with air conditioning and flies in a jet plane understand?"

"Understand the mystery that pours out of the olive groves? Of those who danced there in the moonlight? Or the passion of men and women making love at the harvest festivals? How can they understand the ardor of the chants in the temples?" Cella sounded bemused. "They can. If they know the time."

"It's impossible," Jason said firmly, patiently seated like his own effigy, his eyes half closed. A disjointed silence followed until he spoke again. "There is no starting point, nothing in common. Their humor wasn't our humor. Their brutality wasn't our orderly detective-story brutality. Their passion wasn't our cliché romances. All the human emotions are found in the ancients' art, before they were worn thin by today's conformity."

To the untrained eye, Cella appeared calm and self-contained. She uncrossed her legs and leaned back in her chair, but Jason's words were unnerving. They were too much an echo of her own feelings. "Sometimes I think a teaspoon of their emotions would color a tankload of respectable life today," she said in reluctant agreement.

"It would color a lifetime for today's automatons. That's

why even the most gifted forger cannot re-create the past. The best he can give us is a pale image of the reality. Not the reality itself—not the essence that goes beyond beauty. The spirit is missing. And we're cheated.'' Then, looking very straight at Cella, he smiled and remarked, ''If you didn't agree, you wouldn't have asked the question in the first place.''

His goading acted on Cella like a stimulant, and she knew she would have to go on. Her mother's words came to her lips. ''No, I can't agree. So much of the beauty of the ancients has been lost in mindless wars, in burnings and lootings. If a truly talented artist can restore even a fraction of this splendor, then even if it's a fraud, isn't it a magnificent gift?'' Cella was mesmerized by her vision of her mother's great work. She did not see the subtle look of triumph in the set of Jason's mouth.

''You mean no money would change hands?'' he asked mildly.

Cella gazed at Jason. She could think of no easy reply to his question. ''What difference does money make?''

''By definition, a gift is free. It's given with love, or an approximation of the feeling. But if the forgery is paid for, if it's not a gift of love to humanity, then it's something made to be sold for money. Do you see what I mean?''

''I think I do.'' Cella dropped her eyes abjectly.

''For it to be a gift, money cannot change hands.''

Cella sat still, looking at her hands.

''And if it isn't a gift to the human race, then it's merely a fraud meant to enrich the seller. To make money. Usually as much as possible. Like a whore who makes love for money.'' He took a choked breath. ''Or a woman who could be a whore if she needed the money.'' There was a note of pain in Jason's voice.

Cella found herself staring directly into Jason Lord's sorrowing eyes, and for a moment the two masks slipped simultaneously. Perhaps it was only her embattled imagination—or did she sense, in herself and in the tortured face across the desk, the stirring of a strange kinship? ''I never thought of it that way,'' she said softly.

There were patches of color on Jason's face as he spoke. ''A truly gifted artist must not look back. He must find his own splendor in today's world. Have faith in his own future.''

Cella felt a queer shock. What future? she asked silently. What splendor today? Where do I find it? She felt lured and pursued. What do I do now? Watching Jason, she could see in the tightening of tiny facial muscles the raising of his guard. There was an awkwardness between them that had not been there before. The conversation was going wrong—something had to be done. But what? she asked herself with no real hope of getting an answer.

Then her mind cleared. Suddenly she was flooded with a vision. The Astarte! Not the Aphrodite, but the Astarte! That was it! Would he discover a flaw? In the gold? The soldering? The spirit? Ah, yes, definitely the spirit. He wanted all art work to be a missionary of truth. So be it. Could he tell them apart? He believed the Langobardic earrings had the proper spirit. Why not the Astarte? Jason might even believe this was her real reason for coming to see him. "Have you heard of the Aphrodite necklace that Northbie's sold at auction?"

Jason's eyes widened with attention. "The one from Aphrodisias?"

"The same."

"I've been told it's authentic," Jason said too quickly. He realized he'd revealed too much and forced himself to sit back and wait for Cella to continue.

"We believe it's authentic too," she replied politely, not by a blink revealing that his response had verified Anton's guess. Emory Portland had contacted Abdul Hamid to authenticate the necklace. "The House of Uni bought the necklace, and we expect to resell it at a handsome profit."

Jason's face was a question mark.

"When my father and I return from Italy this fall, I'd like to bring the necklace to you and have you vet it."

"I'd be delighted to, but frankly, I don't see the point."

"Well, you believe the necklace is genuine, and we do too. So think of yourself as our security blanket. I know I would feel more secure if Dr. Jason Lord says the necklace is all we claim it to be. Will you do that for me?" Cella asked, giving him a smile that would last all night.

"I would be honored," he said, managing an apparently spontaneous matching smile.

"That's wonderful," Cella said, rising and extending her hand across the desk to shake his. "We'll meet again in the fall."

Jason clasped her hand, and as had happened when Cella first entered his office, his stomach began to churn. His mind was clogged with desire. Only one other woman had ever affected him as Cella Taggard did. "Yes, we will." He tried to compose himself while his brain raced furiously. He wanted something so badly it was actually a compulsion. He must have it before she left. Abruptly he found his voice. "All my lab equipment is up at MIT, but would you like the nickel tour of my research library?"

"I'd love it," Cella said with quick relief, feeling they were back on an even keel.

Jason directed Cella to a door on her left. The side facing the office was painted the identical white as the rest of the room, but when Jason opened the door and ushered Cella into the library, nothing in her face revealed her surprise. It was so unlike the office they had left. The wall paneling was a dark walnut, and since the wood was on the "endangered species" list, she realized the paneling had to be many decades old. The floor was covered with a rich, deep earth-toned carpet, and two eighteenth-century brass lighting fixtures with green shades hung from the high ceiling. A long rectory table with one wooden chair with the Harvard motto, "Veritas," on the back stood in the middle of the twenty-foot-square, windowless room. There was a single brass, green-shaded reading lamp on the table. And the four walls were lined from floor to ceiling with books on all periods of art.

Jason pointed to the far wall. "Those are my books on ancient civilizations."

"I see," Cella murmured as she wandered over to the shelves and examined the titles. "There's a half shelf on the Assyrians. Two shelves on the Egyptians. Books on the Hittites. Ah! The Etruscans. What a library you have on the Etruscans! Almost a full shelf."

"A highly creative ancient people. As you know. And mysterious too. As you also know," Jason said good-humoredly.

"Enigmatic, the scholars say."

"Enigmatic," Jason repeated, his eyes on Cella. "Would you like to see a fascinating book I have on Aphrodisias?"

"Yes."

Jason pulled a slim volume from the third shelf. "Here."

Cella read the title aloud. *"Aphrodisias, City of Venus Aphrodite.* By Kenan Erim. I know of this book. A friend called it an hors d'oeuvre. Isn't Erim planning a much larger book on his excavations?"

"He is. It's been in the works for years. But until it's actually published, this is what we have." He watched Cella open the book at random and smiled as she gasped at the pictures of the ruins. "Breathtaking, aren't they? And it's all genuine. If you'll excuse me, I have to make a phone call. Would you like to take a few minutes and scan it?"

For an instant there was the shadow of mistrust in Cella's eyes. Then she said, "I'd love to."

Jason turned on the reading lamp. "Make yourself comfortable. I won't be long," he said as Cella sat down.

Once the door was closed, he moved swiftly. Cella's purse was lying on the second Barcelona chair. Jason opened it. He saw what he was hoping for, fished it from the purse and stuffed it into his pocket. He closed the purse and automatically returned it to the exact position in which Cella had left it. That done, he stepped behind the desk and buzzed Emory for messages. When Emory had finished, he asked, "Have you completed typing the report? . . . Good. No, I don't want to talk to Mrs. Bellfont. Call her and tell her that her ring is genuine. An original and three copies of my authentication will be waiting for her. Along with her ring. It's ugly, but it is genuine. One can't have everything. And call Mrs. Herman Schiller. Tell her I cannot attend her party . . . You would?" Jason laughed. "That's very funny. All right. Accept the invitation. You go in my place. And take whomever you please." He replaced the receiver and said half aloud, "That should teach her a lesson in humility."

Jason's hand found its way into his pocket and he fingered the treasure he'd taken from Cella's purse. Momentarily a dreamlike expression came over his face. Then he seemed to shake himself, and dismissing his reverie, he opened the door to the library. Cella was immersed in the book.

"Fascinating, isn't it?" Jason said.

Cella looked up, half startled. Without thinking, she shut the book. "The statues and excavations are extraordinary. I may try to see them this summer."

"In the meantime, would you like to borrow the book? When you're finished, return it by messenger."

"Thank you. But I'd rather buy my own copy. Thank you so much. You've been very kind."

"Nonsense. I've enjoyed meeting you, even if we don't completely agree on the importance of truth in art. At least we do agree on the truth of beauty."

Cella managed a polite smile. She glanced at her watch; she'd stayed too long. Anton would be worried. "I must go," she said.

Jason's face mirrored his disappointment, one of the many emotions with which he was struggling. "I was hoping you might have dinner with me."

"I'm so sorry. I have an engagement."

Jason shrugged. "Another time."

"Yes. Another time."

"Come, I'll get your coat." He followed Cella out of the library. When she picked up her purse without looking inside, he smiled. As she found her way down the long, straight flight of stairs that led to the street, Jason watched her. When she turned at the door to say good-bye, he waved, and waited until she'd closed the front door behind her. Then he returned to his office.

Cella walked slowly through Washington Square Park. Although it wasn't quite dark, the park was almost deserted. Here and there a shadow cast by the park lights grew long, then short, then long again as she passed. She exited the park at Fifth Avenue and considered hailing a cab to go to Anton. But she lingered on the sidewalk, making no motion to signal one. She wasn't ready to welcome Anton home. Not quite yet. Jason Lord still had a hold on her mind.

As she considered his ideas, another mood possessed her. She had the queer feeling of marking time. She was waiting for something to happen. Something unforeseen. The strain of talking to the man, of finding him so attractive, of listening to his speculations on fraud, had shaken her.

It angered her to think that when he spoke of fraud he might easily include her own work, Spina's inspired work, almost all the jewelry sold by The House on Uni since her grandmother's time.

And yet there was such a strong affinity in their thinking. So much of what he'd said about the pagan world struck a sympathetic chord in her heart. All the same, he confused her. Many of his ideas gave her a feeling of unrest that she did not fully understand. Now somewhere inside her, like a smoldering fire, burned the embers of a bitter mistrust. Only dimly did she perceive the existence of this new fear, this new doubt. Of herself. Unwittingly—or perhaps deliberately—Jason Lord had attacked the temples of her private faith: the work that she loved, her family, her ideas of right and wrong. It was as though she had entered a new phase of life and nothing would be quite the same again.

Abruptly, the way the wind sometimes veers over a large body of water, Cella's speculations veered in another direction. Relax, she thought. You're thinking too much. Don't think. Do. It would mean taking a terrible risk, but she would substitute Sebastian's Astarte for the genuine Aphrodite. And when Dr. Jason Lord pronounced it genuine, the question would be settled once and for all. The spirit, yes, the spirit was there. Spina's work, *their* work, was as true as it was beautiful. Then they would return the real Aphrodite to Turkey and rid themselves of the dangerous Abdul Hamid. After a discreet interval, they'd offer the Astarte to an appropriate museum. As a gift.

Cella took a deep breath. She felt a sense of freedom and a careless joy. A cruising cab with its roof light on drew alongside her. Cella hailed the cab. Anton and the Tinia Room were waiting.

Jason Lord opened the book to a page he'd often read, so often lately that he knew the words by heart. But Cella Taggard's visit made it imperative that he reread it again. It was an old, leather-bound volume containing the writings of a fourth-century B.C. Greek historian. It reported on the nature of ancient peoples, among them the Etruscans. Cella was of Etruscan descent, and if there was any foundation to the rumors he'd heard in the art world, then she still held to her ancestors' ways. At this moment, he needed reassurance that she was what he imagined her to be: a sister under the skin to the other woman.

He read the words aloud in a hushed whisper, as though he wanted some unseen listener to share his passion for the Etruscan world, ashamed though he was to admit it, even to himself.

" 'That the Etruscans confused and often shocked the Greeks, we know from the Greek writers who stressed the Etruscan fondness for uninhibited pleasure. They are as beautiful to behold as they are shameless. The Etruscans raise all children without their knowing to whom they belong . . . When friends and relatives gather, they all engage in making love to each other, some watching, some isolating themselves by means of rattan screens . . .' "

With a violence that threatened to do damage to the yellowed volume, Jason slammed the book shut. "She's a whore! They're both whores!"

The statement was a series of strangulated sounds rather than clearly articulated words. His movements were jerky as he climbed the library ladder and reached for the book box. He wished desperately it were possible for the book box never to leave the top shelf, but there were times when Jason could only be what he was.

He placed the box on the library table and opened the clasp. He breathed deeply of the sensual odor of Shalimar. Using the utmost care, he placed the silky chemise on the library table. There was a curious smile on his face. It was the smile of both pleasure and dismay; the kind of distress that a strong man feels when he surrenders to something in his nature that he despises but can no longer deny. He reached into his pocket and removed the item he'd taken from Cella's purse. It was a lace-trimmed linen handkerchief. Jason spread the handkerchief next to the chemise. He lightly fingered the initial C in one corner of the white square, running the forefinger of his right hand around the outer edge of the C and then tracing the inner edge. When he brought the handkerchief close to his face, his smile became concerned. Momentarily puzzled, he looked at the chemise and then at the handkerchief. Then he removed the bottle of Shalimar from the book box and sprinkled a few drops of the perfume on the handkerchief.

With his right hand he held the handkerchief and with his left, the chemise. Raising first one, then the other, he alternately breathed in their aromas. His face became flushed, and a thin film of perspiration formed on his forehead. They were so much alike, those women. And God, how he wanted them!

Jason felt his sex straining against his pants. "No!" he whispered. But his body would no listen. He rocked back and forth, his eyes closed, his mouth open, his face contorted, and as he did a vision from his past thrust itself into his brain. "No!" he moaned again, dropping the chemise and the handkerchief on the table. "I won't." Yet he could no more stop his mind from remembering than he could keep his hands from caressing himself. But they were no longer his hands on his sex. They were a woman's hands on another man's sex, and the man was enjoying her . . .

Where were they? He had waited for them to return to the empty house, like a tiger waiting for its prey. He kept praying they wouldn't come, but then her car turned into the driveway. And she wasn't alone. The final proof that the world had ended for him.

He watched the two of them through a crack in the door that they were too much in a hurry to close properly. The bedroom was lit only by twilight, but Jason's sharp eyes could see the bed and the two people as clearly as if they were bathed in sunlight. They stood looking into each other's eyes. It seemed to Jason an eternity, but actually it was only a matter of seconds. Then their mouths met with a wild violence, and when she averted her face, he covered her cheeks, her eyes, with kisses. He buried his face in her neck. Her arms went around him and pressed his head closer. Closer. At last he raised his head and looked at her. Jason glimpsed an almost savage fierceness in the man's face. Abruptly she pushed him away and pulled her dress quickly over her head. All she had on beneath it was a golden silk chemise. Her legs were bare. They were always bare in warm weather.

"Take off your lipstick," Jason heard him say.

She shook her head. "If you want to kiss me, kiss me."

He brought his face very close to hers. Jason imagined he could smell the scent of her hair, the perfume, Shalimar, that she always wore. Then they were kissing, and their lips clung together it seemed forever, her hands gripping his shoulders convulsively.

"Oh, Hans!" she said breathlessly. "Now!"

Hans moved back from her and put his hand under her chin. He leaned closer, his mouth an inch from her lips.

"Don't stop kissing me," Jason heard her murmur.

Hans pulled her to him, and Jason felt a sudden spasm of desire, as if her body were pressed against his. He watched with avid eyes how incredibly soft and pliant she was, moving into the vise of Hans' arms, as if she had been there many times before, as if she knew every angle of his body and moved to adjust her own so that the bones, the warm flesh, the willing muscles locked into place with his, fitted like the last piece of a difficult puzzle. Hans pushed her back slightly, pulling down the thin lingerie straps, and she wiggled to help him lower the chemise to her waist. The globes of her breasts were free. His hands were on her nipples and she moaned, "Oh, please!" Her back arched as she pulled his head to her breasts. Jason saw her hand tighten on the back of his neck as he kissed her nipples, her throat, his hands caressing her nakedness, her body blushing with passion.

When he finally raised his lips from her body, her head lay back in his arm, as if she had fainted. He swept her up and carried her to the bed. She lay across the coverlet, one arm flung back. He seized the other hand and kissed it feverishly; pulled himself away and rapidly undressed, tearing off his clothes. A button from his shirt flew off and rolled into a corner. His shoes, his socks, his shorts, all torn off. Finally naked, he stood over her a moment before lowering himself onto her, raining kisses on her mouth, her eyes, her throat. She accepted him, moaning, her arms around him as if she would bind him to her forever. And it did seem forever to Jason.

"Oh, my darling. My dearest. My angel." Jason heard his mother say the words, and he closed his eyes, dizzy with the sight of them, the scent of them, the jealousy and pain of the pent-up desire in his groin demanding release. He did what he had to do. As he ejaculated, a barely perceptible "Aaah" escaped his lips. He opened his eyes, and nothing had changed; his mother and her lover were naked as before, their bodies still locked as if they had always been together. And would always be so.

Panting harshly, Dr. Jason Lord became aware of his surroundings. He'd come and his sperm had been captured by the silk chemise with the initials MKL on them and the handkerchief with the single initial C in the corner. Spent, he bent over the table, sick with shame. He could wash the stains off the lingerie and handkerchief. But what about himself? God help him, he loved them. His mother and Cella Taggard. He loved them both.

Chapter Eighteen

As Washington, D.C., hotel suites go, the one shared by Cella and Anton at the Madison was among the more gracious. The sitting room was lavishly furnished with a crystal chandelier, Oriental carpets, twin sofas and a breakfront containing some interesting Chinese porcelains. She gazed around the room, glad to be there.

Anton had completed dressing, his black tie neatly knotted, his sharply pleated dress shirt gleaming with sapphire studs, and for the moment the bar—fully stocked by the hotel—absorbed his attention. While he sipped his Haig & Haig Pinch from a tiny snifter, he watched Cella through the open door that led to the bedroom. She was brushing her hair.

"Would you like a little more Dom Perignon?" he called out.

"Dear creature, I had enough champagne this afternoon to float three battleships. And there'll be more at Darlene's. I think I'll pass."

Cella gazed at herself absentmindedly in the dressing table mirror as she brushed her hair. Then automatically she applied a dab of perfume behind her ears. She tried to concentrate on her hair, her perfume, but it was difficult to get Jason Lord out of her mind. In the light—or was it the darkness?—of the ideas he'd set forth, her view of her present and future was continually troubling. She couldn't tell what was coming next. And in a way, that was more disturbing than the worst certainty.

Now she smiled at Anton. Knowing how wordlessly they could interchange thoughts, she hoped he sensed nothing now. Only the standard female preoccupation with her grooming. She carefully slipped into a strapless, sequined, black silk chiffon that clung and caressed her body. Slowly she turned, swinging her hips, smiling more for Anton than for herself as she watched her reflection in the mirror. The tulle underskirt shifted and swayed rhythmically with the strand of pearls and pear-shaped emeralds that she wore around her neck.

"You look lovely," Anton commented as he watched, amused at Cella's preening. "I'll have to squint as I approach you, or I'll be blinded by your beauty."

"If I'm to play Beauty, you won't be the Beast. You look very handsome, my darling."

Anton came up behind her and kissed her bare shoulder. "By the way, how old is Herman?"

"I believe Darlene said forty-five. But this is the third forty-fifth birthday party she's given for him."

"If he actually runs for President, the truth will out." Anton reached around her waist. "Do you think Herman ever changed his name?"

"No," Cella said, remembering the little whip Darlene had bought. "If his age is the worst that comes out, he might be elected." She turned and licked Anton's earlobe as she nuzzled against him.

"Tease," he said, laughing.

"How dare you say that?" She pouted. "How did we spend the afternoon?"

"Seeing the sights."

"Liar! We spent it in bed."

"We did?" Anton's expression was incrediulous innocence. "It seems so long ago, I simply forgot."

"Long ago? *Povero giovane*. It's barely two hours since we straightened the sheets for the maid. And what did we do an hour ago in the shower?"

"I scrubbed your back and you . . ."

"Yes?" Cella whispered as she put her arms around his neck. Just as their lips touched, the telephone rang.

"Damn!" Anton said. "That has to be Sebastian. He has the most god-awful sense of timing. Whenever we make love, he calls. If we hadn't told the switchboard to hold all calls this morning, he'd have wrecked our 'sightseeing' trip."

The telephone rang again and Cella picked it up. "Hello? . . . Ah, Marina . . . What? . . . No. I don't think so . . . All right, put him on." She waited and as she waited she shook her head firmly. "Father is being ridiciulous," she said, covering the mouthpiece.

"What does he want?" Anton asked.

"Never mind. You won't like it, and I won't agree," Cella whispered. She listened for a moment and then spoke. "Yes, Father, I understand. I understand perfectly. Josie would like to borrow your suite for an indecent massage by Roberto.

And you want us . . . No way, Father, dear . . . All right. If you must, you can come over and explain why it is my sacred duty to agree.'' Slowly Cella hung up the receiver.

"What the devil is going on?'' Anton asked.

"Darlene introduced Josie to the pleasures of Roberto. You remember Roberto, Darlene's personal masseur. And now when the poor, deprived child visits Washington, she no longer thinks of her lost tax shelters in real estate, cattle and the film business, but only of the pursuit of happiness via Roberto's fingers. If you think about it, the Declaration of Independence approves of Josie's efforts,'' Cella said brightly.

"Neither James Madison nor Thomas Jefferson nor George Washington would have approved of Josie's interpretation of the pursuit of happiness. I'm not so sure of Ben Franklin. I think he would have wanted a masseuse. But an older one. Anyway, what have Josie's little depravities got to do with us?''

"Realistically, nothing. But Sebastian sees it otherwise. Wait. He'll be here in a minute and you can—'' There was a knock on the door. "He must have flown down the corridor, black patent pumps flashing, his million-dollar rock-crystal pocket watch from the Hermitage collection jiggling up and down in his right vest pocket. That watch is the one piece of modern jewelry Father owns. His justification is perfect. There were no watches in existence until centuries after the Red Sea parted.'' There was a second, louder knock on the door, and Cella sighed as she went to answer it.

"Father,'' she said gaily to a distraught Sebastian standing in the doorway. "How nice to see you so soon.''

Sebastian ignored Anton as he stepped into the room. "Where were you this afternoon? I tried to reach you five times. Never mind. Cella, Josie Frankenberg has been invited to this party. And our ridiculous friend Darlene introduced her to Roberto some months ago, when Henley, the Senate whip—you know he's Herman's lackey—needed a campaign contribution.''

"Josie actually made a political contribution.'' Cella was shocked. "Anything large is illegal.''

"This is legal. One thousand dollars. But she convinced Moe, that's her father, to form one of those Political Action Committees that I'm always being invited to join. They can make a big contribution. Not tax deductible over five thousand dollars, but Moe, being Moe, formed twenty committees. Very generous man. Anyway, after Henley was reelected, Moe was invited to the White House and introduced to the

President, and Herman and he have become bosom buddies. If Schiller should run for President . . .''

"Moe will form fifty Political Action Committees. Now, what has Moe's contribution got to do with Josie's craving for Roberto's massage?'' Cella asked too sweetly.

"Everything. Darlene invited Josie. But she couldn't invite Josie without inviting Moe and Hyla. She has to consider Herman's future.''

"Who is Hyla?'' Anton asked.

"Josie's mother. Mrs. Moe Frankenberg.''

"So? Don't keep me in suspense, Father.''

"So the entire Frankenberg family is presently ensconced at the Hyatt Regency.''

"How cozy. But I still don't see . . .''

"The connection? Think. How can Roberto give Josie a massage with her father and mother in the adjoining suite? Suppose Hyla popped in to chat?''

"Do you think she'd be jealous?'' Anton asked.

"I think she'd be shocked right out of her girdle. She'd probably cut Josie's allowance in half. Which is why Josie wants to borrow our suite to have her massage,'' Sebastian said plaintively.

"Oh what a tangled web we weave when first we practice to deceive,'' Anton intoned.

"And you don't want to lend it?'' Cella asked.

"Marina doesn't understand that sometimes during these galas I like to escape for an hour and nap.''

Cella stared at him out of the corner of her eye. "Nap? Ha! Tell that nap nonsense to Josie,'' she said.

Sebastian smiled a rigid smile. "How can I? Josie is one of our very good customers.'' Sebastian gazed at Cella and Cella gazed at Sebastian and what passed between them was a wordless argument. "Cella, please. You and Anton have had your sleep. I haven't. Do it for The House of Uni. Your father. Your heritage . . .''

"No,'' Anton said. "Suppose we want to slip away and grab a quickie?''

"A quickie what?'' Cella asked, wide-eyed.

"A quickie nap. You know how I frequently nap in the middle of long nights of partying.''

Cella smoothed her hair needlessly while Sebastian's eyes bore straight into hers, waiting. "That's true, Father. Anton and I enjoy our naps as much as you do. Much as we'd like to oblige, I think it's your turn to be the human sacrifice for

The House of Uni. There is much I have done and will continue to do. But—''

The telephone rang and Cella picked it up. "Hello? . . . Yes, Marina, he's here . . . Of course. I'm terribly sorry that we didn't foresee these complications. We could have taken a third suite for Josie . . . Yes, I'll tell him . . . See you at Darlene's.'' Cella hung up and smiled at her father. "The moving finger writes and having writ moves on. That was Marina. Josie just telephoned and said she was practically on her way over. She's already arranged to meet Roberto at your suite. What could Marina say but 'How nice.' Nap or not, you're both stuck.''

"Damn! Damn! Damn!'' Sebastian exclaimed as he hurried out of the room.

"Don't fall over anything in the dark, Sebastian,'' Anton called after him.

"He's rather good at indignation. I like the way he plays it,'' Cella observed.

"It strikes me the Madison is turning into a hot pillow joint,'' Anton said and paused. "You've got on your enigmatic face, Cella. What's your mood?''

"Pure puzzlement. Why does Sebastian think he can throw sand in my eyes? I'm his daughter. He's never taken a nap in his life.''

"Never?''

"Never. He's up to something.''

"What?''

"I'm not sure.''

"Every family has its secrets.''

"I'm starting to think that's all we have,'' Cella said dryly.

"Enough self-searching for today. Now we go to Herman's annual forty-fifth birthday party. Stand up straight, keep your shoulders back so you'll look pretty and . . .''

"And don't get run over by any strange men. It's all right. I have on clean panties.''

"Very thoughtful of you,'' Anton said, kissing her lightly on the lips. Then harder.

Josie Frankenberg played with her black hair while she stretched out on her bed, listening wearily to her mother on the hotel house phone. In her clingy workout clothes and deck shoes she looked like a health club addict.

"Yes, Mother . . . No, I'll be back before she's put all your eyelashes on . . . No, I can't. I have to work out before the party, not after. Please don't argue. If I don't keep my weight down, I'll split the seams of my dress . . . No! Why in heaven's name should you go along? You live on Chinese roots, alfalfa and celery. I don't have your discipline . . . Yes, dear, of course I love you . . . Good. I knew you'd understand. Bye.''

Josie slowly hung up the telephone receiver. That piece of family madness attended to, she got off the bed, walked to the closet and pulled out her sable.

Darlene prided herself on her parties. Protocol always went to pieces; the atmosphere became ripe for scandal. Promiscuous social kisses were tossed around helter-skelter between senators and diplomatic wives—the young ones; between cabinet officers and congressional wives—the younger ones; between congressmen looking for sex, and a political contribution from Texas, Brazilian or German heiresses of any age. If theoretically the point of the party was Herman's birthday, realistically the reason to be there was to raise campaign funds. Wherever one listened there lurked a sense of business being done.

The chandeliers sparkled; the furniture, mostly French eighteenth century or earlier, was graceful. In fact, the effect was so tasteful that one indulgently forgot that in days gone by Darlene might have thought a commode was something one sat on in the bathroom.

As Cella and Anton entered, a man in a business suit said with intensity to a woman in a short satin bubble dress, ''We already have the capacity to destroy each other totally. So there's nothing more important than stopping this insane nuclear buildup. Nothing!''

''Absolutely nothing! After all, what could be more important than the end of the world?'' The woman glowed provocatively.

''I see one of our great hookers is here,'' Anton muttered as they passed.

Having picked up the key that Marina had left for her at the desk, Josie entered the suite. She was full of a longing for original sin and perspiring with eagerness to be the forbidden apple. She could hardly wait to meet the serpent—Roberto—ah, Roberto. It was the same compulsion that made Josie, on other occasions, using other names, stroll around inner-city neighborhoods at night, a handbag hanging from her shoulder. She knew she should control herself. But it was hard. When she didn't make love on a manic wave of primal appetite, she surrendered to other appetites; and the urge to consume chocolate mousse, napoleons, éclairs and all manner of sensual desserts prepared by the dessert chef at the Bel Air hotel was overpowering. She would eat so much she could make herself sick. But why eat? Wasn't anonymous sex better than a Sacher torte, and then making herself bone tired from jogging it off?

Tonight Josie was very eager and too early. Still, she hoped he might be waiting for her. She searched through the rooms. No Roberto. Not anywhere. What was holding him up? The bastard!

As Cella and Anton moved through the huge crowded room, a fine odor of orchids and power politics assaulted their senses. Cella found a transient relief in the distraction. Contact with the pressures of busy and indifferent people she barely knew gave remoteness to the questions which clung to her like flesh on bone. Darlene had not spared on movers and shakers. On flowers. On champagne. Out of nowhere a splendidly superior waiter materialized and offered them each a glass of champagne.

A passing glitter girl remarked confidentially to a bearded young man taking notes, "Of course it's top secret. But I hear that most of the terrorists come from wealthy families."

Anton said, "I count seven mousse-sprayed senators—they wear more hairspray then a TV pitch girl."

"And more girdles than dowagers," Cella said, licking her lips as she savored a canapé of smoked salmon. "Have some smoked salmon. Have some oyster roe."

Anton swallowed an onion tartlet. "The bloody place is a circus. And smells like one. The odor in the room is pure horse trading. There's the majority leader smiling for the TV cameras. I see three committee chairmen plus the majority whip. Hawkers and barkers. Smelling of the farm with manure on their shoes."

"And notice the Russians walking on a tightwire and listening for the unsaid," Cella murmured, surveying the crowd. The relief she'd felt on entering was only momentary, and the smiles of recognition which greeted her here and there left her with a renewed sense of isolation. The color and excitement, which at another time would have caught her up, now seemed to insulate her in her own thoughts.

* * *

Josie stretched herself, forcing relaxation, and took off her jogging shoes. She wriggled her toes in sheer ecstasy. What a joy to be barefoot. Her head full of X-rated fantasies, she slipped out of her bodysuit, and with no lingerie to hamper her, danced around the suite enjoying her own nakedness. All that she had on was her watch. And only that because she was feverishly watching the seconds tick away until Roberto's arrival. Where was he? Did he have his dates confused? If he didn't show soon she'd scream.

Tired of dancing for no audience, she lay down on the bed and caressed herself. That proved unfulfilling. She'd rather have Roberto. She hurried to the bathroom and grabbed two large luxurious bath towels. She pulled back the spread on the king-sized bed, then the light, soft blanket, and placing the towels by her side, she stretched herself out full length on the cool, silken lavender sheets that Marina had brought with her. She glanced at her watch for the fiftieth time. Where was Roberto? Now he was late, but she wouldn't scold him. In fact, she would pretend to be asleep. That would serve him right. But before she lay facedown on the sheets, she placed one of the towels demurely across her behind. That would serve him right too.

As she buried her face in the pillow, she felt a delicious shiver. It was caused by the sound of the door to the suite being opened. Aaah, Roberto. Darlene had kept her promise—she'd found him a key. Josie would make believe she was sound asleep. Roberto would arouse her.

Cella wandered off slowly in the direction of Marina.

A young woman she didn't recognize waved to her, smiling a friendly smile. She had shining silver-gray hair pulled back like an eighteenth-century marquise, but she couldn't be more than twenty-two, with her gamine face. As she approached Cella, wavering on stiletto heels and wearing something in bustled shot-silk taffeta, her body slanted rearward in a funky Motown street walk that was a startling contrast to her highbrow elegance. Her smile grew warmer the closer she came, and as she reached handshake distance she remarked with embarrassment, "I don't know why I feel clumsy. I've been walking around in high heels since I was ten years old. How are you, Cella Taggard? Papa sends greetings."

Cella smiled back, taking her cue. "Give Papa my best," she said, wishing she knew who the hell Papa was.

"He was so sorry he couldn't be here. He sent me instead. Isn't it wonderful?"

"Wonderful," Cella agreed. "But I don't believe we've met. I couldn't forget you," she added, her tone genuinely flattering.

"Or I you. You are as beautiful as I was told. Much like your beautiful mother, Spina. What a terrible thing—that accident."

It was thoroughly unnerving to Cella to observe the strange young woman's calm contemplation and to listen to the knowing report on her family. "But if you never saw me, how did you recognize me?"

"My father gave me a picture of you. And to make certain, when I arrived, I asked Osman, my brother, to point you out."

Abruptly Cella had a sense of what was coming. "If Osman is your brother, you must be Alexandria."

"And you must call me Lexi."

Cella nodded. "How nice to meet you, Lexi."

"And you!" the young woman said enthusiastically. "Would you be kind enough to introduce me to your father? Unfortunately, I lost his photograph. Do you think I lost it in packing? Papa would be so angry with me. But Papa doesn't know. It is too bad Osman never met him." She gave Cella a wonderful, hopeful, affectionate smile. "But yours I did not lose. You will please introduce me to your father?"

"Of course." This was what Sebastian had been up to, Cella realized. His tactics stank like a piece of rotted fish that had been left lying in the sun. "You want to discuss the Aphrodite necklace?" She forced a smile.

"Yes. I fly to Washington to see it."

"My father told your father he would show it to him?"

"He said that on the telephone. But Papa, he could not leave Istanbul at this time. The Greeks again. So he sent me as his emissary. You do know he wants it back?"

"I know."

"Papa was certain that Anton Vilanova would tell you. Your cousin is very discreet. And loyal. Your whole family is loyal. We Turks understand family loyalty." The silver-haired child spoke with sly deliberateness. "Of course, we will pay a reasonable price. Osman has the checkbook."

"That's very efficient."

"Now, who is your father? Or should I meet him in his suite?"

Cella laughed softly. "I think not. He'd have a problem with that." Sebastian had been pursuing a line he had marked out for himself. And it was equally clear that her share of the business consisted for now of merely observing. "Let me introduce you," she said as she guided the young woman toward Sebastian, who was engrossed with a pale, sculptured beauty.

"Excuse me a moment, Father, but I'd like you to meet Lexi. She's flown five thousand miles to meet you."

"Lexi?" Sebastian asked, instantly charmed by the silvery hair and the flower-fresh face.

"Abdul Hamid's daughter."

"Yes," Lexi said. "Second from the top."

"Ah," said Sebastian. "Your father . . . ?"

"I am his emissary. The president needed Papa."

"Naturally, and what a pleasure to meet you."

"And I you. I lost your photograph, but it doesn't do you justice."

"You must take after your mother. Who would believe that Abdul could have such a lovely daughter." Sebastian was enchanted and giving his all.

"I can see you two have much to discuss. It was so nice to meet you, Lexi," Cella said. Sebastian was just as glad to see her go as she was to leave. Given just one more of his calculated courtesies, Cella might have said things that everyone, most of all she herself, would have afterward regretted.

Josie's breath caught as Roberto's fingers stroked the curve of her buttocks and slipped downward to caress the smooth warmth of her inner thighs. So it began. Then his fingers and tongue explored the humid soft core of her being, finding nerve endings Josie hadn't known she possessed. Heat pulsed through her body with each sweet probe of his tongue. She heard a strange moan of pleasure and knew it was her own. This was better than it had ever been before. With anyone. Her hips shifted with sinuous movements seeking his touch as his hands and tongue roved restlessly, hungrily over her. Then with a single, powerful movement he slid into her center, making her cry out raggedly. He went into her and out and into her again and again, burying himself so deeply that the ecstasy exploding through him seemed to go on forever. Her name caught in his throat, coming out as a broken groan echoing the pulses of his orgasm.

The sound of his voice hurled Josie into a final grand climax, and the heat uncurled deep within her body, expanding outward in rings of tiny convulsions, closing around his rigid flesh and caressing him with the rhythms of her orgasm.

For a long time there was no sound but that of their breathing gradually slowing, and when Roberto finally stirred and she felt his weight roll off her. She twisted slowly toward him. She wanted him again, but in a different position. Face-to-face, mouth to mouth, her legs wrapped around his hips. Eyes still closed, her hands moved hungrily over him, combing through the rough hair that covered his chest. Her nails scraped lightly over his nipples. Slowly her hands drifted lower, searching for and finding his masculine flesh, again rigid and again ready for pleasure. She opened her eyes in delight.

Then she opened her mouth. But it happened too fast for her to scream.

A golden haze had settled over the frivolities when Darlene, wearing a pleated red taffeta that ended in a train and a red silk fedora tilted over one eye, tiptoed up behind Cella. "Did your stubborn-as-a-mule father bring the Aphrodite with him?" she hissed in Cella's ear.

"How should I know?" Cella said, exuding innocence. "Ask him."

"Why are you always coy with me, Cella Taggard? You know."

"I really don't. The last I heard he was considering your last bid."

"Did he tell you I offered four million?"

"He mentioned some number with a lot of zeros attached."

"I'll strangle him if he sells it to someone else."

"I'll tell him that," Cella said, glancing over to where Sebastian was talking intently to Lexi.

"And who is that gray-haired trollop fastened onto his every word?" Darlene snorted.

"Don't you know who you invited?"

"I gave Herman's secretary my list. He added his own. She must be one of his. Who is she?"

Cella shrugged. "Another question I can't answer." She paused. "Father's looking this way. I believe he's coming over."

"Alone, thank goodness."

"Perhaps she's going to the bathroom."

"Oh, damn! There's Herman stamping and pawing the ground like a stallion in heat. Any minute now he'll start to bray. My master's voice." Darlene rolled her eyes heavenward and picked up her train. "Damn this thing! It has a life of its own. It's been fighting me all evening. Would you believe that this homicidal dress cost twelve thousand dollars? You tell Sebastian I want to speak to him after dinner,'' she said between clenched teeth, giving Cella a dazzling—if toothy—smile. ''Coming, love,'' she caroled as she tottered off in the direction of Herman Schiller. The White House Chief of Staff was surrounded by Big Hitters, Big Money and notably Moe Frankenberg.

''Cella, I need a favor from you. A small favor, but important,'' Sebastian said, full of high spirits. As always, he could be in whatever mood he had to be in to accomplish his purpose.

''You want me to get Josie out of your suite?'' Cella said tentatively.

''Exactly. She's had quite enough massaging and she's missing the party. She should be here before dinner is served, and before Moe and Hyla start to miss her.'' He was the soul of friendly concern. ''I say this for her own good.''

''And for yours. You want to take Lexi to the suite and show her the necklace.''

''I promised her I would. She and Osman. After dinner.''

For an instant Cella's eyes glowed. ''You mean to sell it to her? I'm so glad.''

''I mean to show it to them. That's all.''

''I don't understand.'' The miserable truth was she did understand.

''Lexi knows exactly how much Abdul will pay.''

''And you want an upset price?''

''I congratulate you, Cella. You're becoming a business-woman. Yes, that's what I want. An upset price. I think Abdul will offer even more than Darlene's four million.''

''You're making a mistake.''

''Don't talk nonsense. We didn't steal it. We bought it from Northbie's. For a pretty penny. If it happens to be a national art treasure, Istanbul can damn well pay for it.''

''Through the nose, if I follow your thinking,'' Cella said caustically.

''I don't appreciate sarcasm. They should pay what it's worth to them. Furthermore, the Greek ambassador has approached me on the matter of the Aphrodite.''

Cella stared at her father, conscious of a strange sense of isolation, of being cut off from this man she'd known all her life; this man who was more and more a stranger. ''How did the Greek ambassador know about it?''

''How do I know? Word gets around.''

''Or you get it around.''

"Let's not split hairs. The Greek government is very interested."

"I think it would be a mistake not to sell the Aphrodite to Abdul Hamid. At whatever price he offers. I would even sell it to him at our cost."

"This discussion is over. My key is at the desk, Cella. Get it, go upstairs and get rid of her."

"Get rid of Josie?" Anton asked as he joined them.

"Yes," Cella said soberly. "Father's doing a private showing of the Aphrodite."

"For Lexi and Osman."

"How did you know?" Cella asked.

"Once I knew Abdul was back in our business, I ran a check on him. Family gossip can be as accurate as computers." Anton glanced at Sebastian. "I thought you would want an upset price."

"Precisely," Sebastian said impatiently.

"To tantalize the Greeks with," Anton said.

"And thus the Aphrodite necklace becomes an international incident," Cella said softly.

"Cella, stop dramatizing. Just get the key and get rid of Josie," Sebastian said.

"I'll go with you," Anton said.

"You don't have to."

"I think I do."

A mute look passed between Cella and Anton.

"An Etruscan hunch?" she asked.

"Yes."

Anton opened the door to Sebastian and Marina's suite. He entered first and Cella followed. Both felt a little foolish. The sight of the living room made them feel even more foolish. Everything was in order. Everything was as it should be. Everything made them more apprehensive.

"Josie!" Cella called. "It's time to get out of the pool." No one answered.

"I feel like a Peeping Tom," she whispered to Anton. "This is coitus interruptus with a vengeance."

"Try again."

"Josie! Roberto! Playtime is over!"

Still the suite remained silent.

"I'd make a rotten policewoman," Cella said. "There is no gracious way to break into a bedroom where two people are engaged in—"

"Do you hear any moans and groans?" Anton interrupted in a low, puzzled voice.

"No."

Anton put his forefinger to his lips and murmured, "Listen. For deep breathing. Panting."

They listened. There was no sound.

"They're asleep. Or something," Anton said.

"Or something. Here we go." Cella raised her voice. "Josie! Roberto! Ready or not, here we come!"

Side by side, Cella and Anton walked toward the bedroom. The bedroom door was partially open and Anton pushed it back. He stepped inside, Cella following him. They stood together silently, scanning the room. It was neat and orderly enough to please even Sebastian, with the only queer note being Josie; Josie sprawled naked and fast asleep on the bed.

"She's sound asleep," Cella whispered.

"Seems so," Anton said, walking over to the bed.

"We have to wake her," Cella said. "I think I'd better do it."

"Mmm . . ." Anton answered, bending over Josie.

"You wait for us in the living room," Cella stated firmly. "Josie will have a fit if she thinks you saw her naked. You're not Roberto. Deep down under all that lustfulness beats the heart of a dedicated hypocrite."

Anton shook his head. "Not anymore it doesn't."

"No!" Cella exclaimed, but she knew it was true. "She's dead?"

"Very dead."

The next morning Moe and Hyla Frankenberg were in deep mourning and could not speak to the press. Darlene and Herman Schiller had splitting headaches and would not speak to the press. Cella and Anton would not speak to the press. Sebastian and Marina would not speak to the press. Nonetheless the newspaper headlines were bold. And depending on the newspaper, on page 1 or page 3.

JOSIE FRANKENBERG,
SOCIALITE HEIRESS,
FOUND MURDERED
IN WASHINGTON HOTEL SUITE

Different newspapers approached the murder in different ways. Some were severely factual. Some were discreetly sensational. Some bordered on the slanderous, having long ago set their sights on the privately lustful indiscretions of the rich and famous. All of them speculated on the murderer. It clearly wasn't Roberto Poggi, Washington society's favorite masseur. His body was discovered stuffed into the sixth-floor linen closet. The cause of both deaths was strangulation.

PART SEVEN

HOME IS THE PLACE WHERE,
WHEN YOU HAVE TO GO THERE,
THEY HAVE TO TAKE YOU IN.
                    Robert Frost

Chapter Nineteen

Every year, from mid-June to mid-July, Cella and Sebastian covered about twenty thousand miles—Cella thought of it as their tour of duty—before they returned to the villa in Italy where they spent the rest of the summer. They visited clients around the world, both for pleasure and for business. They interviewed sources who had contacted them over the year claiming extraordinary finds. And once in a while they did discover a truly wonderful piece that Sebastian would pick up for a song. Usually Cella anticipated these trips with great eagerness, but this year she felt deeply reluctant about going. The finds were authentic pieces, but they represented a very small percentage of what The House of Uni sold, compared with their own work. And more and more the idea of their own work made her uneasy. In her mind she described the feeling as the "Jason Lord Syndrome." Did the spirit of the ancients coexist in The House of Uni's "re-creations," or had it been driven out by Sebastian's gluttonous appetite for money? The conflict nagged at her constantly.

Still, when the time came, she packed her bags and headed for Kennedy Airport. She met Sebastian in Los Angeles. He had flown on ahead with Marina to pay a condolence call on the Frankenbergs. From Los Angeles, Marina left for Santa Barbara to spend the summer there. Cella and Sebastian flew to San Francisco, each carefully avoiding the subject of Josie's murder. Both were aware of the possibility that Marina might have been the actual target. Cella repeatedly asked herself why anyone would want to kill Marina. Or, for that matter, Josie. All she had were questions, but no answers.

In San Francisco they visited a client on Russian Hill, a longtime patron of The House of Uni. Sebastian considered the visit an outstanding success when his client agreed to the "outrageous" price on the lapis-lazuli-and-jade earrings she'd seen some months ago. She did so love jade. And after all, one only lived once.

From San Francisco, the next stop was Tokyo. Cella listened to Sebastian humming in the seat beside her. He was pleased with himself, thinking about the sale. He'd already sold the earrings, and now he had to "re-create" them again. He would want her help, to give it new individuality, and the idea depressed Cella. The "Jason Lord Syndrome" again.

Cella tried to distract herself by remembering how much she enjoyed Tokyo. There were Kyoto and Karuizawa to see. And the night life of the Roppongi—the cafes, the clubs, the discos—where one could see the Japanese eating Big Macs and Frostees and gyrating to a rock-and-roll beat. Her mind filled with rhythms and color and noise that stopped her from thinking.

This time the brief visit started at eight the next morning. After an early sushi breakfast in one of the hotel restaurants, they took the limousine to meet Mr. Keigo. Mr. Keigo ran a shop in the Akihabara section of Edo, the Old City, that was occasionally open. It was one among hundreds of similar small shops and stalls which sold the latest electronic appliances, the shiniest gadgets, anything that buzzed or hummed or had blinking lights. The small shop hardly accounted for the fact that Mr. Keigo maintained a modern, expensive, luxurious apartment in the southwest district of Harajuku. The shop's purpose was to keep Mr. Keigo in touch with the people of the Old City. The people of the Old City were the source of his wealth. They seldom knew the value of the things that their families had owned for generations. The things Mr. Keigo often took off their hands for a pittance to help them out. Solely out of the goodness of his heart.

This time he'd come up with an extraordinary treasure.

"What is it?" Sebastian asked, examining the odd piece of gold jewelry encrusted with pearls.

"It's a fishhook, Father," Cella said. "An ancient fishhook."

"It symbolizes a widespread myth of the fishhook, stolen by the prankish sea god. The legend is found not only in Japan but in Oceania, Indonesia and other Asian countries," Mr. Keigo said in his flawless English, having graduated from Stanford and lived many years in San Francisco.

"Where did you get the piece?" Sebastian asked.

"You mean what is the provenance?" Keigo smiled sardonically. "I am the provenance. I am the authority on Japanese mythic themes and ancient Japanese art. I stumbled across it washed up at the beach in Kamakura. The sea god chose to return it to me.''

"What do you think?'' Sebastian asked Cella.

Cella glanced at her father. She could almost hear him thinking how easily he could make another version in the workshop, if she would put the little touches to it that would make it indisputably authentic. No, she thought, surprised at her own inner vehemence. I don't want to help you. Fingering the piece gently, she smiled. "Yes. Let's take it.''

Sebastian pursed his lips and turned back to Mr. Keigo. After much haggling concerning the age of the fishhook, the workmanship, the quality of the gold, of the pearls, the condition of the piece as a whole, the two men settled on a price of 26,100,000 yen, or about $190,000.

"It will make a charming pendant. Or a pin. At a nice profit for you. About a quarter of a million American dollars, I think,'' said Mr. Keigo.

Back in her hotel room, Cella stared at the telephone. She wanted to tell someone something, but she didn't know what, or to whom she would tell it. She sat down at the desk chair and picked up the telephone receiver. The instructions on the telephone dial stated clearly how to direct-dial long distance. But long distance to whom? Anton? No. Who? She put the receiver down, feeling confused and slightly silly. The "Jason Lord Syndrome'' strikes again, she thought.

From Tokyo, they flew directly over the North Pole to their next stop, Ireland, where Sebastian had an appointment to play golf and other games with Lady Deidre O'Meara.

"Golf may have been invented in Scotland, but today Ireland has more golf courses per citizen than any other country in the world,'' Sebastian remarked loftily. "Actually, Ireland is a wonderful place for golf. The air. The ocean,'' he said, smiling and preening his feathers. "And, of course, Lady Deidre is here.''

"Of course,'' Cella murmured offhandedly, mindful that Lady Deidre and Sebastian had an "understanding.'' Since Lord Sean O'Meara was far more interested in laying a three iron on the green than in laying his lady, their understanding was quite acceptable to the golfing lord. To add to Sebastian's pleasure, her ladyship lived in a romantic old windy castle with ancient plumbing, and was devoted to everything antique or ancient, including jewelry.

But this time Lady Deidre, to Sebastian's surprise, was not

interested in jewelry of any kind. She was interested in a marker for golf balls.

"A marker?" Sebastian asked, puzzled. "What do you mean by a marker?"

"Oh, Sebastian, you're a terrible hacker but I adore you. A marker is the coin that you put on the green just behind the golf ball. You use American dimes. What I want are ten ancient markers."

"To my knowledge, the Romans and Greeks had no markers. They never played golf."

"Sebastian, I am not a fool. What I want are ten ancient coins for his lordship to use as markers. They should be golden and preferably no larger than a tuppence. And thin. I want a present for him. It's the least I can do to reward him for not making a fuss over our little pleasures."

When Sebastian reported the conversation to Cella, she thought it a splendid idea. She agreed they could find Lady Deidre ten ancient gold coins. At ten thousand dollars apiece. Or more, Sebastian countered. Depending on the provenance. One might be the lucky coin of Cicero. Or Virgil. Or who knew—maybe Nero. Who undoubtedly had gambled.

Cella nodded. Sebastian could make the coins himself. Without her help. Thinking this, she felt suddenly light-hearted. Yes, markers were a marvelous idea.

London was not on their itinerary, but Sebastian wanted to stop at the Grosvenor House Fair. He'd heard about a mystery clock, actually a rock crystal, enamel, onyx and diamond clock in which the hands seemed to float in free space. All an optical illusion.

"It's the absolutely perfect birthday present for Marcus," Sebastian said. "He lives and breathes the mysteries of Wall Street. What he buys and sells are optical illusions."

"J.P. Morgan owned a mystery clock, Father," Cella said, feeling protective of her brother. "And he didn't do badly. Neither will Marcus."

"Because Marcus has us to fall back on. He lives with his feet planted firmly in midair. A mystery clock is ideal."

After the clock was purchased for considerable money, they went to a party in Mayfair thrown by an eager earl for a punk-rock star. A marquis had a boating picnic on the Thames another day, and there was also an embarrassment of dinner invitations from ambassadors—including the Turkish and the Greek. Sebastian was amused and pleased. The Aphrodite necklace had made them diplomatic plums. Cella was tense and angry with her father. Sebastian and she had developed an unspoken, uneasy truce about the Aphrodite. Now, despite his urging, she refused to dine at either the Greek or the Turkish embassy. She wasn't interested in starting a bidding war for the Aphrodite between the two countries. So Sebastian went to the Greek and Turkish ambassadors' dinner parties alone, while Cella sat quietly in her suite at the Dorchester thinking about the Aphrodite, Jason Lord and how doubts seemed to come in clusters.

Next came Marseilles. They visited briefly with Victor Vilanova, who was also in Marseilles to check on the work of his atelier. They had lunch at Le Petit Nice overlooking the sea, and Sebastian said the bouillabaisse was the best he'd ever eaten. Victor was in no mood to rhapsodize over the glories of Marseilles' gastronomic delights. He had just left a meeting with two of his most talented sculptors, the brothers Armand and Maurice Mermoz. And he was exasperated at their denseness.

"It is inconceivable that such imbeciles are so talented," Victor said, shaking his head of white hair impatiently.

"You mean they actually wanted to tell people they created the Cycladian idols?" Cella's eyes were wide with disbelief.

"My dear child, they wanted to hold a press conference."

"Good Lord!" Sebastian said.

"Where did they get the idea?" Cella asked.

"From the publicity the idols have recently received. Thanks to the renowned Dr. Jason Lord." Victor frowned with distaste. "They believe Lord's attack proves their genius, since there are so many experts who believe their work is authentic. They are great artists and they want recognition."

"They are artists," Cella said tentatively.

"No! They are only artisans and fools. I know. I taught them everything. Thanks to me, they are master forgers," Victor said firmly. "That should be good enough for them."

"Yes," Sebastian agreed. "You pay them a very handsome commission when you sell their work."

"Of course," Victor said, wiping his white mustache with his napkin. "But they had the misfortune to read about this Mexican forger, Brigido Lara. He works in pre-Columbian artifacts. He claims much of his work is in prestigious museums. Or highly esteemed private collections. Maurice and Armand are jealous."

"They're lunatics," Sebastian said.

"I've read about Lara," Cella said quietly. "He calls himself an interpreter, not a forger."

"He may call himself an interpreter, but he's a forger. And also a fool," Victor said.

For a moment Cella thought she had misheard or misunderstood. "You don't think there's a difference? Between interpretation and . . ." She spit out the word. "Forgery?"

"I do not. But whether he's a forger or an interpreter, pre-Columbian artifacts do not command a tenth of the price that our statuary does. Maurice and Armand do superb work creating ancient Greek kouros. Two are in the Dallas Museum of Art. Many are in fine private collections. They are world-famous, if anonymous. Armand did a marvelous bust of the Roman emperor Claudius. It is in the Metropolitan in New York in the antiquities section. My two madmen have an annual income of six figures, but they feel neglected. They wanted to write their memoirs. About the great art fakes they created. Or interpretations, as they call them. The Cycladian idols."

"It has elements of humor," Cella said, trying to smile.

"To write their memoirs would end their careers forever," Sebastian said.

"Naturally."

"How did you handle it?" Sebastian asked.

"I pointed out what Brigido Lara does for a living now."

"Which is—?" Cella asked.

"Their hero now ekes out a miserable living making replicas for the gift shop at the Jalapa Archaeological Museum in Veracruz."

"At a minimum wage," Sebastian noted smugly.

"Mexican minimum," Victor said.

"Did that stop them?" Cella asked.

"It made them think." Victor smiled slyly. "And then I delivered the coup de grace."

"Yes?" said Cella.

"I told their wives about their memoirs." For the first time Victor started to laugh. "Margot and Angelique handled the rest. The idea that they would be known as the wives of art forgers put an end to the memoirs."

On the plane to Tangier, their last stop before the villa in Carrara, Cella felt a queer, dazed detachment. There was a voice in her head that sounded strangely familiar, that kept repeating two words over and over: *Interpreter. Forger. Interpreter. Forger.* Why did the words make her think of her own work? Of Sebastian's work? She always thought of The House of Uni's work as re-creations. Was it that? Re-creation? Or interpretation? Or? Her mind froze for an instant. Or was it forgery? Jason Lord would say, "Forgery!" Goddamn Jason Lord! She remembered Sebastian's anger at Marcus when he'd used the word.

Clearly, the truth was no simple matter. It began in the country of one's childhood. Layer upon layer of adult illusion resting on the faith of a child. Thinking this, Cella felt a strong fear that she must not go too far. If she did she might learn more about the truth than she could stand.

They avoided the south of France. Too many clients were summering there, and that meant an endless round of parties. They flew straight to Tangier to visit an old family friend, Jeremy Webb, the second son of the second son of the fifteenth Earl of Mansfield. Jeremy had been a particular friend of Spina's and he'd kept the friendship alive through Cella. Aided by Sebastian's interest in Jeremy's friends, many of them often became clients.

Jeremy himself never bought a thimble. He was a man of limited means; his ivory-painted villa, looking from the outside much like every house in the city, was a unique surprise once one passed through the entrance. The interior was airy, inviting and suggested a faultless taste for beauty, a discerning eye for arrangement. And scattered throughout were mementos and souvenirs of Jeremy's friendships with people in the arts. For the house was run like a hotel. Anyone might drop in. A spy who had come in from the cold; a professional basketball star who had been a Rhodes scholar; Alex Head, a legendary French horse trainer; the Pope's tailor, Francesco Gammarelli; or a premiere ballerina taking a breather from the Bolshoi. Anyone. Cella looked forward to Jeremy's surprises. His talent for enjoying life made it predictable that there would be interesting parties and entertainments and people of all kinds visiting during their stay.

But even more important than the star-studded guests was something upstairs waiting for her. Feeling eager and intense, Cella walked up the circular staircase, counting the steps to keep her mind occupied. At last she reached the second floor, then hurried to the room that had been Spina's until her death and now was reserved for Cella. She opened the door, slipped off her shoes and crossed the threshold, shutting the door behind her. Attached to the bedroom was a boudoir dressing room, and as usual, everything in it seemed perfect: the huge exquisite mantelpiece, the china candlesticks on the dressing table, the large oval mirror framed in gold leaf. It all reminded her of Spina's beauty.

And as always, the photograph was on the dressing room table. The same photograph that, until Spina's death, had been in Spina's workroom at the villa. Then it had disappeared. But Jeremy always took out his copy when Cella came to visit. The angle of the sun streaming through the terrace doors lit up the warm, lovely face in the photograph. It looked out at Cella with all the sweetness and mystery she remembered, so familiar and yet so unknown. It was the Spina of long ago, a very young Spina. And beside her was the young man. Cella noted his features carefully, as she had done so many times before: the hair black as Anton's, black as her own; the straight nose and flaring nostrils; the curve of the mouth in the smile she knew so well. Who was he? She had no answer. Someone she'd always known, someone she'd never met, smiling the ancient Etruscan smile. He and she looked so much alike, he could have been her brother. Except that his age was all wrong. Maybe he was a relation of some kind. But who?

As a child, she would ask Spina who the man in the photograph was, and Spina would get an odd look on her face and say, "A dear friend. A friend of the family." And then change the subject. Sebastian always said he didn't know and didn't care; and the way he said it ended the conversation. In time Cella gave up trying to find out the man's name. But now she admitted to herself that since Spina's death, the presence of the photograph was the reason she always insisted they visit Jeremy in Tangier.

When it was time to leave, Cella packed quickly and half regretfully, glancing at the photograph. Then, feeling like a thief, she went to the bureau and slipped the gold-framed picture between layers of silken lingerie. Somehow she was convinced Jeremy would understand her theft. She only wished she did.

As always, coming home was like a wonderful dream. The blue hills, the streams and the village, the gray stone villa were dreamlike. The days of July were serene and sunny, except when Cella allowed herself to think, which she tried not to do. The nights were harder. Sometimes she would wake with a start and sit up shaking, her body covered with perspiration, her heart pounding. This was no glorious vision of the past. This was horrifying. Trapped in some ugly nightmare world, she would stare around the room and for a moment not know where she was. Her dream was more real than the real world. Then slowly it faded and she remembered nothing. When she fumbled for the meaning of the dream, it escaped her. Why was it so terrifying? She didn't know, but sometimes she was afraid to go to sleep.

August was much like July, punctuated by two weekend jaunts to visit Anton in San Sebastian in Spain, where he owned a house on the heights of Monte Igueldo with a stunning view of the town and the endless ocean. There they spent a disproportionate amount of time in bed. It was an interval of rapturous happiness. During the hours with Anton, the "Jason Lord Syndrome" seemed to fall away. It was easy not to think. To forget. To foget Victor. Forget Sebastian. Forget words like *interpretation* and *forgery*. Above all, to forget Jason Lord. Anton was the finest lover she'd ever known, the most sensual, the most tender, yet the most ferocious. Sometimes their arousal was violent and fast. Feverish. Sometimes they made love with languid passion, while the fire within Cella grew hotter and hotter. At last when her body melted against his, she had no breath, no thought, nothing but a feeling of joyous release. Later, in his arms she always slept peacefully.

It was almost impossible to leave him, and yet she could feel herself being drawn back to the villa by an instinctive necessity. She never stayed as long as either of them wished. But when she returned home, she felt a strange elation in the air around her. It was as if the country too was her beloved, and it came out to meet her, to put its arms around her as Spina used to do, and welcome her home. As though it feared she might not return.

As always, Luisa and Luigi were up at dawn polishing the marble floors, waxing the furniture, mending the linen and doing the laundry. In the kitchen Luisa's aunt, Celeste, still presided over the charcoal stove and copper pots from which emerged food that was equal to the best of the Michelin guide.

Each morning, as she had done for so many mornings of her life, Cella would fling aside the curtains in her bedroom, open the wooden shutters and gaze at the sunlight that seemed to sparkle on the branches of the cypress outside her window, and on the silvery olive trees on either side. One morning she took the photograph out of the bureau drawer where she'd placed it and stood it on the round Carrara marble table in the living room among all the family pictures. Sebastian wouldn't notice it, but seeing it gave her a great pleasure.

One day, after her visit to Anton, Cella went to the village to buy figs. It had rained earlier and as she walked, the warm sun was drawing moisture from the grass. Cella loved the scent; it was green and strong, the scent of summer. In the village she met people she'd known all her life. They smiled at her and gossiped as if she'd never been away. And when they spoke of Spina, it was clear how dear Spina had been to everyone. The memory of her beautiful mother seemed to live in all of them, like an afterglow. People talked about Spina as if she were still alive, and it gave Cella the illusion that her mother was very close. If she turned her head quickly she might just catch her smiling. She always felt her nearness at the villa, and now she felt it again among the villagers. However irrational it seemed, Spina was close. This thought gave Cella a sense of peace.

When she arrived home hours later, Sebastian was sitting on the terrace, a cup of iced coffee untouched, the newspaper unopened as he read a letter taken from a stack of mail.

"From Marina?" Cella asked, slipping into a chair beside him while Luisa brought her a glass of chilled white wine.

"From Marcus," Sebastian said without pleasure.

Cella waited for him to continue. He'd tell her when he was ready, and from the look of irritation on his face, she guessed she wouldn't have long to wait.

Sebastian started to read aloud. "He says we must be extraordinarily happy to be home again. It is the promised land. He wishes he were with us. He longs for Etruria. The olive groves. The lemons. The soft air. The enchantment of the villa. His mind swarms with memories of houses, roads, trees and people. He looks forward to seeing us in the fall and hearing the news of home—et cetera, et cetera."

"He's grown quite poetic," Cella murmured, tasting her wine.

"He needs money," Sebastian said finally.

"Does he say so?"

"You heard what he says."

"That letter hardly sounds like a request for money," Cella insisted, trying not to smile.

"It is. You know your brother as well as I do," Sebastian said sarcastically. "Why else would he drown us in sentimental drivel? Does he think I'm a complete fool? He must be heading into trouble over some idiotic speculation." Sebastian shook his head in irritation. "What he'll get from me is the mystery clock I bought in London. For his birthday." Sebastian tore up the letter.

Cella's smile broke through. "You may be right. What else is in the mail? Besides Marcus?"

"Lady Gwen. She's invited me for shooting in Scotland this month."

"How could I forget Gwenith. And you accepted?"

"I did. It will only be for two weeks and I'm sure you can enjoy yourself without me."

"I can. But what do you propose to tell Marina about Lady Gwenith? And Lady Deidre? And—" '

"We are not married yet," Sebastian said peevishly. "And with your attitude toward Jason Lord, we may never be."

"So you're sowing wild oats while I give you the excuse."

"Are you keeping tabs on me like a housemother?"

"No. Just wondering if Marina will understand your adventures."

"Let me worry about what Marina will understand," Sebastian said silkily. He took a sip of coffee. "At that, there's been a conspicuous lack of men named Gorgeous in your life this summer. Except for Anton, I must say you've been tediously straitlaced."

Cella started to laugh. "Don't despair. I have a rich, sensual inner life."

Sebastian took another sip of coffee. "I looked for you at breakfast this morning. Where were you? I wanted to go for a walk."

"I was in the village. I lunched there with Father Giacomo. And on the way back I stopped to pay my respects to Mother. And Grandmother. And to all the others sheltered by our trees."

"I was there yesterday." Sebastian glanced away and for a moment he looked somehow smaller, humbler. Then he shrugged, himself again, and said in a too-loud voice, as if anyone who wished to hear were welcome, "How would you like to go for a walk with me now and pay our respects to our more ancient relatives?"

Cella glanced up at her father and drew a deep breath. "I visited them yesterday."

"I thought you did. And probably every day since we've been here," Sebastian said a bit aggressively.

"Almost every day," Cella said, watching him with solemn eyes.

They sat in silence for a while and Cella thought how different she was from her father. He usually visited the ancestral tomb once during the long summer. Sometimes twice. "If you think it's time?" she asked in a quiet voice.

"I think it's time."

"Of course I'll go with you."

Cella and Sebastian followed the path running along the
edge of the forest and slowly made their way up the hill. In
the valley the landscape lay calm and golden in the summer
sunlight. Cella walked along slowly and easily; she was at
home on the narrow, twisting, rocky path. Sebastian followed
beside her, a little stiffly and uneasily. It seemed to Cella that
the air was like white wine and brighter as they reached higher
levels, even though the true mountain loomed over them and
shut out some of the sunlight. They continued going steadily
but gently upward—between the boulders that appeared to be
tossed haphazardly along the way by some giant hand—for
what seemed a long time, until at last they reached the clearing that was the goal of their pilgrimage. Once there, they
were so high and the true mountain so far away, it no longer
looked solid. They were standing in sunlight that was too
bright to look at, and they paused to breathe deeply. Somewhere a lark was singing; except for that, a great stillness lay
over the world.

Cella felt a bubbling up of delight. There was the great,
ancient stone. The sight of it made her light-headed with joy.
But Sebastian was pale.

"This is it?" He always asked the same question, though
he'd been here many times before. It was typical of his ner-
vousness, of his sense of not belonging.

"Yes, Father, we're here," Cella said, her heart dancing.
"Or almost." She walked quickly over to the stone. Sebastian followed and positioned himself beside her. Cella placed
both hands reverently on the huge slab. "This is the portal,
Father. Use your hands." Half fearfully, Sebastian placed his
hands next to hers and together, using every ounce of strength,
they pushed.

For a heartbeat nothing happened.

"Father, stand back," Cella said softly. "You're fighting
it." Sebastian took his hands off the rock. Then Cella pushed
again. And slowly, soundlessly, the huge stone moved on
invisible hinges, opening the door to another world. As always, the music of flutes floated out of the cavern, and the
singing and laughter and whispering of voices from the past
flew out to greet them. Cella stepped forward into the darkness and stopped. Her breath caught in her throat. The dark
was light enough. Sebastian trailed behind, carefully shining
his flashlight before him. Cella gazed not onto the steps lead-

ing to the tomb, but into another world. The ancient world had come to life. Cella felt awe and an astonishment of heart. There was a greenish summery light all around her, and sunshine seemed to be falling through vine leaves. There were wild vines and many groves of flourishing olive trees, and bright water—pools, streams and little cataracts. Cella could hear the trickling of the streams and the humming of the bees. She closed her eyes in reverence, and opened them in wonder. Had she stepped back in time? Here was the ancient world as it had always been. She was "seeing" at last what Spina had always seen.

"Isn't it wonderful, Father?" she said in a hushed tone.

"Wonderful," Sebastian said. "But turn on your flashlight. The batteries have given out in mine. It's hard for me to see my way."

Cella gave him a quick look. "See your way? You still don't see?"

"See what?" Sebastian asked.

"Everything. Oh, my! Isn't she lovely?" It seemed to Cella that coming from a recess in the wall was a tall, graceful woman in a gown of shadowy green interspersed with threads of gold. The woman had the bearing of a priestess or a queen, and she smiled at Cella as though she knew her. Then she faded from view.

Sebastian glanced at Cella uncertainly. "Isn't who beautiful? What do you see in the dark?"

"The ancient world."

"Aaah," he said, as though through Cella he knew that something existed. "It's beautiful?"

"Very beautiful."

Sebastian squinted and again looked around at a space that was pitch black to his eyes. "I'll have to take your word for it."

As he said the words, the mirage—or hallucination or whatever it was—faded and the dark came back to greet them. For an instant Cella wondered if she'd really seen anything. Or if some strange spell had been cast on her eyes so that she saw more than at other times. They were standing at the top of the stone steps that led down to the tomb of their ancestors.

"I'll light the way," Cella said softly, keeping her voice steady. "Follow me, Father."

Slowly they descended into the earth, and as they did so Cella's eyes grew accustomed to the blackness. The ancient world was here, all around them, full of the life of their ancestors. But was it here for her father? The vision had shaken and stirred Cella in a hundred ways. Sebastian seemed more the stranger than her long-gone ancestors. The valley with its grass and vines and running streams, the incredible palace with its pillars and arches, the queen who seemed to know her—Sebastian saw none of it. There must be hundreds of things that he couldn't see. Couldn't understand. Her mind grew darker than the tomb. The idea was unendurable.

Cella and Sebastian sat on the terrace later that day sipping cold wine and talking. Actually, Sebastian did most of the talking. Cella was doing her best to conceal her doubts and confusion.

"The tomb is a remarkable experience," Sebastian said. "It's hard to explain. But every time I go there I feel refreshed and revived. My confidence is restored. I remember who I am. My heritage. I know I can re-create the most magnificent jewelry."

Cella nodded. She paled slightly but otherwise betrayed no emotion. "You mean it puts you in touch with the spirit of the time?"

"Something like that. I seem to understand the harvest festivals. Even the burning of Troy." His tone was reflective. "I don't know how Spina did it. She actually lived in the past. You do too. Though not as deeply as Spina did. But I have no gift. It's not easy for me."

Cella had heard all this before. In different words. And in the past it had always made her heart ache. This time nothing happened. She only listened.

"I'm a man of today," he continued. "How can I understand the passion of the temple chants?"

More and more his words were an echo of those Jason Lord had used, and Cella felt a horrid chill. "You mean you go to the tomb to try to understand the chants? The dances? The past?"

"Yes. To capture the spirit. If I never saw the wall paintings, the artifacts, the jewelry, I'd be lost. I couldn't work. I've nothing in common with my ancestors. With their age."

His look seemed to say he was shut in or shut out. Why was she not moved? "If it means so much to you, why do you go so seldom?"

"One visit does it. Two at the most. I soak up the past."

Cella found herself looking into her father's brown eyes, and something happened that had never happened before. She had a flash of insight, a revelation of sorts in the midst of dread. "And that carries you for the year?"

"Yes. That's why I would never sell any of the jewelry we have in the tomb."

On her guard, hoping she was concealing her dismay, she asked casually, "Have you never thought of selling even a small piece? When there's so much there? One or two small pieces? A pendant? Certain rings? A pin? Not the necklaces or the golden wreaths. Or the tiaras. None of the important jewelry, but now and then something small. Even a small piece would fetch a great deal of money."

A look of quiet wariness appeared on Sebastian's face. "But how could I—how could we—do that? That jewelry embodies the spirit of our past. Our heritage."

"I've thought about it." She hoped he didn't see the distrust that must be naked in her face.

But Sebastian noticed nothing. "You don't really mean it?"

"It's a thought," Cella remarked vaguely.

"Not a good one. You'd never forgive yourself for doing it." But the expression on his face was absolutely new and unprecedented, as though he were reading and appraising her.

"People change, Father."

"You don't. I know you."

As he spoke Cella saw within the depths of his too-sincere eyes a trick of cunning she had never suspected. "As I said, just one or two of the small pieces."

"It's a novel idea." His eyes fairly glittered and he gave her a wonderful smile. "But quite impossible. At any rate, this is too big a subject to talk about lightly." He rose from his chair. "I'm going to my room and stretch out."

Cella nodded and smiled at his departing back. Sitting alone on the patio, she stared without sight at the landscape turning gold in the late afternoon sun. At that moment she felt how much her equilibrium depended on the strength of her will, the will to live with the truth about her father. For her nature was in full revolt against his twentieth-century values.

Cella was conscious of a mortal coldness, a feeling that she would never be warm again, as she sat at the escritoire in her sitting room. She stared at the telephone. She argued with herself. The pros, the cons. Finally she knew there was no way out. The miserable truth had closed around her; she was doing what had to be done. She'd not known until today that she would make this telephone call. That she had fought an inner battle over it ever since she'd left New York.

Her heart was pounding as it had the entire summer when she thought there was someone she must call. She'd pretended to herself that she didn't know who. Now she knew who and she knew why. Her hands felt damp; her mouth was dry; her hand was none too steady as she held the receiver, waiting for the long-distance operator to cross the continent and the ocean and put the call through. Minutes passed that seemed like years. Finally the connection was made. Emory answered. His tone was matter-of-fact. If it had taken years to cross the continent and the ocean, it took Emory an eternity to connect her to Dr. Jason Lord.

Dr. Jason Lord. She repeated the name over to herself. Now that she knew him, she accepted the fact of him completely. Blindly self-indulgent, Sebastian wanted to marry Marina. With Marina came Jason Lord, a threat to the very essence of their life. But how could she continue to oppose Sebastian's will? Sooner or later, he would do as he pleased. He always did. So be it. She would let Sebastian have what he wanted. Perhaps there was some small gain in having Jason believe she favored the marriage.

"Hello, Cella. What a pleasant surprise." Jason Lord's rich voice leaped easily over five thousand miles. "You're not back in Manhattan yet, I gather. Emory tells me this is long distance."

His voice was a shock. It was exactly as she remembered, the voice she had been hearing in her head. "Very long distance. I'm calling from Carrara," she said with false serenity. "But I wanted you to be the first to know. I felt I owed it to you."

Jason's thoughts grew still. Her voice affected him as his affected her. He felt an irresistible current drawing him to the woman across the thousands of miles. For an instant the room blurred as wave after wave of desire eddied through his body. He sat very still, silently fighting it, hearing her say, "Jason, are you there?"

He fought his feeling bleakly, willing it away.

"Jason?" Cella said again with less certainty. "Hello?"

At last he regained control of himself, and the room came sharply into focus. "I'm here. Sorry. Can you hear me now?"

"Yes, now I can."

"It's the telephone system. I could hear you, but you couldn't hear me."

"Of course."

"You were saying you wanted me to be the first to know. The first to know what?"

Words and phrases moved feverishly through Cella's mind, flying in and out with astonishing speed. Could she risk a true explanation? Could she tell him what had happened to her? How he had invaded her thinking, multiplied her doubts? How he had opened her eyes to a new vision of her work? Of Sebastian's work? How reluctant she'd become to continue it all? Unconsciously she shook her head. She couldn't tell him any of that.

"I'm sure Marina told you that I objected to her marriage to my father because of you."

There was a brief silence at the other end of the line. "Yes. Something like that," Jason said.

"I've changed my mind. I look forward to your joining our family."

"What changed your mind?"

"You did." It was a half-truth.

"Our little talk?"

Cella was silent for a few seconds. "We do have so much in common."

Jason closed his eyes and rested his free hand between his thighs. He felt immediately calmed, the calm of potency and absolute control. It made his body stir and harden. He would wait patiently to see her.

"It's going to be a little strange thinking of you as a sister," he said, almost laughing.

For a moment Cella was startled. Then she dismissed his remark as an example of Jason's sense of humor. "And I you," she said, matching his tone. "You tell your mother. I'll tell my father."

And so they left it.

Chapter Twenty

Early autumn in New York was Cella's favorite season. There was an undertone of frost in the still-warm breeze, and the air seemed fresh and sparkling. The streets were charged with an electric vitality, and as Cella walked the city up and down and around and back, exhilaration mixed with sadness; fatigue and happiness became one. She felt like a castaway tossed on a familiar reef. Familiar? Yes. And no. For though everything seemed the same, nothing was as it had been. There was the constant blare of the traffic, the looming skyscrapers as beautiful as they were stupefying, the infinite variety of shops lining the avenues, and of course the crowds of hurrying people—bag women and women of fashion, girls in jeans, men in Brooks Brothers suits, or leather jackets and Levi's, Arabs in caftans, and anything else imaginable. A city of the world that exulted in variety.

Voices seemed to leap out at her from buildings. A woman said, ''Darling, Cella. How wonderful to see you back.'' It took a minute for Cella to remember who she was. Or who the man was who asked, ''Did you get my message about the ballet?'' ''Of course,'' she said. ''I'll be in touch. Tomorrow.'' And she hurried on. She seemed to have lost the gift of fitting names to faces. She hoped the lapse was temporary.

She walked up Madison Avenue thinking she ought to buy something. That would prove she was back. But what? Exactly what came to her as she approached a stationery store. She ordered notepaper. She had thank-you notes to write. Yes. That proved she was back.

Marcus knew Sebastian's study in the house at Sands Point all too well. It was the scene of many disputes between them. Over his going to work on Wall Street instead of at The House of Uni. Over the year he'd spent crewing and seeing the world on a freighter. And then there were the books. In the study were floor-to-ceiling bookcases of fine mahogany and a great number of beautiful books, many of them bound in calf and hand-tooled in gold. Those books were quite special, and unlike the books in the library which covered a great range of topics, they were primarily a collection of pornography through the ages. When Marcus was a young boy, Sebastian occasionally found him mesmerized by one of them. This led to admonitions and the eleven-year-old Marcus being barred from the study. That worked for a few weeks until Sebastian realized several books were missing. There was another scene between Marcus and Sebastian, which only Spina could end. Again there was a calm until Sebastian, in search of a dictionary, stumbled across the pornography collection Marcus was building for himself. But by this time Marcus was too big a boy to order around. And Sebastian decided to leave well enough alone and give thanks that any teenager as handsome—almost pretty—as Marcus was fixated on girls. But it did seem to Marcus as if he and Sebastian were destined to have most of their disagreements in this room.

Now Marcus sat at the edge of a chair sipping a vermouth cassise. Relaxed behind his desk, Sebastian smoked a cigarette and stared at the ceiling. He had a clear idea of why Marcus was here and he hoped to make the discussion short and definite. Finally, glancing at Marcus speculatively, he spoke.

"Since you've gone to the trouble to come here within two days of our arrival, logically it follows that you need money."

Marcus' hand paused in the act of conveying the drink to his lips. He laughed nervously. "Yes, I do. But I also wanted to see both of you. You've been away for almost three months. You are my family."

"Come to the point," Sebastian said. "How much money do you need? And why?"

"Not that much and not for that long. It would only be a loan. I'll pay interest on it."

"How much?"

"One and a half million," Marcus said quickly. He had no way of telling from his father's face exactly what Sebastian's reaction was, but he knew his father well enough to know it wasn't good. Money was always a sticking point with Sebastian.

After a moment's pause Sebastian asked, "Why?"

Marcus found it impossible to explain what had happened and still come up smelling like a rose. He was going to eat shit and he might as well start swallowing it.

"I overinvested in Minnerex."

"The people who were putting De Beers out of business?"

"That's right."

"Their diamonds don't cut glass?"

"Their diamonds don't cut butter. It was a promotion. The insiders—the owners of the company—unloaded a lot of stock through my firm to the public. There was a column on them in *Barron's*, and the stock fell out of bed."

"You're a fool."

"I made a mistake. I was overly optimistic." Marcus began to plead. "Look, Father, one and a half million won't even put a small dent in your portfolio. Or your lifestyle. And I'll have the principal back to you plus interest."

Sebastian seemed not to have heard him. "I brought you a present from London. A mystery clock. J.P. Morgan owned one once." He gave Marcus a malicious glance. "It cost a good deal. I meant it as a birthday present. But if you need money so badly I could give it to you now. You could sell it."

Marcus stared at him. He had the feeling that he was looking at a stranger. "Father, this is a very serious matter. I must have the money to cover my losses."

"Sell the clock."

"It's not worth one and a half million."

"No, but it is a beginning. Then you could sell your John Lobb shoes. And your Lamborghini." Sebastian gave Marcus a pallid smile. "Shall I tell Alda you're staying for dinner? Cella will be glad to see you."

Marcus put the glass down on the side table and rose to his feet with some effort. He gazed at Sebastian wearily. "I expected you to say no, but now that you have, I admit I'm hurt." He swallowed hard. "You know I'll go bankrupt. And that's just the beginning."

Sebastian stared straight ahead. "Spare me the details. Are you staying for dinner?"

Marcus was aware that he was adrift on a dangerous sea. He could think of nothing else but his need to be saved. He shouted, "Dammit! I'm your son! Doesn't that count for anything? What the hell's the matter with you, Father? We're suppose to be a family."

Sebastian rose quietly to his feet. "I have some work to do now. So if you'll excuse me, I'll see you at dinner." If Marcus had been listening, he would have realized how edgy and disconcerted Sebastian sounded.

"Dammit! You're not to be believed!" Marcus bellowed. Then he turned on his heel and walked out. He strode through the corridor, brushing past Cella, who had entered the house just minutes before.

"Marcus!" she cried out with pleasure.

He didn't answer but kept going toward the door, dimly aware of a strange face.

"Marcus!" Cella followed him quickly, taking hold of his arm. Impatiently, Marcus tried to shake her off, and when she wouldn't let go, he stopped and stared at her. He thought she said something, and he said something in reply. She shook her head with a familiar exasperation and slowly she came into focus. It was Cella.

"Marcus! What's the matter?"

He took a deep breath, trying to clear his mind. "I've had some words with Father."

"About what?" Cella asked, though she knew the answer.

Their eyes met. Marcus frowned. "You know about what. About money."

"How much?"

"Not more than Father can afford. Without depriving himself of a Ferrari—if he wanted one—a Hermitage watch or an hour's sleep."

"Maybe I can . . ."

"You can't. Unless you happen to have a million and a half lying around. I mean a million and a half that isn't tied up in your stock in The House of Uni. And your salary won't do it. I need one and a half million dollars. Now."

Cella pursed her lips. "Another Wall Street speculation?"

"Call it that."

"And Father said no?" Cella felt a cold, dull ache settle around her heart.

"He invited me to dinner. And suggested I sell the birthday present he plans to give me, to raise the money. A mystery clock. And my shoes and car. I've seen those clocks. They're wonderful. But I never exchange or sell birthday presents. Even his." Marcus then went on with a forced nonchalance. "It's lucky I have other sources. Father was really my worst-case scenario."

Cella could see the struggle in his face, the effort to mask the deep hurt he felt. "He'll change his mind. I'll speak to him tonight."

Marcus stepped back and studied her. "You know, dear, you are a beauty. It's a pleasure to have you back. I'll ring you shortly. Right now I must see a man about money."

He was out the door, even as she called, "Marcus, please stay."

That evening at dinner Sebastian did not mention Marcus. Cella tried a variety of techniques ranging from humor to fatherly love. The silence was deafening. Sebastian refused to discuss his son, and his son's money troubles. He began to look impatient. He wanted to talk about his ideas for the Astarte. The more enthusiastically he talked the more depressed Cella grew.

"Well, what do you think of my ideas?" he asked.

Cella's throat felt dry and tight. "They're quite good."

"And now I have a surprise for you."

Cella waited, then said in a quiet voice, "What kind of surprise?"

"I've decided to create the Astarte myself. Alone. Without your help. It will be my masterpiece."

Cella shut her eyes, drawing in her breath slowly to steady herself. "That's a fine idea," she said at last.

"I thought you would agree. You haven't liked the idea of doing it from the beginning." He paused. "Have you?"

"Not much."

"Then we're both satisfied. You'll run the shop while I spend a month at Sands Point creating the necklace. Tell our friends and clients I'm in France. With a client." He smiled broadly. "And when it's finished, we'll have a masterpiece to sell. My masterpiece."

Cella stared at him. She wondered if she could ever make Sebastian understand the way she now felt about his work. She didn't think so.

Later that evening, Cella waited impatiently in the lobby of Anton's apartment house for the elevator. She had telephoned ahead that she was coming. She needed his advice. She needed his love and comfort. Minutes dragged by while she waited. Where was the elevator? At last, directly opposite her, the elevator doors slowly opened, and there stood . . . Cella gasped.

"Marcus!"

"We meet again." He grinned at her. "Twice in one day. We really are star-crossed."

"You were seeing Anton?"

"Our esteemed cousin."

"I thought you had to see a man about money."

"I did." Marcus shrugged. "But he's losing his shirt in

gold. Then I checked out another friend. But he's up to his ass in Texas real estate. Finally it occurred to me that charity begins at home. Not at our home, of course.'' Cella heard the bitterness in his voice, saw the intensity in his eyes. ''But we do have kin. So here I am.''

''Anton doesn't have a million and a half dollars.'' Cella was in a quandary. ''I mean a million and a half that isn't in the Vilanova family trust.''

''True. But he has other sources. I should have seen him first. It would have saved a lot of wear and tear. Our cousin does know how to turn a buck.'' He looked at her steadily. ''Anyway, he's waiting for you. Thank him for me again. I've already kissed him on both cheeks.''

''I'm glad he was helpful.''

''He was better than helpful. He may save my life. Keep your fingers crossed.'' Marcus gave Cella a long look. ''And you can tell our dear father to go straight to an Etruscan hell. Whatever that is. In the future you and I will meet at my apartment. Or the Oak Bar. Or the Irish bar. Or Lutece. Or other convivial watering holes. Never in Father's house again. Bye, love.'' Marcus saluted her and hurried through the lobby.

''Actually, it's even more serious than Sebastian realizes,'' Anton said as he slowly sipped his gin and tonic.

''He'll be wiped out? Father knows that. I think he sees it as a lesson for Marcus,'' Cella said as she paced the floor.

''Worse than that, dearest.''

''Worse than bankruptcy?''

Anton hesitated. He could see how tense Cella had become. Color stained her cheeks; her eyes were bright. ''Yes, worse. He could go to jail. For a year or more. That's worse.''

Cella collapsed in an armchair as though her legs had been shot out from under her. ''What happened?'' she asked when she found her breath.

''He says he only borrowed the money. He meant to repay it with interest.''

''Borrowed what money? From who? I don't understand.''

''I know. The word *borrow* is a euphemism. What he did was borrow his cutomers' stock.''

''Shares that don't really belong to him?''

''Exactly. Stock that doesn't belong to him. Shares that are held in the firm's name. He used customer stock as collateral to borrow additional monies from the banks. That's a criminal offense.''

Cella heard the words and couldn't stop hearing them. They

kept echoing in her mind until they were drowned out by the clamor of other voices. Uncle Victor's, full of irritation with his "master forgers." Jason Lord's, fervent about truth. Sebastian's satisfaction with the high price of a snake ring he had made, which supposedly came from ancient Greece. Her mother's soft tones, remembering the radiance of the past. Telling Marcus he would kiss the feet of many fools. And warning her to be careful. When had Spina said that? And why? Be careful of what? Or whom? Cella shivered. How would Marcus explain what he did? Would he say it wasn't stealing, just borrowing? And didn't The House of Uni do exactly that? Borrow from the past? Much more than a million and a half dollars, too. Cella felt sick. Were they all merely common criminals? Shame at this thought made her blush.

Anton saw the color sweep up over her neck, burning her cheeks. With a sudden decisiveness, he determined it was time to face what he'd been putting off for so many years. It was time to tell Cella everything. About Marcus. About himself.

"Marcus was too greedy. He went too far. And now he hasn't much time to pay the piper. He didn't tell Sebastian the full truth because he was afraid it would make your father even more self-righteous. Maybe it would. But since Sebastian won't help, I must. So I'm arranging to get him the million and a half dollars."

The silence that followed seemed intensely loud, and to go on forever. Cella broke it at last, asking in a cold, tired voice, "Where do you propose to get that much cash?"

"I have a source," Anton answered almost too eagerly.

"What source?" Cella asked, unbelieving. "The bulk of your holdings is tied up in the Vilanova family trust. As mine is in The House of Uni. You can't touch that money. That's not a source."

"I wasn't thinking of the Trust. I was thinking of my Luxembourg Corporation." Anton was surprised at how disgusted he suddenly felt with himself at the mention of the Luxembourg Corporation and the corruption it stood for.

Cella felt slightly dizzy. So much was happening. "What is the Luxembourg Corporation?"

Her face was intent, her violet eyes watchful, and for a moment Anton had nothing to say. He had planned to tell her about it one day. Someday. When she was more ready. But instead it had to be now. It took a huge effort, but his voice was level, almost matter-of-fact. Only one small gesture, running his hand through his hair, betrayed his anxiety. He told her about the business arrangement he had with Lawrence Lord. He began in a strain of easy confidence, but as Cella listened, she understood that his words were being poured out in an effort to bridge the gap that was widening between them. He explained how he had done the financing, and how Lord had been the buyer and the seller, providing the authority that museum directors needed. He described how they bought paintings at one price from one museum and sold them at a higher price to another museum. Since most of the small, out-of-town museums had little knowledge of the art market, they usually sold Lord excellent paintings well below their value. Lawrence was a truffle hound at finding the gems. Thanks to him, Anton's quarter-of-a-million-dollar investment was now worth about five million dollars.

Cella looked at Anton a long time, the color drained from her face. When she spoke she couldn't hide the fear in her voice. "Museums are usually owned by the city they're built in, aren't they?"

"Not always. There are private museums, like the Frick. But yes, usually they're owned by the city."

Cella felt a blank emptiness. "I see."

Anton saw too. He watched her hands move in a shocked incoherent way, and he knew how much she disliked what he had told her. "It's exactly what you think," he said, too weary and ashamed to pretend. "But it is also business."

"I know. Buy low. Sell high. The great art-world scam. But in this case aren't you conning the American people? Their taxes support the museums."

"I suppose you could say that."

Cella sighed. "I wish you hadn't told me about it."

"Would you rather I lied to you about where the money for Marcus comes from?"

"Maybe. I don't know. Feelings are never simple."

"Neither is the truth."

As he spoke he sensed instinctively a shift, a very delicate change in Cella's attitude. He knew her so well, he could almost feel the pulse of her heart, and now he felt a withdrawal from him; reluctant, sad, but a withdrawal just the same. A barrier was slowly being erected.

Cella rose and paced about the room. For an instant she couldn't think or feel. Then she said with a light self-mockery, "Marcus steals from investors. You steal from museums. I steal from the past. It seems we are quite a den of thieves."

Anton felt split in two. One half longed to comfort and

console her. To tell her she mustn't think of her work in the same breath as Marcus. Or himself. What they did, they did solely for money. What Cella created was an act of love. That was half the truth. The other half argued forcibly that she must face the facts. Whatever Lucca and Spina had thought they were doing when they started The House of Uni, the times had corrupted their dream. Sebastian and even Cella were no different from Marcus and he. They'd all—each in his own way—been seduced by money.

Yet how could he say that to her? Something in the quiet, stoic look of her face made him feel like a bully. She had her own destiny to wrestle with.

After a minute he spoke. "What can I say? Being sorry isn't good enough."

Cella kept looking at him, and she saw that he was suffering as much as she was. His eyes seemed to say, "Help me. Love me. Forgive me."

His appeal came home to her with such force that for an instant she felt the numbness draining out of her body. He reached for her and held her hard against him, comforting her, comforting himself. He felt her body pressing warmly against him, her face burrowing into his chest, her hands caressing him. He stroked her shining hair, and then, aroused by her closeness, he kissed her passionately, beside himself with desire.

It was part of Cella's genius for sensuality that no taint of their quarrel served to diminish the intensity of their love-making. If anything, it served to heighten her senses, and she abandoned herself to an extravagance of kisses and caresses. He took her so quickly he came before she did, leaving her wild with excitement. Suddenly she became all mouth, tongue and fingers, all stinging bites, until he responded savagely again—if they could kill each other this way, they would.

Afterward, out of sheer exhaustion, they fell asleep. Later, lying side by side in bed, spent and entangled, Cella was aware of a process going on deep within her, a process of weighing, considering, deciding. Staring into nothingness, she felt the darkness inside herself. She thought she should be disgusted with him, but what was the sense? It was no use trying to deny she loved him. Yet underneath, all her being was racked with sobs.

She was not aware of having fallen asleep, but she must have, because the light was breaking when she awoke with a start. She stared at Anton's sleeping figure, listened to the even rhythm of his breathing, and an immense weariness possessed her. But her mind was clear. She knew that she had to face the truth directly, make an adjustment to it then and there, so she could stand it. They would not spend another night like this. She must break with Anton now. While she still could. On this point she was quite certain. Quietly she dressed, and while he slept deeply, she slipped out of the bedroom, tiptoing toward the apartment door. This was the way, the only way. But blanketing her was a feeling of numbness such as one might feel on discovering one had a fatal illness. For that was exactly the case.

═══ Chapter Twenty-one ═══

Wherever one looked there was hectic excitement. Turmoil and tumult. Anxious women with briefcases. Feverish men with suitcases. Boys and girls in jeans carrying backpacks, yahooing to each other. Kennedy Airport was a milling crowd of babbling, shouting, talking, chanting people, and finding someone was not easy. Even when one knew where to look. The man should be standing on line at the Air France ticket counter. The woman should be beside him. A pair of eyes stared malevolently over the crowd. They weren't there. The eyes scanned every person and became opaque with boredom.

Abruptly the eyes stopped roving and focused. For a moment they became so confused they actually seemed not to recognize the man and the woman kissing each other. Much as the sight was expected, it was bewildering. Slowly the eyes drew closer, but not so near as to be noticed, or that the ears could hear what the man said to the woman when they kissed again and then broke apart. In the chaotic vortex of the soul of the eyes, what was seen was more important than what was said. The man put a small gold ring on the thumb of the woman. The sight made the watcher dizzy. It was an ancient symbolic gesture of marriage.

The man stepped back and smiled at the woman. His expression was one many men would recognize: that of a man who had spent a satisfying time making love with the woman and was sorry he was leaving her to board a plane.

The eyes watched the man and woman kiss good-bye again. The man seemed to insist that the woman leave the airport before he went through the security check. Impulsively the woman stood on tiptoe and kissed the man hard on the mouth. Then, unwillingly, she turned and walked toward the exit. The eyes followed her from a safe distance, then returned for an instant to watch the man go through the security check.

The man had vanished. Or he had gone so swiftly through the security check that he seemed to have vanished. It didn't matter. The next performance in the soul of the eyes was beginning.

The man had not vanished through the security check. He was hurrying through the cold night air outside the terminal toward a rented limousine. In less than half an hour he would be in Sands Point and free to work on the Astarte. Sebastian was relieved to have the airport charade over with. Marina had insisted on seeing him off. As he stepped into the limo his eyes grew thoughtful. She'd make a fine wife.

Cella and Juliana were busily readying the shop for the fall opening. Cella was trying to decide how to display the ancient Japanese fishhook, and a golden cross. Occasionally Juliana would answer the telephone and say that neither Cella nor Sebastian was present. Until Anton called. For a moment Cella, who was accustomed to managing awkward moments with ease, felt at a loss. She went to her office and picked up the receiver.

"Hello there," she said.

"The same to you. Are we still on for dinner tonight?"

"Marina telephoned. She wants me to come to dinner. To celebrate. She and Sebastian are getting married." Cella laughed dryly. "I gave my permission."

"Sebastian and Marina? You didn't tell me."

"I know. I had other things on my mind," she floundered.

Anton took a moment to steady his thoughts. "I think we have a great deal to talk about. When?"

"I don't know."

"When!" It was not a question.

She took a moment to answer, then said gently, "Let me call you."

Anton gave a deep sigh. "Cella, we've known each other all our lives. Don't behave as if you met me at a dinner party last night."

"Sorry. But I must sort things out first."

"We'll sort them out together. For instance, you seem to have forgotten that Jason Lord is still Marina's son."

"I think I misjudged him."

Anton considered this. Finally he said, "Maybe. All the more reason we should talk." Cella was silent so he continued, trying his best to be casual. "Cella, what are you doing? What are you worried about?"

There was a faint shiver in her voice when she answered, "I'm worried about everything."

"That's why you need me. We'll work it out."

"We can't. I'm worried about you too."

"That's absurd."

"And about myself. Everything has changed."

"Nothing has really changed, you know. Only the way you now see it."

"That's what makes it hard to understand."

"What can I do?" His voice was strained.

"Nothing now. Bear with me."

"As you wish," he said.

"You really are an English gentleman," Cella said with a half-whimsical flash of regret. Then she hung up.

"You sounded very young on the telephone," Marina said as she led Ben Stein into the exquisitely furnished living room. "I've heard so much about you."

"Not all of it flattering, I'm sure." Stein walked to a big, comfortable armchair and sat down in it easily. Another man of his small size would have appeared lost in the chair. Somehow Ben Stein filled it completely.

"Would you like coffee? Or something stronger? Perhaps a scotch?" Marina said, sitting down opposite him.

"Nothing, thank you." Without being aware of the gesture, he secured the bobby pins—brown today—that held his brown yarmulke.

"How about Perrier water?"

"I'm not thirsty, thank you."

"You can't be counting calories." Marina smiled stiffly.

Ben Stein shook his head.

Marina cleared her throat. "You said on the telephone that you wanted to talk about Phillip Mckay. I was wondering when you would contact me." Looking at him, Marina thought how deceptive his size was. At first glance it made him seem diffident, modest. It was a very good disguise.

"You were in Santa Barbara this past summer?" he asked.

"Then you did try to reach me?"

"No. I had a lot of information to organize before talking to you."

Momentarily Marina felt afraid. Then she dismissed the feeling as silly. "You said if you'd wanted to reach me sooner you could have. That makes me think I'm not under suspicion."

"There are no suspects at the moment." Stein took a small

notebook and a ballpoint pen from his pocket. "I wonder if you'll oblige me by answering a few questions."

"I'd be more than delighted to. What do you want to know?"

Noting the exaggeration in her words, Ben Stein glanced up from his notebook, but Marina Lord was studying her fingernails.

"Would it be asking too much if we reviewed the details of your relationship with the deceased? Only the relevant ones, naturally."

"I've nothing to hide," Marina said impatiently to her fingernails.

"I assume that."

"If I did it would be impossible. You undoubtedly know a great deal already about my affair with Phillip. The art world thrives on gossip."

"True. But I'd like to get your version. First there is the question of your possible marriage to him. Let me explain what I mean by that . . ."

Ben Stein went into some detail about the romance between Marina and Phillip and the question of any other suitors who might have been jealous. Anyone in her life? Any women in Phillip's? Stein knew from long experience that anyone who had to listen to his or her own biography recited by another will build up an almost unbearable urge to set the record straight, if it needed straightening. Marina was no exception. When Stein paused for breath, she burst out with all her pent-up energy to give her version.

"While Phillip and I were seeing each other, there was no one else. No one. Not for me. Not for him. We were completely devoted."

She went on to explain that she was not that sort of woman. She never involved herself with more than one man at a time. She gave herself completely. So did Phillip. When Phillip and she parted, it was because somehow she fell out of love. It happens. No third party had caused the breakup. On that point she was adamant. In truth, the only one who might have been jealous was Lawrence Lord. Her former husband. He was always on the scene. Hovering in the background. Though they'd been divorced for a long time, she felt his presence, his pressure.

"He used to say he was my anchor. As if I needed an anchor. I should never have married him. It was the mistake of a young, sheltered girl."

She had married a fantasy, she said. A reputation. Not a

man. Not a person. Not even a partner. She loved art and he was so eminent in the field, even as a young man. It was all a sad mistake.

"I see," said Ben Stein, diligently writing in his notebook.

"By the time I realized my mistake, I couldn't leave him," she said soberly. "I had to wait for Jason to grow up. One shouldn't take one's son away from his father at too young an age. It was actually a bad joke on me. When I finally left, Jason chose to remain with his father." Then, unexpectedly, she asked, "Do you have children?"

Ben Stein shook his head, allowing himself a small frown of disappointment.

"But you are married?"

"Yes. Very happily, as a matter of fact."

"We can't all be lucky," Marina said. "I wasn't unhappy. But I wasn't happy. I simply existed. My whole life was bound up with Jason. Until I met Hans."

A short lull occurred while Ben Stein took refuge in more notes. "Hans?" he asked at last, looking up. "Who is Hans?"

"He was Jason's instructor in draftsmanship at college."

"Draftsmanship?"

"At that time Jason was studying to be an architect. He would have made a marvelously gifted architect if he'd continued his studies."

"Interesting. Why did he give it up?"

"I don't know. It happened after I divorced Lawrence. I've always blamed myself for his change of career. Somehow I think the divorce affected Jason's interest in architecture."

"He does important work now. He's quite celebrated. Perhaps it was for the best," Ben Stein said soothingly.

"Perhaps. I don't know. Heaven knows, we're all human and we make mistakes."

"Well, we were speaking of your connection to Mr. Etzel." Ben Stein paused, waiting for Marina to ask him how he knew Hans' last name. When she didn't, he continued. "You were saying . . . ?"

"Hans. Hans Etzel. He was a visiting instructor from Heidelberg. Very talented. Jason adored him. Brought him home to dinner constantly." Marina's face was turned away as if she were studying the fall of the draperies. "I adored him too. To be perfectly frank, I fell in love for the first time in my life."

Again Ben Stein took his time. He looked at his notes and

then back to Marina. "Did you divorce Dr. Lord to marry Mr. Etzel?"

"No! I divorced Dr. Lord for good and sufficient reasons," Marina said with some impatience. "Hans Etzel had returned to Germany by the time that happened."

"I see. You had ceased to be, er, in love?" Stein's voice was moderate and consoling.

"No, I was still in love with Hans. He refused to see me," Marina said more quietly.

"I see," Ben Stein continued sympathetically.

"You see nothing. Hans never stopped loving me. But something terrible happened to him. One night after he left me, he was attacked. By a vagrant, the police said. And hospitalized for a month." Marina shook her head and shuddered. "I think he blamed me. He believed that it was Lawrence who did it. Or paid someone to do it. Out of jealousy." For an instant she clenched her right fist. "I think so too."

Ben Stein did not reply at first but went on writing. "Could you give me details, Mrs. Lord? The dates and the name of the hospital?"

She could and she did; reciting the hospital name, the hour the next day that she'd been informed of the assault, as well as the hour the doctor had told her that Hans did not wish to see her. Ever again. Her voice broke a little when she completed her story. Marina went on to say that she believed her ex-husband was still insanely jealous. She couldn't see how it was possible, but she half believed he was involved in the death of Andrew Henderson, the man she had planned to marry five years ago in Barcelona. She gave more names, dates and places.

When she finished, Ben Stein stood up, dropping his small notebook back into his pocket. "You've been very kind," he said. "And very helpful."

After a few moments more of meaningless chatter about Marina's fondness for Phillip Mckay, she walked him to the door.

Almost imperceptibly, Marina's relationship with Jason began to take on a different tone and color. There were still the patches of gray and shadow, but more and more it seemed to have a golden cast. At dinner, while Marina sipped a martini and Jason his white wine, he looked at his watch. "Mother," he said, "who or what are we waiting for?"

"Someone you should know. She's not usually late."

"A virtue," said Jason.

Marina's smile was offhanded.

When the house phone rang, the maid answered it quickly with a "Yes, she's expected."

Shortly afterward, Cella Taggard entered the softly lighted room. Her dress was the color of deep violets, her face alight with easy animation.

"Cella," Marina said, moving toward her.

"Marina, I'm sorry." Cella greeted her with warmth. "Please forgive me. A call from Istanbul." As she spoke she must have felt the force of Jason's silent presence, for she seemed to gather herself together as she turned toward him. "Jason, how pleasant."

"Hello, Cella."

"Hello." Cella felt a sensation of shyness and an acute unwillingness to have him think the meeting was planned. "I didn't know you were coming."

"I didn't know you were." For a moment they exchanged glances, then Jason said, "But I am glad to see you again. And you don't mind?"

"Oh, no. I'm delighted."

"Then we are both pleasantly surprised. My mother is a Machiavelli among hostesses."

"I take that as a compliment," Marina said. "I think it's time this family got to know each other better." And to keep the tone of the evening frivolous, she hurried on with chitchat about theater and ballet and opera until dinner was announced.

They sat at one end of a long candlelit table, Jason and Cella on either side of Marina.

"Usually I despise dinner parties," Jason said. "But small ones can be interesting. Large ones are atrocious. Too many people who don't know each other and have nothing to say to one another eating together. Then there are the after-dinner faces. The women look particularly exhausted."

"You sound like Lord Byron."

"I'm hardly a poet."

From her seat Marina watched them and listened. A very handsome pair. She saw Cella's neck and shoulders glow like marble; the shining black hair; the incandescent face. Jason's gleaming blond hair was slightly disheveled and his strong face was full of an enthusiasm she remembered from his boyhood. He was talking constantly, almost babbling, and ate very little. Cella sat hugging silence, sometimes bubbling to the surface in a splash of talk, then sipping her wine and listening again.

"You really like claret?" Jason asked.

"I love it."

"Unusual. Most women prefer white wine."

Jason found it impossible to look at her dispassionately. She wore no makeup, and her complexion looked soap-and-water clean, like a schoolgirl's. Yet there was a radiance about her face that was almost hypnotic. He desperately wished that the dinner would end. And that it would go on forever.

Later on, over brandy, the three of them talked with animation about Marina's forthcoming marriage to Sebastian.

"Actually, I expected to meet Sebastian this evening. Where is my future father-in-law during this festive family gathering? Shouldn't he be here?" Jason asked amiably.

"He's in France with a client," Cella answered quickly.

There was a short silence as Cella thought about the lies that must be told from now on. "He has many clients abroad," she added.

"Perhaps when we're married, I'll go with him," Marina said.

"Perhaps," Cella said, wondering how thin hypocrisy could wear. "His trips are rather hectic. Sebastian is very preoccupied." She smiled at Marina.

"At the moment, it's an unimportant question. Let's talk about the wedding. Large or small? What is your view, Jason?"

"Small. I like small weddings. Small dinner parties. Small families."

"Ours is large," Cella said, smiling at him.

Her steady gaze was not flirtatious, but it aroused in him sensations and thoughts and desires that he couldn't ignore. The continued response of his body to her presence frightened him. Images of inconceivable sexuality ricocheted through his mind. It was impossible for Jason to look at her coolly. He tried to make his usual judgments, but his rational mind refused all help. It was canceled by the urgent demands of his senses.

"You are Etruscans. I forgot. The extended family, I believe," he said politely.

"In the past. Now we make do with modern forms."

"Jason, you can give me away," Marina interrupted. "And you'll be maid of honor, Cella."

"Who will be Sebastian's best man?" Jason asked. "Victor Vilanova?"

"Marcus. Perhaps," Cella said, inventing as she went along. "But I really think Sebastian may suggest an elope-

ment, Marina. My father is an incorrigible romantic. As you
know.''

"I know." Marina glowed. "Maybe we will elope. Or do
something quietly in a judge's chambers.''

"Have you actually set the date?'' Jason asked in a neutral
tone.

"No. This is my way of getting accustomed to the idea of
marriage again.''

"A happier marriage,'' he said almost humbly.

"Yes, something like that, dear,'' Marina agreed. "I haven't
even thought about where we might honeymoon.''

Cella moved through the conversation as one moves through
a jungle in a dream. The smoothness of her manner overlaid
a chaotic agitation. So much was happening so fast. Nothing
would ever be quite the same. A wedding. A new Mrs. Sebastian Taggard. Her stepmother. Jason Lord. Her new stepbrother. A honeymoon. A complete stranger marrying into a
family such as theirs, with its customs, its history, its inter-
connections. If it weren't so impossible, it would be almost
high comedy. She had a sense of moving swiftly out of the
past toward the future. She thought of Anton and their deep
attachment and wondered if the end of the past meant the end
of their loving. She had bathed in a tub of warm water. One
does not bathe in the same water twice. She had taken a risk
and now must live with it.

It was not very late, but Jason decided that he would walk
Cella home. To save her the expense of the cab, he said jok-
ingly. Marina was delighted. They were hitting it off.

The evening was warm.

"Cella . . .'' Jason said.

She smiled. She liked the way he pronounced her name. It
had an Italian accent.

"What changed your mind?'' he asked.

"About my father and your mother marrying?''

"Yes.'' Jason's face was still, his features composed.

"In a way, you did. I thought about what you said the
afternoon we met, and after a while it made more and more
sense.'' Her violet eyes regarded him levelly.

"About the ancient world?''

"About the ancient world.''

"I don't see the connection.''

"You don't have to. I do.'' She smiled. "And I wish you'd
stop looking as if you'd seen Medusa. I thought you'd be
pleased with your influence.''

"I am very pleased.'' Jason gave her his most sincere smile.

Their eyes met, and for an instant Jason felt drunk. He made himself stare straight ahead to avoid the sight of her wide mouth, her full hips, her high breasts, her long, strong, deceptively slim legs, all promising sexual strength and passion. When he looked at her striding gracefully beside him, he felt his flesh harden and leap. Her slightest movement made his breath shorten as he thought of the possibilities.

While they walked, they talked little, each lost in his own thoughts. Here and there were bursts of conversation from other evening strollers that neither of them noticed. At a corner two young girls laughed and flirted with Jason. A boy walked past and gave Cella a special whistle. A couple of teenagers in green sneakers started to bar their way, gave Jason a measuring look and moved on.

Cella paid no attention to any of it. All she heard was the beating of her heart. All evening her mind had argued with itself. How could she feel so drawn to a man she had so recently despised? As they approached the Taggard home, their steps grew slower. They passed a still brightly lit outdoor cafe.

"Would you like to stop for a nightcap?" Cella asked, feeling awkward about wanting to prolong the evening.

Jason sighed. "I would, but I still have a report to write tonight."

Cella gave him a teasing look. "I suppose the next time we'll meet will be at the wedding."

Jason cleared his throat, then glanced up and down the street casually, trying to wipe out the pain and confusion of leaving her. "Perhaps sooner. You were going to show me the Aphrodite. Or have you decided against it?"

For an instant Cella looked at him curiously, then dismissed the feeling as unworthy. "I mean to. When my father returns from France."

"Good. Call me. We'll set up an appointment. I admit to considerable interest."

"I'll call," Cella said, feeling put off. Still, it was better than nothing.

Suddenly he gave her a disarming smile. "Marina asked me to escort her to the Rheims opening at the Hathaway Gallery on Thursday of next week. It's an unusual photography exhibit. As I understand it, Eric Rheims used nude models in ancient archaeological sites. The Pyramids. The Acropolis. And such. It's taken him five years to complete the collection. Might be well worth seeing." He tilted his head in a question. "Will you be there?"

"With a vengeance. I'm on display," Cella said with sudden embarrassment.

"You are?"

"I was one of Eric's models." To her own surprise, Cella felt herself blush. "It's a voyeur's delight."

Jason looked away quickly. He understood the blush. And desire flared in his eyes. "Then I mustn't miss it," he said, regaining his calm.

"Maybe you should." Cella grinned impishly. "I was younger then. And a bit of an exhibitionist."

"But no less beautiful."

Again their eyes met, and he looked away first.

PART EIGHT

THE GATHERING STORM

═ Chapter Twenty-two ═

Cella slipped a double strand of red Bakelite hearts with a gold tassel clasp around her neck. Then she slid over each wrist a sumptuous armload of Bakelite bangles, all richly colored; some plaid, some polka-dot, one studded with rhinestones, another inlaid with amber. It amused her that the jewelry she wore was plastic. Loading herself down with Depression-era costume jewelry that once had sold for a few cents to a few dollars was something of a put-down to the diamonds that would be present at the exhibit. Staring into her full-length cheval mirror, she studied the effect of the necklace and bracelets against her scarlet dress. If one could call an open-crocheted, thigh-high, see-through slip of a garment with two dental-floss straps to hold it up a dress. A pair of pink stockings and a cache-sexe sewn into the garment were all that kept her from being arrested for indecent exposure. This costume—for it was a costume quite suitable for an orgy—was equally suitable for tonight's gala opening at the Hathaway Gallery.

At first, when she remembered that Jason Lord would be there, Cella had almost changed her mind about the costume. Something more discreet, perhaps. In the end she had said to hell with it. Why should she itsy-poo around for Lord Jason? The same perverse and independent nature that had egged her on to pose nude for Eric's photography now insisted she not change her dress. If Dr. Jason Lord was shocked, dear Dr. Jason Lord would be shocked. She started to laugh. What a hoot and a holler if he actually blushed. But he would have to accept that his future stepsister was an exhibitionist. At that, she suspected he was something of a voyeur. She could smell it. They should get along famously.

As Cella brushed her hair, the second button on her telephone lit up. Someone was calling on the private line. Inexplicably, she was startled. Who was it? Anton calling about the opening? She hoped not. Marcus? That was impossible. Not in his mood. And Sebastian couldn't possibly be telephoning from Sands Point. She picked up the receiver.

"Hello?" Hesitancy was evident in her tone.

"Cella. This is Jason Lord."

Cella's hand shook.

"Marina and I thought we might escort you to the Rheims opening since Sebastian is in France. Or do you have another engagement?"

"No. I'm free."

There was a silence.

"Well, how about it?" Jason asked.

"I'd love to go with you," Cella answered. "And Marina."

Jason Lord waited for Cella in the second-floor living room, almost at his ease with the evening ahead. Freshly showered and shaved, holding a cigarette for the first time in years, with no savage fantasies whispering in his ears, Jason looked forward to a fine October evening in Manhattan. When Cella appeared, he whistled.

"That's quite an outfit," he said.

"I thought I'd introduce the real me in stages," Cella responded, laughing. "You'll see more of the real me at the exhibition."

"There isn't much more to see," Jason said easily, joining in her laughter.

"If you think so, you're in for a shock."

Before Cella could say any more, Jason added, "But you do look wonderful."

"Thank you." Cella smiled back. She looked hard at Jason; he looked wonderful too, like a man and a gentleman, turned out and masculine, wearing an impeccable dinner jacket with a small black bow tie perfectly knotted. "You look very handsome yourself."

"Come. Your chariot awaits." Jason glowed. "And so does Marina. We'll drink dreadful champagne and stare at what are hopefully great photographs." As he helped Cella into a black fox stole, he asked, "What do you think of Eric's work?"

"I haven't seen the photographs."

"But you posed for them."

"Eric says he wants to surprise me."

Jason's face lit up as he smiled. "Then it should be a stimulating evening for all of us."

* * *

The October evening was cool, and Cella shivered nervously under her black fox stole as the limousine pulled up in front of the Hathaway Gallery. Jason Lord offered her his hand when she stepped from the car to the sidewalk, and then turned to help Marina out of the limousine. People were coming and going, talking, laughing, greeting one another as they entered the crowded gallery. One end of the huge room was devoted to an open bar, but for those who preferred looking at the photographs to bellying up to the bar, a half-dozen young men dressed as Roman legionnaires and young women done as vestal virgins carried trays laden with glasses of champagne and canapés. A female musician—also dressed as a vestal virgin—playing a lute slithered through the crowd, never missing a note as she improvised what might have been a medley of ancient tunes. Cella wondered if Anton had arrived.

"Extraordinary," said Darlene Schiller. "Eric is really a talent."

"For photography, it's exceptional," said Toby Phipps. "I think he used a new Japanese camera."

"Darling, I wouldn't know. He does do his own developing, of course. You know, she is extraordinarily beautiful," Darlene conceded with unusual generosity.

"Yes, quite extraordinary. I must admit if I were a photography buff I'd be impressed. That altar is quite convincing. The very spirit of human sacrifice. Authentically bloodstained."

"A real beauty."

"Oh! You mean Cella. I was thinking of the altar."

"Yes, I mean Cella," Darlene snapped. "What do you think of her posing in the nude?"

"What is there to think? Pagan. And breathtaking."

As Cella, Marina and Jason entered the gallery, Eric Rheims, a small man in evening clothes with an ugly, agreeable face surrounded by an entourage of friends, admirers, detractors and climbers, watched only Cella. Since *The New York Times* critic had not only put in an appearance but shown some enthusiasm, Eric was feeling his oats. Now that the critic had left, he felt less cramped, freer to indulge his quite considerable talent for selling. He detached himself from the human zoo surrounding him, and with a face full of predatory high spirits, bounded off to greet the newcomers. It was not simply because of their artistry that some of the larger photographs being shown were those of Cella Taggard. On the way, he bumped into the ample form of Tobias Phipps.

"Toby, you old goat, what do you think?" He grasped Toby's hand warmly.

"Looks like a success, Eric. But you never were one for failure."

"You ought to consider photography, Toby. It's the coming thing. Soon there won't be enough paintings around for Northbie's to auction."

"I'll think about it. You're very convincing."

"I mean to be." Then, grasping Cella, Rheims guided her away from the throng surrounding her and whispered in her ear, "Darling, the Petty and the Getty are wildly enchanted with the photographs. They are at swords' points over who gets what. Peter wants every photograph in which you appear. Tersius, the photography curator for the Getty, insists the Getty have the three of them. Petty says they can have none. He says he'll double any offer that Tersius makes. Tersius told Hathaway to add a third to any offer Peter makes. Which way do you think I should bounce? Both collections are highly respected."

"Solomon's choice in reverse. Split the baby in half. Half to each."

"Marvelous. Marvelous. My thinking exactly. After they raise the bids somewhat more." He paused. "Unfortunately, neither can have the Cycladian maiden portrait. Pity. It's caused a genuine sensation. And a true bidding war. But it goes for not a tuppence," he muttered sourly.

"Why not? Why can't either of them have it?"

"Darling, don't fuss at me. You know why. It belongs to Anton."

"It does?"

"Your great and good friend purchased it from the negative. In fact, it was only my strong opposition that stopped him from purchasing all the photographs of you."

"You showed Anton the negatives?" Cella was astonished.

"Well, of course, darling. He's my sponsor. He has seen everything. He financed me. Don't pretend you didn't know." He smiled teasingly. "Or was it a lover's secret? Yes, his little secret."

"He never mentioned it," Cella murmured thoughtfully.

"Now I see why. You know he objected quite strenuously to my using you as a model. But when you said yes, he had to agree." He sighed contentedly. "But I do wish Anton would arrive in time to watch Petty and Getty try to devour the entire collection. Anton will make a substantial dollar on his faith in me.'' The smile was beatific. "And of course on my faith in you,'' Eric added with satisfaction. Then his glance swept swiftly over the milling throng in the gallery, many standing openmouthed, with glasses of untasted champagne, transfixed by the photography. "Actually, the photographs of you should hang in the Modern. But at least one will hang in your boudoir, I'd say.'' Then he put his arm around Cella's waist and led her to two hired photographers.

"Boys! Here is our star.''

The photographers noted Cella with appreciation.

"Say cheese, dear girl,'' said Eric.

"Cheese,'' said Cella, and there was a flash of bulbs.

Out of nowhere Peter Petty materialized.

"Hello, Cella. Those photographs are wonderful. Beautiful women are not always so photogenic.''

"I've heard you don't collect photography,'' Eric said. "What a loss!''

"My grandfather wouldn't buy a photograph of the Christ child,'' Peter said. "Snapshots are what fathers take of naked babies. And what old men take of their equally naked girlfriends.''

"Your grandfather always did have a dirty mind,'' said Toby disdainfully as he joined them.

"It runs in the family.'' Peter grinned. "Actually, times are changing. I think the Petty ought to have a small room for photographs. Not a wing, you understand. But a room. For something like that,'' he said, nodding toward the photograph of Cella on the altar. "In fact, I'll start my collection with these photographs.'' He sipped from his glass of champagne. "That one. And that one. And that one. And that.'' Peter turned his body slowly around the mobbed room. Each choice was punctuated by the jabbing of Peter's forefinger in the direction of the nine photographs in which Cella appeared. "I like the transparent, almost ghostlike quality of the girl, the human flesh against the stone Ionic columns. And with the lifelike marble statues of deities and people. I like it very much.''

"A wonderful idea,'' Rheims said. "But old Hathaway tells me that Tersius has put in quite a high bid for that one.'' He nodded toward the altar photograph. Eric was deliberately needling Petty. He stalked him with all the skill reserved only for the biggest game.

"I told Hathaway I'd double any bid Tersius made on the photographs I want."

"Really?" said Eric as if this were news to him. "But I know you missed out on this one. It has real grandeur." Eric indicated to a photograph of Cella in the same pose as that of an exquisite seminude, full-size marble statue of a beautiful woman of antiquity. "In fact, Tersius has claimed three of the nine in which you're interested."

"Well, let him unclaim them. Hathaway knows my position."

"But I believe Tersius told the old man he'd add a third to anything you offered," Eric said blandly.

"So? Let him add his third. I'll double it."

Eric was in seventh heaven. If he played his cards right, he'd be in both the Petty and the Getty collections.

"You know I dislike disputes," he said, hoping to egg Peter on and on. "Now look at this colossal head of Medusa and the lion peering out of the shadows. All part of a series of magnificent consoles that decorated the Baths of Hadrian. It is magnificent, isn't it?"

"Yes, it is. And I'll consider it after we have the other nine photographs crated and ready to be freighted to the Petty Museum. I've told you which ones I want."

"Yes, of course," Eric said, clasping Cella to him tenderly. "Well, I'm glad you like my work."

"It's the way you handle light," Peter said with amusement. "Eric, you are the Vermeer of photography."

"Offhand, I'd say it's the way he handles his model," Toby remarked snidely.

Eric's foxlike eyes gleamed shrewdly at Toby's perception. He remarked with just the right note of humility, "All great photographers owe a debt of gratitude to great models." He smiled at Cella winningly. "Thank you, Cella."

"You're welcome, Eric."

"You should thank her," Peter said. "She gives life and vitality to the world of the ancients. She imbues your photographs with a heroic spirit." Peter was astonished at his own rhetoric.

Cella had to stop herself from laughing. "Eric, with or without me you'd have been a success."

"No false modesty. Thank you again." But in truth, Eric had never discounted Cella's value as a model. Even so, the results had far outstripped his wildest dreams. Apparently Peter Petty had more than a passing interest in the young woman. What luck.

"Well, I think I ought to see old Hathaway now," Peter said, suddenly all business. "I'll give him a blank check and he can fill in the amount as soon as the show is over. I'll send the Lear for them."

"What about Tersius?" Cella asked, half teasing.

"What about him? He can have anything. That is, anything I don't want."

"Peter, are you sure? As I said, he is raising your offer by a third," Eric reminded him.

"Talk is cheap," Peter said with mild exasperation. "He's Tersius, curator of photography for the Getty. But he is not John Paul Getty. He can't write a blank check. If he overshoots his budget, they'll stop him. I am Peter Regis Petty. I answer to no one but granddaddy's spirit." He smiled cheerfully. "And Grandfather loved beautiful women. I believe he listed at least twelve in his will. Excuse me for a moment, Cella, while I get this straightened out with Hathaway."

Cella and Toby watched Peter make his way through the crowd. His high-handed attitude toward money was both awesome and funny. Even among the richest of the rich, Peter was a phenomenon.

Eric was ecstatic. With Peter in a bidding battle with Tersius of the Getty, the sky was the limit. It would end with him being rich. Yes, thanks to Cella, he had a chance for immortality. He kissed Cella on the cheek in true gratitude.

"Peter Petty is a man with the courage of his convictions," he said.

"And his inheritance," Toby added maliciously.

The photographs were discussed in various corners of the gallery. A brilliant group of society people, art-world people, the beautiful and the bulletproof rich, as well as theatrical types, were there. By and large the crowd was filled with jealousy or lust. Many conversations ended with the words "Shocking! But what a body!" Occasionally one heard words like "amusing" or "inspiring."

Anton arrived at last, and for him the show was not shocking, amusing or inspiring. What it was was infuriating. At the moment he was sick of the art world, sick of himself, sick of his association with Lawrence Lord, which had contaminated his relationship with Cella.

"Have you seen Cella?" he asked Marina.

"She's with Eric somewhere," came the reply.

"Have you seen Cella?" he asked someone else.

"She's with Eric. Or Jason Lord, somewhere."

"Where?" he asked in exasperation.

"Try the bar. The champagne's not bad. Or the powder room. Or a movie."

Jason had wandered off to look at the photographs. Cella found him alone, transfixed in front of a stunning shot of a naked Cella, covered only by her hair, welcoming a handsome nude warrior, Ares, the ancient god of war. He'd been looking at it the way a hungry dog eyes a dripping bone.

"How do you like the photographs?" Jason asked when she stood beside him.

"I modeled for them, didn't I?"

"How do you like them?" Jason asked again.

"How do you like them?" Cella countered.

Jason glanced away from the photograph, resurrecting a smile. "Very impressive, I'd say."

"Is that all? Are they art?"

"Yes. Quite distinguished!" Jason said in too loud a voice. "For once a photography exhibition wasn't overrated." He felt an urge to move closer to her, but the loneliness of which he was so jealous didn't permit it.

"I'm glad you approve. They really are distinguished. And I think they are their own art form," Cella said.

Jason faced the photograph resolutely. The nude shots of Cella disturbed him and he was doing his best to cover it. He had loved a woman a long time ago but never liked her. Now he loved two women. Detachment was his only protection. He had never spoken words of love to a woman. Nor had there been any woman who expected such words. In the solitude of his mind he sought his only truth. Looking at the photographs, he faced what he had to face and saw that it was unavoidable. It had no name, no future. But if one could not feel hope, at least one could act with justice. There was only one thing to be done. And when the time came, he would do it.

Just then Peter Petty showed up to join them. Ignoring Jason, Peter smiled at Cella. "Well, I've settled old Hathaway. He understands perfectly." He paused and gazed at a photograph hanging to the left of the one Jason was admiring. "I believe I particularly like that one."

Jason glanced at it, then at Peter. "I particularly dislike that one. It's the only one in the collection I dislike."

"I find it stunning," Peter said with good humor. "Extremely effective—Cella and the Cycladian maiden. Two beautiful women standing side by side. Linking together three thousand years. One modern, one pagan.''

Both pagan, Cella thought.

"One beautiful woman. One fake," said Jason.

Cella felt bad weather coming. "Which is your favorite photograph, Jason?" she asked, hoping to derail the conversation.

But Peter was persistent. "I'd love to see that idol, Cella. It's quite impressive. I've never seen a life-size Cycladian maiden."

Cella smiled. "It's trick photography. That's not the real size of the statue. Eric blew it up in the lab until it was as tall as I am."

"What a shame! What a stunner a life-size Cycladian maiden would be in my Greek antiquities room."

"And what a stupendous fraud," Jason said sarcastically. "I'll give you a tip, Peter. If you like it so much, I'm sure Victor Vilanova can be persuaded to have a life-size Cycladian maiden made especially for you."

It was as if an abyss had opened before Cella. She was tormented by the pictures in her mind. The Cycladic idol Anton had given her two years ago on her twenty-fifth birthday. Now she remembered all too clearly his cynical acknowledgment that most of the other idols on the market were fakes from Victor's studio. Vividly she saw again in her mind's eye Uncle Victor and Sebastian and herself having lunch in Marseilles. Victor complaining impatiently about the foolishness of his prize forgers. The sunlit scene in the tomb that her father was blind to. The dreams she had. The world she'd lost when Spina died. The faith in her heritage that Jason had shaken. She felt herself fighting her sight. Fighting her dreams. Struggling for an absence of thought.

"I'll bet you're the celebrated Dr. Jason Lord, dedicated to the Holy Grail of Truth. The scourge of the art world," Peter Petty said, laughing.

"Truth is my Grail. I despise fraudulent art."

"And you mean to protect me from myself."

"Someone should. I hear you've collected quite a few of those fake Cycladic idols."

"What the hell are you talking about?"

Cella spun about at the sound of a dear, familiar voice, harsh with fury. There was Anton dressed in faded jeans and a blue turtleneck sweater. She'd never seen so much anger in his face or heard so much rage in his voice.

"There's only one man with the talent to forge one hundred

Cycladian maidens and the skill to distribute them through the art world.'' Jason laughed in Anton's face. ''Yes, Peter, call Anton's uncle Victor. Offer him a commission he can't refuse and he'll turn up a magnificent find. An ancient, life-sized Cycladian maiden complete with the provenance of where it was dug up—at least two hundred years ago—and in whose basement it's been languishing ever since. What's one more fraud among so many?''

''Jason, don't talk like that about the Vilanovas. They are highly respected and your attitude is uncalled for,'' Marina said briskly.

Jason seemed not to hear his mother, who had joined the group in time to hear this remark. As he spoke he continued to stare at the picture of Cella. There were things that made him tremble and other things that filled him with anger. The photograph did both. It was a straight-on shot, a beautiful nude, twin of the Cycladian idol with her arms crossed in the same position, and with the same mysterious dream on her face.

''You seem fascinated by the picture. Is it the naked woman or the fraud that intrigues you?'' Anton asked.

Jason blinked and glanced away from the photograph as if he'd been caught stealing. Suddenly he spun about, completely out of control. ''Apologize to Cella, you bastard,'' he said in a hoarse voice.

''For what?'' Anton said. ''For the fact that you enjoyed the sight of her nude body? She posed for the photograph. She knew what she was doing. Judging from your reaction, she got just the effect she wanted.''

The photographs, the champagne, the lowering of his guard, combined to free the latent savagery in Jason. He seized Anton's sweater and held him. The two men were about the same height and their shoulders were equally broad. But where Anton was as lean as a rapier, Jason was as brutally powerful as a mace. He shook Anton.

''Stop it, Jason,'' Cella cried.

''Jason! For heaven's sake!'' Marina echoed Cella's distress.

''Stay out of this, Cella,'' Anton said, his voice surprisingly calm. ''Lord, you've got three seconds to let go before I break your arms. One. Two. Three!'' With that Anton raised both his hands and chopped down hard on Jason's biceps.

''Anton! You'll hurt him!'' Marina shrilled.

''I mean to,'' Anton said.

''Stop it this minute!'' Cella said.

Anton slowly shook his head. "Victor is your uncle, too."

"I know that," she replied.

"Spina's brother," he said in quiet fury.

Cella let this remark register, saying nothing more.

Jason shook his hands to get some feeling back in them. He then raised his fist, slowly, almost ponderously.

"Don't try it, Lord," Anton warned.

"That's enough! Both of you!" Cella exclaimed, stepping between the men.

"You're acting like children," Marina said softly as a crowd began to gather around them. "Jason, people are watching."

"Go away, Mother. Do yourself a favor." Jason dropped his fist and turned to Cella. "I'm sorry," he said. "I regret that you two are cousins."

"Please, Jason. No more. I can't stand any more," Cella said in a low voice.

"I said I was sorry," Jason repeated, and then, eyeing Anton, he went on coolly. "And I am sorry for you. In fact, I pity you, Anton Vilanova. The nephew of a liar. And a thief. Probably a liar and a thief yourself."

"Jason! How dare you speak to Anton that way!" Marina fumed but was unnoticed.

"While you're pitying me, pity yourself," Anton snapped. "Listen to me, Dr. Jason Lord, our celebrated art sleuth— you're about to step into a swamp. Get your own house in order before you start throwing bricks at my family. And Cella's. Try a little detective work in your own backyard, buddy. Look into a few closets and under a few rocks. See if you like what you find."

Cella thought of Anton's story about the Luxembourg Corporation and Lawrence Lord. She couldn't bear what he might be going to say. "No!" she said loudly, holding up her hand, commanding silence.

"I'm telling him something," Anton said, and their eyes met for a moment.

"I know that," she replied. "Don't, Anton. Please."

"What are you talking about?" Jason asked, suddenly calm.

Cella had never before had the feeling she had then. It was like a blow to the face. A treacherous blow. The man who had given her a new vision of the world, who had shown her the meaning of truth, was behaving like a contemptible swine, slinging mud at her family name. And the man she loved most in the world was behaving with equal ugliness. For a moment anger so great surged in Cella that she thought she would scream. Then a small, cold, rational voice told her that she really must not play their game. She drew a long breath, composed her face and looked straight at Anton.

"I think this has gone far enough," she said quietly. The appeal in her eyes had hardened to sternness. "Anton, stop now."

"No. Let him say what he wants to say. I'm curious." Jason's voice was stiff.

Anton swallowed. Cella saw the muscles in his throat move. Then he broke away from her eyes and muttered, "Sorry, Cella. Two wrongs don't make a right, as the old American axiom says." With that he walked away from them, disappearing into the crowd.

"Anton Vilanova, come back," Jason called. But Anton was beyond hearing. Or if he did hear, he ignored it. Jason looked at his mother. "Do you know what he was talking about?"

"No, and I don't care. I think it's time I had another champagne. Jason, sometimes you really do worry me." And she, too, vanished into the crowd.

Cella cast her eyes desperately around, looking for escape. From Jason. From the photographs. From the odor of violence that still hung in the air. "Peter. Peter Petty," she said. "I'm hungry. How would you like to take me to dinner?"

"Be my pleasure."

Cella left the exhibit without looking back at Jason or for Anton.

Cella and Peter stood side by side on the pavement, staring into the darkness around them. People were still pushing in and out of the gallery while the headlights of cars could be seen charging up Madison Avenue. With the light from the lamppost shining on her, the paleness of Cella's skin accentuated the gleam of her hair as though what was left of her vitality had centered itself there. She was still beautiful, but at this moment her face was glazed with pain; with the dreadful faraway look of an animal that hurts but cannot tell anyone what the matter is.

"Take a deep breath," Peter said protectively.

There was a long pause, neither knowing exactly what to say now that the noise of the gallery was behind them. Then, unexpectedly, Cella gave a wry smile. "I'd wager that Anton and Jason will never be buddies."

Peter laughed. "Jason isn't anybody's buddy."

"That was quite a performance they put on," Cella said, probing for Peter's reaction.

"It seems to me Jason opened the show," Peter noted. "That man is not exactly the life of the party."

They strolled hand in hand down Madison Avenue looking for a cab. Anyone glancing casually at Cella would have guessed that at that moment she had everything she wanted. But a more discerning eye would have noted the almost feverish brightness of her manner and sensed that she was walking on the edge of a cliff; that each step she took was proof that the ground was not falling away under her.

When they finally caught a cab and reached their destination, it was exactly what Cella wanted—a neighborhood restaurant bar in Chelsea. Not fashionable. Not glitzy. Not glamorous. And no one noticed them when they wandered in. Just a well-dressed man adrift on the town with what might have been his floozy—considering the way she was dressed. But at least she was beautiful.

"I'd like a real drink," Cella said, seating herself in a booth. "Order a Bombay gin for me. Neat. No ice."

Peter motioned to the waiter. He gave Cella's order and added, "Bring me a double Jack Daniel's. Also neat."

"Good idea. Make mine a double. I rarely drink enough to get drunk, but tonight I'm making an exception. Our ringside seat at that wrestling match unsteadied my nerves."

"No, Cella, you're wrong. That was no fight. Just another pissing contest between two angry men. Two unhappy men," Peter said. "But then most folks are unhappy."

"You think so?"

"I do. Think about it. There are probably three components to happiness: enough money, love and good health. I know some people who have none of the three. I know a great number of people who have one out of the three. I even know a few people who have two out of the three. Me, for instance. But I don't know a single solitary soul who has all three. Including me, you, your father, Anton Vilanova, Jason Lord, Eric Rheims. No one has all three components." He leaned forward. "Do you know anything about me except that I'm rich, presumed to be lazy and trying to build a world-class museum? And as has been said, I have probably the largest collection of second-rate paintings by first-rate painters in the world." He made a wry face. "I'd like to do better, but first-rate paintings by first-rate painters rarely come on the market."

Peter reached into his pocket and took out his wallet. He

extracted a snapshot and handed it to Cella. It was a picture of a strikingly beautiful blond-haired woman, a tall, handsome man in a Marine officer's uniform and a young boy, about ten or eleven.

"The man in the photograph is my father, the woman my mother. And I'm the fair-haired boy with cheek. I'll come back to the picture in a moment, Cella. As you know, my grandfather was an oilman. He was also, if you'll pardon the expression, a cocksman. He screwed anything that moved. Actresses, models, maids . . ."

"You don't have to tell me this," Cella said softly.

"I want to," Peter said. He paused as the drinks were served. After taking a big swallow he continued. "The list isn't complete. Acrobats, athletes and his son's wife. The fact is I'm probably his son. Which is why he left me everything."

Cella simply stared.

"At any rate, when that picture was taken, my father had just enlisted in the Marines. He'd found out, quite accidentally, about his father and his wife. He died in the Tet offensive in February 1968. She died drunk in an automobile accident."

"Why are you telling me this?"

Peter Petty was not the kind of man who talked openly about his history without a reason. But a dazzling perception had dawned on him. He knew he had a fear of the deepest kind of human relationship. He'd never felt equal to it. Thanks to his mother and father and grandfather. Yet now with Cella he felt there was a possibility of a bearable intimacy, despite her flamboyant sexuality. There was a straightness about her that made it possible.

"I've been thinking about us." His tone was lower, more a feeling than a sound.

"I had that impression." Cella drained her drink.

Peter felt his dignity slip away like a blanket fallen from his back, and his pride, which had never before deserted him, was for the moment shamefully missing. "I think I've fallen in love with you." He finished his drink and motioned to the waiter for a second round. "It's a new experience. I'd appreciate it if you'd think about it."

Cella stared at him, bewildered. "I'll think about it," she promised. "But don't hope too much. Remember, I'm an Etruscan. And you may expect more from me than I can give you. Etruscan women have mores quite different from yours."

"I know the mores," he said, struggling with his emotions. "I've had a lot of research done on your culture, your heritage. I know all that the scholars know about the Etruscan people." He braced himself. "I know how they regarded fidelity. It wasn't one of their strong points. A husband wasn't always the father of the child. And I know . . ." He paled slightly. "I know, please forgive me, what my detectives tell me about you."

Cella nodded her head gravely, guessing at all the possibilities for embarrassment which any further explanations could lead to.

"I was thinking that we might be good for each other. We know each other's limits." Here Peter stopped long enough to draw a deep breath. "For instance, I've even thought about all the Gorgeouses. All of them."

"You really have had me checked out."

"I never do anything halfway."

"What else do you know?"

"I know about Anton. I know he is probably the only man you love."

"You know too much." But there was dissent in her voice. "And do you know I've loved him all my life? How do you feel about that, Peter?"

"Mildly jealous. But only mildly. Like a torn fingernail that will be forgotten in a minute." He smiled.

"You are a strange man, Peter Petty. Strange, that is, for an American."

"I know who I am. I don't lie. I'm straight with myself. The way you are. In fact, the idea of Anton—the idea of your fidelity—doesn't interest me in the least."

It was a standard so different from anything Cella had ever encountered in an American that she had no idea how to respond.

Peter looked at her intently. "Say you will think about me as . . . as a lover." He reached across the table to hold her hand as the drinks arrived. "And as an added incentive to your agreeing, I'll tell you my secret plan to make you immortal."

Cella had been thoroughly surprised by Peter's entire outburst, and she wondered what could possibly be coming next.

"Because I feel about you the way I do, I'm adding a Cella Taggard wing onto the Petty Musuem. To house the ancient jewelry I buy from The House of Uni."

Cella felt faintly giddy. "A Cella Taggard wing?"

"That's what I said."

"You may change your mind someday," she said, thinking of the revelations the future might bring.

"Not where you're concerned. Remember, I've fallen in love with you. That hasn't happened to me before."

"I hope you don't regret it. I mean, the Cella Taggard wing."

"I never regret how I spend my money. Now will you give me some thought?"

Cella took half of her drink in one swallow. The gin made her feel warm and mellow. "Yes. I'll give you some thought. In fact, I have already," she said in a husky voice. "Here is my answer. Order me a slice of roast beef, very rare." She paused, running the tip of her tongue around the rim of her liquor glass. "Will you do that for me, Gorgeous? After dinner we'll have a brandy at my house."

═ Chapter Twenty-three ═

It was Sunday. The sky was a rich blue, and as Cella reclined on a chaise in the small garden behind the house, the sun, bearing with it the warmth of Indian summer, fell like a gentle caress across her shoulders. The paperback volume of Baudelaire that she wasn't reading lay in her lap open to the same page for an hour as she stared into space seeing images that weren't there. She was alone, more alone than ever before in her life, and she preferred it that way. During the past few weeks she'd moved through life infused with a sense of the familiar but with a twist. Marcus had disappeared into the woodwork while waiting for Anton to help him climb out of the financial swamp he'd dug for himself. She'd refused to answer Anton's frequent phone calls, nor had she contacted Jason Lord. His behavior at the art gallery had been too outrageous. Peter Petty was—as Gorgeouses went—more than adequate. He had flown back to Dallas full of plans to prepare the Petty museum for the opening of the Cella Taggard wing. As for herself, though she appreciated the honor, the idea was constantly shouldered out of her thoughts by other concerns. In fact, she didn't think about it at all.

The sound of footsteps made her turn. Sebastian stood inside the French doors that led to the garden, smiling.

"It's been almost a month, but I've something to show you," he said, exuding self-satisfaction.

"I've been waiting," Cella said.

"You'll be pleased."

Cella pursed her lips and didn't answer at once. "With the Astarte?" she finally said.

"It's lovely."

"I'm glad."

"You didn't think I could do it without you?" Sebastian asked.

"Not true. I was sure you could," Cella lied.

"You'll be pleased," he repeated.

"When do I get to see it?"

"Now. Come." He turned and walked quickly into the house without looking back.

Cella closed her book and stood up. She followed Sebastian out of the bright garden into the dim interior of the house, where the air felt refreshingly cool against her warm skin. Together they went up the stairs to the library on the second floor. In the softly daylit room he nodded toward the desk. There, set in the middle of the desktop, were two long velvet boxes. One pale blue, the other white.

"Open the blue box," Sebastian instructed proudly.

Cella slowly did as she was told.

"The Aphrodite!" she murmured, startled. Then she frowned. Looking at the necklace intently, she felt something was missing and didn't know what; that something was wrong and didn't know why.

"The Astarte," Sebastian explained.

"The Astarte," Cella repeated. Now she understood. She couldn't repress the shiver that ran through her body. Eventually she found her voice. "It's lovely," she said. "But impossible."

"It's perfect," Sebastian retorted, and as far as Cella could tell, he believed his proud boast.

"It's totally impossible!" she repeated sharply.

"What's the matter with you? It's a perfect copy."

Cella's fear was overwhelming. She wanted to cry out, "But that's all it is! The spirit is missing. It's a copy. A forgery!"

Instead she simply asked, "Why?"

"Why a copy? A beautiful twin?"

"Why a copy? I don't understand."

"I know you don't. Think of Marina."

Cella's imagination spun about, grasping at straws. "I see. It's for Marina. To wear at private parties. A duplicate of the Aphrodite."

"You're half right." Sebastian picked up the white velvet box. He opened it reverently. Against the white velvet, the luminous pearls and golden pomegranates exuded a mystic splendor. "For Marina, the Aphrodite itself. The gift of the goddess of love. My wedding present."

Cella looked at the necklace as though in the presence of some final mystery. It had a power, a magnificence, that to her made the copy seem lifeless by comparison. "You'd give Marina the Aphrodite?"

"My gift of love."

For a second Cella couldn't trust herself to speak. When she did, all she could say was "Why? Why, Father? You've loved many women."

"Why then give her this priceless gift?"

"Unless you love her that much."

"How much is that much? I've never pretended to be what I'm not. Spina once said my Etruscan blood ran true. I was a natural philanderer. That is the American word."

"Then why?"

"She loves me. You do understand that?"

"Other women have loved you."

"I'm older. My perspective has changed. I don't want to be alone. Ever. And I feel if I give her the Aphrodite I will never lose her. Never." He smiled impudently. "In fact, now that you've agreed to my marriage, I may even give up philandering. Who knows—I might settle into staid monogamy."

"I doubt it. And I didn't agree because I thought you needed to experience fidelity."

"You didn't?" He laughed. "Then why?"

"I have my reasons." She hesitated. "I hope they're the right ones."

"Whatever your reasons, they satisfy me. At any rate, the Astarte is identical to the Aphrodite. No one on earth, not even Jason Lord, my celebrated son-in-law-to-be, will know the difference. My work is the equal of the ancients. You guessed because you knew there were two necklaces." Sebastian ventured a small smile. "So my bride gets the Aphrodite. The world, the Astarte." He studied the two pieces of jewelry for an instant. "Of course, we will rename the necklaces. The Aphrodite becomes the Astarte and the Astarte, the Aphrodite."

Cella tried to control her anger. "Father, it will not do. Have you forgotten Lexi?"

"I think of her all the time. At least of her father's ten million."

"You'd sell Lexi the Astarte?"

"I'll sell Lexi my Aphrodite. I told you, Abdul Hamid will never know the difference. Should she object, there are always the Greeks. Their agent has contacted me. Right now—for my own reasons—I'm leaning toward the Greeks."

"The shrine of Aphrodite would know . . ." Cella hesitated. "Father, don't do it."

"Cella—"

"Please!"

"I dislike family arguments."

"But it's wrong."

"You're not on my side anymore."

"I am on your side. That's why I'm telling you not to do it."

Sebastian shrugged his shoulders. "I'm sorry you feel this way."

"So am I." Cella had grown very pale. She carefully closed the blue box. Then she leaned against the desk as though to steady herself.

Sebastian was caught short by a sudden concern. "My dear, are you all right?"

"I've been better," Cella said as she left the room, walking with a stiff grace.

Later that evening in her room, Cella faced her dilemma. There had been too many lies. There must be a stop. She must break the pattern. Now! She had a feeling that one more lie—one more forgery—would kill her. When she got into bed she stared at the ceiling for a long time before falling into a sleep plagued with wild dreams. In her dreams her mind soared free of time and space; it dipped into the past, careened into the future. She heard Spina's voice telling her she must leave all in the hands of the gods.

At daybreak she woke up with a start. She tired to remember her dreams. To remember Spina's words. All kinds of thoughts leaped into her consciousness. Jumbled thoughts. Restless thoughts. Fragmentary thoughts. Then, gradually, the pieces sorted themselves out. A word became an idea. An idea a plan. A plan a final decision. As though guided by Spina, her mind formed the question: Why not? Why not end it all? This was her chance. She had already taken the first step by agreeing to Sebastian's marriage to Marina.

Now she would let Sebastian go his own way. She would not try to protect him. Or herself. Or their heritage. Or their reputation. She heard Spina's voice. The forgeries—if that was what they had become—must be left to the gods, to bring about what would be. Long ago Spina had taught her that they lived and flourished by the will of the gods. And only by their will. If sometimes that will should seem hard and relentless, so be it. It was no easy thing to serve the gods. No matter the outcome, she would not be afraid.

When she sat down to breakfast, she offered Sebastian an apology for her obstinacy about the Aphrodite. Sebastian accepted her new attitude gratefully, with little surprise.

"I'm glad you changed your mind," he said. "I thought you would in time."

"Sometimes you know me better than I know myself."

"Why did you?"

"Isn't it a woman's prerogative to change her mind?" Cella smiled.

"I'm seeing Marina this evening."

"With the necklace?" She watched as Sebastian nodded contentedly. "Lexi will be flying over next month."

"Very likely," Sebastian said. "The Greek representative is here now."

Cella said almost humbly, "Don't ask me to help you persuade her to buy it."

"That won't be necessary," Sebastian said. "I've been in touch with Abdul. He's very eager."

Cella studied her father and saw herself and him, two people alone in a sunlit room discussing a fraud worth many millions of dollars as if it were a plan for a dinner party. "In the meantime, do you mind if I study the Astarte? Excuse me, the Aphrodite? I won't help you make the sale, but the necklace must be flawless."

"Please. I would appreciate your doing it." He gave her an appraising look. "Or perhaps you now agree that the world deserves my Aphrodite? Can I take that as qualified approval?"

Cella picked up her spoon and studied the design. "Yes. Take it as that."

"Good." Sebastian pushed his chair away from the table. "I have an appointment with Felix."

"Your tailor?"

"We must discuss a morning coat. Marina has decided on a formal wedding."

Cella gazed at her father standing very straight and handsome in his loose, tweedy, houndstooth jacket. He had a talent for making all women feel more attractive. He was facile and arrogant and shallow, and of course he had enormous charm. And of course she had always known it, and of course she was devoted to him.

"I'll see you in the shop tomorrow morning," he said as he left.

Cella continued sipping her coffee. She felt a quiet, sad strangeness. Something had gone from her irrevocably. Trust, and a belief she would never know again. She could see the start of things she had never imagined possible. And the end of things she had thought would last forever.

* * *

At three-thirty in the morning, Sebastian left Marina's building on Seventy-first Street, opposite the Frick museum. He could have stayed the rest of the night at Marina's, but he needed to change his clothes.

It was refreshing to stroll home in the unusually warm November night. There was a full hunter's moon shining over the leafless trees in Central Park that made him think unexpectedly of ancient woodlands long ago. He smiled inwardly, thinking that Cella must often have such associations. Yes, he'd walk down Fifth Avenue past the Frick and eventually cross over to Madison Avenue and enjoy the boutique windows until he reached Sixty-third Street.

Sebastian walked quite slowly, not wanting to hurry, wanting to remember. Marina had been rapturous about the Aphrodite, and Sebastian relished reliving the scene—her delight, her excitement, her sexual intensity afterward. Later they had laughed at their own wedding plans because they were older and wiser; but they were serious about their marriage because they felt surprisingly young and vulnerable. At the moment Sebastian was so self-involved the rest of the world hardly existed for him.

So he was totally oblivious of a pair of eyes watching him, lurking behind one of the trees that lined the park side of the avenue. In his lighthearted mood, Sebastian played a child's game as he walked. He moved from concrete square to concrete square that made up the sidewalk—always careful not to step on the cracks. It took two steps to encompass one square and one step the next. A burst of energy surged through him each time he stretched his legs to cover the square with one step. Although in his early fifties, he prided himself on his fitness. He thought his stride was that of a young man.

Keeping about a half block behind him, the pair of eyes flitted after him from behind the trees, watching him, following him, scorning his silly game.

At Sixty-eighth Street, the pair of eyes took advantage of the traffic light to cross from the park side to the apartment side of Fifth Avenue, always remaining about a half block behind. The eyes belonged to a man dressed in black warm-up pants, a black warm-up jacket and black jogging shoes that made tiny squeaky whispers every time he took a step, but were completely inaudible from more than a few feet away. A black knit cap covered his hair, and his black skin easily absorbed the moonlight. The man was almost invisible in the dark night.

At Sixty-seventh Street, Sebastian turned east toward Madison Avenue. The mouth smiled, the watching eyes narrowed. The shadow figure quickened its pace and in seconds was around the corner. Sebastian was no more than fifty feet ahead. The black shadow began to move faster, silent as the night at his back.

About one hundred feet down the block between Fifth and Madison avenues, a series of old four-story buildings—the kind that in the past had made New York a gracious city—was being demolished in favor of a huge high-rise apartment house. To protect pedestrians from falling bricks and dirt, the demolitions company had built a roof over the sidewalk. As Sebastian walked under the construction, he wrinkled his nose, smelling the brick-and-plaster dust mingled with the sour odor of urine. The moon had temporarily disappeared behind a bank of clouds. Sebastian felt a sudden depression and quickened his pace, anxious to be home.

But as rapidly as Sebastian moved, the shadow moved faster—determined, quiet, steady. Now it was twenty feet behind Sebastian. Ten feet. Five feet. Suddenly Sebastian heard the squeak of rubber. He turned, stared and for an instant he froze. He saw the shadow looming over him. Clearly, sharply, as a camera must see things. He saw everything, but could not react. Then the rubber squeaked again, jarring him into consciousness. How long is an instant? However long, it was too late. Sebastian tried to dodge, to shout, but steellike arms wrapped themselves around his body, lifting him clear of the ground. He felt his bones rattle as he was hurled onto the construction site, and his cries for help were smothered by a gloved hand over his mouth. A fist smashed against the side of his head. Stars flashed before his eyes. Then he lost consciousness. The night was silent, dispassionate. Blood and violence in the dark were a familiar sight. Familiar as kisses.

The arena was filled with people. Running, jumping and javelin-throwing contests had preceded the wrestling matches. Now thousands of eyes were riveted on a pair of naked wrestlers. In the beginning there had been eight pair, then four, then two, now one pair—their muscles bulging, straining and sweating, fighting for supremacy. The winner would have his choice of three maidens. Even of Gaia Caecilla. The crowd stirred, roaring for blood. Thousands of eyes watched every move critically. The audience bobbed up and down, rose, leaned forward, then stood up and bellowed. One man was thrown to the ground. Hundreds of voices, each like an immense discordant horn, swelled up and rolled over the wrestlers. Over Gaia Caecilla. The men's bodies were glistening as the perspiration poured over their skins.

Then, ever so slowly, the sharp outlines of their torsos began to melt, to dissolve into each other, until what remained was one huge body and two heads, each head with its teeth bared trying to bite the other. In the distance Gaia Caecilla heard the sound of the crowd. Then it was over. As if somebody had slammed shut the door on Babel. . . .

Cella woke up slowly, struggling to the surface of reality. What a dream! It took little imagination to understand its meaning. But knowing the conflict that was tearing her apart did not make the conflict easier. She reached for her ringing telephone, glancing at the bedside clock. Five-thirty in the morning. Who the hell was calling at this hour?

"Hello," she said blearily.

"Is this Cella Taggard?" It was a man's voice that sounded vaguely familiar.

"Yes."

"This is Sergeant Peter Reilly."

Instantly Cella was alert. "Sergeant Reilly from the Sixty-sixth Street precinct?"

"Yes. We spoke some months ago."

"I know, Sergeant. What's happened?"

"Your father . . ."

"Oh, no!" The sound that emerged from Cella's throat was less than a word and more than merely a gasp. "Is he all right?"

"No, Miss Taggard. He was attacked about an hour ago. But he's alive," the sergeant added quickly.

"My God! Where is he?"

"In Lenox Hill Hospital emergency."

"I'll be over in fifteen minutes."

"Officer Max Browsky is waiting in front of your building in a patrol car. He'll drive you here. He's the officer who found your father and probably saved his life."

"I don't understand."

"Lieutenant Ben Stein will explain when you get here."

"Lieutenant Stein? What's he got to do with this?"

"Miss Taggard," Sergeant Reilly said, his impatience evident in his tone, "please hurry. Browsky is waiting for you."

"I'm sorry. But you're sure my father is all right?"

"He's alive. Please get here."

Cella slammed the receiver down, feeling an acute nausea. Instinctively she started to dial Anton, then pushed down the button and dialed Marcus instead. She told him what had happened and to please call Marina. Then she ran to her closet to get dressed.

An hour later Cella, Marcus and Marina, holding on to Jason, were sitting in a semicircle in the visitors' room on the fourth floor of Lenox Hill Hospital. It was a grim room, with the thin-legged, plastic-covered chairs, white walls and white asphalt tiled floor that typified many hospital waiting rooms. Everyone present knew that Sebastian was in emergency surgery. In the center of the circle, Lieutenant Ben Stein, wearing his brown yarmulke, was speaking quietly. Sergeant Reilly was at his side taking notes.

"As near as we can tell," Stein said, "Mr. Taggard is a lucky man. Fortunately, Officer Browsky was on foot patrol last night. He was across the street from the construction site when he heard Mr. Taggard's weak cry for help. He started running in the direction of the voice, shouting that he was a police officer. The assailant heard Browsky and ran. I repeat, it was fortunate. The vicious attack on Mr. Taggard was never completed."

"What was the nature of the attack?" Jason Lord asked. "You make it sound somewhat strange. Was it something more unusual than the standard New York mugging?"

"It was."

"I begged him to stay with me," Marina wailed. "The streets aren't safe at that time of night."

"When can I see my father?" Cella asked.

"You'll have to ask Dr. Noah Greenberg. He's in charge of emergency admittance."

"Where is the doctor? I want to know exactly what happened to my father. And how he is."

"I'll tell you what happened to him," Ben Stein said. "But as to his present condition, I'll leave that to the doctor."

"Stop talking around it, Lieutenant Stein," Cella burst out.

"Your father was not very coherent when he was admitted. As near as I can tell, he was jumped by a huge black man who attempted to castrate him." Lieutenant Stein ignored the round of hushed gasps. "The attack may have been successful. We don't know yet."

Marina slumped and was caught up by Jason and placed in her seat.

"Castrated?" Jason sounded disbelieving. "Muggers don't castrate. They rob."

"This one didn't rob."

"Castration makes no sense. Murder would make more sense. Why would anyone want to castrate Sebastian?" Jason asked.

"I don't know," Ben Stein admitted. "But someone did. A thin piece of nylon fishing line was wound around his testicles. Given another minute, they would have been severed."

At that moment they were joined by a young doctor with prematurely gray curly hair.

"Which of you are Cella Taggard and Marcus Taggard?" The doctor spoke with a rich Southern accent.

"We are," Marcus and Cella answered in unison.

"Good. First, your father is all right. He has a deep concussion and his testicles were partially severed."

"My God!" Cella exclaimed. "You call that all right?"

"I've repaired what I could, but he may lose the use of one testicle," the doctor continued. "It's all right. Many men have gone through life with only one testicle and produced a football team of kids. Dr. William Lamont, our head of surgery, has taken over now. Mr. Taggard couldn't be in better hands. He should be good as new when Lamont is done." Dr. Greenberg paused, frowning. "There's one thing I don't understand about this case, though."

"Only one thing," Ben Stein said with a wry smile. "That puts you way ahead of the police."

"No, I don't mean that," the doctor said quickly. "You see, the way Mr. Taggard explained it when he was admitted, he never had a chance to defend himself. The man was on him, lifted him in the air and literally threw him onto the construction site. And Mr. Taggard remembers getting hit only once. The contusions bear that out. Mr. Taggard is about five feet ten or eleven inches tall and must weight about one hundred eighty pounds. I can tell you that physically he's not a weak man. Yet the man who attacked him handled him like a child. The man must be a giant. A man of enormous strength."

Jason Lord looked up from Marina, who had slumped against his shoulder. "If I ever get my hands on the son of a bitch, we'll find out how strong he really is," he said, eyes flashing.

"Jason Lord!" Dr. Greenberg exclaimed. "What are you doing here?"

"I'm almost a member of the family, Noah. Sebastian Taggard is engaged to marry my mother."

"Congratulations. I assure you he will be able to function

once he recovers from the surgery. Listen, Jason, you still owe me a chess match. When are you going to show up and play it? I haven't seen you at the club in a long time.''

"I've been there, though not as often as I'd like. Too much work. But don't worry, you'll get your match.''

"Good. I'm ten dollars down. By the way, did your father ever reach you? He called the club one night looking for you."

"When was that?"

"Months ago. Last spring."

"He found me."

Dr. Greenberg took a deep breath. "I must get back to my other cases. Dr. Lamont will see you when he finishes the examination. So if you'll excuse me . . .'' Without waiting for a reply, he hurried off.

After Dr. Greenberg had left, Sergeant Reilly and Officer Browsky left too. Their job was done. Then Marcus shrugged on his jacket, which he'd thrown over his shoulders. He explained that he had to get to the office before the market opened. He expected some heavy trading in one of his stocks. After kissing Cella and saying he would call her later in the morning, he hurried away to face his mounting personal problems.

Jason Lord also stood up and excused himself. Marina had recovered her self-possession, so there was nothing more he could do here. And there was a lot he had to do in his office.

All that remained of the police presence was Lieutenant Ben Stein, who was busily transposing Reilly's notes into his own notebook.

The hours passed as the three of them sat waiting for Dr. Lamont to appear. The coffee cups were untouched, and Cella and Marina grew more and more tense. Finally at eleven o'clock—more than five hours after Cella had arrived at the hospital—Dr. William Lamont did appear. His surgical gown was spotlessly white, as were his rubber-soled shoes. As he walked rapidly toward the waiting room, he exuded self-importance, quickly writing prescriptions and instructions for the care of his various patients. Instead of handing them directly to the nurse who followed him, he dropped them on the floor, making it necessary for her to stoop to pick them up. Then she had to run to catch up with the great man. And in truth, he was a handsome, imposing figure of a man. Large, well over six feet tall and two hundred pounds, with a shock of white hair, a florid face and a rich, cultivated baritone voice. He often felt he sat next to God.

His glance took in Cella and Marina, but when it fell on Lieutenant Stein, he looked puzzled.

"It would be simpler," he said, "if you'd identify yourselves." Cella and Marina did. Then the doctor turned to Ben Stein. "And you, sir. Where do you fit in?"

Resignedly, Stein reached into his breast coat pocket and pulled out his New York Police Department shield. "Lieutenant Stein, homicide," he explained.

"You're Ben Stein? The Ben Stein who broke the Jackdaw case?" The doctor asked incredulously.

"Yes."

"Doctor, how is my father?" Cella asked somewhat impatiently.

"Better than might be expected. I pride myself on the fact that I managed to save both testicles. However, he does have a deep concussion."

"How long will he have to stay in the hospital?" Stein asked.

"At least a week. And if you'll forgive me, Lieutenant, why was homicide called in? There's been no murder."

"There was an attempted murder," Stein said.

"Not in my expert opinion." The doctor made an elaborate production out of the word *expert*. "There was an attempted castration, not a murder. If the assailant wanted to murder Mr. Taggard, Mr. Taggard would be dead. The use of the fishing line, instead of the usual knife, would have pinched off the veins and arteries. That way the victim could not bleed to death. Mr. Taggard was meant to live."

At the mention of Sebastian's condition, Marina started to sway, and Cella put an arm around her to steady her.

"It's all right, Marina," she said gently. "Sebastian will be all right." She looked up at the doctor, who was staring down at Marina unsympathetically. "That is accurate, isn't it?"

"Quite accurate. And now I hope that's the end of the question-and-answer period. I have other patients to attend to and very little time to waste." He sounded irritated.

"Fine." Cella had had enough of Dr. William Lamont. "No more questions," she said in a flat voice. "And considering your lack of manners, I hope you're as good a surgeon as you seem to think. But I don't like you. Can we get Dr. Greenberg to take care of my father?"

"Dr. Greenberg is a resident. He's not allowed to have private patients," Dr. Lamont remarked from on high.

"Really? Is Joshua Heath still on the board of directors of this hospital?"

"Yes. Why?"

"I know Joshua Heath very well. I want Dr. Noah Greenberg personally to see to my father's well-being. I think Josh can arrange that. Don't you agree, Doctor?"

"Well, yes. If that's what you really want. But everything that can be done has been done. What your father needs now is rest," the doctor stated firmly and then walked down the corridor, followed by his nurse.

After Dr. Lamont was out of earshot, Cella looked at Ben Stein. "What now, Lieutenant?"

"Now we do detective work. We'll chase down every black man with a known record of weird assaults until we find one who happened to be in the neighborhood—"

Marina interrupted him. "You're wasting your time. You ought to arrest my ex-husband, Lawrence Lord. He was responsible for this." There was still a note of borderline hysteria in her voice. "Just as he was responsible for Hans and Andrew and Phillip. He hates anyone I love."

"Mrs. Lord," Lieutenant Stein said patiently. "Mr. Taggard identified his assailant as a huge black man. A man of great strength. Does that description fit your husband?

"No," Marina said slowly as she studied the tiles on the floor. Then her face brightened. "But he could have hired someone who fits the description."

"That's possible. I promise you I'll talk to Dr. Lord myself."

"Would you?" Marina pleaded. "When you arrest him, the jinx will be broken."

"We'll see. May I speak to you privately for a moment, Miss Taggard?" Lieutenant Stein asked.

"Certainly," Cella said.

"Walk me outside. There's nothing more I can do here."

Cella glanced at Marina. "I'll be right back, and then the two of us should go somewhere for breakfast."

As they stood outside the hospital, the detective said, "Do you remember that I asked you who disliked Phillip Mckay?"

"Yes."

"Now I must ask you who disliked your father."

"A lot of people. But no one disliked him enough to do what was done."

"Are you sure?"

Cella hesitated. There were the Turks and the Greeks and

the Aphrodite. Somehow castrating the man who owned the necklace of the goddess of love made sense in a weird, crazy way.

"I'm not sure," she admitted finally.

In as few words as possible, she told the lieutenant about buying the necklace at Northbie's auction and how the Turkish government and the Greek government both claimed the necklace as their own. But Sebastian had pitted them against each other, insisting on an auction to get the highest price. In passing, she mentioned Darlene Schiller's Washington party, where Sebastian had planned to show the necklace to the daughter of the Turkish minister of culture. He had been stopped by Josie Frankenberg's murder in his suite.

"What was Josie Frankenberg doing in Sebastian Taggard's suite? I though Marina Lord occupied his full attention," Ben Stein remarked with elaborate casualness.

"Marina does. Sebastian and Marina shared the suite."

"I see. Who knew that Miss Frankenberg was going to be in their suite that night?"

"Well, Sebastian and Marina, of course. Anton Vilanova and I knew. So did Darlene Schiller. I don't know who else. Oh, yes! Roberto, the masseur. He knew because he was supposed to give Josie a massage there. Marina had given Josie her time with Roberto."

Lieutenant Ben Stein was quiet for a long moment. Finally he said, "And as I recall, Roberto was also murdered. So we can eliminate him as a suspect."

"Darlene was heartbroken. He was her masseur. She introduced him to Josie."

"Darlene Schiller? The wife of Herman Schiller, the White House Chief of Staff?"

"Yes."

"Did Herman Schiller keep it out of the papers that Miss Frankenberg was murdered in your father and Marina Lord's suite?"

"Actually, I think Moe Frankenberg had more to do with that."

Stein fussed with his yarmulke which he always did when he was upset. "I really shouldn't blame myself," he said, more for his own ears than for Cella's. "There was no way to have made the connection. But I do blame myself."

"What connection?" Cella wasn't following the logic of Ben Stein's mind.

"The connection between the murder of Josie Frankenberg

and that of Phillip Mckay. In Sebastian Taggard and Marina Lord's suite.''

"Is there a connection?''

Ben Stein sighed deeply. "There may be. And if so, both those murders are connected to the attack on your father. All this could have been prevented if I'd used the brains under my yarmulke. Damn!''

"Then I wish we'd talked sooner. Something I said might have helped you. And my father would have been spared this awful experience.''

"There was a piece of the puzzle missing. You've just given it to me.''

"I have? What is it?''

"It's the suite.''

"Why the suite?''

"Do you remember that I said Dr. Mckay's murder was a crime of passion?''

"I remember.''

"Josie Frankenberg's rape and murder were obviously crimes of passion too.''

"Yes, and I'm starting to see something as well,'' Cella said softly. "The attack on my father was also a crime of passion, wasn't it?''

"Precisely. Sexual passion.''

"Is it possible the same man who killed Phillip killed Josie too? And then attacked my father?''

"It's possible. It's a theory. But I try not to have theories. Theories have a nasty habit of distorting the facts. One instinctively tries to twist the facts to fit the theory.''

"But this theory *does* fit the facts. Each crime involved sexual passion,'' Cella said with conviction.

"My dear young woman, this crime may also have involved the Turks and the Greeks. And the Aphrodite. They too have passions.''

"I forgot about them.''

"Don't. And I'll try not to. But I'm only a New York City homicide lieutenant. My State Department connections are not very good. The attack on your father may have been an attempt by one of those governments—or some religious fanatic—to frighten him into giving up the necklace. I hope it's as simple as that.''

"You think that's simple?''

"Of course. Then the crimes will end when the necklace is returned to the rightful government,'' Stein said. "Not that we'll ever get a conviction.'' He shook his head. "Now, if you'll excuse me, I have a long report to file. And you have a breakfast appointment with Marina Lord."

With that Lieutenant Stein headed off in the direction of the Lexington Avenue subway. In a matter of seconds he had disappeared completely right before her startled eyes. She shrugged and turned. Marina was waiting. Marina! It struck her with the force of a blow that Ben Stein had deliberately mentioned Marina. In his way he was telling her each crime was connected to Marina Lord. She started to run after him but knew it was useless and stopped.

Chapter Twenty-four

What gives life its glib party smile for many is the realization of its unpredictability. The very moment when we feel "on top" is when the bomb casually explodes.

On a late, golden November afternoon the telephone rang in Anton Vilanova's apartment. He was on his way to La Guardia to catch the shuttle to Boston and had just closed and locked the door to his apartment. When he heard the telephone ring, he was already late. He controlled his impulse to reenter the apartment and answer it, waiting instead until he heard the message service pick up the call. Then he ran for the elevator. The doorman was holding a cab for him downstairs, and if he took much longer the traffic would get worse, he'd miss the plane and have to take a later one. A later one meant dinner. He didn't want to have dinner with his Boston friend.

When the plane landed at Logan Airport, Anton told the cab driver to take him to the Harvard Club on Commonwealth Avenue. The cab soon pulled up in front of a handsome gray stone building with a wrought-iron fence protecting a small grassy plot in front of the structure and twin Doric columns on either side of the door. Anton thought how symbolic the structure was of old Back Bay Boston.

Lawrence Lord was waiting for him just inside the entrance to the club. He greeted him with elaborate courtesy.

"Anton! What a pleasure. How was the flight?"

"The shuttle is the shuttle. It was crowded."

"As always. And often delayed."

"As always. That's why I'm late."

"I half thought you might have changed your mind." Lawrence smiled benevolently. "Now that you've arrived, why don't we have a drink in the President's Room?" he said, starting through the lobby.

Anton followed Lawrence's lead into a small room whose papered walls were covered with pictures of the past presidents of the Harvard Club. And of those graduates of Harvard who had been President of the United States. There were a surprising number of these, including both John and John Quincy Adams, both Franklin and Teddy Roosevelt, and John F. Kennedy. Harvard graduates believed that if they were not necessarily the best or the brightest men for the job, they were the right men for the job. in some cases, the only man for the job. Glancing at the pictures, Anton thought that he liked the air of confidence the portraits exuded.

"What shall I order for you?" Lawrence Lord asked.

"A Bombay gin martini. Tell them not too much ice. It dulls the taste of the gin."

Lawrence ordered the martini and a stein of Beck's beer for himself, then settled comfortably in the leather chair to wait, determined to conceal his curiosity at the reason for Anton's unexpected visit.

Anton said nothing. The longer Lawrence waited the better. Instead, he glanced around the room, taking in the people. On all sides were distinguished-looking older men, eager-looking young men, reading *The Wall Street Journal* or playing backgammon or chess. Here and there a woman drank alone or with another woman, occasionally with a man. Apparently the fact that Harvard was now a coed college made little difference here. The Harvard Club of Boston remained primarily a men's club.

Having surveyed the room, Anton resorted to meaningless conversational fill-ins about Boston's weather versus Manhattan's, the presidential candidates and such. He wanted Lawrence on tenterhooks.

The arrival of their drinks along with a generous bowl of peanuts and pretzels provided a useful break in the tension. Both men busied themselves with their drinks. Finally Anton looked over the rim of his glass and remarked in a neutral tone, "You keep the books. What's the current net worth of the Luxembourg Corporation?"

Lawrence sat up a bit straighter. "Why do you ask?"

"I would like to know."

"Are you having a crisis of confidence in me?" Lawrence asked with false heartiness.

"Of course not. I depend on you completely. For five years you've kept the books. Very accurately."

"I take that as a compliment. You are a man of unusually sound business judgment."

Listening to Lawrence compliment him, Anton had to remind himself that Lawrence's true personality contained much dishonesty and little more than a gracious, cultivated, well-concealed greed. Still, he usually enjoyed the man's company. It was only after they parted that he wished he never had to see him again.

"And since my judgment was so sound when I chose you for a partner," Anton said, "tell me what our current net worth is. You know what we have in the bank. And what paintings we have in inventory. What we may be buying or selling. That all adds up to our projected net worth. What is it?"

"It will take a little figuring on the part of our accountant," Lawrence said with a show of great sincerity. "That is, if you want it down to the last penny, rather than a ballpark number off the top of my head."

"I'll settle for a ballpark number."

Lawrence gave him a queer look. "Would you tell me why?"

"I'd like some quick cash."

"You need quick cash? Why?"

Anton had expected that question and for days had been trying to come up with a reason that had a semblance of credibility. But nothing held water. So he settled for no reason at all. "I do. Leave it at that."

"You don't trust me enough to tell me why." Lawrence sounded hurt.

Watching him, Anton thought how misleading Lawrence could be. He actually appeared to be offended. "I made some bad investments," he finally admitted.

"I don't believe it. Not you." Lawrence studied Anton and leaped to one of those prescient conclusions that made him so successful in the art world. "You don't need cash. Not for yourself, at any rate. It's for someone else. A great deal of cash. More than you can manage even out of the income from the Vilanova Trust. Now, I wonder who is in over his head."

Anton had realized that Lawrence would be difficult. He was too subtle a man to be easily bluffed. "It's a personal affair," he said.

"Personal tells me it's Cella Taggard." Lawrence inhaled deeply. "But that's impossible. I don't know the financial situation of the Taggard family, but I know they're worth many, many millions. Sebastian would loan her the money if she needed it. And he wouldn't miss it."

"No, he wouldn't."

"Then who? Your uncle Victor? Impossible." For a second time in as many minutes, Lawrence's instincts served him well. "Marcus!" he said with a note of triumph in his voice. "Marcus Taggard needs money!"

"Why would he? He's a Taggard." Anton realized too late that he sounded defensive. His tone was a giveaway.

"He's not a true Taggard. Not in Sebastian's eyes." Lawrence gave Anton a smile, so sudden, so shrewd, so triumphant that it might have been switched on. "It's Marcus. He's done something foolish. And Sebastian won't help him. He's never forgiven Marcus for his flirtation with Wall Street. So Marcus has come to you for money. That's logical."

Anton was silent.

"You intend to play the Good Samaritan. That's why you want to know our cash position." Another smile, this one malicious, fanciful, twisted Lawrence's lips.

"For openers."

"Openers?" Lawrence's eyebrows shot up quizzically. This time his prescience failed him. "I don't follow you."

"You will."

The first sign of apprehension showed on Lawrence's face. If knowledge of their cash position was for openers, what did Anton want for closers? "When Peter Petty's check clears the bank, we'll have an additional million on hand. That's over and beyond the five hundred thousand or so in cash we already have in the bank. I'd guess one and a half million dollars is enough to take care of Marcus."

"What's our inventory at the Morgan Manhattan worth?"

"Are you asking what we paid for the paintings or what we'll eventually sell them for?" If Anton was calculating on the sale of paintings, then a cool million and a half dollars wasn't enough for Marcus. He must be in one hell of a jam.

"Give me both sets of numbers."

"Close to another two million at cost. But I'll sell them for five million before I'm done. Remember, these are rough figures," Lawrence explained. "I'll have to check the books to give you firm numbers."

"They'll do," Anton said. "More than seven million in all. I'll sell you my half interest in the corporation for three million."

The two men stared at each other without expression; with the faces of men who had learned more thoroughly than most to give nothing away.

"You'd sell me your half. For three million." Lawrence sounded as if he were talking to himself.

"That's what I said."

"Why?"

"Personal reasons."

"I don't believe it. The Luxembourg is too profitable," Lawrence said stoutly.

"You don't believe I could have personal reasons for giving up a profitable venture." Anton laughed. "I am not you, Lawrence. Actually, I've been considering this move for several years. It's no longer fun."

"Fun?" This was a new idea for Lawrence. "Yes, I can see your point. Making money is fun. Why is it less fun now than it was?"

"In a small way I've proved my point."

"Which is?"

"That in a money-mad world I could be as greedy as the next. And beat the greediest at their own game." Lawrence gave him an odd look. "Don't try to understand me. You won't. At any rate, I want out. For three million dollars."

"And you needed this Marcus fiasco to give you the excuse?" Lawrence was probing, afraid he had missed something. Anton's willingness to sell remained a mystery to him.

"I said that my reasons are personal."

Lawrence's eyes were hot and inquisitive as they surveyed Anton. "You're right. I don't understand you. How much cash does Marcus actually need?"

Anton ignored the question.

"Three million," Lawrence repeated out loud, privately confident that Anton was asking for more than he expected to receive. Marcus probably needed two million. "All right. If he's in that bad a jam, I'll buy your half of the Luxembourg for one and a half million." Anton could make up the rest out of his other investments.

"One and a half million," Anton said, making a fine show of outrage. Then he looked around at the backgammon players. Not a head had turned away from the game at the sound of these numbers. "I told you I want three million."

"And I told you I'm offering one and a half million," Lawrence parried.

Anton finished his drink. "Thanks for the drink, Lawrence. No deal." He started to stand up.

Lawrence placed his hand on Anton's shoulder to hold him in place. "Wait a minute. I'll stretch to two million, but on two conditions."

"Two million for my half," Anton said thoughtfully, leaning back in his chair. "What are the conditions?"

"One, our Luxembourg lawyer will draw up the sale agreement. In the meantime, you can sign the check."

"You know you have to sign it as well."

"That brings up my second condition. I'll countersign the check after I talk with Marcus." Lawrence chuckled. "I must admit I'm fascinated to learn why he needs all that money."

"I never said it was for Marcus."

"You don't have to. It is. Do you want to close now?" Anton nodded. "Fine. Let's go to my office."

Lawrence signed the chit and together they left the Harvard Club.

The two men headed for Lawrence's office in the Fogg Museum on the Harvard campus, where he kept the corporate books and the checkbook in a small, strong safe. Lawrence drew up a memo of understanding to give to the lawyer, which both he and Anton signed.

When it was done, Anton said, "Make out two checks."

"I can write a check for a million and a half now. I'll have to postdate the remaining five hundred thousand for about two months from now. It will take me that long to sell off some of our current inventory."

"And you'll get five million eventually for the entire inventory?" The amount was probably closer to seven million, Anton thought. Lawrence was a born swindler.

"I think I can get that. Don't worry, you'll get your five hundred thousand."

"I'm not worried. Make out the check for a million and a half. I'll sign it now."

"To Marcus Taggard?" Lawrence asked slyly.

"To Marcus Taggard," Anton said wearily. He'd grown impatient with Lawrence's games.

"You have to meet my second condition," Lawrence said. "I want you to set up a meeting so I can ask him why he needs the money."

"You have the makings of a first-rate bastard, Lawrence."

"That is not correct. I am the only son of a former chairman of the art history department at Yale. Mama was a member of the Daughters of the American Revolution. She would never have borne a child out of wedlock. But it's true, she could be a bit of a bitch at times. So I may be a son of a bitch. But never a bastard."

"Very funny," Anton said sarcastically. "Marcus won't tell you why he needs the money."

"If he won't tell me, so be it. All I want to do is ask. I am not the kind of man who threatens. He'll get his check either way. But my second condition stands. I won't cosign until Marcus meets with me.''

"All right. I'll see what I can arrange," Anton said after signing the check for a million and a half. "But remember, no horsing around. You will give Marcus this check whether or not he lets you play Ann Landers.''

"Scout's honor," Lawrence said. "You know I'm a man of my word.''

And strangely enough, Anton thought as he left, the bastard was a man of his word. The trouble was his word was often a lie.

Back in New York, Anton had Marcus over to his apartment to discuss Marcus' financial dilemma. Nothing had changed. Even so, Anton did not mention the deal he'd cut with Lawrence Lord. The thought of a naive Marcus Taggard in a room with Lawrence Lord made him nervous. He'd wait. Sebastian might relent. But the pressure on Marcus to produce his customers' stock was building. He could cover for a week or so. That was it. If Sebastian didn't act, Anton would have to set up the meeting with Lawrence Lord.

When Lawrence Lord returned to New York, neatly folded in his wallet was a check for one and a half million dollars made out to Marcus Taggard. All it needed was his signature before Marcus could deposit it. With rising impatience, each day Lawrence waited for Marcus to call. He itched to see a return on an investment. Though, thinking it over, he decided it was probably just as well Marcus didn't call immediately.

Buying out Anton had stripped the Luxembourg Corporation of its liquid assets. Now he needed operating capital. Plus the remaining five hundred thousand he had agreed to pay Anton. Clearly this was no time to rest on his oars. It was time to sell off one or two of the gems in the Luxembourg Corporation's collection. Undoubtedly Toby Phipps was the right man to help replenish the corporate cash position. After he'd been properly wined and dined, of course. The thought made Lawrence nauseous.

Lawrence and Toby had another of their gargantuan lunches and dinners. Lunch was at least deliciously French. Dinner was something else. Suddenly Toby had a yen for Chinese food and they wended their way down to Chinatown, this time Toby in the lead. For this freedom, Lawrence silently thanked heaven and Emory Portland. Chinatown and Chinese food were not his responsibility. Fortunately, the restaurant was a family-run affair, and the preparation of dinner took forever. This gave Lawrence more than enough time to chat. And as usual, he chatted with a purpose.

For Tobias Phipps he'd settled on a drawing of a kneeling monk by Michelangelo that Anton had picked up in Europe. Over the dessert of kumquats and litchi nuts, which Lawrence detested, he brought up the subject. Was Toby interested? Toby was.

Not because he was taken with old master drawings. But Amy and his cousins had gone gaga over drawings. Their grandchildren were bringing them home from school. With the Michelangelo as a centerpiece, he might convince them to fund a new, "old master drawings" room. It would be a nice touch.

When they struck a deal for a cool half million, the price was so reasonable Toby had to shovel two kumquats into his mouth not to ask for the provenance.

What Toby didn't know was that he was no longer the biggest game in town for Lawrence. That honor belonged to Marcus Taggard. And a few things Lawrence had in mind. Now, with the final five hundred thousand in hand, Lawrence felt more secure. His impatience took over. Where the blazes was Marcus? he asked himself as he drank another cup of tiresome, thin Chinese tea.

The next morning, with Toby safely birthed in Delaware, Lawrence impulsively gave way to his need. He refused to wait any longer. He called Marcus. After chatting about nothing for minutes, Lawrence said sympathetically—and when Lawrence Lord chose, there was no one more sympathetic— "Anton tells me you could use some money."

"Not some money. A bundle," Marcus replied sourly, wondering why Anton had mentioned his predicament to Lawrence Lord. If Lord stretched his resources, he might come up with a hundred thousand dollars. And why should he stretch in the first place?

"Perhaps I can be of some help. Why don't we meet in my apartment in Lincoln Towers this afternoon?"

Marcus started to say, "Why waste your time and mine?" then stopped himself. His cousin was a very clever man. If Anton thought enough of Lawrence Lord's ability to help to tell Lawrence his financial troubles, Anton must know something he didn't. "One o'clock?" he asked.

"Make it two."

"Two o'clock it is," Marcus said with a forced cheerfulness. He wanted desperately to believe that there was a good reason for this meeting.

What had started as a golden morning had clouded over by eleven, and a soaking rain was punishing the city. When Marcus arrived at Lawrence's apartment, he carefully shook out his Burberry before entering the vestibule. Like most things Marcus owned, the Burberry wasn't an ordinary Burberry. Marcus had purchased the coat at Brooks Brothers and had the Brooks' tailors alter it to meet his high standards. In addition to the coat being recut, special buttons of bone were substituted for the plastic ones. And Marcus had his initials woven in red into the plaid lining. Even Lawrence Lord was impressed with the coat when he hung it in the closet. But he wasn't impressed enough. He forgot it as soon as he closed the closet door. Lawrence Lord usually had the instincts of a survivor. This time they failed him.

He invited Marcus to make himself comfortable, indicating a chair next to the window. Lawrence seated himself in an identical chair with a small round table between them. Ready for business.

Lawrence had no real idea of how badly Marcus needed cash. But for Anton to have accepted his deal was proof enough of a great need. He opened the conversation by offering Marcus a drink.

"Brandy, if you have any," Marcus said.

"At this time of day?"

"At any time of day."

Shortly Marcus was warming a snifter of Rémy Martin while Lawrence nursed a glass of red wine. Instead of sipping the brandy as Lawrence expected, Marcus tossed the drink down and asked for a second.

Noting Marcus' agitated state, Lawrence decided he might safely shortcut the preliminary softening-up process he'd been preparing. He opened a drawer in the table and pulled out a file folder. With a flourish, he opened it and shoved a piece of paper in Marcus' direction. "Here," he said. "From what Anton tells me, this should solve all your problems."

Marcus glanced at the paper and blinked, unable to hide his amazement. A check made out to him for one and a half million dollars was exactly what he needed. And the check was already signed by Anton. As he reached for it, he wondered why Anton hadn't given it to him personally. Why use Lawrence Lord as a go-between?

Lawrence smiled indulgently. "It's no good, you know. I mean, the bank won't accept it."

Marcus' hand stopped inches from the check. "What the hell do you mean it's no good? Why would Anton sign a check without the money in the bank?"

"I didn't say the money wasn't in the bank. Look at the check carefully, Marcus. What do you see?"

Avoiding touching the check, Marcus examined it. He looked puzzled for a moment, then his face cleared. "It's drawn on the Luxembourg Corporation and it takes two signatures."

Lawrence nodded. "Anton's and mine."

"Then sign it," Marcus said. In the back of his mind it registered that Lawrence Lord, the celebrated professor of art history at Harvard, was Anton's mysterious partner in a venture that was borderline legal at best. And downright crooked at worst. He wondered why Lord was coming out of the closet.

"I intend to sign it," Lawrence said, smiling. "But I have a few questions I want to ask you first."

"I need the money for my business," Marcus said flatly, "if that's what you want to know."

"You took a beating in something. I don't understand. The market's been going up recently. Unless you were shorting the market."

"I gambled on a new issue and lost."

"That was quite a gamble," Lawrence said gently.

"It was a damn fool gamble. There's an old Wall Street adage. 'The bulls and the bears get rich. The pigs go to the slaughterhouse.' I was a hog. I've always been a hog. Too greedy." The long-ago prophecy of Spina came into his mind. *You shall kiss the feet of many fools,* she had said. Lawrence Lord wasn't a fool, but he was demanding his feet be kissed. "Now that you know why I need the money, will you sign the check? Please," Marcus begged humbly.

"I have one more question to ask you."

"About what?"

"Not about you. Or your financial blunders."

Marcus leaned back and sipped his brandy. "Ask away," he said expansively. As long as he didn't have to admit that he'd used his customers' stock to borrow money from the bank, he couldn't think of any question that he wouldn't answer.

Speaking so softly that Marcus had to concentrate on every

word, Lawrence murmured, "Where does The House of Uni get its supply of ancient jewelry?"

Marcus choked on his brandy, coughing a little of it back into his glass. "What do you mean?" he sputtered.

"Precisely what I said. Where does Sebastian get his supply of ancient jewelry?"

Marcus took a deep breath. "He has his sources. Estate sales. Old friends. Leads," he fumbled. "I don't really know what they are. I've never worked with my father."

"Don't take me for an idiot, Marcus. My sources are almost as good as Sebastian's, and I couldn't come up with a fraction of the finds he does."

"Maybe your sources aren't as good as you think."

"And maybe you don't need this check as badly as you think."

"That money is mine. I want it," Marcus said, his anger rising.

"That money is yours when I sign the check. Not one second before. I want to know The House of Uni's sources."

"I told you, I don't know what they are," Marcus insisted in too nervous a voice.

You know them, and you'll tell me, Lawrence said to himself. Aloud, he said, "Look, Marcus, I have no intention of hurting The House of Uni." His tone had grown conciliatory. "Why should I want to hurt them? You know I get a five percent commission for steering customers to the shop. To hurt them would be like killing the goose that laid the golden egg. All I want is what you want—what we all want. A fair share of the pie. A higher commission. And your father is a stubborn man. I need some leverage to persuade Sebastian that it's to his advantage to raise my percentage."

"Your percentage of the take of The House of Uni. That's what this meeting's about?"

"Yes. It's a simple business proposition. I've asked Sebastian repeatedly for an increase to ten percent. He won't give it to me." Lawrence sighed. "It's like his not giving you the money you need."

"How did you know he wouldn't?" Marcus shouted suddenly, as combative as a fighting cock.

Lawrence raised both his hands. "Easy, Marcus. I'm on your side. Try to remember that. Would you be here if your father had given you the money?"

"No! He turned me down!" Marcus all but howled. "Me! His own son! He turned me down!" The anguish that Marcus felt exploded to the surface.

"Your father, like you, like so many of us, is a greedy man. But he is a bit too greedy. You're not my son, but I would never have turned you down. I won't turn you down now," Lawrence said seductively. "In fact, if you'd been my son I'd have been proud of you for taking the risks. Your father doesn't understand the reach of your dreams. He's not that smart."

"Only his own dreams," Marcus said sullenly.

"Exactly. Only his own. Not yours. Not mine." Lawrence shook his head sadly. "All I ever asked him for was a fair return, a chance to get what I deserve. A mere ten percent."

Marcus rested his elbows on the table and rubbed his forehead with his fingertips.

"If I hadn't checked a piece or two, I'd actually suspect the jewelry wasn't genuine. But my son, Jason, swears that everything in The House of Uni is an honest-to-God piece of ancient jewelry. And if Jason Lord says a piece of jewelry is authentic, it's authentic."

"Ha!" Marcus muttered into his brandy snifter.

"Ha? What do you mean, ha?" Anyone not totally locked into his own hurt, as Marcus was, would have seen the change in Lawrence's expression.

"I mean, ha!" Lawrence's words—*You're not my son, but I would never have turned you down*—pounded into Marcus' brain. "Will you give me your word of honor that all you want from my father is an increase to a ten percent commission on the customers you bring in?"

A flash of exultation played for an instant in Lawrence's eyes. "My word of honor? Absolutely."

Marcus stared at Lawrence, trying to ferret out his secret motives. Lawrence's eyes were open and guileless; his face, the portrait of an honest man, a man of integrity. In the glare of his fear Marcus lost his judgment altogether. Everything seemed equally probable or improbable. He wanted desperately to trust the man. So he did.

"Sign the check first," Marcus said.

"After that will you tell me about Sebastian's sources?"

"Yes."

Lawrence nodded as though acknowledging Marcus' honor. In this game of deceit and counterdeceit, Marcus was an amateur; Lawrence, a consummate professional. Lawrence took a pen from the table drawer and signed his name with a flourish, then handed the check across the table to Marcus. But Marcus wouldn't touch the check. He just stared at it, his pale face showing the misery he felt.

"Take it," Lawrence said. "It's yours."

Marcus still did not touch the check. Instead, slowly and precisely, he told Lawrence everything: where the ancient metals and jewels came from, and how Sebastian and Cella made the jewelry in the workroom in the subbasement of the house in Sands Point, using the old techniques.

When there was nothing more to tell, he picked up the check, glanced at his watch and dashed for the door. In his hurry he forgot his raincoat. Only when he reached the lobby and stood facing the rain did he remember it. He glanced at his watch again. He still had time before the bank doors closed. To hell with the raincoat. He'd pick it up another day. A woman was getting out of a cab and he ran for it.

Few men who have longed for success have known the exact minute when it arrived. But Lawrence Lord knew. He stood at the window watching the rain. But he didn't see the rain. Instead of rain, he imagined a meeting with Sebastian. Ten percent? Knowing what he now knew, that was a joke. Fifty percent minimum. A half partner in the profits of The House of Uni. Within five years he'd be a very rich man. And the profits would continue as long as The House of Uni existed. He'd receive that huge income perhaps as long as he lived.

After Marcus had made his deposit at the bank and paid off his loans, he collected his customers' stock from the bank vault and took a taxi to his office at 111 Broadway. His heart didn't stop pounding or his breathing slow down until each stock certificate had been returned to the proper customer's file. Then he opened his mouth and inhaled as much air as his lungs would hold. At last he was safe. He was free and clear.

As he slowly let his breath out, his brain started to clear. A residue of sense brought him back to reality, and he became riddled with suspicions. There was a sharp fitting together of pieces. Suddenly he knew that he had committed another crime. Perhaps an even greater one.

Yes, he was safe. But at what cost?

Abruptly Marcus slumped into his chair. Lord had performed a brilliant masquerade and he'd been a frightened fool. He remembered Lawrence's words. That oblique flattery that delights a son—telling him how much smarter he was than his father. It wasn't the check that had tipped the scales. It was the fatherly tone of admiration. The tone that he longed to hear from Sebastian and never would. For this he, Spina's son, had betrayed his family. He had revealed to an outsider the secret of The House of Uni. Lawrence Lord had sworn that all he wanted was a higher percentage on his sales. But every fiber of his being now warned Marcus that Lawrence was a liar.

He couldn't bring himself to tell Cella. And as for his father—he was still too furious at Sebastian. But the tie of the human bond lay deeper than his rage. He had to protect his family. He must tell someone who would warn Sebastian to expect a visitor. A visitor who knew everything. In a cold sweat, Marcus picked up the phone and dialed. When the ring was answered, he said, "Anton, this is Marcus. Listen to me. I think I just made a terrible mistake. I saw Lawrence Lord this afternoon, and . . . And why the devil did you tell Lawrence Lord about me?"

His sudden outrage at Anton was a mere echo of his own bitter fury at himself.

Chapter Twenty-five

Cella stood in front of the building, going over in her mind how she would put it. Considerable thought had gone into what she meant to say. But he could be stubborn as a mule; there might be a very nasty scene between them. She straightened her shoulders and walked briskly toward the small brownstone on Madison Avenue between Sixty-fourth and Sixty-fifty streets.

Twenty-five years ago, Sebastian's tailor had purchased the brownstone, showing a canny insight into the rising real estate prices of Manhattan. First he remodeled the ground floor and added a small elevator. He used the entire third floor for his work and leased out the other two floors. A fashionable, very expensive boutique paid an exorbitant rent for the use of the street floor with its twin display windows, and an expensive beauty salon occupied the second floor.

Cella stepped inside the aluminum-and-glass door that served as an entrance to the small lobby leading to the upper floors of the building. A tiny elevator with a cab just large enough for four slim people waited on the ground floor. Cella entered, pressed the third-floor button, and the elevator doors closed. Groaning, the elevator rose slowly from the ground floor and came to a stop on the third floor.

In the outside corridor she stared at the door to the tailoring establishment. It was brown with a small round window. But once Nettie, the receptionist, had admitted her to the premises, the impression of genteel poverty disappeared.

Mendelssohn & Son, Haberdashery for Discriminating Gentlemen, was a flourishing operation. The showroom was large, covering almost half of the third floor. It was divided into two areas. One wall of the floor was devoted to a series of mahogany shelves on which bolts of cloth rested—everything from muted Harris tweeds for sport jackets to dark blue and gray vicuna for warm but lightweight overcoats to tan gabardines and woolen serges of all colors and stripes for suits and slacks. If a client wanted a summer suit, Mendelssohn & Son recommended Brooks Brothers or J. Press or Paul Stuart. They refused to work with lightweight fabrics. The material never hung correctly.

In the far corner of the room was a single cheval mirror before which a customer—at this moment Sebastian—stood on a round platform and studied himself from all angles. There was only one such mirror. Under no circumstances would Felix Mendelssohn—a direct descendant of the famous composer; they were a creative family, he often said—permit more than one client in his establishment at the same time. Near the mirror was a tailor's dummy, a wooden figure made in such a way that it could be expanded or contracted at any number of points so that it duplicated the torso of the customer being fitted. At the moment it duplicated Sebastian's body.

The rest of the room was arranged much like a small sitting room in a good men's club, with several deep leather chairs, lamps, a low wooden table, a leather couch and two straight-backed chairs for elderly clients or women who found it awkward to wrestle themselves free from the clutches of the low chairs.

As Cella walked toward an armchair, she glanced around the big room, thinking it had the aura of a shrine—one dedicated to some Great Tailor God in the sky. Actually, it was much like many of the couturier houses she visited. And there was Sebastian, much like a woman having a fitting, posed on the round pedestal while two small, thin men—Mendelssohn and son—danced attendance, working on the morning coat he had ordered for the wedding. After the basting, the dark gray cloth would be temporarily stitched together and Sebastian would come for another fitting. After father and son were satisfied, the coat would be sewn, the lining added and Sebastian invited for a final fitting. Only when the jacket was pronounced perfect was the garment allowed to leave the premises. There were many men who had neither the time, the patience nor the money required to patronize Mendelssohn & Son. Nor did they understand the striving for perfection. Sebastian did. He had the money. He had the patience. He made the time.

When Cella entered the shrine, Sebastian smiled but remained still as a statue. He didn't dare move his arms, or the pinning and stitching might become undone.

"We'll be done soon," he said, barely moving his lips.

Felix Mendelssohn regarded Cella with a faint, polite distaste that reminded her of the secret distaste felt for men who visited women's hair salons.

Cella settled herself in one of the deep club chairs and crossed her legs. She picked up a magazine, then put it down. She uncrossed her legs. Feeling anxious, she closed her eyes and waited for Sebastian. She thought about her father.

Fortunately, he suffered no ill effects from the attempted castration, and since he'd seen Marina on at least three evenings that she knew of and each time had returned home with the satisfied look of a man who has had a successful encounter with a woman, evidently the doctors were right. Sebastian had not been injured.

Her thought veered to Anton. How she missed him! Peter Petty was an adequate Gorgeous, but nothing more. She wasn't and would never be in love with him. As for Jason Lord, that was another kettle of fish. The man was magnetic—if more than a bit obsessive—but something told her to stay away. No matter how much he attracted her.

What it came down to was Anton. Damn! Of course she could call him. The idea brought a vague, tender smile to her lips, the smile of a girl reading an unexpected love letter. Unconsciously she fingered the golden ring of Isis on her finger. Anton had given it to her years ago. Damn it! she silently swore again. Why couldn't Anton have Jason's ethics? His integrity? His sense of right and wrong? Were all the Taggards, all the Vilanovas, motivated by greed? Spina had been different. The jewelry Spina had created was real and even true. Spina had been able to "see." But she herself was only a pale replica of her mother. Was she also tainted? She could feel her body played upon by currents of hysteria and guilt rising like smoke in shining spirals.

A hand touched her shoulder, and she opened her eyes, startled.

"It's time to wake up," Sebastian said. "I'm ready."

"I wasn't asleep. I was thinking."

"Pleasant thoughts, I hope."

"Actually, no."

"Then let's forget them and go to lunch," Sebastian said, determined that nothing spoil the pleasant glow of satisfaction he always felt after being waited on hand and foot.

"I want to talk to you. It's important. And Felix and son have vanished. We can speak privately here."

Sebastian looked around. The Mendelssohns had indeed

disappeared into the back room, where the actual work on his morning coat was done.

"All right. Why not here," he agreed genially.

"Good." Cella took a deep breath and plunged in. "Marcus telephoned me this morning. He sounds dreadful. Like a man going down for the third time."

"I warned him about speculating on Wall Street. He has no talent for it." Sebastian sank into the chair next to Cella.

"He's very bad at it, but he is your son, and he needs your help."

Sebastian nodded in agreement. "He does need help."

"But you won't help him?"

"If he'd quit Wall Street, I'd help him in a second."

"He won't quit," Cella said emphatically. "And if he did, he wouldn't return to The House of Uni. Your attitude has made it impossible for him to work with you."

"I gather his fine-feathered Wall Street friends won't rescue him. Pity! He may have to bite the bullet."

"Father, I dislike saying this, but if you won't help him, I will." Cella's eyes flashed.

"And where do you have a million and a half free cash stashed?"

"Mother left me enough stock in The House of Uni. It's worth considerably more than a million or two. I'll use it at the bank as collateral for a loan."

"I'm the executor of Spina's will. You can't borrow on that stock without my agreement."

"And I have a friend who is a banker. I could challenge your right as executor. I could claim mishandling of funds, or some other rubbish. Would you like me to start washing dirty family linen in a public laundromat?"

"You'd do that?"

"I'd do it. I won't sit still and see my brother drawn and quartered." She paused to catch her breath. "In fact, I'll do more. I'll call Money Maurice and offer him for auction any pieces he chooses from The House of Uni."

"You wouldn't dare!"

"Of course I'd dare. I'll offer him the Queen of Ur's headdress. The one I wouldn't sell to Peter Petty."

"I won't permit it!"

"You couldn't stop me. And our battle would make headlines! Journalists love bloody family feuds. The Hatfields and McCoys are legendary."

Sebastian spoke slowly and deliberately. "You do know

that no matter what you try to do, you'll never get the money in time to save him."

"I know that very well, Father, dear," Cella said sweetly. "I don't stand around under neon lights hoping to get a suntan. I know exactly what I'm doing. But I'll do it anyway." She continued to smile angelically. "Call it tit for tat. And you just think about your loss of face. Of your prestige. Of the reputation of The House of Uni." She chucked Sebastian under the chin. "You won't like the swamp you'll find yourself wallowing in any more than Marcus likes his."

"Cella, you're talking about blackmail," Sebastian said.

"How clever of you to figure it out."

"Pure blackmail." Sebastian started to laugh. "I must admit you could make a man's life very difficult."

"I mean what I say."

"I believe it. Fortunately, we're on the same side."

Cella blinked. Sebastian was not a man to use words idly. "What do you mean—we're on the same side?"

"We are. I'm sorry you wasted your time shooting off fireworks. Though it was a good show." He stroked her cheek. "No, I won't help Marcus. Not quite yet. I want him to sweat just a little longer. But at the right time . . ."

"You'll pull him out?" Cella asked tensely.

"When his back is against the wall, I'll step in. Didn't you know I would? As you pointed out, he is my son."

"You must act quickly, then."

"As soon as it's absolutely necessary."

"How will you know when it's absolutely necessary?" Cella's relief was abruptly replaced by this new concern.

"Darlene Schiller is advising me."

"Little Dolly Drop Drawers?"

"Little Dolly Drop Drawers is married to Herman Schiller, who may not be much of a statesman, but is there anyone who knows more about Wall Street than he does? Think of Schiller, Schmidt and Weintraub."

"But—"

"Darlene wants my Aphrodite. I've promised her that if she helps me, I'll give her an opportunity to top the Turks' bid." Sebastian's pleasure at the prospect of the bidding war made him expand like a pouter pigeon.

"You can't. It belongs to Turkey," Cella said numbly.

"Turkey will have it. Or the Greeks. Haven't you guessed?"

"Guessed what?" Cella asked wearily.

"Darlene isn't buying for herself. The price is too high

even for Herman. She represents the Greeks. If I know Darlene, they're paying her a commission to deliver the necklace. Isn't it a wonderful joke?"

Cella started to say something biting, then stopped herself. "A wonderful joke. Letting them buy your Aphrodite. A brilliant forgery . . ."

"Stop it," Sebastian said sternly. "I warned Marcus many times, but I didn't expect to have to warn you. I don't like that word."

"Sorry. A poor choice of language. A brilliant re-creation." She smiled brightly, knowing there was no way to spare him. The gods would use him for their own purposes.

"Brilliant!" Sebastian couldn't be more pleased with himself. "It's the cream of the jest. Two NATO powers in a bidding war for something I made in our basement last month. It's really funny."

"It does have a humorous aspect."

"And Marina gets the Aphrodite—Turkey or Greece, the replica. It's a perfect copy. None of those fools will know the difference."

"Perhaps Aphrodite herself will be pleased."

"I don't care about her. She's superstitious nonsense."

Cella shook her head to clear it. "All right, let's drop the subject," she went on in a firm tone. "But you will help Marcus?"

"Before they take him away in chains, I'll cover his borrowings at the bank."

"I'm glad."

"I'm not, but I have no choice. He is my son. Now let's go to lunch. I'm starving."

The fluted chimes that announced a visitor to The House of Uni rang. Cella glanced about the store. Juliana was nowhere to be seen. And Sebastian was engrossed in a heart-to-heart conversation with a customer. Cella passed them unnoticed as she went to the display window to see who was there. She took a deep breath at the sight of Jason Lord.

Cella opened the heavy door and greeted Jason with a welcoming smile. "Come in," she said.

Even though the weather had turned cold, Jason wore only a turtleneck sweater and a loose-fitting jacket, not an overcoat. His eyes took in the treasures on display with an avidity that made Cella uncomfortable. Then he turned and looked at her.

"Don't say anything. Hear me out. I have three reasons for being here."

"Yes?" Cella said, tilting her head.

"First, I would like to apologize for that night," he said with a show of embarrassment. "I'm not used to drinking, and the champagne did me in. I had no business saying what I said. So I am sorry. Will you forgive me?" Cella smiled, accepting his apology, and as he watched he felt sure that her lips must taste soft when bitten, and there was a delicious weakness in his legs. The blood raced to his brain, and he hoped it was not apparent how easily she disturbed him.

"Anton behaved just as badly. He didn't have to make an issue out of it," she said a little unsteadily.

Jason shrugged his shoulders, his face expressionless. Then suddenly he grinned. "Now for the second reason I'm here. I'd like to purchase a Cella Classics."

"Did Frank Ford tell you about them?"

"He raved. I saw the ring he picked for his bride. It was inexpensive and quite exquisite. It would have fooled most experts."

"No, it wouldn't," Cella said, her smile glued on. "At The House of Uni we don't try to deceive anyone. Things are what they seem. What we say they are."

"That's why I have such a high respect for this shop," Jason said softly. "And now I would like to see your collection. I have to pick out a present for a . . . a friend."

Cella guided Jason toward the rear of the shop. She pressed the button that allowed them entry to the Clients' Room. "What are you looking for?"

"A ring or a bracelet or a necklace. I'm not sure," Jason said.

"Wait here," she said. "I'll be right back." She left the room, returned with a half-dozen jewelry trays and spread them out on the table. "This is the best of my work. Pick what you like."

Jason looked sideways at Cella. "Which do you like best?"

"I made them all, so naturally I like them all."

"But you must have a favorite."

"I suppose I do. But that's no guarantee the lady will agree with me."

"No. But the two of you have certain similarities. Show me which one."

Cella ran her eyes over the trays. She hesitated at a pair of gold filigreed pendant earrings hung with the figure of Eros. She clipped one onto her earlobe and shook her head. The earring swung back and forth charmingly. "What do you think?" she asked.

Jason studied it dreamily, then shook his head. He picked up a necklace in which rock crystal, lapis lazuli, pearls and coral were alternated with small profiles in gold of a woman and clasped at each end with two winged animals. "What do you think of this?"

"One of my more successful efforts," Cella said. "You have wonderful taste."

"Beauty is my business," Jason responded.

"I thought truth was your business."

"Truth and beauty. This has the beauty of your truth. I'll take it. How much?"

"A gift. From a stepsister to her stepbrother."

"I couldn't accept . . ."

"You can and you will," Cella said firmly. "Shall I send it to the lucky lady? Or do you want to deliver it in person? And collect the reward?"

"It's for my mother," Jason said. "I don't think the reward will be exactly what you had in mind."

Cella started to laugh. "That's unfair. You led me on."

"You led yourself on," Jason said. "Anyway, now for the third reason I'm here. It will make a fair exchange for the necklace."

Cella looked quizzical.

"You wanted me to vet the Aphrodite, and I will. At no charge. My gift to my new stepsister. From her stepbrother."

Cella swallowed quickly. "How kind."

"I don't suppose you keep the Aphrodite here?"

Cella managed to shake her head calmly. "No, we don't. I must speak to Sebastian about it."

Now that her idea of having Jason Lord authenticate the Astarte/Aphrodite was becoming a reality, Cella saw how perfectly it fitted into her plan. Originally she had suggested it to test Jason, not The House of Uni. But the tables had turned. Without her skill the necklace might well be flawed. She wished she had examined it in more detail. Suppose Jason did find something wrong? She rubbed her forehead, struck with a pang of grief, almost of guilt. Well, if it were flawed, perhaps that would teach Sebastian a lesson. Teach them all. She must let it be.

If Jason found the piece flawed, the chain of darkness could prove endless. Do what he would, Sebastian would be caught in a snare. If he tried to return it to Northbie's and claim it was spurious, he'd cause violent suspicions. Wasn't Sebastian an authority? What had taken him so long to discover the fraud? In the uproar and disputes that would follow, something would be irrevocably lost. The trust and belief of the art world in The House of Uni. The faith of the Greeks. Of the Turks. Except for Abdul Hamid. Only he would guess the truth, that Sebastian had counterfeited the necklace of the goddess. For only he knew there was a true Aphrodite. And Abdul Hamid would never forgive the sacrilege.

Cella felt a deathly chill. It would be no better if Dr. Jason Lord authenticated the false necklace. Then Sebastian would sell it to the highest bidder. And a twentieth-century fraud would rest in Aphrodite's shrine. Aphrodite the goddess of love and birth. Aphrodite the queen of darkness and death. Would she take vengeance? Or would she laugh? As Sebastian had. Cella thought, with grim humor, that she would find out the mood of the goddess soon enough. They all would.

Jason broke into her reverie. "Tell me what you're thinking. You have an odd expression on your face. Or don't." He smiled. "If you don't want me to vet the necklace, forget it. I'm positive it's authentic."

"I do. I was simply thinking when would be a good time. We keep it stored in a special vault. I'll call you next week and arrange to bring it to your office."

"We'll have dinner afterward and celebrate," Jason said, all smiles.

"Celebrate what?" Cella asked uncertainly.

Her question lingered in the air between them as they exchanged looks.

"I don't know," Jason said. "Your forgiving me. The Aphrodite. Do we need a reason?"

"No. We'll celebrate Marina and Sebastian," Cella said gaily, wanting to show she could meet him halfway.

"Marina and Sebastian," Jason echoed. But this time his smile was missing.

Cella pressed a button under the table and within seconds Juliana appeared. "Here," Cella said, handing Juliana the necklace Jason had chosen. "I think The House of Uni box in scarlet velvet would be perfect for this necklace."

Juliana nodded and disappeared, and Jason began to examine other pieces of jewelry, asking about them as if he really cared.

Cella was relieved when Juliana reappeared with the jewelry box elegantly wrapped. Jason thanked her and started toward the door, Cella walking beside him.

"Perhaps I'll see you next week. When you bring in the

Aphrodite.'' He paused, and feeling embarrassed as a school-boy, he repeated, ''We'll have dinner afterward?''

''Yes. I'll call in advance.''

Jason turned to leave, and when Cella opened the door, he almost collided with Anton. The two men stood stiffly, less than a yard apart, studying each other. Then Jason extended his hand. ''I apologize for what happened that night. I had no right to sound off like that.''

Anton gracefully acknowledged the apology. ''I didn't handle it too well either, Lord.''

The men shook hands, and Cella could tell from the way their hands gripped that each made an effort to make his handshake firm without using excess pressure. She remembered Peter Petty's words about a pissing contest. Apparently Jason and Anton wanted to avoid a repetition. With a jaunty wave, Jason was gone, leaving Cella to face Anton alone.

''You won't answer my phone calls,'' Anton said in a low voice. ''But I have to talk to you. It's too important to wait for you to recover from your tantrum.''

''It isn't a tantrum. But anyway, I'm over it,'' Cella said. ''And I have something important to tell you. Let's go to my office.''

Cella's office was so small it barely had room for her desk, chair and file cabinets. They stood there separated by inches, looking at each other.

''Please forgive me,'' he said, his eyes searching hers. ''I don't sleep well anymore.''

''I don't forgive you. But I don't sleep so well either.''

''I've even been faithful. The American way,'' Anton said.

''Have you joined the Rotarians?''

''Almost. But I have worshipped the almighty dollar. Isn't that the American way?''

''I remember. Stay with tennis. Dollar worship is a life sport. It leaves no time for . . .'' She stumbled. ''For anything else.''

''I know. And speaking of what it leaves no time for . . .'' Anton let out his breath in a harsh sound. ''Do you think you might come a little closer?''

Cella stood still.

''You haven't forgiven me?''

Cella said nothing.

''You look at me and you see a man you can't trust.''

''That's right. But what are you waiting for?''

''For you. You're too far away. Come here.''

His arms closed around her in an embrace that was both

powerful and gentle. Cella slipped her arms around his neck. The familiar warmth and force of him enveloped her in a single, shattering instant.

She looked into his eyes. "You scoundrel."

"Closer," he said as his hands slipped down her back, her waist, to her buttocks, pressing her firmly against his hard sex, and her whole body pressed against the beating of his heart. Then their lips met and the world slid away for both of them and they longed for nothing more than each other. Cella broke away first, gasping for breath. "That was an adrenaline-generated response." She escaped to the chair behind her desk.

"It's not your adrenaline that's acting up," Anton said.

"Don't argue. You've behaved like a scoundrel, and here I am welcoming you back as if you were a great warrior king."

Anton perched on the edge of her desk, taking her half-unwilling hand in his. "I know. I've been a wheeler and a dealer." He smiled—almost laughing—with the breaking of the long tension between them. "If I had the taste for it, I might have been a corporate raider."

"And because I love you I let you take advantage of me. I am not your toy and plaything."

"That's nonsense. We take advantage of each other. Like all people do who love each other." He shook his head. "Now listen. We have serious matters to discuss. Something has happened."

"Here too."

"All right. You tell me your news first. After I tell you mine, we may have to sign a new peace treaty."

He reached for her hand and their fingers intertwined.

"Sebastian has promised to pay Marcus' debts," Cella said carefully. "He just wants him to sweat a little more. He thinks it will teach him a lesson."

"Damn! Damn! Damn!" Anton exploded.

"Aren't you pleased?"

"Teach him a lesson! Torture never taught anybody a lesson. Except how to hate. Didn't he think the victim would react?"

"I told Sebastian that. It wouldn't teach Marcus a thing. He's as stubborn as Sebastian. He . . ." Cella saw the stricken look on Anton's face and stopped talking. Tentatively she asked, "What is it? Tell me."

"I hope you can stand it." Anton's fingers tightened about hers, almost hurting them. He took a deep breath and said in a flat, unemotional voice, "Lawrence Lord knows everything about The House of Uni."

The color drained from Cella's face, and the pressure of her teeth biting her lips turned them white. When she said "I don't understand," the effort to speak strained the muscles in her throat, and her voice was hoarse.

Without releasing Cella's fingers, Anton walked around the desk and drew her to her feet. He put his arms about her again and, holding her close, told her what had happened. His voice was soft but harsh as he described the deal he'd cut with Lawrence Lord. But Lawrence hadn't waited. He had broken their understanding and gone directly to Marcus himself. Dangling a check in front of the desperate man, he'd played on his need for money while probing for information about The House of Uni. Inevitably Marcus had cracked. He'd given Lawrence even more information than Lawrence had expected.

Cella's face was muffled against Anton's jacket as her body shuddered with the force of her emotions. "How could he do it?" she said. "How could Marcus betray his family?"

Anton felt the trembling of Cella's body, heard her ragged breaths. "Darling, when a man is sentenced to execution, he'll do anything to save himself. And Sebastian was not any help."

"I'm to blame too," she mumbled. "I should have done something. It's my fault as much as Sebastian's."

"We're all to blame. None of us thought the thing through." He bent his head, searching for the softness of her lips, and found the taste of her tears. "I'm sorry," he said gently. "I'm sorry for all of us."

"Didn't he realize Father would never let him go under?" Cella asked irrationally.

"Did you?" Anton replied.

"No."

"Listen to me," Anton said, gripping her tightly by the shoulders and pushing her away to look at her tear-stained face. "Listen to me carefully. We have to make a plan."

"You mean how to deal with Lawrence?" Cella said unsteadily as she tried to gather her strength.

"That's exactly what I mean. A method for dealing with Lawrence Lord. He's nothing like his son, Jason. I have a pretty damn good idea what Dr. Jason Lord would do with this information, but Lawrence Lord is something else. He's pure greed. He told Marcus that what he wants is a ten percent commission on his sales. I don't believe that for a minute. What it will come down to is a negotiation. And there are very few negotiators better than Sebastian."

Suddenly Cella freed herself from Anton's grip. She stepped back and looked up at him. "If I understand you correctly, Lawrence got the money to give to Marcus from you?"

"That's right. I sold him my interests in the Luxembourg Corporation. For two million dollars. And signed a check for a million and a half for Marcus. That was the money he used for the seduction. But Lawrence refused to cosign the check until he talked to Marcus."

"Then you're no longer in business with Lawrence?" Cella asked, her eyes fixed on his face.

"No. I thought of getting out for a long time. Marcus' need and your reaction to my business venture gave me two very good reasons for doing it."

Their eyes met for a moment and held.

"You did it for me?"

"For both of us. And our future."

Even as he said the words Anton felt his mind loosen and spin, filling him with exhilarating recklessness; it made him feel both drugged and excited at once. Almost roughly he drew Cella to him.

"Our future." And this time his touch unleashed in her a feeling even more heady than when they had first embraced. She felt her body surge with a desire so intense she trembled. A sudden, intoxicating impatience possessed her. If only they could be alone.

"I love you, Cella," Anton said into her ear.

"I love you, Anton," Cella whispered against his lips.

"We will marry. The American way."

"By an American judge," Cella said.

"Marcus can be my best man," Anton said.

"Father can give the bride away, and Marina will be the matron of honor," Cella said

"And no other guests," Anton said.

"As soon as this Lawrence Lord fiasco is settled."

"As soon. You warn Sebastian. I'll try to hold Lawrence off until we come up with a plan." Anton wound up dryly, "What it comes down to is how much for how much."

"That's what it always comes down to." She raised her lips to his. "Meanwhile, could you please kiss me again?"

They were interrupted by a knock on the door. Juliana called out without opening the door, "Cella, your father wants to talk to you. Mrs. Schiller has been telephoning him."

"I'll be right there," Cella said impatiently. She kissed Anton briefly, lightly, on the lips, then stood back to look at him. Her eyes met his, and the clamor of their world was stilled. No Marcus. No Lawrence Lord. No Darlene. No Astarte. No Aphrodite. No heritage. No House of Uni. Only their pure delight in each other.

"I'll make dinner tonight, at your place," she said. "And I'll show you what a homey American wife I can be."

Anton slapped Cella on the behind. "Fine. But I want Cella Taggard. From Tages. Not the newest American model." Anton then turned, opened the door and started through the shop while Cella watched with a sigh as his broad back disappeared.

She blinked her eyes to clear her head and gathered herself for the coming storm. The two of them, Marcus and Sebastian, had played with fire, and The House of Uni could well go up in flames. Was that the judgment of the gods? Of Aphrodite? Suddenly she felt free. She didn't care. The future was before her, open and empty but for Anton. She felt an urgent desire that Jason Lord authenticate Sebastian's Aphrodite. It would be her gift to her father before she told him about Lawrence. Then he might forgive Marcus. He might even forgive himself for what they'd done to each other. And to The House of Uni.

Chapter Twenty-six

Cella paid no attention to the wind and rain beating on the roof and walls of the house, nor to the chop of the waves the wind was whipping up in Long Island Sound. She hardly noticed the passage of the hours. In her mind time didn't exist. She was not in Sands Point but in the world of five thousand years ago.

Seated at her bench in the subbasement, she examined each pomegranate with a magnifying glass. The small golden spheres were so regular in form that it was incredible to imagine how they could have been made by hand by the ancient beading tool. But they had been. Nowhere on any of them was there evidence of mechanical aid. And as in the original, every other pomegranate was delicately engraved with the head of the goddess Aphrodite. Sebastian must have used the bronze engraving tool. Or the agate one.

She studied the infinitesimally thin gold leaves surrounding each golden fruit. The gold was almost transparent. Sebastian had hammered the leaves finer than a fingernail. Clearly, this time he had not hurried. He had done that once in the past with a bracelet and spoiled it. As for the pearls, they were luminous and lovely and of the right age. Finally, Cella ran her fingers lightly over the four fine strands of gold loop-in-loop wire chains from which the pomegranates and pearls were suspended. They had been twisted and cross-linked with great skill to make a highly flexible, exquisitely plaited necklace.

Cella sat back and gazed at the Astarte, almost with pleasure. The necklace was perfect. Jason Lord would find nothing amiss. She was glad she had made their appointment for tomorrow morning. Monday. Better to get it over with at the week's start. She would deliver the necklace to him at ten. And then there would be nothing more to do but wait.

Cella rose from the bench, stretched and looked hard at the necklace glowing on the velvet cloth. A curious smile played across her lips. She could impair the piece ever so slightly. She knew exactly what to do and how to do it, so that Jason Lord's suspicions would be aroused. She could—but she mustn't. That wasn't her right. Whatever happened must happen of itself. She put away her tools and magnifying glass. The Astarte went back into the safe to stay until tomorrow, when she would retrieve it before driving back to the city. That done, she left the subbasement for her room on the second floor of the house.

Upstairs in her study, she picked up the telephone receiver and dialed Anton. He answered on the first ring.

"All right, now, tell me!" Anton exclaimed. "Why the hell did you get out of bed and disappear at dawn this morning? Running away while I was fast asleep?"

"I wasn't running away. I had something to do. I told you when I called at eight that I was fine."

"Yes. But where are you? You hung up without saying."

"In Sands Point."

"Sands . . . ? What the devil are you doing out there? In this weather? Is Sebastian with you?"

"Sebastian is probably in bed with Marina. Snoring, I presume."

"You're out there alone? I could have gone with you, if it's so important. Why the devil . . . ?"

"I wanted to be alone, or I would have asked you."

"Cella, exactly what is this about?"

"I owed Sebastian something. Before I give him the cheery news about Lawrence Lord and—"

"Owed him what?" Anton interrupted. "What are you doing? Baking him a cake? Mowing the lawn?"

"I got religion."

"What religion? On this rainy Sunday we could have had more kisses, more caresses, more of everything, plus champagne with our late brunch in bed. To celebrate our forthcoming nuptials. And did we? No. Instead I read *The New York Times* from cover to cover. While you were doing—what the hell were you doing?" Anton was exasperated. "And now you telephone again! Cella, satellite communication has no sex appeal. I want you back here in bed."

"I'll see you tomorrow night and tell you all about everything."

"You're staying over in Sands Point." Anton paused. "I'll drive out."

"No! Don't."

"Cella, didn't we agree? No more Gorgeouses in your life."

"There's no Gorgeous here."

"Then why shouldn't I drive out?"

"I said I'll tell you all about it after I do what has to be done tomorrow."

"For Sebastian?"

"For Sebastian," Cella said softly. "And for me too. Now I want to be alone. And think. Please."

"I can see it now. On our golden anniversary you'll tell me about your secret life."

"I'll tell you tomorrow night."

"We won't have time to talk."

"Between times." She laughed.

That evening Cella lay on her bed thinking of the Astarte. Technically, the Astarte/Aphrodite was perfection. And alone in a velvet box it was impressive enough. But alongside the real Aphrodite, it became a mere trinket, almost costume jewelry. She sighed. She was borrowing trouble when she worried about someone making comparisons. Neither Jason nor the world would ever see the two necklaces together.

But that didn't change the difficult new ideas she'd been living with. She let herself think about her work—Sebastian's work—for The House of Uni. All of it, even the very best of it, was a lie, an evasion, an untruth. They stole from the past, not to restore the beauty of the ancient world, but to dupe the rich and gullible. They were forgers, just as Marcus had said. Forgers—that was the only word for it. They deceived others so effectively that it was relatively easy to deceive themselves. Marcus had been right. And since he had grown up in such an atmosphere, it was no wonder he behaved as he did. Perhaps Lawrence Lord was their punishment.

Only Spina was an exception.

Spina had had more than technical skill. Technically, Cella's work and Sebastian's were the equal of Spina's. But Spina's work had contained a soul. Spina had actually been able to step back into the world of their ancestors, at least in her spirit, in her heart. She, Cella, could only dream of it, not live it. And that one difference between them made all the difference. Spina's work had been true—theirs was a lie. And

Sebastian's Aphrodite was the blackest lie ever offered by The House of Uni.

Cella closed her eyes, and then opened them again. The room around her was exquisite, elegant. But she saw it with new eyes; it had been bought with money from frauds. It belonged to another woman. She was free of it, free of the woman who had lived in it. She felt a queer, light-headed detachment. How ironic that Lawrence Lord should force her to accept what she had never accepted. The knowledge of what she was. A forger.

On Monday morning, she drove back to New York. Sebastian's Aphrodite in its blue velvet box was locked in a special steel fireproof case that had been built into the trunk of the Jaguar XJS. When she arrived in the shop she telephoned Jason Lord. Jason must have alerted Emory, for she was on the line only seconds before Jason picked up his extension.

"Good morning, Cella," he said in a too-hearty voice.

"Good morning, Jason," Cella said quietly.

"Good to hear from you," he said.

"Did Emory give you my message? I called Friday to say that I'd have the Aphrodite. And I'll bring it down about ten."

Jason sounded slightly chagrined. "I got the message. But why not come late this afternoon? We can go to dinner afterward. Do you like Cajun cooking? There's a new restaurant that opened in the Village that's rumored to have the best Cajun cooking north of New Orleans. Is five o'clock all right?" His assumption that they would have dinner was so complete that Cella had no chance to object. "I'll reserve a table for seven o'clock. That'll give me time to have a look at the necklace and give you my preliminary reaction. Although I'm certain it's quite genuine."

"You are? Why?" Cella asked.

"I have my sources," Jason said. "But I can say that too many knowledgeable people know about and want that necklace. These people are not naive art collectors. Or foolish curators. Rather, they are cynics who have had considerable experience dealing with thieves and their fraudulent 'finds.' They are not easily deceived. Given their real interest, the necklace should be authentic. Still, as you said, it does no harm to put it through its paces."

"I'll see you at five," Cella said and added gently, "By

the way, after I tell you my news you may decide to skip dinner.''

"That's impossible."

"If you say so."

"What is your news?"

"I'll tell you when I see you."

"Why so mysterious?" Jason asked. He tried to make light of his sudden apprehension. "After all, I'm almost a member of the family.''

"Then you'll be very happy for me," Cella said. "See you at five." She hung up before Jason could answer.

There was something about sitting in a taxi carrying ten million dollars' worth of necklace in a Saks Fifth Avenue shopping bag that amused Cella. By the time the cab drew up in front of Jason's building, it was dark and had begun to drizzle.

Cella scampered out of the cab and up the few steps leading to Jason's front door. She realized he must have been watching at the window, because the buzzer admitting her sounded before she could ring his bell.

Jason appeared at the top of the stairs. "Watch the third step," he called out. "I still haven't fixed it."

Cella took the stairs quickly, two at a time, her long slim legs flashing. When she reached the landing and stood next to Jason, she was breathing lightly. Jason stared at her, his face reflecting blatant admiration.

"You're remarkable," he said. "Half my clients can't make the stairs. They send up their servants or assistants. It's become such a nuisance I'm considering putting in an elevator. But you, you run up like a bloody mountain goat."

He continued to gaze at her, for the moment oblivious of where they were standing. Abruptly he shook himself as though awakening from a hypnotic state. "I'm sorry. My manners seem to have deserted me," he said, opening the door to his office. "Please come in. And let me hang up your coat. Did you bring the Aphrodite?"

Cella slipped off her raincoat and handed him the Saks bag.

Jason's face grew serious. "You carry a fortune in jewelry in a shopping bag? That's a little too lese majesty for my taste."

Cella laughed lightly. "What better disguise? Besides, the steel safe was too heavy."

After hanging her coat in the hall closet, he guided her into his private office. Then he led her into an alcove that had been turned into a small laboratory with miniaturized versions of highly technical equipment. "I want to look at the necklace under the proper lighting," he said.

Cella handed the blue velvet box to Jason and watched with fascination as he lay the necklace on a table. Under the brilliant laboratory lights it glowed with authenticity.

"Magnificent!" Jason said in a hushed voice.

"It is, isn't it?" Cella agreed. Neither her words nor the tone of her voice gave the smallest clue to her real feelings.

Jason motioned Cella to sit in a chair while he rapidly put the necklace through two tests, nodding contentedly after he'd completed each one. Then he looked up, smiled and ran his fingers through his blond hair.

"Gold forgeries can always be spotted by their metallic composition. The gold available to forgers today is invariably less than one hundred years old. Or it's been melted down from other jewelry. I just used a scanning electronic microscope and X-ray fluorescent spectrometry to study the composition of three of the pomegranates and a segment of the gold chains. These tools would reveal traces of solder or other impurities that genuine ancient gold jewelry doesn't have."

"How fascinating," Cella said, feeling her throat constrict.

"This is only preliminary, of course," he said, "but the gold that I've examined in the necklace is pure. Quite as pure as I would expect in a piece of jewelry almost five thousand years old. I'll have a final report for you within one week."

He replaced the necklace in the blue case. "If you don't mind, I'll put this in my safe." As he spoke he walked to the back wall on which his Harvard degree hung. He swung the frame to one side, revealing a wall safe.

"It's not much of a hiding place, but finding it is the easy part. Opening it is a bit of a killer." He smiled at the word *killer* in a way that made Cella shiver.

She noted the dull gray steel, the three dials, and wondered what other, more complicated electronic devices were connected to the safe. After Jason had spun the dials, he closed the safe and slid the framed degree back into place. Then he turned to Cella, took her arm and walked her back into his main office. "Are you hungry?" he asked as he stood before her, grinning. "I am. Working increases my appetite."

Cella sat down in a chair facing his desk. "Hungry enough," she said. She then made an elaborate pretense of studying her fingernails. "But first I want to talk. You've forgotten. I have something to tell you."

"No, I haven't forgotten," Jason said. "I thought you could tell me over dinner."

"No," Cella said gently. "It's wiser if I tell you now." Whatever else Dr. Jason Lord was, he was no Gorgeous. She had to tell him and put an end to whatever might have developed between them before it caused any pain. "Really, it's wiser," she repeated. "I must."

Jason perched on the edge of his desk. He raised his hands in mock surrender. "If you must, you must."

"Anton and I are getting married."

There was a short intake of breath and then Jason said without a blink, "Congratulations. How charming."

Cella grew flustered. "What I mean is . . ."

"Don't try to explain. When in America, one does as the Americans do," Jason said calmly.

Cella shook her head vehemently. "It's nothing like that. Anton and I are getting married because we love each other."

"Of course. How charming. Now let's—"

"You sound as if you don't believe me."

"I do believe you. Cella, you're Etruscan. Anton is Etruscan. Etruscans always get married. So?"

"So it makes a difference. We'll be married by an American judge." She paused, trying to organize her thoughts, to say the right words so that he would understand her feelings.

"Most Americans are married by American judges. Or American priests. Or rabbis. But I don't think there are any religious authorities available these days in Etruscan society. A judge does nicely."

"When we get married, it will be one man, one woman, till death do . . ." What she was trying to say, and somehow not saying, was that even without having discussed it, she was certain that Anton would no longer put up with her Etruscan ways. Any more than she would put up with his.

"One man, one woman, till death do you part. That is the litany."

"It is also the reality."

"Cella, it is certainly not the reality for Etruscans. In fact, it's not even the reality for millions of Americans. So why don't we go to dinner and you can tell me how you happened to choose that con man."

"He is not a con man. And I've loved him since childhood. We grew up together."

"Obviously that explains it. A form of brother-sister relationship. Moderately incestuous." Jason considered the idea. "Well, why not? Times are changing. Please come. I'm starved."

"Jason, I'm really sorry—" Then she broke off distractedly, trying to think of what she could say that would not offend him. "I'd love to have dinner with you but I can't. I've another appointment."

"How romantic. You're seeing Anton. Your groom-to-be." There was only the slightest hint of a sneer in his voice.

"Actually, I didn't think you would want to have dinner after I gave you my news."

"But I always have dinner. And I much prefer dinner with a beautiful woman. Why don't you call Anton and tell him that your previous appointment refuses to be canceled?"

"I can't."

"Can't? Or won't?"

"Both." Cella forced herself to speak with quiet steadiness.

"Ah, the forms. The forms must be observed." A thousand expressions struggled beneath the surface of his features but were erased before Cella could decipher their meaning.

"I have to go," she said, rising from her chair.

Jason slid off his perch on the desk, put his hands on her shoulders and pulled her against him. His suddenness surprised her, but she managed to break away. "Jason! Stop that!"

Cella could see the huge muscles in his arms stretch the fabric of his shirt as he searched for body control. "Only an expression of brotherly love. You now have more than one brother."

"No! Think of us as kissing cousins. Cheek-kissing." Cella started toward the door.

Jason's eyes followed her with candid animal greed. Half laughing, he remarked, "Cella Taggard, you're a very beautiful woman. And I think you're afraid of me. Perhaps I attract you. Is that it? And you are an Etruscan."

There was an implication in his words that made Cella turn and stare.

"Yes, you are an Etruscan." Jason kept his eyes fixed on her. "If not tonight, another night."

A quiver went through Cella at the note of purpose in his look and tone. "What makes you so sure?"

"You do. Blood will tell. Blood always tells." His eyes were mocking, but he continued in a voice that bore no trace of the strain he was feeling. "I promise never to try to seduce you in public." He gave her an official smile. "And I'll do my best to have your final report ready by the end of the week."

That evening Cella managed to adroitly sidestep Anton's questions about what she had been doing at Sands Point on Sunday. She had no desire to tell him yet about Sebastian's Aphrodite. Not when it was tied to her visit to Dr. Jason Lord. The whispering of Jason's voice still sounded in her head; she still could see his lustful eyes challenging her, daring her, laughing at her. When it was over and done, when the necklace had been authenticated, that would be time enough for Anton to know about Sebastian and her visit to Dr. Jason Lord. In the meantime, she wanted nothing to spoil their time together.

They spent that evening sipping champagne and making love. She felt his breath brush her skin, then the touch of his lips, then his hands. When she closed her eyes in surrender, there was no sound, only a caressing that washed her mind clear. It took very little foreplay on his part for him to enter her. That they were going to marry—really marry, in a double-ring ceremony—acted like an aphrodisiac on both of them, and their lovemaking went beyond physical passion. In truth and in lies, there was this bond between them. They were as married then as they would ever be.

Later, when Anton slept, Cella lay there tense and wakeful, and terribly afraid as she thought about Jason. For no reason she could give, she was absolutely certain that he was dangerous. She told herself that she was wrong. She said it over and over. He would soon be in the family. She had to be wrong. But something deep within her, ancient and instinctive, stubbornly warned her she was right.

Technically, Ben Stein never brought work home from the homicide bureau. But Sophie knew that when Ben was on a case, it was impossible for him to leave his brain at the station house. And when he brought his brain home, it went right on working. As it was doing now, dissecting, analyzing, reasoning, while he sat at the kitchen table whittling on the king—the king he called Tunis, after the great Etruscan god—for his chess set. And while Sophie attended noisily to the kitchen, cleaning the table, washing dishes, rattling the knives and forks, Ben heard nothing. He was thinking.

Occasionally Ben caught his wife looking at him accusingly. After twenty-five years of marriage, he knew what that look meant: "Your fingers are so capable when you whittle those pieces, why is it whenever you help with the dishes, you always drop at least one. Sometimes two."

Ben was conveniently clumsy when it came to dishes.

When she had finished cleaning the kitchen, Sophie said, "I'm going to bed now."

"Yes, dear," Ben Stein answered mechanically, listening to Sophie's heelless mules going *slap, slap, slap* as she walked up the stairs.

Now that the kitchen was quiet, he could concentrate fully on the case at hand. In his mind, he'd named the mystery "Pavanne for a Killer Lover." Using the chess pieces he'd carved, he set the white queen—Uni in this set—in her proper place at the far end of the chess board. That was Marina. The other pieces were assigned roles as Marina's lovers. First Lawrence Lord; a bishop. Very respectable, the bishop. As respectable as a Harvard professor. Ben Stein set Lawrence Lord on the seventh file but one row to the right. They had been lovers and husband and wife, but were no longer. Was Lawrence Lord a killer, as Marina thought? Next came Hans Etzel. Ben chose a knight to represent Hans. Hyperactive, leaping all about, yet with the limited mobility of a knight. Hans had been attacked in the dark. He was a victim, not a killer. But he was still alive. So the piece representing Hans was moved to the seventh file one row to the left. Then came Andrew Henderson. Another knight-errant. Ben Stein selected the second knight and placed the figure behind the knight representing Hans Etzel. Carefully he tipped the figure over. Andrew Henderson was dead. Died in an automobile accident in Europe. Very definitely a victim. Marina's next serious lover had been Phillip Mckay. A respected art curator. More the bishop type. Also dead. Ben selected a second bishop and placed the figure on its side behind the Andrew Henderson knight. That left Sebastian Taggard. About to marry Marina Lord. He'd been attacked but not killed. A Tages if I ever saw one, Ben thought as he set another piece he'd been working on directly in front of the Marina piece.

Then, without knowing exactly why, he moved the Sebastian Taggard piece one row back. As a final touch, he placed the black queen next to the white queen and tipped it over. Josie Frankenberg was also dead. Alongside the dead Josie he set a pawn on its side. Roberto was dead.

He then surveyed the board. The story it told was graphic and dismal. All of Marina's serious lovers had either been killed or maimed. And through it all, Marina had remained unharmed. Absentmindedly he set a rook between the Sebastian/Tages and the Marina/Uni. The mysterious rook was Marina's protector. If it weren't for the deaths of Josie and Roberto, which could have been a mistake, it almost looked as though someone was protecting Marina from her lovers. Now why would anyone do that?

Ben picked up the phone and dialed the Sixty-sixth Street precinct. "Sergeant Reilly, please."

"Who wants him?" asked a bored voice on the other end of the line.

"This is Lieutenant Ben Stein."

"Yes, sir." The boredom disappeared from the voice. Within seconds, Sergeant Reilly was on the phone. "What dirty work can I do for you, Ben?"

"What's Max Browsky doing?"

"Walking a beat and hating it."

"Get him into plain clothes. I want a tail on Marina Lord. Especially at night."

"He'll love it. She's got a pretty nifty tail."

"Quit clowning, Sergeant. I'm drawing a blank on this damn case."

"You always draw a blank just before you put the puzzle together."

"Well, the pieces are all in front of me, but they make no sense."

"The inimitable Ben Stein has missed something?"

"The inimitable has. And I'm damned if I know what. I'll talk to you tomorrow." Ben hung up the phone without looking at the cradle; his eyes were locked on the chessboard. "Taggard almost castrated," he said half aloud. "Mckay bludgeoned to death. Henderson run off a cliff. And Etzel . . . ?" He buried his head in his hands. "You schmuck. You incompetent schmuck. What was it with Etzel? What happened to him?" He reached for the phone and dialed Boston information. After some politely impatient back-and-forth, he finally got the number for the records department of Massachusetts General Hospital.

He leaned back and thought for a while. It mightn't tell him a thing. But then again it might. He dialed the number, and after identifying himself, he asked the nurse who answered for all information on the assault of a Professor Hans Etzel. The nurse was agreeable and everything went swimmingly until he told her the attack had occurred about fifteen years ago. Abruptly she became exasperated.

"That information is in storage on microfilm."

"How long will it take you to retrieve it?"

"Forever."

"What's your name, Nurse?"

"O'Hara. Mary Margaret O'Hara."

"Miss O'Hara, are you going to put a nice Jewish boy like me through the trouble of talking to a New York judge who will call a Boston judge? Then I'll have to fly to Boston. And the Boston judge will issue a court order for you to produce the records. Now, would you do that to me?"

"You betcha, Lieutenant Stern."

"Stein."

"Sorry. Stein. Yes, this Irish colleen will put you through all that trouble. And if I could, more. Do you have any idea how long it would take me to search the records? And how dirty that storage room is? Our files predate computers."

"How long will it take?" Ben Stein asked calmly.

"If I'm lucky, a month."

"And if you're not lucky?"

"Two months."

"Suppose an associate of mine, Sergeant Peter Reilly, flew to Boston to help you?"

"Does he know how to load a microfilm machine?"

"You can teach him."

"Thanks, Lieutenant. You've just added a month to the search time."

"Mary Margaret O'Hara, you are being difficult."

"True," came the cheerful reply.

"Nurse," Ben Stein said in his patient way, "there have been four murders and two assaults connected with this case. I need that information."

There was a silence on the other end of the line. At last Mary Margaret asked in a tight voice, "Did you say four murders and two assaults?"

"I said that."

"What's your phone number, Lieutenant?" Ben Stein gave her both his office and his home numbers. "I'll speak to my brother, Captain Kevin O'Hara of the Boston police. He'll call you, and if that business of four murders and two assaults is straight, he'll get you your court order. I wasn't bluffing—you do need one, police or not."

"I know. And thank you."

"Don't thank me yet. I hope the report gives you the clue, or whatever it is you're looking for."

"So do I," Ben said grimly. "Good-bye."

He went back to studying the chessboard. After some minutes he checked the Manhattan phone book for a number and dialed.

"Lenox Hill? Is Dr. Noah Greenberg available? . . . Thank you. I'll hold." He waited, and then a voice said, "Hello?"

"Dr. Greenberg, this is Lieutenant Stein. Do you remember me? I was at the hospital—"

"I remember. I follow your cases. I'm a detective-story fan. And you're the real thing. You were there when Sebastian Taggard was in the hospital." The doctor paused for breath. "I know all about you. This isn't a social call. How can I help?"

"Dr. Greenberg, you mentioned something that morning at the hospital about Dr. Lawrence Lord calling your chess club looking for his son, Jason. Do your remember when that was?"

"I know exactly when it was. Toward the end of April. It was a pleasant warm evening, and I was looking forward to the chess match I had with Jason. I waited until midnight but he never showed up."

"I see. The end of April. Do you remember the exact date?"

"I play chess on Tuesdays and Thursdays. It would be in my appointment book. Wait, let me check. I'm pretty well organized. Can you hang on?"

"I can hang on." Ben Stein waited patiently, carving slowly, while the good doctor leafed through his appointment book. Suddenly his voice was back on the phone, full of pride in his own efficiency. He'd found exactly what he was looking for.

"I found the day I was scheduled to play chess with Jason," he said heartily. "It was April twenty-sixth. How do you like that number? I've written on the page, 'Jason, chess.' Then, 'The bastard never showed up.' "

"April twenty-sixth."

"It should have been Friday the thirteenth. I waited all night. Is it important?"

"How important is important? At any rate, I wouldn't like you to mention my call to anyone."

"I won't," said Dr. Greenberg, enchanted with the mystery.

"Well, thank you and good night."

After hanging up, Ben Stein picked up the bishop representing Lawrence Lord and studied it. "Hmm," he said as he patted his yarmulke. "It's possible, but what's the motive? Does Dr. Lord feel that much passion for Marina Lord? Hmm.'' He was beginning to get the glimmering of an idea.

Ben stood up. He knew the world was crazy, but if he were right, this was more lunatic than usual. As he reached to turn out the light and go up to bed, the phone rang.

''Lieutenant Stein here,'' he said.

A light tenor voice sounded in his ear. ''This is Captain O'Hara. What can Boston do for one of New York's finest?''

Chapter Twenty-seven

The cablegram arrived at The House of Uni about noon. It was from Istanbul and was addressed to Sebastian. But Sebastian was with Felix again, having another semifinal fitting.

Cella sat quietly at her desk, doodling on the cablegram envelope. She didn't have to read it to know what it said. She'd taken the telephone call earlier that morning that told her its contents. Lexi would be arriving a week earlier than planned. Her father was insisting. She must pick up the Aphrodite. The Greeks were getting on his nerves.

Without shutting her eyes, Cella could visualize the look of excitement, of triumph, on Sebastian's face when he read the cable. He would notify Darlene immediately. She would have to top Lexi's bid or lose the Aphrodite. Then Lexi would call her father and top Darlene's offer. And Darlene would again top Lexi. And Lexi, Darlene. Sebastian would try to kick the price sky-high.

Her hands began to shake so badly she clasped them together in her lap and sat absolutely still. For a moment the room blurred before her eyes. Then, abruptly, she felt a wave of pure relief. At last it would be over. She had only one more thing to do, one more promise to herself to keep, before she faced Sebastian with the grim fact of Lawrence Lord and, even worse, with her own decision. She stared fixedly at the telephone. She composed herself, wetting her lips for a smile. When she picked up the receiver, she meant to sound bright and friendly.

Jason's voice was neutral as he dictated into the tape recorder. ". . . tells us whether the piece came from Paros, Naxos or the Pentelikon—all in Greece—or from Italy or Turkey. Early works from Asia Minor are forgeries if they display high zinc concentrations when subjected to analysis by X-ray fluorescence . . ."

Jason paused reflectively, then continued. "Consequently, after an analysis of materials from which the necklace was made, a study of how it was made and an evaluation of its symptoms of aging, the conclusion is that the Aphrodite necklace is authentic . . ." Jason glanced at the necklace glowing in the blue velvet box resting on his desk.

The intercom rang. Jason Lord switched off the tape recorder as he picked up the phone.

"Cella Taggard is on the line, sir," Emory said.

"I'll talk to her," Jason replied and pushed down the second lit button.

"Cella—this is telepathy. I was just thinking of you."

She was glad he couldn't see her face, because her skin felt cold as ice. But her tone was lighthearted. "We've perfect timing. I was thinking of you and . . ." The moment she said the words she knew she'd struck the wrong note.

"Our timing is not so perfect when it comes to dinners."

"Jason, we have at least ten thousand family dinners ahead of us."

"All boring. Perhaps you've rethought your position and called to tell me so."

"Actually, I called about the necklace. Are the tests completed, Jason? You said you would have them in a week."

"I do. As promised."

"And?" she asked.

"In my opinion, the Aphrodite is authentic. I was dictating my report when you called."

Cella felt a relief that lasted only a few seconds. She had the sense of Jason as large, as dangerous; more dangerous to her than anyone else she'd ever known. In the back of her mind she began to think of how to handle him in the future. "That's what we both expected," she said with forced calm.

"Yet you are relieved."

"Relieved is too strong a word. I am pleased to have you second my evaluation."

For an instant Jason said nothing. Then in a clipped, businesslike tone, he went on. "Emory has three reports to type. The one on the Aphrodite will be ready by four or so. You can pick up the necklace and my signed report at about four-thirty."

"Fine," Cella said, wishing to say good-bye quickly without being rude.

"And don't concern yourself about dinner engagements. My evening is already spoken for," Jason remarked cheerily.

"Perhaps another time, stepsister, dear. When we're both in the mood."

Cella was close to losing her temper, but she was not that foolish. Instead she said lightly, "In this world anything is possible."

"Anything. Meanwhile, good luck with the Aphrodite. May the highest bidder win," Jason said and hung up.

Cella stared at the phone and hung up slowly. She was feeling edgy and disconcerted. Half the job was done. Now, should she wait for Sebastian to return from the tailor to talk to him, or should she do it after she'd actually picked up the Aphrodite? She decided to do it after she retrieved the necklace. She'd hand Sebastian a triumph to chew on before she stunned him with future plans. Silently she thanked the gods that she would not have to see Jason when she picked up the necklace.

Jason had left the office early and gone to his bedroom suite to shower and change for dinner. He had taken great pains with his choice of clothes. He wore his custom-made Brooks Brothers three-piece charcoal-gray flannel suit, usually reserved for professional dinners or when making speeches. His tie was the red-and-gray stripe Marina had given him the previous Christmas.

Now he stood at the doorway to Marina's apartment, trying to tame his excitement. It was no use. His stomach was turning over and his throat was stopping up.

He rang the bell, and his mind seemed to loosen from its moorings and go spinning through space. For an instant he had the sensation that he was falling from some great height, a free fall that was as terrifying as it was exhilarating. They were going to have dinner together. He would give her his gift before they left the apartment. He hoped she would like it, and he felt his hand perspire as he clutched the package. He rang the bell again; while he was still pressing it, Marina opened the door. She seemed to be laughing to herself.

"Jason, my dear. How wonderful to see you," she said as she finished wrapping her shimmering dressing gown around herself. Obviously she wore nothing under the robe. One could see the shape of her breasts lifting up, alert, her legs outlined sturdy and strong through the flimsy material. "I wasn't expecting you so soon."

"I managed to slip away a little earlier."

"I'm delighted. It gives us more time alone. How wonderful you look."

"So do you," he said. "Simply splendid."

"Come in," she said, gesturing and leading him into the softly lit living room.

He followed her, trying to look around with interest, shooting only furtive glances at the sway of her hips.

"What would you like to drink?" she asked.

"Perrier water."

"Oh, Jason! Perrier water has become so cliché."

"What would you like me to drink, Marina?" he asked, his heart thudding heavily in his chest.

"How would you like a glass of champagne? After all, this is a celebration."

"Champagne would be fine."

"I have the champagne on ice. I thought you might like the idea." She left him for a moment before returning with a bottle of Dom Perignon chilled in a bucket of ice, and two fine crystal glasses.

"Remember when you bought me these for my birthday?" She laughed, glancing at the glasses.

"Of course," he said, clearing his throat. "Pure rock crystal."

"Iridescent and exquisite. Thank you, darling." She leaned across the bucket stand and kissed him lightly on the cheek, and his pulse stopped for a minute. "You pop the champagne. You're strong as an ox."

They made meaningless chatter while Jason worked at the wiring around the cork.

"Have you set the date?" he mumbled, intensely aware of her physical presence.

"Not yet."

"Have you picked the judge? Or won't it be a judge?"

"Oh, no! Not a judge. Nor a justice of the peace. A real church wedding. Our church. Sebastian doesn't care. Etruscans have no religious convictions," Marina observed with animation.

"So I understand," Jason said, having far more trouble with the champagne cork then either his strength or the cork warranted.

"Anyway, I think we'll do it at Saint Thomas."

Suddenly the cork flew loose with a loud pop. Jason quickly poured the champagne into a glass to keep it from dripping on the carpet.

"Hooray!" Marina said, applauding. "Now show me what you have in that package."

"Yes, of course." Jason grew flustered. "It's a . . . well, a sort of wedding gift. I mean, something I thought you might like." He had to stop because he was afraid his hand might shake and he would spill the champagne. "I'll show it to you as soon as I finish pouring the champagne." And making a strenuous effort to control his nerves, he filled the two glasses with champagne.

"A toast to you," he said.

"To Sebastian and Marina."

"Yes," said Jason and swallowed the champagne in one gulp. "I'll show you the present now. I hope you like it." He put his glass down on the coffee table.

"I know I will," she said encouragingly.

He took the red velvet box out of the red tissue wrap. "Here it is," he said.

Marina examined the box with a puzzled look. "Red velvet. Isn't that the color Cella uses for Cella Classics?"

"It is a Cella Classics," Jason said with some satisfaction. "A gift designed by your stepdaughter-to-be."

"Oh—it must be lovely. She's extremely gifted."

"Extremely," Jason said, watching her agile fingers open the box.

"A necklace!" Marina said with delight. "Oh, my— how beautiful. Rock crystal. Lapis lazuli. Pearls. Coral— and the profile of a beautiful woman. Isn't she lovely! Who is she, Jason? Who is the woman in the necklace? Some great ancient queen or princess?" Marina was full of wonder.

"Undoubtedly. Cella has a taste for royalty. But the woman is no more beautiful than you," Jason said, pleased at her pleasure. "The truth is she reminded me of you. That's why I chose it."

"Jason, it is stunning. Absolutely stunning. And what a wonderful coincidence. Now I have two exquisite necklaces. From the two men I love best in the world."

"I don't understand."

"Well, of course, I have more than two necklaces. But only these two matter. The two men I love best both thought to give me a necklace as a wedding present." Marina smiled gaily. "I must have an attractive neck."

"As fine as Nefertiti's."

"Now, let's not overdo it. But I am pleased. Both necklaces are so beautiful. Let me show you the one Sebastian gave me.''

''Yes, do,'' Jason said, feeling both tense and curious.

''I'll only be a minute,'' she said, exiting quickly from the living room.

Waiting for her to return, Jason had no idea what they had talked about, only that he had felt a continuous heat at her closeness and a kind of sexualized awkwardness about his body that he hadn't felt since he was a teenager.

''Here it is,'' Marina called as she entered the room. ''What do you think? It's not a Cella's Classics, but it has its own splendor. Isn't it superbly pagan?''

Jason stopped breathing. For an instant he couldn't accept anything that was going on as real. His hands felt gritty and sweaty. His heart seemed to change its position in his chest, and his mind was blank. He couldn't speak.

He wasn't sure how long he remained like that, until finally he found his voice. It couldn't have been that long, because Marina was busily poring them both more champagne. So as casually as possible he asked, ''Isn't that the Aphrodite necklace?''

''No, this one Sebastian calls the Astarte. Another name for the goddess of love. It's also from the tomb of Aphrodite. Only the Taggards know that there were two,'' Marina murmured dreamily.

''I see,'' Jason said, though he didn't see at all.

Jason had the kind of imagery that children have and adults usually lose. He had total recall about anything connected to his work. He could visualize a painting, an artifact, a piece of jewelry, a vase, with an exactness that would have astounded Ben Stein. And looking at the Astarte, he visualized the Aphrodite and knew it was an exact twin to the necklace in his safe in the office. Down to the smallest gold leaf and chain link.

But there was no second necklace from the tomb of Aphrodite. He knew it. The Taggards knew it. Abdul Hamid knew it. One of those necklaces was a perfect forgery. Perfect. And he knew with the certainty of revelation, and a sickening feeling of self-disgust, that the necklace he had tested, the one he had certified as genuine—that one was the fraud. Cella Taggard knew it too. There was no comparison between the one he had vetted and the magnificent strands glowing around Marina's throat.

''Sebastian had this one in the Taggard vault for several decades,'' Marina was saying. ''It was so beautiful he never wanted to sell it. But after we met, and when he bought the Aphrodite at Northbie's . . . Well.'' She blushed ever so slightly. ''He thought it would make the perfect gift of love. Love from the goddess of love. Do you like it?''

''Yes,'' was the best Jason could mumble.

''Of course, your necklace is beautiful too. I'll wear them both.'' She fumbled, laughing uneasily, knowing something was wrong but not what. ''I mean, not at the same time.''

The house phone rang.

''Oh, dear! Sebastian's early too.''

''Sebastian?''

''Didn't I mention it? He's joining us for dinner.''

Jason felt suddenly afraid of what he might do. ''Good. You see, Mother—I mean Marina—I have to beg off dinner. I meant to tell you when I arrived. But the champagne—and the necklace—made me forgetful.''

''You're not coming with us to dinner? I thought it would be a marvelous way for you two to get to know each other.''

''We'll get to know each other,'' Jason said harshly. And then, with an effort at geniality, he echoed Cella. ''We have thousands of family dinners ahead.''

''I suppose,'' Marina said, heading for the house phone.

''If we meet in the elevator, I'll give him my apologies,'' Jason muttered.

Emory had Jason's report on the Aphrodite ready for Cella at five. She only had to wait a half hour. He placed the report in a blue manila envelope, the blue velvet box containing the Aphrodite necklace atop it.

Cella reached first for the jewelry box, then the report, and slipped them both into her attaché case.

''There is no bill for our services.'' Emory sounded puzzled.

''I know,'' Cella answered as she moved toward the door and nearly collided head-on with Jason.

For an instant the silence between them was almost explosive.

Jason spoke first. ''Cella! How come you're still here?''

''I was a little late in typing the report,'' Emory explained.

''At least I have the chance to thank you for your work,'' Cella said, smiling politely. ''I do appreciate it.''

''And I can thank you. For a chance to examine a truly splendid piece of jewelry. An almost magical necklace. It's rumored to have belonged to Aphrodite herself. The goddess of love. Theoretically, it brings with it all kinds of powers.''

"That is the rumor," Cella said. "The necklace of the goddess herself. Again, thank you, and I'll see you at the wedding," she said as she stepped into the hallway, closing the door on her words.

Jason stared for an instant at the closed door. Then glanced impatiently at Emory. "Go home. I'll see you tomorrow."

Jason sounded quite out of temper, something so rare for him that Emory grew uneasy. Thinking it wisest to leave without comment, Emory walked to the closet, took out his jacket and left with a quiet "Good night, sir."

There were images flickering in Jason's head and whisperings in his ears that he could not shut off. There was no arguing with the need they aroused. Slowly he entered his office, and closed and locked the door after him.

As he sat down in the chair behind his desk and stared around the room, he saw nothing. He had gone blind. And it was in these blackest of black moments that he would sit like this, alone in his office, clinging to some unstated hope in the midst of the bleakness of his life. Without thinking of what he was doing, he rose from his chair and padded like an animal to the library.

When he reached the exact spot, he glanced up at the top bookshelf. There he saw the book box and he felt his flesh harden and leap. In a daze he climbed the library ladder and reached for it. Carefully he pulled it out and carried it down the steps to place on the table.

Jason looked at the book box a long time before moving a muscle. He could feel its emanations: they were as discernible as a perfume in the air. Then slowly his hand reached out and opened the box as though moving without the knowledge of his mind. His fingers touched Marina's chemise. And this time he played with the roll of nylon fishing line he'd bought so many years ago, coiling a piece of it tightly around his finger. His huge body shuddered as though struck by a bolt of electricity.

Marina and Sebastian. He could see them together. Making love. His penis grew rigid at the vision, as it had the other time. And his body fell forward, facedown in the box. He kissed the chemise. The aroma of jasmine was overpowering, as it had been that other night so long ago. His senses grew dazed. Again visions of the past were thrust into his brain. So many men had made love to his mother. "Why, Marina? Why them? Especially why him? Why not me?" he said. His voice was muffled. But the vision was too powerful to be stifled. He saw it as clearly as if it were taking place in front of him this very moment. . . .

Jason knelt at the crack of the door. As at other times they'd been in too much of a hurry to close the door carefully, and watched the kneeling, naked woman lift her head and look up at the man with passion-drugged eyes. "Lie down, Hans," she murmured. "I want to make love to you."

The man placed his hands on her head and forced her mouth against his sex. "Please," he said.

"No. Not this time," the woman said with mild irritation. She brushed his penis against the nipples of her breasts. Now the man's penis was between the woman's breasts, and she pressed her breasts together, enveloping it.

"Be careful," the man warned. "I can't take too much more of that."

Immediately the woman stopped. She rose and led the man to the bed. Eagerly, he fell backward, and the woman knelt over him. She guided his penis into her, arching herself toward the ceiling. "Yes, Hans. Yes!" she panted.

Jason's teeth clamped on his lower lip. The boiling in his loins grew. His hand moved to the rhythm of the woman.

"Yes, I say. Yes!" the woman moaned as her orgasm approached.

"Darling!" the man cried.

"Hans!" the woman shrieked.

Jason's hand moved faster and he pushed against the door.

"Now!" the woman screamed.

Hans lifted himself off the bed. Passion contorted his face. As he came, he made strange, unintelligible sounds that were barely audible beneath the woman's cries.

"Marina! My love!" Hans said as he drew her to him, kissing her wildly.

Horrified at what his mother had become, and frightened at how close he'd come to bursting into the room and thrusting himself between them, Jason stuffed his hard sex into his pants and tugged at the zipper. He remained silent, watching his mother and her lover hold each other. His hand reached into his pocket and fingered the coil of nylon fishing line. Gradually his fear and shame turned to anger. Hans, his friend, his teacher, had done this thing to his mother. His beautiful mother.

For months Jason had lived in the same house as his mother, eaten at the same table as his mother, gone on long walks

with his mother, kissed his mother good night on the evenings when she was home; and all the while, he had known
she and Hans were making love. Hans, whom he had un-
thinkingly brought home to dinner one night months ago.
Hans, who he had thought was his friend, his favorite teacher.
This man had turned his mother into a wanton whore. A
month ago he'd made a plan to rid his mother of Hans. Then
he'd discarded it. But the idea refused to die. It grew and
grew in his mind until it consumed him. He had no choice. If
he did not do it, his mother's lechery would drive him mad.

On this night, Jason slipped out of the house and waited.
Soon Hans would leave. He'd walk home along darkened
streets. There was one long stretch that included a small
park. One of the streetlights was out. He'd meet Hans there.
He wouldn't kill the man, although he deserved to die. But
when Jason did what he had to do, Hans would never touch
his beautiful mother again. He'd never touch any woman
again.

Jason crouched behind a thick shrub. From where he was
he had a clear view of the house. As the minutes passed,
Jason's agony grew. Hans and his mother were doing it again.
Images of their naked bodies locked together flickered before
his eyes like a film being run too fast. Jason rocked back and
forth in agony. It took all his strength for him not to run
from . . .

At last the front door opened, and Hans appeared. He
strolled toward where Jason was waiting. As he passed under
a dim streetlight, Jason could see the smug satisfaction on his
face. Now he was abreast of Jason. Silently, Jason slipped
from behind the shrub, his tennis shoes making no sound.
Unconcerned, Hans walked slowly along the narrow sidewalk. Jason flitted from tree to tree, always growing closer
to his target. Now he was only ten feet behind Hans. Now
five. Now . . . With a single, catlike bound, Jason had the
man in his grasp.

Hans was a tall man, but a man with thin bones and little
physical strength. One of Jason's huge hands circled his neck
and the other covered his mouth. Helpless, Hans was dragged
into the trees. Jason loosened his grip on Hans' throat just
long enough to crash the side of his fist against the man's
head. Hans fell facedown on the ground. Jason was on him,
pounding at his head. He rolled Hans over and, his fists moving like pistons, he battered Hans' face. The cartilage in Hans'
nose splintered, and blood spurted from his nostrils. A final

blow tore Hans' jaw from its socket. Only then did Jason stop.

He remained crouched over the unconscious man, his fists—only inches from Hans' broken face—trembling violently with the effort it took for him not to kill the man. ''I must not kill you,'' Jason whispered into the ear of the unhearing man. ''It would be wrong to kill you. This is right.'' As he spoke, he pulled Hans' pants down around his knees. The man wore no underwear. Jason looked at the man's sex. It was flaccid and still sticky from his mother. Tears streamed down Jason's cheeks as again the vision of his naked mother and this man rose before his eyes. He was horrified to feel his own penis growing hard again. Then he smiled a strange smile. Yes. That was also right.

He reached into his pocket and pulled out a coil of nylon fishing line. His hands moved swiftly, forming a slipknot. He found the place he'd read about in the medical journal—the exact spot where the testicles hung from the body—and fastened the line around the skin. With a jerk, he tightened the nylon until the thin line almost severed the skin. And then he pulled the noose still tighter.

Jason stood over the fallen man. When he opened his fly, his sex sprang free. His hand went to his penis and he closed his eyes. It was his mother's hand holding him. In seconds his orgasm came, and the thick white fluid spurted over her breasts. Over Hans' face . . .

Gasping for air, Jason closed the book box and stared at it. He meant to put it away, but for a moment he couldn't move. His mind flickered with images of Marina in various states of undress. He saw her with a heightened clarity. Her gestures, her face, her body movements, her nuances of speech, were vivid and clear to him. But it all had been hopeless. When he finally got up the courage to make love to her, he'd failed. She'd eluded him—thanks to Josie Frankenberg. But it wasn't over yet. He shook his head, trying to rid himself of his desire. He tried to stand up. But he still couldn't move. He had a feeling he wanted to do something, but he wasn't sure what. And then it happened. He saw a woman coming toward him, coming slowly as if in a dream. He saw in a silence that was deafening that her eyes were violet, not gray like Marina's; her hair was black too, not brown. It was Cella Taggard. Marina receded and Cella grew clearer. He had an image of a naked Cella with rolling grasslands in the background. The instant he saw it he knew how much he longed to possess her. He wanted to throw her down to the soft, warm, wet earth and hold her there.

He drew in his breath sharply as the picture became more vivid. The sensation he felt was like the one he had when holding an egg in his hand. Not that Celia was fragile or even seemed fragile. It wasn't that. It was her completeness, her egglike self-sufficiency that made him want to take her and crush her. She was so like Marina. A whore. A liar. A cheat. All the secret things he'd wanted to do to his mother—but never had—he could do to Cella. And he would too. He had loved Cella as he loved Marina. Helpless, he raged against the dying of that love.

PART NINE

THE WRATH OF THE GODDESS

═ Chapter Twenty-eight ═

Cella lounged cross-legged in brown stretch pants and a brown tunic on her favorite hassock in the library, absorbed in a book about Africa. It was the description of the landscape as much as the story that drew her. Picturing it as she read, she thought how familiar it seemed. It was a landscape such as she had seen in her dreams. There had been no cities then—until her ancestors and people like them had started to build. They had made them out of earth and rock and flesh and bone and the sweat of thousands of years. They had made them out of hope and need.

"Cella! What are you doing home?" Sebastian asked as he entered the library.

"What are *you* doing here? I thought you and Marina were having dinner tonight."

"We did. Now I'm home."

"That's apparent. How come?"

"I have something to discuss with you," he said, frowning.

"I have something to discuss with you," Cella said, looking equally serious as she closed the book.

"Is that why you left in such a rush at four o'clock?"

Cella sat quietly, her long, elegant fingers playing with a strand of her hair. As they moved, her unpainted nails glinted in the light, and her fingers seemed to be saying something. Sebastian waited.

"I was picking up something. A kind of gift for you."

"A gift for me? It's not my birthday."

"A gift—let's say for future birthdays." Her smile faltered slightly.

"Stop talking in riddles," Sebastian said as he poured himself a snifter of brandy. "We have serious business to discuss."

"Who goes first?"

"Ladies always go first." Sebastian settled himself in his chair.

Cella's mouth felt parched. At first she couldn't think of what to say. "I'm not sure how to begin."

"At the beginning," Sebastian said with impatience. "Or in the middle. Or at the end. Just begin."

Cella opened her mouth and then closed it. Then started to talk. "All right, I'll start with the good news first. It concerns your version of the Aphrodite. I took the necklace to Jason Lord to have it vetted."

"No!" Sebastian stared at her as though estimating her sanity. "How could you do such a thing!"

"Why not? Suppose you had missed something when you duplicated the original? Or I'd missed something when I checked it? I didn't want you to be at risk." Cella's smile was animated by a luminous intensity.

"But suppose he doesn't authenticate it?"

"If that happened you could return it to Northbie's. I wanted to protect you from your silly mistake—giving the true Aphrodite to Marina."

"You should have told me." Sebastian's expression of utter confusion had frozen on his face.

"I intended to tell you, once I knew Jason's opinion. Now that I know, I'm telling you." Cella sat up, straight as a ramrod, resolute. "Dr. Jason Lord, the eminent archiometrist, authenticated your version of the Aphrodite. I put the documentation on the desk in your study. You should be pleased. Our Dr. Lord has provided a written document that your Aphrodite is genuine." Cella paused and gazed at her father. "Why aren't you clicking your heels? Dancing a jig? That gives you a backup if there should ever be flak from Abdul Hamid, Darlene or the Greek government."

"But you did it without telling me," Sebastian repeated dully.

"Will you please tell me what was wrong with what I did?"

"Marina showed the Aphrodite to Jason this evening. Explaining it was my wedding gift to her."

Cella heard herself sigh. "Oh, my God!"

"That's why I came home early. I wanted to discuss with you what we do next."

Cella said soberly, "I thought you told me she would only wear the necklace in private."

"She considers Jason private. He is her son. He was supposed to have dinner with us and he brought with him his own wedding gift. Another necklace. A Cella Classics, by the way.''

"I helped him choose it," Cella said weakly. Her instinct, that rare and delicate instrument, had gone wrong. After years of service, it had failed her. "Did Marina call the necklace the Aphrodite?"

"No—thank heaven for that. I told her it was the Astarte. That it had been in our vaults for years. That it too was from the tomb of Aphrodite. Nonsense like that.''

"I see. But Jason didn't go to dinner with you?" Cella was remembering their meeting in his office.

"No. He had something to do.''

Cella didn't like it. She didn't like any part of it.

"So now Jason has seen both necklaces. And knowing Jason Lord, I'm sure he's noted that they're identical twins.''

"Yes.'' Sebastian's face was flushed.

It was in this one stricken moment of open fear that Cella realized her instincts hadn't failed after all. By some special grace, the wheels of the gods continued to spin smoothly along. Whatever was supposed to happen was happening. But whatever it was, Jason Lord would not be the instrument of disaster. Dr. Jason Lord had personally authenticated Sebastian's duplicate. His own reputation would be on the line if he made so much as a squeak.

She kept her thoughts to herself, but she shared her conclusion with Sebastian: Jason Lord had as much at stake in the look-alike necklace as they did. Listening to her, Sebastian relaxed and leaned back in his chair, nodding sagely, more than willing to accept her analysis. It was indeed lucky she had had Lord authenticate his masterpiece.

"Now that I've heard your good news.'' Sebastian said, sipping his brandy with relief, "tell me your bad news. It might be an improvement.''

Again Cella didn't know how to begin. "This is going to be hard to explain.''

"I'm a very good listener.''

"You'll have to be," she answered. Then, slowly, she told him about Marcus and his treachery. How Marcus had gone temporarily crazy in his panic for money, which had led him eventually to Anton. And how this, unfortunately, had put him in contact with Lawrence Lord.

When she had finished, Sebastian asked quietly, "Marcus actually told Lawrence everything?"

"Everything. Even about the subbasement in Sands Point.''

Sebastian was stunned. His face became like chalk. "Didn't he know I intended to bail him out?"

"He did not. Neither did I, until you told me you would. You never gave him a glimmer of hope."

Suddenly Sebastian exploded. "That ungrateful, good-for-nothing—"

"Father, please," Cella said.

"Don't 'Father, please' me!" Sebastian shouted. "He's a wastrel and a scoundrel and an ingrate!"

That was the beginning of his attack on Marcus, which, as it went on, left no doubt in Cella's mind as to the extent of his rage at his son. Marcus was entirely to blame, while he, as a father, had acted in a thoroughly responsible fashion. As far as Sebastian was concerned, it was all Marcus' fault. Jail would have been a well-deserved punishment. He should never even have considered giving Marcus the money. He would speak to his attorneys tomorrow and have Marcus written out of his will.

Listening to Sebastian rave, Cella realized that to suggest a somewhat different view would only feed the flames of his anger. And further unleash a storm of ridicule for the skulduggery of Wall Street. Sebastian would never see a connection between what Marcus had done and the way they made their money at The House of Uni. So she deliberately tried not to hear his rantings.

Noticing the loss of her attention, Sebastian said harshly, "Cella, I need your help. What the devil are you mooning about? What are we going to do about this Lawrence Lord mess?"

Cella did not dare shift her eyes away from Sebastian's. "Believe me, you won't like what I'm going to say."

"I can't like it less than what I've already heard."

"You will. But I have to say it. I know I'm right."

Cella knew that once she told him her thinking, they might become like strangers. Worse, like enemies. She loved her father and she was trying to do what was best for them both. Love tries. Love is desperate to help, but it must also question and take chances. She had to try to make him understand. But if he didn't, so be it. At least once she'd told him, she would be cleansed, relieved of the anxiety that had been eating at her this past year.

"Listen, Father," she said in a low voice, "I think you should tell Lawrence Lord that there'll be no percentage at all for his bringing clients to The House of Uni. The House of Uni is going out of the business of forging ancient pendants, forging necklaces, earrings, rings—you name it.''

"Cella! That word! I won't stand for it!''

"Stand for it, Father. Because that's exactly what we do. We forge ancient jewelry! Oh, we do it expertly. Even with some inspiration. Our tools, our methods—all those are exactly right for the time and place. Our ancestors left perfect records. And our materials come from the tomb. They're as old as Troy. No wonder we can throw sand in the eyes of Dr. Jason Lord. And others like him. There isn't an experienced collector or a trained art curator who has ever doubted the truth of what we sell. But we know the truth, don't we? I know. And I for one can't continue.''

Sebastian was beside himself. "Cella, I won't listen to you. This Lawrence Lord business has temporarily unbalanced you.'' His rejection of her position was definitive.

"No, I'm not unbalanced, Father. I've made up my mind. You can go on as you've been doing. That's why I had your Aphrodite authenticated by Jason Lord. You can conduct business as usual. But I won't. I'm getting out. I can't stand the deceit anymore.''

Sebastian listened to her tensely. And then his face softened. Shrewd as always, he recovered his composure. He prepared to negotiate, saying gently, "All right. I understand you've been under a great strain. You need a rest. In the meantime, all I ask is that you help me work out what I say to Lawrence Lord. Because there's no doubt about it—he means to try to blackmail me.''

A sudden panic gripped Cella at the thought of all she was risking. If she stood her ground, she'd lose her father. He'd never forgive her. She'd lose it all. Their work together. Their being a family. His love. As Marcus had lost his love. Her eyes blurred with tears.

"How can I help you when I no longer believe in what we're doing?'' It was like some wild disjuncture between them.

"You don't have to believe.'' He smiled in a kindly way. "Just spend the weekend with me at Sands Point and help me work out a plan of action. I can't ask Marina. I'm alone, Cella, but for you.''

"You won't give up The House of Uni?''

"I won't. Though I understand that you may want to.'' He took a deep breath. "Someday you may change your mind. And I don't propose to throw away your birthright.''

Sitting erect, almost woodenly, listening to the soft and

mending sound of Sebastian's words, trying to maintain the status quo, Cella hesitated about opposing him further. Briefly she wondered if her decision had come too quickly. Tread lightly, a voice within her warned. Consider deeply.

"All right, Father," she said softly. "I'll meet you at Sands Point this weekend. And we'll talk over how you should handle Lawrence Lord."

As she said this, there was an exchange of looks between them, the bestowal and acceptance of each other's confidence. They both understood all too well that the decisions they made from here on would affect the rest of their lives. Nothing would be quite the same again.

Sebastian paced up, down and around the library in Sands Point. The windows were partially open, and when he glanced in their direction, the sky beyond was gray and overcast. A small breeze drifted in, bringing with it a smell in the air of mist and a cold dampness, the smell that comes when frost is in the air. As he strode about he pulled nervously on the lapels of his brown velvet smoking jacket. For one of the few times in his life, Sebastian was uncomfortable in his own company. His anger at Marcus had faded into the back of his mind as he considered the immediate threat of Lawrence Lord.

Sebastian was as hardheaded and realistic a businessman as any, and automatically, he placed himself in Lawrence Lord's position. Lawrence would never settle for a ten percent commission on the business he brought The House of Uni. Not given what he now knew. Marcus, desperate for money as he was, had eagerly snapped at the unrealistic promise. But Sebastian knew better. And at that, no matter what percentage Lord had in mind, the idea of a friendly man-to-man discussion with that bastard about the gross sales and profits of The House of Uni—the mere thought made Sebastian want to throw up. It was an impossible conversation. The question was how to avoid it.

For the tenth time Sebastian checked his watch. Where was Cella? He picked up the *Times* again and started turning pages without reading them. He had a queer sense of marking time. He was waiting for something to happen, something unforeseen. The fact of the two Aphrodites, the business with Marcus, and now Lawrence Lord breathing down his neck, all combined to give him a feeling of apprehension that he intensely disliked.

Jigsaw-puzzle pieces came tumbling thick and fast upon

him. Disjointed pictures flashed one by one through his disturbed mind. Marcus pleading with him for money. Cella's face when she said she would no longer create jewelry for The House of Uni. Marina wearing the Aphrodite in front of Jason. And, worst of all, that cheating bastard Lawrence Lord knowing what he did. Sebastian wondered how much his forthcoming marriage to Marina had entered into Lawrence's desire to muscle his way into The House of Uni. Offhand he thought, Not much. Sexual jealousy was not in Lawrence's nature. Money jealousy was.

Again he looked at his watch. Cella had said she'd drive out to Sands Point around two. Two o'clock was three hours ago. He swore silently; she could damn near walk to Sands Point in three hours. Dammit, where was she? They had to talk over what to do. Lawrence Lord wasn't going to wait for them to come to him. Not Lawrence. He'd probably come knocking on the shop door next week.

The headlights of an approaching car shone through the windows of the library. Sebastian sighed with relief. Cella. Repressing the urge to hurry to the door, he returned to his favorite chair and composed himself. It would be wrong to show undo concern. As head of the house, he had a dignity to preserve.

When the chimes announced a visitor, Sebastian was momentarily startled. Then he shrugged. Cella had forgotten her keys. Slowly, even casually, Sebastian sauntered into the entrance hall. As he neared the door, the chimes sounded again.

"It's all right. I'm here," Sebastian called out. He opened the door with a flourish. "What took you so—" He tried to shut the door, but a big tennis shoe planted in the way prevented the door from closing.

There stood Lawrence Lord in a red tennis warm-up jacket and pants, with a raincoat slung over his shoulders. "Shame on you, Sebastian. Is that any way to treat an old friend?"

"Lawrence, I am very busy. Actually, expecting guests. And Cella should be here momentarily. Wouldn't it be better if you stopped by the shop in the morning?"

"Who are you expecting? Anyone I know?"

"Now, if you'll excuse me. And take your foot from the door."

"I will if you ask me in for a drink. I'm staying at the Brooks house, down the road. They have a bubble over their heated tennis court, so one can play all winter. I was thinking they would make marvelous clients for The House of Uni."

"Lawrence, this is not a good time for a visit. Another

Sunday afternoon perhaps. Why don't you return to the Brookses?''

''Impossible. Alden Winston was kind enough to drop me off on his way to say hello to the Peels. He won't be picking me up for at least a half hour. You can't expect me to trudge back three miles to the Brooks home.''

''It's as good exercise as tennis.''

''True, but we've so much to talk about. Actually, I'd like to discuss real estate and land values in Sands Point. I'm considering buying a house just up the road. We'll be next-door neighbors.''

''Not next door, Lawrence. I own that land.''

''Purely a figure of speech. A neighbor. A home owner in the vicinity.'' Lawrence smiled graciously. ''And by the way, I would have dropped this off at the shop, but since I knew I'd be out this weekend, I thought I'd bring it over. Marcus forgot it at my apartment.'' With these words he took the raincoat off his shoulders.

''Thank you, but that is not Marcus' raincoat.''

''My dear Sebastian, it is.'' As he spoke Lawrence Lord turned the raincoat inside out, so that the initials MT, in red, were clearly visible on the lining. ''Yes, it is your son's raincoat. One of his many. And very handsome too,'' Lawrence remarked cheerfully.

Sebastian said nothing, simply staring at the initials.

Abruptly Lawrence folded the raincoat and tossed it at Sebastian. To catch it, Sebastian let go his grip on the doorknob. The door swung open and Lawrence sidled into the house.

A flush spread across Sebastian's face as he felt the throb of blood in his temples, and a spasm of rage rose in his throat. With a strenuous effort he controlled himself.

''And what was Marcus doing at your apartment?'' Sebastian asked as if this were news to him.

Lawrence gave him a hard look. Was it possible Sebastian didn't know? ''Visiting. Just visiting,'' he said affably, watching Sebastian hang the raincoat in the hall closet while forgetting to shut the front door. Clearly Sebastian was jumpy.

''Thank you for returning it. For that I owe you a drink. But a quickie. Then I will have to ask you to leave.''

Lawrence ambled into the house. He looked around the foyer, and generally studied the doors leading off it with great curiosity. Then he entered the library and peered at the well-stocked bar.

''Nice place you have here,'' he said, turning to Sebastian, who was right behind him. "Very tasteful. Very elegant. But quite what I would expect."

"What are you drinking?" Sebastian asked.

"Whiskey and soda," Lawrence said as he settled himself on the couch.

Sebastian made a whiskey and soda for Lawrence and poured a small vodka neat for himself.

"I don't think you can afford real estate in this area, Lawrence," he said calmly. But his composure was too calculated to pass for indifference.

"At the moment, no. But I can when we settle on my new percentage at The House of Uni."

"You mean five percent is not enough?" Sebastian did a good imitation of surprise. "I think I've been more than generous. Your take on Peter Petty was spectacular."

"Not spectacular enough. I believe I deserve more." Lawrence savored his drink.

"How much more?"

Lawrence leaned toward Sebastian, seated opposite him in an armchair. "Quite a bit more."

"Lawrence, I don't mean to be rude, but I think we should save this kind of discussion for my office at the shop."

"Now, now, Sebastian. Don't be difficult. You're acting as if I'm the big, bad wolf. Truly, I'm a perfectly ordinary, harmless fellow. The essence of reasonableness."

"This is neither the time nor the place to discuss your commission. Or how reasonable you are."

"One must strike while the iron is hot. And it's white-hot now," Lawrence said, raising his voice slightly. "I mean to be fair."

"By being fair, you mean you expect an increase in your commission?"

"For openers. You and I both know five percent is hardly fair. Don't we?"

"No, we don't."

"Listen to me, Sebastian," Lawrence said slowly. "You've done very well with The House of Uni. Far better, I'm sure, than anyone in the family ever expected. Far better than you had a right to expect."

"I don't follow your thinking. Our jewelry is exquisite."

"It is. But considering its provenance . . ."

"Which is impeccable."

"Impeccable to the uninitiated."

Sebastian frowned and put his drink down on the side table. He started to rise from his chair. "There is something decidedly tasteless about your implication, Lawrence. Do you mind leaving this house, or do I have to throw you out?''

"Wait a bit, my old friend," Lawrence said. "I haven't finished yet. You realize that I can make things damned unpleasant for you if I choose?''

Sebastian sat down again, his eyes fixed on Lawrence.

"And how do you propose to do that?" Sebastian asked.

"I don't—if you are as reasonable as I am. All I want is what I deserve. A fair share. After all, Sebastian, I have your best interests at heart. Because your best interests turn out to be my best interests.''

"And your best interests involve a higher commission?''

Lawrence stared for a moment at Sebastian. "Considerably higher.''

Sebastian took a sip of vodka. "All right. I can probably see my way clear to raising it to seven and one half percent.''

"Please don't take me for a fool, Sebastian. Seven and one half percent.'' He pronounced each syllable. "That's not even a bad joke.''

"Lawrence, I think we've come to the end of our drinks and our conversation. And we may have come to the end of our association.''

"Steady, old man. Don't be so jumpy! After all, you are doing business with the ex-husband of the woman you plan to marry," Lawrence said with a half smile that Sebastian didn't like. "You ought to think of us as a modern extended family. And whatever I get is all in the family.''

"How much do you want?''

"A family partnership. A three-way split. Thirty-three and a third percent of the profits of The House of Uni for not telling the world what I know. Of course, I could ask for another sixteen and two-thirds percent for not telling Marina what kind of a man she's marrying. But I never was a hog.''

Sebastian went very white and a little pulse began to show on his forehead. "I've asked you before to leave this house. I'm not going to ask you again. You know where the door is. Use it.''

"Come on, Sebastian. You know as well as I do that you have too much to lose when you lose my good will. As I said before, I can make things unpleasant. I can also make them dangerous.'' Lawrence lowered his voice. "Listen to me, and listen hard, Sebastian Taggard.''

Sebastian did not move. He never took his eyes off Lawrence.

"I'll speak plainly so there's no misunderstanding. I know

there's a subbasement in this house. Right down there." He pointed toward the floor. "A subbasement that contains all manner of ancient tools, ancient gold, ancient gems and other things necessary for your profession. In the subbasement of this house you create your own instant antiques. You're a brilliant craftsman. I'll give you that. Brilliant enough to fool my son. But unless I get what I want, the game ends now."

"Where did you get this wild idea?" Sebastian asked quietly.

"From your dear son, Marcus."

"Who is furious at me and will say anything to smear my reputation."

"I think not. He told the truth." Sebastian had never seen such venom in a smile. "In the subbasement of this house exquisite ancient jewelry is made. Or perhaps the right words are 'exquisite ancient frauds.' "

"The House of Uni does not sell 'frauds,' to use your revolting term," Sebastian flared.

"It does and will continue to. And all I want is my fair share of the take whether or not I supply the clients for these frauds. Though I will continue to do so. I never bite the hand that feeds me."

"I told you I object to that word," Sebastian said, his temper rising.

"I'll refrain from using that word again. It does have an unsavory ring," Lawrence temporized. "And of course you do sell authentic works. But they're the exception, not the rule. The rule is you make them. In the subbasement." Lawrence paused as though planning something in his mind. "I've laid my cards on the table. It's in both our interests to come to an agreement. Or in no time what I know will become public information."

"And you'll be the source of the public information."

"You give me no choice. Unless we have a meeting of the minds, there will be unpleasant consequences."

Sebastian gave him a queer smile. "Lawrence, you bore me. You seem to have forgotten that blackmail is a two-way street." Lawrence gave him a look so sharp that Sebastian almost smiled. "Now, just suppose I went to see the dean at Harvard. To discuss the shenanigans of his Gulbanian professor of art history. And his Luxembourg Corporation. I doubt that the consequences would be pleasant."

Lawrence Lord looked searchingly at Sebastian. "What Luxembourg Corporation? What are you talking about?"

"No doubt it's another fiction of Marcus'. The same as the subbasement here is one of his fictions."

Lawrence had gone very white. He pursed his lips thoughtfully, dazed by the sudden mention of the Luxembourg Corporation. Sebastian could tell from the expression on his face that he understood. There was doubt written on it, then wonder, then hatred, then conviction. He began to talk again in a loud, domineering tone.

"It does seem we have a stranglehold on each other, doesn't it?" He gave Sebastian a look that was ugly, and calculating. "So let's call a truce. You keep your mouth shut and so will I. You open your mouth . . . and so will I."

"Agreed. And that ends the question of higher commissions."

"Not at all." Lawrence produced a miniature Minolta camera from his jacket pocket. "I intend to photograph the subbasement. You can show it to me. Or I'll find it myself."

Sebastian rose from his chair and walked slowly toward the seated man. He stood over Lawrence. "There is no subbasement, and I have no intention of allowing you to wander about the house alone. There are too many things of value. One might just happen to fall off the table into your pocket."

Lawrence heaved himself to his feet. He was several inches taller than Sebastian but not nearly as broad. Layer by layer, the trappings of twentieth-century civilization were being stripped away from each man. "Get out of my way, Sebastian." For the first time Lawrence's nerves began to show signs of fraying. "Or I'll bring The House of Uni to its knees."

Neither of them heard the sound of the Mercedes outside.

"And lose The House of Uni as a source of income? As well as the Luxembourg Corporation? I think not."

The two men stood facing each other tensely for a second. Neither of them moved. Silently Lawrence swore under his breath.

Neither of them heard a man enter the open front door.

"Lawrence, come along. The Brookses are expecting us for drinks before dinner. And I need a shower." A man with a decidedly British accent was speaking.

Sebastian turned and for a moment he felt paralyzed. At the door stood a tall black man in a blue tennis warm-up outfit. He had a tennis racket under his arm. Who the hell was he? Sebastian eyed him with dread. Was this the man who had tried to castrate him? His height and his skin color were about right. But something was different. The man was tall and well built, but more lean than powerful. Was he the same man?

"You lay a hand on me again," Sebastian said to the intruder as he went behind his desk and pulled a small-caliber revolver out of a drawer, "and I'll kill you." Sebastian's usual self-control was replaced by mindless hysteria.

"I've never seen you before in my life, sir," said the man with a scornful British accent. "And stop waving the pistol about. Someone might get hurt."

Lawrence gave Sebastian a quick, curious glance. "What are you talking about, Sebastian? Alden Winston is with the Nigerian delegation at the UN. If he says he's never seen you before tonight, bank on it."

"Maybe yes. Maybe no. Either way, I want the two of you out of here now!"

"Lawrence, we are clearly not wanted," said the black man. "So let's move."

"I can't, Alden. I have some pictures to take first," Lawrence said, holding his position.

Sebastian waved the gun about before lightly rapping Lawrence on the side of his head. The blow triggered a violence in Lawrence that he hadn't known he was capable of. He grabbed for the gun, caught hold of the barrel and tried to wrestle it from Sebastian's hand. Sebastian didn't take the attempt seriously and, almost casually, he shoved Lawrence away. But Lawrence hung on and the two men staggered about the room. Alden Winston watched, searching for an opportunity to step between them. Suddenly he swung his racket at the gun, hitting it and knocking it from Sebastian's grip. Sebastian tried to catch his balance by grabbing hold of the edge of a table. Inspired by his success, Winston whipped the racket a second time, smashing Sebastian across the knuckles. Sebastian stepped back in shock, holding his hand. For a moment, Lawrence wondered what had happened. Then he saw Sebastian's right hand. The edge of the hard graphite racket had struck Sebastian's knuckles, shattering several of them.

The lights from a car shone through the window of the library. Someone was coming.

"Let's get out of here," Lawrence shouted. "Sorry about your hand, Sebastian. But for the sake of The House of Uni, keep your mouth shut." The two men hurried from the room, slamming the door after them.

Sebastian stood in the middle of the library, turning his ruined hand so he could look first at his palm and then at the smashed knuckles of his forefinger and middle finger. Although his hand was bleeding profusely, it hadn't yet begun to hurt. That would come later.

In the distance he heard the sound of a car being started and the screech of tires as it sped away. Then the front door was opened and he heard the light tapping of Cella's heels coming toward him.

When she entered the library, she exclaimed, "What were those men doing here, Father?" Only after Sebastian had turned to face her did she see his hand.

"Oh, my God!" she cried. She hustled the numbed Sebastian from the house and into her car. She had to get to the nearest hospital.

═══ Chapter Twenty-nine ═══

No amount of surgery could restore full movement to Sebastian's right hand. For Sebastian, it was a personal tragedy. For those close to him, it was almost as painful an experience. Sebastian had been the keystone of an arch built with many stones, many lives. When the keystone was crushed, the arch crumbled, hurling the many stones every which way. But then the lives were put together, as lives and stones often are, and arranged in a new design.

Marcus started drinking too much. His days went by like the ticking of a clock that has no hands and doesn't tell the time. He had learned a humiliating lesson. There were smarter cheats in the world than he. Cagier con men. It was an old story—a man proving how dangerous it is to be an amateur in a world of professionals.

It was hard for Marcus to be alone. Harder still to be with another person. When he thought of his father, his heart heaved in a storm of guilt. Through naïveté and desperation he was the coconspirator in Lawrence Lord's crime. There was no escape from this truth. Soon he could no longer stand himself. He tried psychiatry. EST. Hypnosis. TM. Biofeedback. And a neighborhood guru. Nothing helped. The yeast went out of the bread, and he developed a taste for pessimism. He took to obsessively washing his hands. He started seeing flashes of light before his eyes. One day he decided to see an ophthalmologist before visiting a mind healer.

Waiting impatiently in the reception room, he couldn't read the magazines piled on the table in front of the couch. He didn't care if skirts were going up, down or sidewise, or how to make Black Forest chocolate cake. He didn't—and then he stopped and stared. One of the cover headlines on a magazine called *Psychology Now* got to him: Recognizing Criminal Tendencies in Normal Children. After examining the article, he felt it had something to tell him. The piece had been excerpted from a classic book on child psychology called *Love, Guilt and Reparation*. That was what he needed desperately—more love, less guilt and a way to make reparation. Suddenly he felt he no longer had glaucoma and left the office quickly with the magazine under his arm.

At home he poured himself a scotch, settled in an armchair and began to read. Though he was a crime fan and the piece hardly read like a detective story, still it held him.

Lines like "Our own hatred, fear and distrust tend to create in our unconscious mind frightening and exacting parent figures . . . Thus making reparations for these hostile feelings is an essential part of the ability to love, and is a fundamental element in all human relationships . . . If we become able to clear our feelings toward our parents of grievances, to make reparations and forgive them for the frustrations we had to bear, then we will be at peace with ourselves . . ."

There it was. That was his answer. That was the way to peace. What he needed to do was to make reparations to his father. He poured himself a fourth scotch and fell asleep before he finished it.

Marcus was awakened by the telephone ringing. Anton wanted to know how he was, and without waiting for an answer, suggested they meet for dinner. Marcus agreed.

Over dinner Marcus could hardly eat, and he would not listen. He had too much in him that he must get rid of.

"I mean he's in deep trouble. The poor s.o.b. As if near castration wasn't enough, now he has this. And this is a real killer. The loss of movement in the fingers of his right hand is major. He's only got one right hand. They don't have right-hand transplants. And the poor s.o.b's—I mean my father's—right hand is shattered."

"At least it's not a matter of life and death."

"It is! Don't you get it? It is life and death. Oh, sure, his hand will mend. Good as new, the doctors say, once they do reconstructive surgery. Good as new, my ass. So eventually he'll be able to handle a steak knife, shake hands, hit a golf ball. Great! But so what! That's it. It ends there. His ability to do re-creations of ancient jewelry—to make a gorgeous pendant or a wow of a ring—all that depended on the dexterity of his hands. The control of his fingers. That ability's gone. Finished. Lost forever. In short, his lifework is over. Thanks to his loving son."

"I'm sorry I have to agree with you," Anton said.

"Agree or don't. I know what I know. It's all my fault. If

only I'd kept my flannel mouth shut when I saw Lawrence Lord." His mouth grew tight. "Now what I want is vengeance. Something ancient. Inevitable. The hand of fate. I want to make reparation to my father. An eye for an eye."

Anton's gaze was curious and intent. "What do you have in mind?"

"Nothing yet. First I started with the damn fool idea of bringing charges. But that won't play. The only evidence that it was Lawrence at the house is that he returned my raincoat. Which brings us to the subject of how he got the raincoat in the first place. Which gets us all into deeper trouble. That slippery scum would never go to jail. We would." Marcus grimaced. "He'll say the raincoat was his excuse for barging in on Sebastian. Because he has long suspected The House of Uni of selling forgeries. He did it to save the trusting public and museum curators from being hoodwinked. His lawyers will insist they get out a search warrant for the subbasement. And so on and on."

"It's too dangerous," Anton agreed. "All kinds of rocks could easily be turned over."

"They'll call him Saint Larry," Marcus said sourly.

It was Anton, then, who helped him work out his reparation. And salvation. Anton had a thought. He described it in terms that were vivid but discreetly detailed. When he finished, Marcus blinked. Their eyes met for a moment, and though he did not express it, Anton's coming up with the solution touched Marcus deeply. Giving him at last breathable air.

"It's the quintessential revenge." He gave Anton an ironical smile, irony without bitterness now that the balance would be set right.

"He deserves it," Anton said, meditating.

"Poetic justice."

"Poetic justice."

"Love, guilt and reparation," Marcus said.

"Reparation certainly," Anton said.

In Sebastian's study on the second floor of their house on Sixty-third Street, he sat behind his desk and gazed at Cella and Marcus, half challenging, half defensive. With the exception of his thumb, his right hand was in a cast from his wrist to his fingernails; the existence of the cast was a constant reminder that the life he'd led since marrying Spina thirty years ago was over.

"Well, the time has come to do what must be done." He

sounded tired. "I have to give it up. I mean The House of Uni."

"Father!" Marcus said, at a loss to say more.

"I can't work with this hand," Sebastian said, holding up his right hand. "It's now a useless tool."

"I'm so sorry, Father," Cella murmured, feeling that she too was responsible for this final stage in her father's career. She hadn't trusted him to behave decently. If she'd challenged him sooner, everything would be different today.

"It's all my fault," Marcus said. "Everything."

"It's not your fault," Sebastian replied softly. "I tried to teach you a lesson. It was the wrong lesson using the wrong method at the wrong time. I underestimated how desperate you were."

"The idea of prison terrified me," Marcus said. "I was stunned that you'd let me down. You never did before."

"That's the one thing that surprised me. That you would think I would let you down this time."

"I didn't think."

"Neither did I," Sebastian said.

"Nobody did much thinking," Cella said. "Including me."

"I should have guessed you'd bail me out," Marcus said drearily.

"You're not a mind reader. What's done is done. Let's forget it," Sebastian said. "We must get on with our futures."

The entire conversation sounded false and terribly sad to Cella. Marcus and Sebastian were both taking the blame for something that in reality each felt was the other's fault. And the truth was it was no one's fault. Or everyone's. They could not help being other than what they were.

Using his left hand, Sebastian handed Cella and Marcus an agreement in a blue folder.

"Will you each sign the documents and give me one dollar, please?" he said. "I want the sale of my shares in The House of Uni to be perfectly legal."

Before speaking, Cella had to clear a space in her mind from the suffocating rush of sensations. Did he think she would create more forgeries? That would give him joy. She would hate it. "Father, you know how I feel about our work"

"You made yourself very clear."

"And you still want to give me half of your holdings?"

"I do."

Cella looked at him, feeling breathless in her effort to make this new adjustment to reality.

"Look, Cella, I don't agree with you. But I have no right—not anymore—to stand in your way. Who am I to decide between your code and mine? I can no longer be active in the business." With an effort to repress his misery, Sebastian stood up and walked around the room. "I've tried to see things from your standpoint, but I don't." He came over to Cella, reached for her hand with his good one and held it tightly, like a child trying to gain confidence. "I have only one suggestion that I wish you would consider."

"What is it?" The grip of his hand was almost painful.

He released her hand and started pacing again, staring at the rug. "A compromise of sorts." Cella said nothing, so he went on. "Continue The House of Uni as before. For one year. Or until our current inventory is sold. If, during the year, you change your mind, I will return and act as business manager. Not attempt any re-creation of jewelry. I can't."

"What if I don't change my mind?"

"We'll take all the jewelry that remains into our private collection." He made a gesture of surrender. "If there's no way to bring you around to my way of thinking, then that's it. Finis."

Cella could feel her father's need, even as she struggled with her own. She owed him so much. But where did it stop? What she wanted was a sign to tell her which road to take. "I need time to think," she said.

"You will have time to think. In the meantime, I give you your share of The House of Uni. I want you to make your decision without pressure."

"Thank you, Father," Cella said softly.

"What are the two of you talking about?" Marcus asked petulantly.

"You'll know soon enough." She smiled confidentially. "I'll tell you about it."

"It's nice that you're keeping me in your confidence."

"Do I have a choice? We're partners now." She'd recovered her calmness. "Sign the agreement, Marcus," Cella said.

Marcus produced a huge, black Mont Blanc pen and signed both copies without reading them. Cella followed suit.

"The House of Uni now belongs to you," Sebastian said. Then with a flash of his old spirit, he added, "Paragraph three, subparagraph c states that you cannot sell the stock to anyone not related, either by marriage or birth. And you cannot use the stock to borrow money except to add to The House of Uni's capital." He looked directly at Marcus when he said, "That means there will be no speculations on Wall Street done with money borrowed from The House of Uni."

Marcus laughed defiantly. "With Cella's cooperation, I can think of three ways to get around that clause. And I haven't even scratched the surface of possibilities."

"Don't count on my cooperation," Cella said, her tone carrying a warning. "In fact, you may find me a lot less indulgent than Father."

"That's possible." Sebastian nodded. He had the air of a man who had observed more than anyone suspected.

Marcus flushed. "Will the two of you please relax. It was a hard lesson. I love the Wall Street game, but I've no talent for it. Who knows? I may work for The House of Uni as a salesman. I'm a born salesman. The problem is, like most salesmen, I'm my own best customer."

Sebastian raised his bandaged hand. "They tell me my hand will be almost as good as new. I'll open doors, garden, drive a car. What they didn't mention was a prodigal son. That my hand might reach out and bring one home. I can almost thank Lawrence Lord for that."

The Air France terminal was crowded with wealthy travelers. Marina and Sebastian had only one suitcase apiece to check through, and they each held a small bag they would carry onto the plane. With Cella, Anton and Marcus behind them, they passed through the checkpoint and went directly to the luxurious lounge reserved for those using the Concorde. There were only a few other people in the lounge. Much to Sebastian's thinly disguised disgust, Marina insisted on ordering champagne for everyone. The champagne was Mumm's, a fine brand of commercial French champagne that Sebastian detested, and the hors d'oeuvres were a variety of American caviars—actually lump fish, which set Sebastian's teeth on edge—and French pâtés, which he grumpily admitted were not too bad.

Marina babbled nervously, almost feverishly, about how much fun it would be to be married in the Taggard family residence in Tuscany and maybe Jason would take a quick trip over for the wedding, or at the least surprise them by stopping by this morning to wave them off. Through all this Sebastian was guarded and silent. Her constant chatter about Jason came so close to getting on his nerves that he had to struggle to keep from saying something he'd regret. To hold himself in check, Sebastian took a restless turn around the lounge. He gestured to Cella to join him. She had been sitting between Marcus and Anton with her head on Anton's shoulder. When she saw Sebastian's signal, she excused herself and walked over to him.

"One final point." His tone was quiet. "I've restrained myself from raising it, but now I must. As your father, I ask you a favor."

Cella gazed at him with a kind of solemnity. "I've wondered when you would ask."

"You know the favor?"

"Yes. To sell your Aphrodite necklace." Cella gave him a frank smile.

Sebastian paused, trying to choose his words with deliberation. "I respect your new principles. But postpone your decision until my Aphrodite is sold. That is, if you actually do decide to close The House of Uni. Or somehow change it."

"I promise to sell your Aphrodite."

"Good!" Sebastian sighed with relief.

"I understand. It's because you feel it's your finest work."

"My masterpiece."

Their gazes flowed together. "I know," Cella said. "And because it's that and not the money, I'll sell it for you. It will be a wedding gift to you. And to Marina."

"You'll sell it to the highest bidder?"

"You'll see how I do when I give you the check. I won't keep the money for The House of Uni. I'll give it to you at your wedding breakfast."

For an instant Sebastian frowned. "But you will get a good price? It's a matter of pride." He raised an entreating hand. "I was a good artist, you know."

"You were a fine artist. And the price will be right. Depend on me."

"I take you at your word," Sebastian said, smiling again.

A young woman in the uniform of a stewardess interrupted them. "Please, Mr. Taggard. It's time you and Mrs. Lord boarded the plane."

"So soon?" Sebastian growled. "Oh, well." With a shrug of his shoulders he led Cella back to where Anton and Marcus were sitting. "She's yours now, Anton." He kissed Cella and Marcus, shook left hands with Anton and sauntered over to where Marina was standing waiting. As he approached, her face brightened and the sparkle returned to her eyes. "I'm so excited. I only wish Jason were here to see us off."

Standing with one hand clasped around Anton's arm and the other holding Marcus' hand, Cella thought how much his shattered hand had changed Sebastian's life forever. She watched her father walk toward the boarding gate. He walked as if he were completely alone, like an abdicating king.

The week before Thanksgiving, the cold wind of shock whipped through the art world. In rapid succession two of the titans of the world had been toppled.

First there was the retirement of Sebastian Taggard. At gallery showings through the season, there was more hum and buzz about Sebastian than there was about the paintings.

"I hear he caught his hand in a printing press."

"What were they printing? Money?"

"Don't be so pedestrian. The House of Uni never prints money. They coin money. Old Roman coins. That shop is a money machine."

"Who'll manage it now?"

"Cella, of course."

"Can she do it?"

"Why not? It isn't hard. She opens the door. The customer walks in. Spends a fortune on some ancient knickknack that Cella picked up for pennies from some indigent grave robber. I could do it and I can't even balance my checkbook."

"But where would you find the grave robber?"

Then there was the weird behavior of Dr. Lawrence Lord. Metaphorically, he thumbed his nose at the Metropolitan Museum of Art, the Whitney, the Museum of Modern Art and all the other museums and galleries that made up the Manhattan art world. He had decided to take a position as curator in a small museum in Orange County.

"Orange County? Where is Orange County?" asked a pretty woman with blazing white hair.

"California, my dear. It's full of orange groves," the man said, smoothing his Vandyke beard. "It's all very strange."

"Not at all, Vincent. California has everything. Tennis courts. Beaches. Sunshine."

"But he resigned his position as Gulbanian professor of Art History at Harvard. What does it all mean?"

"It means he won't have to put up with another hideous winter in Boston."

Jason Lord was thunderstruck when he heard of his father's resignation from Harvard. After trying unsuccessfully to reach him, he made one last call. It was this call that in its way was the end of Jason. It was his final degradation, the agent of his shame. When he thought of his father at all, he thought of him as a man who was reasonably upright and, if not noble, not a cheat. As it turned out, the call proved a monstrous irony.

He contacted the dean of the School of Fine Arts at Harvard. The conversation was short and unpleasant. While the dean saw no reason to tar the son with the sins of the father, he took a malicious pleasure in telling the celebrated and righteous Dr. Jason Lord exactly what crime his father had committed as president of a corporation that bought and sold paintings to many city museums. When he bought, his price was outrageously low. When he sold, his price was disgracefully high. Either way he defrauded the taxpayer.

"The man's lucky he's not in prison," the dean concluded sanctimoniously, feeling that in the future, perhaps, Dr. Jason Lord would not be so quick to throw stones.

Jason listened without making a sound. The horror within him grew. As he listened, the image of his father's face in his mind became that of a cartoon. Swallowing his revulsion, he asked, "How do you know all this is true?"

"Anton Vilanova and Marcus Taggard visited me two weeks ago. They filled me in on every detail, with documents and invoices. Anton Vilanova was Dr. Lawrence Lord's partner for many years."

The cartoon who was his father grew larger in Jason's mind, evil, odious, blatant. "Thank you," was all he managed to say as he slowly hung up the telephone receiver. The force of the shock, and the rage of hatred it aroused, made his head spin.

He sat with his fingers clamped around the edge of his desk. The whole thing was inconceivable, hideous, disconnected from any reality; yet it was true. He had been "sold" down the river. If his mother was a whore—and she was—his father, God help him, was a pimp. He felt ravaged and despairing. Briefly he considered the ways of ending Lawrence Lord's days on earth. Then he put the thought aside. There was Cella Taggard to be taken care of first. And the entire Taggard family. His mother among them. The eminent Dr. Lawrence Lord would have to wait. The art world was a small world. A very special kind of prison. His father could run, but he couldn't hide.

══════ Chapter Thirty ══════

As usual, Lexi was dressed in the height of fashion. She wore the shortest skirt, the highest heels, the blackest, sheerest hose and a black beret. Her jewelry was bold, new and geometric. But as a concession to the fact that her visit was official, her charcoal-gray suit was pin-striped. It struck Cella as amusing that Lexi, so much the essence of the now generation, should be the official Turkish emissary sent to buy the Aphrodite necklace, worn by the goddess of love of thousands of years ago.

Cella had given instructions to Juliana that the shop was to be closed for the morning and that she could take the time off. The telephone was to be shut off. There was to be no interruption while Lexi was present. This gave an almost monastic silence to the shop as the young woman examined the Aphrodite necklace. Lexi had been studying it for a long time, looking like a charming, inquisitive little animal.

"It's quite lovely," was all she said after the first fifteen minutes. Then she said nothing for a long time, turning the necklace over delicately between her fingers, examining each pearl, each pomegranate, each chain and the way it all intertwined.

As the minutes ticked away, Cella began to suspect an overzealousness in Lexi's minute examination. She had the sense that her silence was not sympathetic. What was she looking for? Lexi was neither uncultivated nor a fool.

"Yes, it's very lovely," Lexi repeated again as she continued to study the necklace.

When it seemed Cella had waited longer than was sensible, Lexi turned to her with a faintly embarrassed smile.

"I'm so sorry, Cella."

Cella let this remark pass unchallenged, asking instead with puzzlement, "Do you think age has impaired its beauty? I feel it's added to its magnificence. I would think you'd feel the same.''

"Ordinarily, yes." Lexi's lips tightened to the vanishing point. "I would agree with you under the right circumstances. But these are not the right circumstances.''

Cella's face showed intense surprise. "I'm sorry, but I don't follow you.''

"I'm afraid you will not like what I am going to say." Lexi arched her dramatic eyebrows and gazed again at the necklace.

"Why not?''

"This is not the true Aphrodite.''

Cella felt as if she'd entered a room in which the lights were suddenly turned out. "That's absurd," she exclaimed. "This is the same necklace that we purchased from Northbie's. That your father wanted.''

"This is not the necklace of the goddess," Lexi murmured again. She raised her eyes from her thoughtful contemplation of the piece.

"Your father seemed to think it was. He said as much to Anton.''

"He did. And he does. My father wants the true Aphrodite. Desperately.''

"I understand that. He told Anton it came from the tomb of the goddess. In fact, he said he found it originally himself. And he described its passage and provenance, owner by owner, over the past forty years.''

"The necklace was found in the tomb of the great goddess. But my father tells small lies. The fact is he didn't find it.''

Cella didn't understand the turn the conversation had taken. "What difference does it make who found it?''

"Because it does.''

"It had to be someone close to him, someone he trusted, who found it. Or he wouldn't have been so sure it was the necklace of the goddess.''

Lexi's reply only increased Cella's startled sense of strangeness. "Someone very close to him did find it. His nephew, Tancredi Vilanova. His sister's young son. He was three at the time.''

"A three-year-old found the Aphrodite necklace?''

Lexi leaned against the counter. "Enrico Vilanova, my uncle, Tancredi's father, used to take him along on exploring expeditions. He believed in teaching him young. One morning they were examining the stones around what is now known to be Aphrodisias. And Tancredi, wandering into a cave, saw a crevice between two large rocks. Because he was so small he could slip through the opening into the dark below. Enrico and my father went wild. Where was the boy? They shouted to him down the crevice. It was no bigger than a rabbit hole, too small for grown men. They went crazy. They started to dig frantically around the rocks where he'd fallen through. But beneath the dirt was solid rock, and they could make no headway. They sweated all day with pickaxes, shovels. Enrico was weeping as he worked. So was my father. The sun was starting to set. And then it happened." Lexi paused.

"What happened?"

"The earthquake happened. Turkey has earthquakes, you know."

"And Tancredi . . . ?"

"I am not capable of saying anything profound about the workings of fate. All I know is it seems to act most generously—or miserly—when people least expect it. The earthquake threw large rocks around. The cave collapsed. Enrico was killed. My father was knocked unconscious. But somehow—and how can a small boy explain a great earthquake?—Tancredi was tossed to the surface of the earth. When my father awoke he found him wandering in the ruins, sobbing, calling for his father. And wearing the necklace, holding part of it in his mouth. You know the way a child puts everything in its mouth."

"He'd found the necklace under the ground?" There was a note of skepticism in Cella's voice.

"He found it in the tomb of Aphrodite, goddess of love."

"Do you believe that? The tomb has never been found."

"Nor do I think it will ever be found again. Too many earthquakes. Too many thousands of tons of rock and dirt. Who knows how far it has sunk into the earth? I believe Aphrodite prefers to sleep undisturbed."

"You do believe it, then?" Even as Cella said the words she felt that Lexi knew a great deal more than she was telling.

"Don't you?"

"My mother would have believed it," Cella mused.

"I believe in UFOs. My father doesn't. But he believed Tancredi, implicitly." Lexi's smile was elusive and ambiguous. "After all, there was the Aphrodite necklace as proof."

"But you don't believe that it's real."

"The Aphrodite necklace is real. What you show me here isn't."

"I wish I understood your reservations. I've even had it

tested by Dr. Jason Lord. And he has given it his stamp of approval."

Lexi made a slight gesture. "I've no doubt that it appears to be authentic. It is simply not the necklace of the goddess."

Cella felt a faint chill of apprehension. "What makes you so sure?"

"You may not believe me if I tell you."

"How do you know until you tell me?"

"Because you don't believe that the boy, Tancredi, found it. And what I would tell you is so much more incredible."

"Try me, Lexi," Cella insisted.

"Then listen," Lexi answered. "When the small Tancredi could talk coherently, he told his mother what he saw. In the tomb of the goddess. He said he entered a beautiful and spacious hall. This great chamber had a white marble floor and the walls were golden and jeweled. It was a magnificent place and there were many beautiful young men and women moving about, laughing and dancing. And there was one who he said was as pretty as his mother, asleep on a golden altar. As Tancredi stumbled toward the altar, the woman awoke from her slumber and smiled at him. She gestured to him to come and sit on her lap. He did, and she drew him to her bosom. She wore an exquisite necklace, and like any little boy, Tancredi played with it. Seeing his fascination, the goddess allowed him to take the necklace and put it around his neck. Then she lay down, closed her eyes, and the earthquake started."

Cella stared at Lexi in amazement. "What an incredible story. Perhaps it was all his vivid imagination. Probably the dancing couples were paintings on the walls and the woman with the necklace was a statue."

"Perhaps yes, perhaps no. But, imagination or not, the Aphrodite necklace does exist."

"All right, Lexi. This may not be the true Aphrodite." Cella flung out her words in a burst of abandonment. "But it is an ancient necklace and could have been hers."

"No, it's a perfect forgery. Created by Sebastian," Lexi said with a note of amusement. "If you'd done it I might not have guessed. You'd have been more careful."

Cella flushed to her forehead. She now wished she'd been able to compare Sebastian's creation with the original. "Why do you say it's a forgery?"

"For me, it looks drab. It lacks the splendor I expected. And then, of course, there's more concrete proof."

Cella thought about Lexi's word *drab*. She had felt the

same. But that was not reason enough. "What's the concrete proof?"

"The toothmark on the golden pomegranate is missing."

"The toothmark?"

"Tancredi's." Lexi looked at Cella earnestly, without a trace of irony in her tone. "I told you that when they found him, he had a portion of the necklace in his mouth. Like any little boy who is wandering around and afraid, he was sucking on his thumb. And on one of the pomegranates. Occasionally biting into it. Of course, he had almost no teeth. And what teeth he had were his first milk teeth. Small and weak. But he did leave a tiny dent in one pomegranate. My father saw it later when he examined the necklace. He called it the mark of Tancredi. He knew no collector would ever notice it. Or would think it a mark of age. But my father, being my father, knew it was the mark of Tancredi. He told me to search for that mark. And there is no dent anywhere on any pomegranate in this necklace."

"Then I suppose you don't mean to bid?" Cella asked wearily.

"Not for this one. For the real one."

"I was going to offer it to you for exactly what we paid for it at auction. One million two."

"A pittance, when you know my father is offering ten million. You have scruples, Cella Taggard. Imagine, scruples—in this day and age."

"I have my reasons."

Lexi's eyes flickered with amusement. "I have a counteroffer. One that Sebastian will like far more."

Cella gave her a blank look. "What kind of counteroffer?"

"Ten million, as my father promised."

Cella was stunned. "Ten million for a necklace you don't believe is the Aphrodite?"

"But Darlene Schiller thinks it is." Lexi gave her a frank smile. "She is going to top my bid by ten percent."

"How did you know?"

"My father knows everything."

"I never meant to accept Darlene's bid."

"Accept it." There was a pagan freshness in Lexi's opportunism.

"I can't. Unless you make a real offer."

"You mean it's a point of honor?" Lexi leaned toward Cella in an intense, almost childlike effort to understand.

Cella shrugged her shoulders. "That's one way of looking at it. I can't even consider her bid unless yours is genuine."

Lexi thought about this. "I like that. And I do bid ten million. On one condition."

"Which is?"

"You are the daughter of Spina." She gave Cella a shrewd look. "Can't you guess?"

"You want the real Aphrodite." Cella make an impatient motion. "For, let us say, one dollar."

Lexi giggled joyously at Cella's discernment. "Like Spina, you are gifted with insight. Yes, I want the real Aphrodite. For one dollar."

Cella gave her a singular look. "What makes you think I know where the real Aphrodite is?"

"You have to know. Sebastian copied it. Almost exactly." She let her eyes rest on Cella. "Think what a wonderful joke it is."

Cella stared at Lexi, grappling slowly with her confusion, which loomed larger and darker as it closed in around her. "Yes, I suppose it is."

"A joke on the Greeks too."

"On the Greeks too."

"It happens that I am lunching today with Darlene Schiller. I shall tell her my offer." Lexi beamed. "She should call you this afternoon."

"I may not take her offer," Cella said quietly.

"Why not? Do you think it's what they call a rip-off?" She laughed. "The necklace has been authenticated by Dr. Jason Lord. Why shouldn't Darlene pay top dollar for it?"

"She thinks she's buying the Aphrodite."

"So?"

"So I have to think about it."

Lexi gazed at her with a kind of awe. She who had been trained to weigh motives and calculate chances felt Cella's hesitancy astonishing. "I find your attitude extravagantly wasteful. But," she added thoughtfully, "it would relieve you of all obligations to return the true Aphrodite to my father."

"I could do that anyway."

"No, you couldn't. We both know Sebastian too well. He will want his money." Lexi made a motion to adjust her beret, meaning to end their conversation. "He is of a different breed than you. Or Spina."

The two young women exchanged a long look: searching on Lexi's part, sad and indefinable on Cella's.

Suddenly Lexi smiled. "I almost forgot. I have something for you." She fumbled in her purse and drew out a small black velvet jewelry box, which she handed to Cella.

"What is it?" Cella stared at the box in wonderment.

"It's for you. A gift from Spina, from Tancredi. For returning to us the Aphrodite. Spina gave it to Tancredi's mother many years ago to keep for you."

"Lexi, who is Tancredi Vilanova?"

"Open the box when you are at home. Then you will see and understand. I am certain it will help you make up your mind about Darlene."

Who is Tancredi? Cella wanted to ask again but didn't. She watched Lexi take her wallet out of her purse and put one dollar on the counter.

"We are of the same race, but we have different views of honor. I understand how you feel. Still, I think it would be best for all to let Darlene buy Sebastian's Aphrodite."

"But that would put me so deeply in your debt."

"And I in yours. It's the way the world works," the young woman said as she moved toward the door. Then she paused with her hand on the doorknob. "That dollar, as you know, is payment in advance. For the real Aphrodite." She smiled as she closed the door after her.

Cella locked the shop and left shortly after Lexi had. Her brain was tingling with the shock of all she had heard. About the false Aphrodite. About Sebastian. About this strange, new name: Tancredi Vilanova.

She had to get away, to escape, to think. Or, to be accurate, not to think. Almost instinctively she knew she had to get to Sands Point. There she would open the jewelry box that Lexi had given her. The gift from Spina. From Tancredi.

As she drove along the Northern State Parkway, the name kept spinning around in her head. Tancredi Vilanova? Where had she heard it before? She was glad the traffic was heavy; it made her concentrate and let her mind rest. More than an hour went by before she arrived at the house. And since the housekeeper came only in the mornings, Cella was entirely, blissfully alone. She felt like a person swimming away from a flooded town who is taken up into a boat. Here she could rest.

She carried her confusions and questions to her suite and hung her coat in the entrance closet. Here there was nothing to disturb her; everything was familiar; there was nothing to think of but the black velvet box, which she placed on the desk in her study. She stood for a moment and stared at it. The truth she had been at such pains to acquire, the questions to which she had no answers, were somehow inside that box.

Now she had no thought of calling Anton. She wanted her inner tumult to subside before she met his eyes again. She wanted no one to influence her decision about the Aphrodite. Only Spina. Only Tancredi. Why Tancredi? Each time she thought his name, she felt as if she were locked in a struggle with herself. A struggle for what? She didn't want to know. Not yet. She left the velvet box on the desk and walked swiftly to her bedroom.

Inside it, she slowly slipped out of her clothes. Dress. Shoes. Lingerie. Pantyhose. And still deliberately not looking at anything more than she had to, she reached for a navy blue terry-cloth robe, slipped it on and padded barefoot back to the study.

She knew she had things to do, but she couldn't do them. There were household bills to be paid and letters to write—to Sebastian, to Marina. But she could do nothing until she had opened the jewelry box. She sat down at her desk, contemplating the small size of her courage. Her fingers trembled as she slowly opened the box. She gasped. It was the ring. The magical ring.

The present seemed to slip away as she looked at it, and her hand went unconsciously to her heart, her memory flashing pictures of another time. She saw a landscape with trees. A light summer rain had stopped. The afternoon air was almost cool. Golden sunlight and quiet blue shadows divided the landscape between them. A rainbow arced in the sky, and she and Spina were trudging out of the woods. On all sides the birds were singing. In the dripping wet woods the young leaves were still soft and silky, swaying in the forest air like seaweed in shallow water. . . .

"You won't believe me," her mother remarked, "but long ago many things had life which are now lifeless. The mossy, rotten old logs in the forest could talk. I have never heard them, but once I think I did hear one snore in its sleep as I passed it at night."

"Oh, Mother." Cella giggled. "What did the snore sound like?"

"It sounded like Sebastian. A charming but self-centered snore."

As they approached the villa, Cella felt a mild panic.

"Do you think Father has returned?"

"No. He would not miss having lunch with the principessa."

"He'll be home in time, won't he?"

"Yes, dear, he'll be home in time for your twelfth birthday party," her mother reassured her as they went up the steps of the villa. "He has nothing to sell the principessa," she added with mild irony.

When they entered the huge doors, Angelina, the cook's helper, came running toward them. "Madam! Come quickly. Celeste is in a storm."

"Angelina! Find Madam! Find her!" Celeste's voice resounded from the kitchen, hearty and strong.

Cella and her mother hurried to the kitchen, and there stood the cook, looking both triumphant and dazed.

"What is it?" Spina asked.

"It's this," the cook said. "Stretch out your hand."

Spina did, and Celeste dropped into the palm of her hand an exquisite ring in the shape of a spiral serpent with gems for eyes. At the sight of it Spina gasped and slowly backed off. "Where did you get this?" she asked, raising her eyes to Celeste.

"From there." The cook nodded to the kitchen counter on which a ten-pound turbot lay stretched out with the belly slit. The fish was destined to be the main course at Cella's birthday dinner.

"From the fish?" Spina asked incredulously.

"From its belly. The fish carried this gift in its belly for you, madam. He has brought you a ring from the sea. Aren't you pleased?"

Spina gave Celeste an odd, crooked smile. "I am very pleased, Celeste. Thank you." She closed her fingers around the ring and backed slowly out of the kitchen with Cella following her.

When Cella and her mother stood on the patio in the afternoon sun, Spina opened her fingers, a dazed expression on her face.

"Oh, Mother, it's so beautiful," Cella said as she stared at the ring. "And the blue stones are very blue."

"Sapphires. Blue as the sea the ring came from."

"What does it mean, Mother?" Cella asked in an awed voice.

Spina stood quietly staring at the ring for a long time. "Praise Uni!" she said at last in a hushed tone. "It's so strange that I almost cannot speak of it. The last time I saw this ring, you had just been born. Your father made it for me."

"Father made this ring!" Cella was amazed.

"It was something I'd once seen—centuries old—in a

dream.'' A look of deep introspection was on Spina's face. ''And I wanted one exactly like it.'' She paused for a moment, lost in thought. ''The first one was worn by the Queen of Sumer!''

''Mother!''

''On her right hand. It was her favorite ring. I could never re-create the ring. It seemed wrong to make it for myself. But I had described it to your father once. And when I was carrying you, he made the ring for me. It is as beautiful as the queen's ring.''

''What happened to the queen's ring?''

At first Spina did not answer, and Cella wondered if her mother had heard what she said. Watching her, Cella felt that in the soundings of Spina's being were passions, memories and longings of which she knew nothing.

''It was lost,'' Spina said at last in a low voice. ''Lost ages ago.''

''Maybe this is the queen's ring.''

''Maybe it is.''

''What happened to your ring?''

''After you were born, your father and I took a vacation to Amalfi. We were in a boat off Ischia, not far from the shore. While we sailed I trailed my hand in the blue water. My fingers are strong but slim, and the ring was a little too large. Your father told me to be careful or I would lose the ring to the sea. And I would not get another one like it. But I wasn't careful. And I did lose it to the sea.''

''Is this your ring, Mother?'' Cella asked wonderingly. ''Or does it belong to the Queen of Sumer?''

''I don't know, Cella. If it belongs to the queen, then she was gracious and kind to send me her ring by the fish. Although she may wish it returned. If it is the ring your father made for me, perhaps I can keep it,'' Spina said gravely. ''And one day it will be yours. A gift from me and your father. To bless you on your way.'' Spina gave her a long, strange look.

Cella shook her head as she studied the ring. ''I never knew Father was so gifted. I must tell him tonight how beautiful it is.''

Spina's brooding eyes grew dark. ''You must not mention this ring to Sebastian. Ever.''

For an instant Cella gazed at Spina, then looked away saying nothing. She dismissed all questions from her mind. Cella had a deep and wordless communication with her mother. The two of them were aware that they were very much like each other, in a world that was different from either of them. And at moments like this she could feel how different too was their world from that of her father.

That was the last time she had seen the ring. Until now.

Feeling dazed and suddenly exhausted, Cella sat quietly, staring at the ring. What did it mean? She gazed around the room, but it told her nothing. It was still midafternoon, all white clouds and blue sky. Over and over again the room became suddenly bright and then subdued, as the shining white clouds rolled north across the sky. The fitful illumination was reflected in the polished surface of the desk and on the teakwood floor, carpeted only here and there with Oriental rugs.

Cella felt the floor becoming cold and she wanted her slippers. She rose from her chair and started toward the bedroom. Abruptly she stopped herself. There was some kind of answer waiting for her there. But she didn't want to know it. Not yet. She sat down again at her desk to stare at the ring. She yawned and rubbed her eyelids, trying to think of something else. She must write to Sebastian so that he would not worry about The House of Uni. She would take it over with firmness and authority. There was much to tell him without mentioning his Aphrodite . . . or this lost ring that Lexi had returned to her. Mists and confusion filled her brain. Sand drifted across her eyes as her head dropped forward and her eyes closed.

Fragments of the conversation with Lexi went swirling through her mind.

"I never heard of Tancredi. Tell me—who is he?" Cella fixed her eyes on Lexi with a terrible intensity of appeal.

"You mean Spina never told you? You don't know?"

"I know nothing," she said.

"I may have spoken out of turn. I thought you Etruscans always told each other. The ancient laws never questioned fatherhood." Lexi paused with puzzled brows. "Is it my place to do this?"

"You brought it up. Now you owe me an answer," Cella protested.

"That's true," Lexi said and sighed. "And if I've done damage, then it's already been done. What do you want to know?"

"Everything about Tancredi. Tancredi Vilanova."

"If you want to know more, ask Spina."

And even as Lexi said these words, there was a merging

and an interplay of identities. Lexi became Spina and Spina, Lexi. Until the two faces blended and all that remained was Spina. When Cella opened her eyes again, the room had grown darker. She had fallen asleep; the conversation with Lexi had been a dream.

Unconsciously she rose from her seat at the desk and this time deliberately walked into the bedroom. Her eyes seemed to see everywhere, but nothing registered. Only the photograph on top of her dressing table that she had taken from Jeremy Webb's home.

As she gazed at the picture of Spina and the beautiful young, black-haired man, her surprise was complete and overwhelming. She stood silently before it, her hands trembling. This was a revelation she was unprepared for.

That was Tancredi Vilanova. That was the man. As she gazed at his face she couldn't bargain or argue the recognition away. That was Tancredi. But who was he? And what did he have to do with the ring?

She went back to her study, walked slowly to the desk and took the ring out of the box. She slipped it on the third finger of her right hand. Spina had sent it to her. Spina and Tancredi. She stared around the room, looking for something, and her eyes came to a stop at the curtained alcove at the far side of the room. Afterward she could hardly define the impulse that had finally possessed her. She only knew that the depths of her nature had been loosened and that she was borne forward on their current to the very fate she had sought for years. She walked toward the alcove, parted the curtains and entered slowly. The candles were never lit during the week, and the only light entering the alcove came when she drew the curtains aside. She watched with reverence as the soft, late afternoon light flowed over the altar of Uni.

She knelt at the altar, admitting the inexplicable and strange to an increasing familiarity.

She was aware of nothing beyond her need to know who Tancredi was. Nothing but that knowledge would satisfy her. As she accepted her need, the questions she asked seemed to be answered by the goddess even at the moment of their being asked. And while she listened, the world became peacefully clear. It was almost as if the course she must follow were being dictated to her. Her people were of an ancient race, and their blood was as venerable and chaste as truth. Their knowledge was her knowledge; she must let herself find the way.

She took a deep breath, letting the world vanish little by

little. She shivered with sudden cold as the mist gathered around her.

Then, like a curtain being pulled back, the mist vanished, and she watched the young Cella follow the doctor down a long corridor and into an elevator that took them to another floor, the number of which she did not notice. The young Cella saw nothing except the back of the doctor. When she entered the room where her mother was lying in bed, she began to tremble. She "saw" her mother was dying.

Spina waited for the doctor to leave before beginning to speak. "Cella, come here, darling." Spina's voice was very weak. Her eyes were closed, and Cella wondered how she could speak at all. She walked quickly to her mother's bedside and kissed her lightly on the forehead. Her skin was damp and cool. She showed no sign of having felt the kiss. "I want you to listen carefully to me," she said. "I haven't much strength. Or much time."

"Yes, Mother," Cella said from a world that had been drained of color.

"My dear one, I have always felt a duty to the past and have tried to keep the old religion of beauty and joy alive." Spina was silent then, as if she weren't sure where she was or whom she was speaking to. After a while, Cella didn't know how long, she seemed to grope her way back. "Cella, every piece of jewelry I have created glowed with the beauty of the ancient religion. A religion of sunlit freedom and joy. Of savagery too. But of rich life." Her purpose was back and she seemed to grow stronger. "For me to forget our past, to annihilate it in the present, would have been a sin."

"Mother," Cella said gently, "I understand. I will do the work as you did."

"No, darling, you do not understand." Spina raised her upper body perhaps an inch from the bed and then slumped down.

Cella all but screamed, "Mother, please! You mustn't. You mustn't strain yourself."

"I know. But I must make you understand." Spina's voice faltered again.

"I do understand, Mother. I'll do whatever you tell me to do." Spina's hand fumbled toward Cella's, and Cella took her mother's limp fingers into her firm young grasp. A look of love passed between them.

"All right. Now listen carefully." Spina's voice seemed to come from far away. "There is another kind of religion abroad in the world today. One I do not love."

Cella had a sudden feeling that her mother was looking not at her but into her. "Yes, Mother," she said.

"You will understand. You are my daughter." Spina sighed. "But Marcus has never understood. Marcus has been infected. He knows and he is glad that this is not a time for the old gods of joy and passion. This is the time of money. Money is the god of the people." Spina seemed to be drawing her thoughts from deep down in her being. "So now it will be up to you."

"What will, Mother?" The look of tenderness in Cella's eyes was muddied with fear.

"The House of Uni. The house that your grandmother started. That I have built. Its days are coming to an end."

Cella would have been terrified if she still had it in her to be terrified. She stared at her mother, not knowing what to think. The House of Uni? It was coming to an end? Yet never in her whole life had her mother said anything that Cella doubted. "Tell me, Mother," she said at last. "Why must it end?"

"Because it no longer has a purpose. In The House of Uni we re-create the beautiful jewelry of the ancients, glowing with the wisdom of the old gods." Her mother's voice was very tired. "But today the people are blind. The beauty, the wisdom of the past, are not what they desire."

"What must I do?"

"Sebastian, like Marcus, worships the god of money. It is for that god that he works so conscientiously. But Sebastian cannot create without me. Or without you. He needs your help. Or one day he will begin to make exact copies of the things the ancients did. When he does this, you must not help him. You will know that is the time when The House of Uni is over."

"You don't want me to help my father?"

"Cella, darling, Marcus is Sebastian's son. Marcus is in his image." There was another long silence during which Spina didn't speak. "But you are not like him," she finally said.

"I know."

"Do you know why?"

Cella swallowed. "No."

"Because you are not his daughter."

Cella stared at Spina dumbly. Finally she managed to ask, "Sebastian is not my father?"

"No. Tancredi Vilanova was your father. He was brilliant, gifted and passionate. His glance had a rare depth and clearness such as one sees in the eyes of a young lion.'' She gazed at Cella unseeingly as the low and clear cry of a bird drifted in through the hospital window. ''Did you hear the bird? That used to mean that something fortunate was to happen to me. Maybe it is fortunate that I tell you the truth before I go.''

Cella had found her mother's words almost unintelligible. ''Tell me something about my father.''

''There is nothing much to tell. He grew up in Istanbul. His mother was a Turkish woman. His father, Enrico Vilanova, was a distant cousin of your uncle Victor. And when he was a young man, we met at one of our vast family parties in Genoa. We fell in love.''

''But you had many lovers.''

''This was different. Tancredi was the handsomest man in the world. There was a legend that the goddess of love, Aphrodite herself, had kissed him. And given him her necklace. He was beautiful. We loved each other deeply.''

''Then where does my father—Sebastian—come in?''

What Spina was telling her was as unexplainable as a fragment of meteorite dropped on a sidewalk.

''He knew about Tancredi. He didn't care. You know the Etruscan way as well as I do. Tancredi and I lived a glorious life. Then he died. We both knew he was to die. He could 'see.' The way I can 'see.' That was why I stayed with Sebastian.''

''How did he die?''

''It was an accident.'' Dusk was beginning to fill Spina's eyes.

''How?''

''The Red Guard blew up his car. By mistake.''

''He died in a car?''

Spina smiled an odd smile. ''Yes, we knew we would have the same death.''

''Oh, Mother!'' There was grief in Cella's voice, and tenderness.

Spina had sunk into her own thoughts, but the sound of Cella's voice called her back. ''No, child. We will be together, returned to our true place in the order of things.''

They were both quite still for a minute.

Cella had complete faith in her mother. She closed her eyes for an instant as if in prayer. When she opened them she said in a whisper, ''I promise you, Mother, I will do as you say about The House of Uni.''

Her mother's face began to glow with a strange, triumphant brightness. Cella saw again what she had seen before: that her mother had the same face and the power behind it as the ancient statue of Uni. The atmosphere of the room became resplendent, as if the old gods had suddenly revealed themselves, smiling, enigmatic, full of joy and beauty. Her mother's deep, dark eyes looked straight at Cella. She spoke softly.

"Cella, my daughter, we fail because we are too small in our vision. Too small for the ways of the gods."

Then with a sudden, weary movement she turned her head to the side and closed her eyes. The light slowly faded from the room.

Chapter Thirty-one

Jason Lord returned to his office feeling frustrated and furious. He'd spent most of the day checking people and chasing about New York, looking for Cella Taggard. Through his art-world contacts it was easy for him to learn that she'd canceled a lunch date with a Met curator and an afternoon appointment with a noted collector. Juliana was completely useless. Yesterday, Cella had given her the morning off, and then last evening had telephoned her at home and told her to open the shop herself today. At the earliest, Cella didn't expect to return to the shop for another week. Juliana had no idea where she was. Cella being Cella, she could be in Rome, Bombay or Copenhagen. What infuriated Jason was that he believed Juliana had told the truth. And another week of waiting was more than he could stand.

Cella had made a fool of him. The way all women made fools of men. He didn't hate women. But he saw clearly what they were. And what they wanted. Sly and devious, they took a man's love. His very soul. And then they cheated on him, laughing at the poor bastard. He had loved two women and they were both cheats. Both liars. Secretly they wanted to make him crawl on his knees and beg for their love. It was their nature. But he'd had enough. Cella was the last straw. He would punish her the way she deserved to be punished.

Then the blinking red light on the answering machine caught his eye. A message had come in after Emory had left for the day. Absentmindedly, he turned the machine on, and the unmistakable voice of Toby Phipps filled the room.

"Emory, dear boy," Toby boomed forth. "My birthday party has had to be postponed. I'm devastated, but Cella Taggard called me from her home in Sands Point. She's resting. If she weren't an Etruscan, I'd think she was a Catholic and had gone on a retreat. I don't know what's wrong with her, but she doesn't want to mingle. So until she recovers, there's no party. That's the way it goes. I'll talk to you tomorrow, you beautiful boy. Oh, yes. This is Toby Phipps, just in case you thought it was Prince Charming. Bye.'' The machine turned itself off.

Jason rewound the tape and listened to the message for a second time, his head throbbing.

No wonder I couldn't find her, he said to himself. He dialed information and asked for the Taggard number in Sands Point.

The operator asked, ''Which Taggard do you want? There are three. Sebastian Taggard. Marcus Taggard. And a C. Taggard.''

''That's the one,'' Jason said, struggling to hide his impatience. ''C. Taggard. What's the number?''

''Five one six - six seven two - eight nine three four.''

''Thank you. Could you give me the address?''

''They all have the same address. Lands End. Hofstetter Lane in Sands Point.''

''Thank you,'' Jason said again, then hung up. He walked briskly to his office and went directly to the library. This time there was no reluctance in his manner when he brought down the book box. Before bringing the freshly laundered handkerchief to his nose, he sprinkled a few drops of Shalimar on the cloth. He then breathed deeply of the heady fragrance. Almost immediately he could feel his penis lengthen and begin to harden. Controlling himself, he returned the handkerchief to the box and closed the lid.

''Not this time. This time I'll do better,'' he said aloud to the empty room as he replaced the box on the top shelf. What had been, had been. It was time to add new pictures to his store of memories, not just relive the old ones.

Jason entered his sleeping quarters at the back of the office. They consisted of a bedroom and a bathroom. From a large oak chest at the foot of the bed he removed a black jumpsuit, a pair of black jogging shoes and a makeup kit. He dropped the jumpsuit and shoes on the bed and went into his bathroom to apply the black makeup. But halfway through the application he stopped and stared at his image in the mirror. No. The makeup was wrong. He wanted Cella Taggard to recognize him before she felt the heat of his pleasure. Marina would come after Cella. The Great Whore herself. He smiled grimly at the mirror. He was an exterminator whose duty was to cleanse the world of corruption.

With rapid, savage motions, Jason cleaned his face. He combed his hair in preparation for the evening ahead. His

one regret was that he couldn't live this night over and over
again.

Anton Vilanova entered the Sixty-sixth Street police sta-
tion. He walked up to the desk sergeant and said, "I'm Anton
Vilanova. I received a message from Lieutenant Ben Stein.
He asked me to meet him here as quickly as I could."

When the sergeant heard the name, he left the desk and
went into the back room. He returned in a minute and said,
"Stein expects you. He's back there." The sergeant jerked a
thumb toward the door he'd just closed.

Anton opened the door and blinked. The room was painted
a dull brown and was brilliantly lit by a single bulb hanging
from the ceiling. The only furnishings were a small, oblong,
gunmetal-gray table and six hard wooden chairs. At the far
end of the room was a second door consisting of steel bars,
and beyond the bars he could see part of a series of small
cells. Holding pens for prisoners being transferred from the
precinct to one of the main city or county jails. Ben Stein,
his overcoat and suit coat hanging from the back of a chair,
wearing a black yarmulke, lounged in another chair, eyes
closed. When Anton appeared, he opened his eyes.

"Where's Cella Taggard?"

"Why do you want to know?" Anton had his own questions to ask.

"Where is she?"

"She's resting in Sands Point. Something happened. She
won't tell me what, but I think it has something to do with
her father. And she wants to be alone while she works things
through. Is she in some kind of danger?"

Stein ignored the question. "Does Jason Lord have any
idea where she is?"

"I don't know."

"He's looking for her."

"How do you know that?"

"He dropped in at the House of Uni and quizzed the
woman." Stein consulted his notes. "Juliana. She isn't the
only one he questioned. There's a list."

"All right, he's looking for her. You haven't told me why."

"Probably to rape her. And then to kill her," Stein said in
a matter-of-fact tone.

Anton stared at him. Then found his voice. "Christ! He
must be crazy."

"An astute observation. Rivaled only by the comment that
'life is unfair.' Yes, he is crazy. A homicidal psychotic, to

use the technical jargon. Or one could say a paranoid schizophrenic. That's okay for the psychiatrists.'' Stein's face showed mild resentment. "But not for me. In my mind he's a rapist and a killer. A homicidal maniac."

Anton's mind was in a turmoil. Dr. Jason Lord, the celebrated seeker after truth, a homicidal maniac? "For God's sake! How do you know? And why Cella? I don't want to scare the daylights out of her just so you can have a field day in the press."

"I don't need any more field days in the press," Ben Stein said with some distaste. "What I am trying to do is save a couple of human lives. Do you understand?"

"I am trying. I dislike Jason Lord. But when you ask me to believe he is a killer . . ."

"You have heard of Sigmund Freud?"

"Of course."

"And you have heard of the Oedipus complex?"

"The Greek tragedies are full of it."

"So are the American tragedies. It applies to all small boys who want to fuck their mothers. Some small boys never grow up."

"You mean Jason wants to—hmm—fuck Marina?"

"Very badly. He's been in a sexual frenzy to do it for a number of years," Ben Stein said thoughtfully.

"How do you know all this?"

"I have evidence that he attacked Hans Etzel, one of Marina Lord's former lovers—when she was still married to Lawrence Lord. He castrated Hans Etzel."

"You know that for a fact?"

"I know it for a fact."

"How do you know it wasn't Lawrence Lord?"

"On the evening Etzel was castrated, Lord was giving a lecture to The Society of Painting Lovers in Newton, Mass."

Anton said nothing for a minute. "Sebastian was nearly castrated."

Ben Stein's eyes gleamed. "At last you begin to see connections. Taggard was nearly castrated by someone bigger than he—he is not a small man—and by someone far stronger. In fact unbelievably strong. Taggard is no weakling. This description of great strength does not fit the slim Lawrence Lord. But it does fit his son."

Anton shook his head in bewilderment.

"You want to know why. I'd say in the case of Etzel and Taggard that vengeance was Dr. Lord's motive. They were lucky he wasn't ready for murder. Jason Lord is an intelligent man. A thinking man. But beneath his official, composed, outward exterior lives a human being pursued by lust for his mother. And jealousy. It has driven him mad. He feels rejected and scorned by her. So his passion has grown more and more violent through hatred, and a repeated realization that he can't have her. That's why he raped and murdered Josie Frankenberg. He was seeking the ultimate orgasm.''

"Josie was in Marina's suite that night," Anton said in a low voice, remembering.

"Very good, my friend—you made another connection. That's where Josie was. In Marina's suite. And Jason Lord entered in the guise of her masseur. When he discovered Josie wasn't his mother, he was furious. He felt he'd been betrayed.''

"What if it had been Marina?"

"Then he might simply have raped her and let her live.'' Stein shrugged his shoulders. "Or he might not. Remember, we are groping around in the dark jungle of the heart. Trying to sniff out the secret caves of passion. Of lust. Because lust is what we're dealing with.''

"Did Jason Lord kill Phillip Mckay?"

"Yes. Thinking Mckay was still his mother's lover.''

Anton was trying to absorb it all very quickly. "You have proof of what you've been saying?''

"I have enough evidence to ask the district attorney for a warrant to arrest Jason Lord for murder, attempted murder, assault. The warrant is being prepared now.''

"You'll excuse me if I feel slightly sick. But I believe you,'' Anton said. "Only one thing I don't understand. Why Cella? What makes you think he's now after Cella? She's not his mother.''

"I'm a detective. I've spent my life confronting wild beasts. Human animals. With bloody fangs. I've saved the lives of quite a few people. By my wits. I've stayed alive the same way. Now I have a hunch. Cella Taggard is Jason Lord's next stop. And his intentions are violent.''

Anton stood up quickly. "I'd better get out to Sands Point immediately.''

"I agree. Be prepared. He's very strong," Ben Stein said in a dry voice. "Sands Point is out of my jurisdiction. But I'll inform the Nassau County police to watch the Taggard house. Though at the moment it seems Lord doesn't know where Cella Taggard is.''

"I'll leave as soon as I get out of here.''

"Good. You keep a twenty-four-hour guard on her.'' He

handed Anton a card. "Here are my home and office numbers. Should Jason Lord appear, find a way to call me. And don't try to take him on yourself. I don't need any dead heroes. Too many people have died or been mutilated already."

He watched as Anton hurried from the room. "Reilly," he called out. When the sergeant poked his head in the doorway, he said, "Did you get all that down?"

"Yes, Lieutenant."

"Do you think he can handle Lord if he shows up?"

"As easily as pigs fly."

"That's what I think too."

With Spina's words still in her head, Cella picked up the telephone and called Air France. She reserved two seats on the Concorde to Paris for the day after tomorrow. One for herself, one for Anton.

She had asked for a sign, and a sign had been given. The memory of Spina's final words, buried for so many years in her brain, had surfaced at last. When she needed them most. Now she knew what to do. With both Aphrodite necklaces. And with The House of Uni.

Sebastian had begun making copies. That was the signal the powers had sent: that The House of Uni must end. Now she understood why she felt so different than Sebastian about making money. And forgeries. He was not her real father. Tancredi Vilanova was. Spina and Tancredi must have been a lot alike. And Spina had expected her, when the time came, to behave in a manner that would make their love proud. She nodded at the sapphire eyes sparkling on the ring on her finger.

As she walked around her study Cella thought about Sebastian, Spina and Tancredi. Especially Tancredi. From Spina's dying words and the picture of him on Cella's dressing table, he looked like a romantic adventurer, a man of great courage and charm. Also intelligence. Killed in a crazy accident by the Red Guard. Simply in the wrong place at the wrong time. She wondered if her mother would have divorced her father to marry—Cella shook her head. Sebastian is not my father. Tancredi is. Will I always think of Sebastian as my father and have to correct myself?

She picked up the picture of Spina and Tancredi and stared at it, trying to see herself in him. Physically it was easy. They were so much alike. But psychologically it was very difficult. She had no idea what he was like. All that was knowable about Tancredi Vilanova had died with Spina. She held the picture close, trying to breathe life into it. Dreaming of the wonderful man her real father must have been, for Spina had loved him so much she bore him a child. Cella was a love child, the kind of child she would have with Anton. Such children were especially valued by the Etruscans. They believed such children had a fearlessness toward life that children born of cooler matings never knew. The primal forces of life having been present at their birth, when they met them again as adults, they would know how to deal with them. Yes, Cella decided, Spina and Tancredi must be pleased with her.

In a way she was glad. Now she had two fathers. Even as in the old Etruscan way of life. And it made her think of a quotation from another religion. From the New Testament. Something like, "Render unto Caesar that which is Caesar's and unto the goddess that which is hers."

She would do that. She would render unto Sebastian that which was his. The eleven million dollars Darlene would pay for his perfect forgery. And she would render unto the old gods, to the goddess of love, to Tancredi's Turkey, the true Aphrodite necklace. She would insist that Sebastian take it back from Marina and let her sell it to Lexi for one dollar. He would have his eleven million for his masterpiece. She'd brook no objections.

And The House of Uni would change. She would tell Sebastian she'd made up her mind. They must take the current inventory and one way or another sell the jewelry as Cella Classics. None of the pieces would be sold as ancient jewelry.

The weather had turned blustery and she stretched and yawned, looking forward to the late evening and telephoning Anton. But first she would rest in front of a warm fire. She needed to put a little cushion of sanity in her bank account on which she might draw in the future; living with the truth often made hard demands.

As twilight turned to dusk, her telephone rang.

"Anton?" she said, picking up the receiver. "I was going to call you."

All she heard was a click as though someone had hung up. Unconcerned, she replaced the receiver in its cradle.

She was in the middle of preparing dinner, wearing only a quilted dressing gown and slippers, when the front doorbell rang. She answered the door and was surprised and disconcerted to discover that Jason Lord was standing a few feet away. He was wearing a black raincoat, below which she saw he had on black warm-up pants and black jogging shoes.

"Jason!" she exclaimed. "What are you doing here?"

"Aren't you going to invite me in?" Jason said in a strained voice. "It's bloody cold outside."

"Sorry. Come on in. Take off your coat and relax. I've got a good fire going, and I'm making dinner. How did you know I was here?"

A satisfied smile crossed Jason's face. Now that he knew the future, he could ignore Cella's sexual effect on him. In fact, it added spice to the game. He tossed his coat on a chair and said, "I phoned earlier, and you answered the ring."

Cella recalled the click after she had picked up the receiver. "That was you? Why didn't you say hello?"

"I didn't want to talk to you. I wanted to see you. Besides, you might have told someone I called. That would have been a mistake."

An oppressive wariness rose in Cella. There was something odd going on with Jason, and she had no intention of allowing him to come too close to her.

"Look, Jason," she said bluntly, "I came out here to be alone, and frankly, you're intruding. At any other time I'd be happy to see you. But not tonight. So why don't you be a nice guy and get the hell out of here?"

"But I'm not a nice guy. Haven't you figured that out?"

"Then be a shit for all I care. Just go away." With that she turned her back on him and headed for the kitchen. There was a phone in there. She'd call the police in Port Washington. They'd get rid of Jason Lord for her. But when she lifted the receiver, she felt the first tremors of fear. The line was dead. She snapped the buttons that shifted the extension to her father's line—it was also dead. So was Marcus' line.

She spun about and there was Jason standing in the doorway, dressed in a black jogging outfit. Exactly as Sebastian had described his assailant. Everything fitted except for the black face, but Cella suddenly knew that Jason Lord had been her father's attacker. And she was next on his list.

Before she could say a word, Jason volunteered the information. "I cut the lines," he said calmly. "I told you I didn't want anyone to know I might be here. Or have any interruptions."

Since her physical strength was only a fraction of Jason's, Cella made an effort to dominate the situation by force of will. "And I said I don't want you here. Go away!"

"Not until I've done what I came to do."

As Cella said, "All right. Let's have it. Exactly what have you come to do?" she reached behind her and fumbled for a kitchen knife in the knife stand. When she held the carving knife in front of her, the expression on her face was fierce. "Game's over, Jason. I don't give a damn what brought you here. Go away!"

Jason's laughter had a crazy edge. "You think that silly little toy can stop me? Any more than the two policemen guarding this house could?" Before Cella could do more than make a futile threatening motion with the knife, Jason was on her, his huge hand clamped around her wrist, twisting it painfully until she dropped the weapon. He then kicked the knife halfway across the kitchen floor. With a sudden, backhand blow, he struck Cella across the forehead, stunning her. He picked her up easily by the legs, and draping her legs over his shoulders with her head and body trailing down his back, he carried her into the living room and up the stairs. Once on the second floor, he searched for her bedroom. The third door he opened revealed an unmade bed and all the markings of a woman's room. Unceremoniously, he dumped the still-dazed Cella on the bed. He then ripped a pillowcase into strips and bound her hands to the headboard and her feet to two small posts that were part of the footboard. That done, he gagged her mouth with a portion of the ripped pillowcase. Finally he tore open her dressing gown, exposing her nude body, and stared hungrily at her breasts, her belly, her crotch. Then he sat in a chair and waited. He had plenty of time. He wanted Cella to be completely conscious. It was important that she know everything that was happening to her. Until the very end.

Anton fought his way through the Northern State Parkway traffic. The rain slick had caused an accident somewhere up ahead. Finally the traffic slowed to a bumper-to-bumper crawl, and all he could do was grip the wheel tightly with whitened knuckles and curse.

Jason Lord dampened a washcloth and patted the bruise that was developing on the side of Cella's head. He hoped he hadn't hit her too hard, and when she opened her eyes, groaning lightly, he exhaled slowly with relief. Her eyes opened wider with terror when she became conscious of her nudity. And how vulnerable it made her feel. The muscles in her arms and legs strained to break free of the bonds. The effort was useless.

"I know you're wondering what I'm going to do to you and why," Jason said in too rational a voice. "I'm going to make love to you. The way a man should make love to a whore. The way I never could make love to that other whore. My mother. And then I'm going to kill you. You'll be first.'' He might easily have been talking about taking her to the opening night of a show. And after the show they would go to a theatrical hangout and wait for the reviews to come out.

"You're a whore. All Etruscans are whores. You corrupt anyone you come in contact with. Look what Anton did to my father." The tears gathered behind Jason's eyes as he said these words. "My father was an honest art history professor until he met Vilanova. Now he's disgraced. Forced to leave his position. A laughingstock. But no one cares about Vilanova.''

Cella heard a very slight sound and turned her head toward the door. Her heart stopped with relief. Anton was lounging against the jamb.

"I would say it was the other way around, Lord," Anton said in a lazy, relaxed voice. "Your father didn't need to be seduced. He was as corrupt as a rotten piece of melon, ripe, juicy and too sweet. Anybody who was passing by could have plucked him. But as it happened, I didn't pick him. He picked me. The whole swindle was your father's idea. All I did was put up seed money.''

"You're a liar," Jason Lord screamed as he hurled himself at Anton. But Anton slipped to one side and caught Jason with a backhand chop to the neck. Jason was moving so fast, Anton's aim was a shade off, and his hand bounced off the knotted muscle protecting Jason's shoulder. Like a ballet dancer, Anton slid to the center of the bedroom and waited for Jason's next charge. If Jason ever got a firm grip on him, the fight would be over, but if Anton could keep the man at arm's length and box him, he might just be able to wear him out.

Anton warily circled Jason, drilling left jabs at his unprotected head. Jason had no real idea of how to box. With each punch, his head snapped back but his body kept moving slowly, ponderously, forward. His arms were extended like two arms of a nutcracker, waiting to close on Anton. Jab, jab, right cross. As hard a right cross as Anton had ever thrown in his life. It could have felled an ox, but all Jason did was step back two paces, shake his head to clear it and move forward again. Blood was oozing from cuts over his eyes, from his nose, from the corners of his mouth. An uninformed observer would have said that Anton was winning the fight hands down. But a knowing critic would have no-

ticed that Anton was starting to breathe heavily and that his
punches were losing their snap.

Suddenly Jason stepped inside Anton's jab and wrapped his
arms about him. His arms closed tighter and tighter as Anton
rained ineffective chops to the back of Jason's neck. Jason's
muscles were so thick and corded it was like pounding concrete. Gradually the breath was being forced from Anton's
lungs while Jason's arms tightened inexorably. With a desperate strength he didn't know he had, Anton drove his knee
into Jason's crotch, and a gagging sound came from Jason's
throat as he relaxed his grip. It was only seconds, but that
was all Anton needed to twist himself away from the bone-
crushing hold. Before Jason could recover, Anton hit him
with a left and a right and a left and a right. His fists were a
blur. Jason didn't try to avoid the blows. All he did was lean
forward into the punches. When he recovered himself, he
moved forward again, his face a hideous mask of blood but
his strength unimpaired.

Desperately Anton tired to think of something different.
He could not keep playing toreador to Jason's bull. Sooner or
later the bull was going to catch him again. He'd been lucky
the first time. He doubted he'd be as lucky again. Tables and
chairs went flying as Anton tried to put some furniture between Jason and himself. But as quickly as he was able to
push a chair in Jason's way, just as quickly did Jason hurl it
to one side. And through it all, Cella's wide-open, horror-
filled eyes were following the struggle while she strained fu-
tilely to break free of her bonds.

The fight was fought in silence, each man conserving his
strength as best as he could. Jason reached for Anton, but
when Anton set himself for one last punch, his foot slipped
on the rug and it was too late. Jason had him. He lifted Anton
off the ground and hurled him across the room. Anton was
groggy as he staggered to his feet. Slowly, enjoying Anton's
useless attempt to gather himself, Jason moved toward him.
Again his arms were outstretched like a lover seeking to embrace his beloved.

Suddenly sirens broke the sound of the men's heavy breathing. A high-pitched *whoop! Whoop! Whoop!* Several police
cars were moving fast up the driveway. Jason hesitated,
stopped and listened. The cars pulled up in front of the house,
and a man's voice amplified by a bullhorn could be heard.

"Jason Lord, this is Lieutenant Ben Stein. Come out with
your hands up, or we're coming in after you."

Jason's eyes roamed wildly around the room, staring first

at Anton and then at Cella. He wiped his bleeding mouth with the back of his hand. "I'll be back," he said in a voice that was unrecognizable. And he hurled himself through the door.

Anton staggered more than walked to Cella's bed. Quickly he removed the gag from her mouth and untied the knots that held her arms. As soon as her arms were free, she hugged him close to her.

They both looked up as a volley of shots was fired outside the house. Then there were more shots. And more shots.

"He got away," Anton said quietly. He loosened Cella's arms from around his neck, stood up, took a deep breath and winced. "Christ, I've never known anyone that strong."

Anton untied Cella's legs, and she pulled her robe around her. "He was going to rape me and kill me," she said unsteadily. "He called me a whore like his mother. What's the matter with him?" When Anton didn't answer, Cella felt a terrible shudder run through her.

A half hour later, over drinks in the library, Ben Stein explained that he had a warrant for Jason's arrest. After he had tried to call Cella and found the lines were out of order, he'd known there was trouble. That had started him moving immediately. He had called the Port Washington police and, by using his police siren and driving hell-bent for leather, had arrived just in time.

"Just in time," Anton echoed. "I'm pretty good with my hands, but in another five minutes he'd have had me."

"We have to call my father and warn him," Cella said. "Jason said as soon as he finished with me, Marina was next. His own mother," she concluded lamely. "The man is crazy."

"He is," Ben Stein agreed. "Whatever happened to Lord happened when he was very young. A teenager or younger. Call your father, Miss Taggard, and warn him to be on the lookout. I'll have the airlines watched and notify Interpol. Sooner or later, we'll get him."

"I hope it's sooner. None of us are safe until Jason Lord is behind bars," Anton said.

Cella checked her watch. "It's five-thirty in the morning at the villa. I'll call around eight. That'll give my father time to notify the Italian police to be on the watch. But I don't believe Jason Lord will ever be taken prisoner," she said with uneasy certainty. It was as though she could see the future through her mother's eyes.

═══ Chapter Thirty-two ═══

Early the next morning, while Anton still slept, Cella changed their flight reservations for that afternoon at one o'clock. Then she telephoned Juliana and woke her up. She told her she would have to mind the store for about two weeks. And she was to sell nothing until Cella returned, except Cella Classics, if a customer was interested.

"What about Darlene Schiller?" Juliana inquired drowsily. "She called three times yesterday for you. She's anxious to get her hands on the Aphrodite necklace."

"All right. I'll call her. If the price is right, I'll call you back."

Cella then put in a call to Darlene Schiller in Washington D.C. Yes, Mrs. Schiller was up. She was an early riser, the maid said. "Your name again, please?"

"Cella Taggard."

Reluctantly the maid agreed to interrupt Mrs. Schiller with the name Cella Taggard. Within minutes Darlene's voice was singing away on the telephone.

"Cella, darling. How sweet of you to call."

Cella had no time for social pleasantries. "I'm leaving for Paris at once. I'll be gone for a while. Juliana told me you called three times yesterday."

"I did." Darlene was all charm. "I had lunch yesterday with Lexi and she told me her bid. She said you were thinking it over."

"She told you what she bid?" Cella sounded surprised.

"Well, she's so young. New to the game." Darlene's voice was all smiles. "So, as promised, I'm topping it by ten percent."

"That's eleven million dollars."

"You took a course in higher mathematics. Will you tell Lexi?"

"No. I won't conduct a bidding war. Eleven will do. When do you want to pick it up?"

"This morning," Darlene said eagerly. "Before Lexi decides she hasn't offered enough."

"Juliana will have the necklace boxed and ready. Bring a cashier's check."

"Dear Cella. It's a pleasure to do business with you." That ended the conversation.

Cella called Juliana back and told her Darlene would appear that morning to pick up the Aphrodite. She would leave with Juliana a cashier's check for eleven million dollars. Juliana was to deposit it in Sebastian's personal account at the Morgan. Cella would pick up the deposit slip on her way to the airport.

Then Cella went into the bedroom and woke Anton for the drive back to Manhattan.

"Right," said Anton as he slid out of bed. He watched Cella dress hastily. She seemed taut as a stretched wire. Touch her and she'd twang.

"Take it easy, darling, or you'll levitate."

Cella nodded. "I know. Please get dressed."

"I'm on my way."

Once she was in Manhattan, the time difference was such that she could call Sebastian. Just the sound of his voice relieved her anxiety. When she told him all there was to tell about Jason Lord, his comment was typical of the man:

"Are you sure you're all right?"

"Honestly, I'm fine. Anton and Ben Stein rescued me."

It fascinated Cella that even though Sebastian had known from the day she was born that she was not his daughter, his attitude had always been that of a loving father. Now he dismissed the danger to himself with a cavalier arrogance.

"I'll carry my pistol with me at all times. If I see Lord I'll shoot him on sight. Like any mad dog."

"Just be careful," Cella pleaded. "And Jason aside, I have some wonderful news for you."

"You sold my Aphrodite?"

"For a very pretty penny. I'll give you the deposit slip at the wedding breakfast."

"How much?"

"Can't you wait until the wedding?"

"I'm curious."

"Then call the Morgan bank and find out. I'm having Juliana deposit the check in your personal account."

"Aaaah." Sebastian sighed contentedly. Then he went on.

"Have you given any further thought to our discussion about The House of Uni?"

"A great deal of thought. We have lots to talk about. Jason Lord and your marriage aren't the only reasons I'm flying over."

"The House of Uni is a very good reason."

"So is the real Aphrodite." The words just slipped out.

"The Astarte. You mean Marina's necklace?" Sebastian sounded guarded.

"We have a lot to talk about," Cella repeated weakly.

"I've wanted to talk to you about the necklace, too." Sebastian's voice was odd. "But aside from all that, I look forward to seeing you."

"So do I, Father." Cella said "father" out of habit. And then smiled. "I'll see you shortly."

She had barely put the phone down when it startled her by ringing.

"Hello?"

"Miss Taggard, this is Lieutenant Stein."

Cella's heart gave a great leap of hope. "You've caught Jason Lord?"

"Not quite," Ben Stein said dryly. "He boarded a Lufthansa flight last night before Interpol got its act together. But they know he landed in Frankfurt this morning. Lord could be anywhere now."

"Not anywhere. He's on his way to our villa in Tuscany," Cella said stonily.

"I have the unpleasant suspicion you're right."

"I am. He means to find his mother and my father. I just called Sebastian and warned him about Lord. I told him Anton and I are flying over today. From Paris we'll catch a flight to Genoa. Given the speed of the Concorde, it's the quickest way."

"At least Interpol is alerted," Stein said wearily. "Maybe they'll pick him up at the border. And if he goes near the villa, the Italian police are ready. They'll get him."

"They won't. Jason Lord will never be caught by any policeman." Cella had never been as sure of anything as she was of that fact. It was the Taggards and Vilanovas versus Jason Lord. The gods would decide who would be left alive at the end of the struggle. "Thank you, Lieutenant. I must call Anton now."

Anton picked up the phone immediately. As he listened, he quietly cursed Interpol. "I'll be by in twenty minutes."

* * *

Due to the time difference, Anton and Cella landed at Orly Airport at eight o'clock in the evening. Even so, they were able to arrange for a night flight to Genoa. But once in Genoa, they had to wait until morning before they could rent a car for the drive to the villa.

Before they left Genoa, they called Stein in New York. There was no word concerning the whereabouts of Jason Lord. He'd dropped off the face of the earth.

"Not very likely," was Cella's comment. He was somewhere near the villa. They were racing against time.

Anton drove at a clip that made even the undauntable Italian drivers blanch. As they neared the villa, Cella felt—as she always did—as if she were entering a world deeply and sweetly familiar to her. She was coming home, to a place that belonged to her and where she belonged more deeply than anywhere else in the world. The villages they hurtled through, the carts and cars lining the sides of the road, the luminous blue sky and the tall, straight cypress trees that reached for the sky all seemed to be slowly and gravely acknowledging her return.

Finally they arrived at the gate to the villa. The bumpy driveway forced Anton to brake his speed, and he skidded to a stop at the entrance. The door to the villa was open, and Cella ran from the car into the house. The entrance was ominously silent.

Cella found Celeste on the floor, blood running from her mouth. She knelt on her knees and held Celeste's head in her lap while Anton hurried into the kitchen for a damp cloth. "What happened, Celeste? For heaven's sake! What happened?" Cella asked.

Celeste tried to talk. "A man. Big, big man. He hit me. He was looking for Commendatore Taggard. And Madam—Madam Lord."

"Where are they?" Cella asked. Anton wiped her mouth gently with the cloth. But Celeste could only stare at Cella with glazed eyes.

Anton left again, and when he returned he placed a pillow under Celeste's head. "I called Dr. Antonio," he said to Cella and then, turning to Celeste, asked softly, *"Dove* Signor Taggard?"

Celeste seemed to find some strength. "With la signora. A picnic on the mountain."

"Which mountain?" Cella asked cautiously.

"You know, signorina. Your mountain. La Signora Spina's mountain. The old one." Her serious eyes were on Cella's face. "Signor not want to go, but the signora insist. She think it be good."

"And the big man? Does he know where they went?" Cella asked.

"*Sì.* "

"Rest, Celeste. Dr. Antonio will be here very soon," Cella said, standing up quickly. "Now we must catch the big man."

"Catch him. He is a bad one," Celeste said faintly.

"Come on, Anton," Cella said as she turned and headed for the side door. She knew exactly where she was going and sprinted for the path that led up the mountainside. A flock of birds nervously circled skyward. Cella stopped for an instant, her face going pale. "Exactly the same as when Mother died," she said in a whisper.

She was off again. Up the mountainside, following the winding trail. Then she stopped. Frozen. The earth beneath them was trembling. She had heard of this happening, but it never seemed real. Now it was. Something which Cella always believed was immovable had started to move. The earth under them rose and stretched itself. Shaking with colossal laughter. It seemed to send her a message even while it tossed and shifted beneath their feet.

Cella went sprawling on the ground. Anton tumbled on top of her. Another shock came seconds later. The earth rumbled and made a loud, lamenting sound. Now it was sobbing. High above them, the mountain shuddered, tossing boulders and dirt down its sides. Anton lifted Cella in his arms and carried her to the side of the trail.

Earth, rocks and boulders were plunging toward them, eager to bury them. Cella thought, We are going to die. Let it be so. There was a third shock, and incredibly, the landslide stopped. As though it had hit a wall. Something jammed it up about a thousand feet above them. The slide piled up, up, up and became a barricade. The rocks that thundered down the slope flung themselves against the high barrier of earth. And fell back.

The earthquake ended in seconds, the rockslide in less than a minute. But all over, the landscape was changed. The level area where Cella and her mother had once picnicked was buried under hundreds of tons of dirt and stone. The entrance to the ancient family tomb had disappeared as magically as it had appeared sixty years ago when Lucca discovered it, after a similar earthquake.

Cella scrambled to her feet. "Father!" she called and

started up the path toward the mountain of rock. When she reached the foot of the landslide, she cried again, "Father!" This time the word was despairing.

"It's no use, my dearest," Anton said in a gentle voice. "We've lost him. He couldn't have survived. He could have been showing her the tomb."

"He'd never do that. And besides, he couldn't enter it. The portal won't move for him." Cella saw Anton's puzzled look. "Never mind. I can't explain. He can't enter the tomb."

"In it, or near it, that's where the landslide centered. Now the tomb is buried." He hesitated. "And so are they. Dynamite would only blast out the mountain. More dirt and rocks would fall into the tomb and over the whole area, into the valley."

"And Jason?" she asked stiffly.

"Jason too. He went after them."

"There's nothing we can do?" She begged for another answer.

"Nothing. If they were caught in the slide, they had no chance. And if they were anywhere near the tomb, they were trapped and buried under . . ." Anton stopped talking as Cella's face grew more ashen.

Cella let her eyes wander around the landscape vaguely. If anyone but Anton had tried to make her accept what had happened, the attempt would have been useless. Now she felt as if she had been handed a burden too heavy to hold, with no place within reach on which to set it.

"Aphrodite," Cella said in an awed whisper. "The wrath of the goddess. I warned him to return the necklace." She was silent a moment, in deep thought. "Why did she spare me?"

"Remember what you told me. You would render unto the goddess that which was hers. You'll return the necklace to Lexi."

"Yes." For the first time that day Cella thought of her other father, Tancredi. Now she had lost both.

Her eyes blurred with tears. She had no more to do here, so she started slowly down the trail, walking like an old woman, though she felt herself storming forward in a mad flight. Cella was so despairing, so shocked and hurt that she couldn't talk. With all her strength she had to hold back a long wail of grief.

Each time the pain in her body mounted, it squeezed her throat so tightly that she really believed she would die. Then it went still higher and settled behind her eyes. It was no longer only her own grief; it was the sadness of life itself. Feeling chilled, she went step by step back to the villa. She thought, I shall never get home, and was astonished when she saw before her the villa.

Anton followed her silently, ready to catch her if she fell. He knew her too well to offer sympathy. And with this knowledge there came over him a profounder conviction: that her coming here and the earthquake had once and for all set her free of the past. Like a river which at last spills into the sea, she had arrived at her destination. And their being together now brought them together forever.

Once back at the villa, Cella went in search of the Aphrodite. It wasn't in Marina's jewelry box, where it would normally be kept. It was nowhere around. For an instant, Cella had the horrid feeling Marina had been wearing it on the picnic. In a panic, she went to Sebastian's suite and opened the safe behind the Rembrandt drawing. There it was, the white velvet box. She stared. Had Sebastian taken it back from Marina? Now she'd never know. She took the box out quickly and opened it. The necklace was as she remembered it, glowing in all its mystic splendor. She telephoned Lexi in Manhattan and arranged to have her pick up the Aphrodite necklace. Lexi had already paid her one dollar.

There was no funeral service held for the three entombed people. Instead, the following afternoon Cella and Anton, with Celeste and the other faithful servants, trooped as far up the mountain trail as the rockslide permitted. No villager was invited.

Prior to the service, Cella and Anton had had a strong disagreement about including Jason Lord in the ceremony. But Cella refused to be vindictive. She pitied Jason for what he was and grieved for what he might have been. The great goddess Uni, the old books said, forgives us all, forever. She could do no less.

Cella knelt at the foot of the slide, clasped her hands together and lowered her head. She spoke softly an ancient Etruscan prayer in words intelligible only to Anton.

By the time Cella finished, Anton had dug three holes in the ground, filled them with loam and peat moss and, using the pitchers of water carried by the servants, watered the holes. This task completed, Cella planted three small, slender cypress saplings and tamped the rich earth around the roots. With the passage of years, the trees would grow tall and straight in remembrance of those buried in the hills above. As Cella stood back and gazed at the saplings, the country seemed changed. The hills stood up gravely; they knew and understood what the ceremony meant. The shadow of destiny that she had felt so strongly had now taken charge of almost all her family.

Cella straightened up and looked around. All that she could do, she had done. Sebastian was gone. Spina was gone. Tancredi was gone. Now she must return to the twentieth century. The age of Uni and Tunis had ended for her. The ancient world of the Etruscans would survive only in her memory and that of scholars.

EPILOGUE

Cella, Anton and Marcus sat in the library of the Taggard town house, their eyes fixed on six blank CRTs resting side by side on the parsons table. While they waited tensely for the auction to begin, they talked with excitement about their hopes.

"Anyway, this time you don't have to break Northbie's modem auction code, Cella." Marcus laughed. "Maurice invited you to watch the bidding."

"In fact, Cella is the guest of honor," Anton noted.

"I'm scared stiff," Cella said.

"I know," Anton said, putting an arm around her shoulders.

"What an experience. To see the private collection of The House of Uni auctioned off." Marcus shook his head.

"Marcus, please remember that what Maurice is auctioning is not the private collection of The House of Uni. There is no private collection. They're Cella Classics. I did not claim that any of it is more than a few years old. Hardly ancient jewelry. They're my re-creations of everything we once sold in the shop," Cella said firmly.

Marcus snorted. "It's a very clever way out of Father's scam."

"It astonishes me that Northbie's took the collection," Cella said. "There's no big money in modern jewelry, even if it perfectly reproduces the ancient necklaces and rings."

"Maurice thinks otherwise. He said ancient jewelry is becoming as scarce as paintings by Van Gogh," Marcus enthused.

"I know. He insisted. He adored the idea of Cella Classics. He said if I hadn't told him that these pieces weren't authentic, he'd have sold them as genuine ancient jewelry. As it is, he expects to do very nicely."

"He should do brilliantly. You are a great artist, Cella," Anton said respectfully.

"But suppose he's wrong. Suppose nobody bids. Or the bidding is a pittance. That's not a good omen for Cella Classics," she said uneasily.

"Shh!" Anton said. "Here it comes."

The six computer screens at six different sites, each wired to an IBM AT computer, came to life. Six different faces appeared.

"He invited Darlene," Marcus whispered. "There she sits in her bath towel."

"And there's Toby Phipps. And Emory," Anton noted. "I hear Emory now works for Toby. Poor Toby."

"And there's Tersius from the Getty. And Peter Petty looking like Peter," said Cella.

"Of course Peter Petty. They ought to play Fanfare for the Big Spender," Anton said dryly.

"And Mari Schlieffen, the mudslinging queen," Marcus chortled. "She's come up in the world, to be invited to one of Maurice's auctions."

"And there is the man himself, wearing his red-and-blue bow tie and his navy flannel jacket with hand-sewn buttonholes. Yes, the real Maurice Wheelock stands before us." Anton laughed.

But, in fact, it wasn't the real Maurice. For the first time in his entire professional life, Maurice looked embarrassed, awkward and ill at ease. Something had gone wrong. For an instant Cella felt a terrible pang. He regretted selling her Cella Classics. What else could it be?

Sensing her disquiet, Anton smoothed her hair. Then Maurice launched forth with fake joviality. "Ladies and gentlemen, you are a carefully selected chosen few who Northbie's felt would appreciate this auction of the inimitable jewelry by Cella Taggard. Known to the cognoscenti as Cella Classics. Here we have the Queen of Ur's diadem. A perfect re-creation. The Queen of Sumer's bracelet. Equally wonderful. And various other marvels Miss Taggard has re-created which perfectly embody the spirit of their time."

"What is he getting at?" Marcus whispered.

"I don't know," Cella said in an unsteady tone.

"But unfortunately," Maurice continued, "at the last minute I regret to have to inform you that the auction has been called off."

"Called off!" Darlene Schiller snapped. "Maurice, I put off my facial just to bid on my favorite Classics."

"I could be shopping in Bergdorf's," Mari Schlieffen whined.

"They're holding a table for me at Sofi's," Toby said with resignation.

"Yes, called off, dear friends. And you must forgive me. You see, Mr. Peter Petty has made arrangements with North-

bie's to buy the entire collection. At a very handsome price."
Even the famed Money Maurice was having difficulty keeping
under control his shock at the price Peter Petty had offered.

Cella, Anton and Marcus turned to the screen of Peter
Petty, who was smiling like the Cheshire cat as he sat there
in his custom-made white silk suit and his white leather,
handmade boots.

"If I see something I like, I'll top Petty's price," said
Tersius of the Getty with irritation.

"Impossible," said Maurice. "He has paid in advance for
a further topping bid of ten percent over anything offered. So
I think we'd all best take it like good sports and wish Cella
Taggard well. Northbie's thanks you for coming. Please remember there will be other auctions in which you will have
better fortune. I wish you good day."

Abruptly the screens went blank.

"He bought the entire collection! Good God!" Marcus
said.

Anton leaned back and gazed at Cella. "The poor man's
in love with you."

"You know?" Cella was suddenly embarrassed. "You
never told me you knew."

"I don't tell you everything."

"You don't? I tell you everything."

"Bullshit," Anton said, and he kissed her. Anton's black
eyes were faintly amused. "Everyone knows. But I knew
months ago. I'm now your American husband. As such I have
attacks of jealousy. You can write Peter a thank-you note. But
that's all."

"I've an idea," Marcus suddenly exploded. "Cella, I can't
do it without you." Cella glanced at Anton briefly, then back
at Marcus. "You'll be proud of it. So will Anton." Cella
nodded, so he hurried on.

"With Peter Petty buying Cella Classics, everybody will
want them. Let's set up a chain of stores. Call them Cella
Classics. Or The House of Uni. We can decide that later.
Eventually we can go public."

Cella swallowed hard. The idea of a small chain of exclusive stores selling Cella Classics—authentic copies of the jewelry of the ancient world—sent tremors through her body. In
her own way, she would continue the legacy of The House of
Uni. As Spina had said she should. Re-creating the beauty of
the ancient world for the world of today. But was that her
road? "I don't know, Marcus," she said hesitatingly. "I don't
know if I'm up to it."

"Of course you are," Anton said, his own excitement mounting. "You have a brilliant instinct for the ancient world. The Cella Classics collection has always done splendidly." Anton looked at the exquisite ring on her finger. The spiral serpent with sapphire eyes shooting sparks of blue fire. "You told me Tancredi made this. Then your father was as great a designer as your mother. You are their daughter. You can create a line of ancient jewelry for Cella Classics just as fine as what your mother and Sebastian did for The House of Uni."

Cella's smile was radiant. She accepted that the decision of fate to return the ring to her contained a value, a depth, a message. Go forward in the world as it is.

And so the future of Cella Taggard Vilanova and The House of Uni was resolved.

**Everyone Loves
A Lindsey—**

**Coming in June 1989
from Avon Books**

the next breathtakingly
beautiful novel of love and passion
from the *New York Times* bestselling
author